Liberated

Liberated

A Novel of Germany, 1945

Steve Anderson

YUCCA

Yucca Publishing books may be purchased in bulk at special discounts for sales promotion, corporate gifts, fund-raising, or educational purposes. Special editions can also be created to specifications. For details, contact the Special Sales Department, Yucca Publishing, 307 West 36th Street, 11th Floor, New York, NY 10018 or yucca@skyhorsepublishing.com.

Yucca Publishing® is an imprint of Skyhorse Publishing, Inc.®, a Delaware corporation.

Visit our website at www.yuccapub.com.

10 9 8 7 6 5 4 3 2 1

Library of Congress Cataloging-in-Publication Data is available on file.

Cover design by Rain Saukas

Print ISBN: 978-1-63158-001-7
E-book ISBN: 978-1-63158-029-1

56479892

Printed in the United States of America

To my parents,
Carl and Jean

One

I SHOULD'VE BEEN MORE SCARED, but the truth was I had never felt more ready and raring to go. I was heading deeper into the heartland of our bitter enemy. I drove this country route all alone, my jeep so new I could smell the tires. The sun rose above the birch trees lining the road, so I dropped the canvas top. I blitzed on past farms and villages. On the way I saw no German locals, no stray soldiers looking to surrender. They would see me soon enough. Within minutes, I'd be running a whole Bavarian town on my own.

I passed through a valley with fields of young green wheat. I'd never seen a sky so blue, like some vast, upside-down ceramic bowl of flawless azure all around me. The road smoothed out. I knew I was close. I slid on my helmet for effect and unclasped my holster, though I wouldn't need a weapon. My olive green American uniform would do the work. I might even be the first *Ami* most of these people ever saw (*Ami* meant Amerikaner, the German version of Yank). We were something new, all right. We called it US Military Government, MG for short. I was MG for a burg called Heimgau. I didn't have a staff yet, but Munich MG had told me to get in there, make contact and get the place running again.

In Heimgau, the US Occupation was going to be yours truly. As I drove on, the thought of me as liberator and likely mentor gave me a surge of warmth that not even this early May sun could match. Self-support was our goal for these people, and I'd get them off rations even if the *Bürgermeister* had to work the fields himself. One day I could stage an American-style mock election, show them the ropes of a working democracy. This was going to be the Germans' New Deal and I would bring it to them. Call it idealistic, quixotic even. I didn't care. Not after so many had died.

A vista of red roofs appeared, a steeple shooting up from the middle of it. I passed timber-framed houses, then blocks of stone buildings appeared and I was turning corners, my tires thumping on cobblestone. Second stories still had white linens hanging out as flags of surrender for US combat troops that had never come. US Tenth Armored had bypassed this whole county as it headed south into Austria. Today was May 8. The Unconditional Surrender was now official, but the war's long, unruly cessation had left remote areas like this hanging for days, weeks even.

I entered the old city gate and drove the Ludwigstrasse to the Domplatz—Cathedral Square. Still, I saw no people. What sort of square didn't have locals? This place was like a ghost town. Were they really that spooked? Even the usual stern faces would do.

The streets narrowed. I gave the jeep taps of gas, coasting along. On the Stefansplatz I stopped before a rose-colored building with arches and high gables. Here was City Hall. I stood in the jeep, leaned on the windshield frame, and waited because someone had to be watching. And I had to shake my head at the irony—even disorder was orderly here.

I removed my helmet, slid on my flyboy sunglasses, and lit up a Lucky Strike. Then, the people started showing. Locals. Heimgauers. They kept their distance. Men crouched behind carts and barrels. Women stood behind a fountain, hugging baskets and purses. Boys and girls crammed back in an alley, the group tight like a spring ready to bolt. Others watched from windows, from behind barely parted curtains. Obedient was one thing, but why the meek act, folks? I fought the urge to smile, to pass out smokes and Hershey's bars, and had to remind myself it was these very people who had helped cause so much horror in the world.

I dropped back down in my seat and steered the jeep into the City Hall courtyard.

A large sign stood propped against a wall:

US MILITARY GOVERNMENT HEADQUARTERS

What? How did that get there? But there it was, with MG-issue black-on-white stencil, ready to be hung front and center. A US Army command car and a jeep were parked here too.

My stomach had tightened up. I fought the shock with my head, with reason. Okay, so I wasn't the first man in. No big deal. A few lieutenants and corporals were here sitting on their hands waiting for me, their commanding officer. I got out, pocketed my flyboys, brushed the road dust off my Ike jacket, and lit another Lucky but then stomped on it, deciding that smoking was too casual for a new CO.

I grabbed my brown leather briefcase and chromium thermos and marched on in. The hallways were vacant, silent. More signs stood waiting to be hung. Off Limits. Authorized MG Personnel Only. English is the Official Administrative Language of US Military Government. Was this some kind of prank? Some top-secret maneuver? The town mayor's office was on the third floor. There I found a large white plaque on the door:

MAJOR ROBERTSON MEMBRE
MILITARY GOVERNMENT COMMANDER,
LK HEIMGAU

Who? I was CO. Munich sent me here. Surely, this was a case of misdirected orders. I'd heard of detachments landing in the wrong town, towns having the same name. That was it, I told myself. This was just a matter of two sensible MG Joes hashing it out. Taking a deep breath, I moved to knock—

A booming voice sounded from behind the door: "Who's there? Come in before I give you one merry wrath of hell!"

In I went. A major stood before a grand desk, this Major Robertson Membre no doubt. I remembered to salute though I hadn't done it in a while, riding so close to the front.

"The signs out there. Did you see them? They're important," the major said. His voice lowered to a colorless Midwest tone. "The signs instruct, and signs clarify, and they leave no doubt."

"Yes, sir."

His face was handsome in a mild and sunny way—pink skin, plump cheeks, a mop of thick blond hair. Yet his tie was high and tight at his fleshy neck and his uniform working overtime to hold in heavy shoulders and a pronounced paunch, an imposing body but one that lacked muscle. This was a man of thirty-five in the body of a giant twelve-year-old. In this spacious mayor's suite, he looked out of place as if he'd locked himself in his father's office and refused to leave.

"At ease." Membre peered at my trousers. That morning, for my big entrance, I'd made sure my pleats were crisp. "You always dress so spit-and-polish?" the major said.

"I try to, Major ..." I wasn't sure how to pronounce the man's name, I realized. Maybe it was "Mombra," or "Membree"? The last thing I needed was to sound un-American.

"It's pronounced 'Member.' Major Robertson Membre."

"Yes, sir."

"We should always give a commanding impression," Membre added. "We must impress upon the conquered our fortitude and our rectitude to be sure."

I made myself nod in approval. I wanted to roll my eyes. Here was that brand of MG swagger that I loathed. We all had plans for this place, but you had to show it, not preach it.

"Well, who are you, Captain?"

"Kaspar. Harry Kaspar. It seems there's been a mix-up. You see, I've been posted CO here."

The major laughed. "What? Come now ..."

I set my thermos on a chair and opened my briefcase, fumbling for my orders.

The major dropped the laugh, sucking in his gut. "Who sent you, Captain Kaspar? Who?"

"Munich Regional. I checked in there. They sent me on."

"Hah! Nuts. Frankfurt sent me. Pinpointed."

His eyes fixed on me, Membre reached back and pulled a page from the desktop—the only document there, I noticed.

I read it. I read it again. This was no prank or secret maneuver, but rather good old army overlap, a snafu. Someone had laid an egg. My problem was, Frankfurt Zonal overruled Munich Regional and the major outranked me.

"Right there plain as day, in quad-rup-li-cate," the major said, stressing every syllable like I didn't know what a carbon copy was.

"Munich had held me back, something about the situation unsettled."

"It's all fine now, Kaspar. They just got in, a few hours ago."

"They, sir?"

"Rest of the detachment. You're one of the last to report."

"The last?"

"Not to worry. I won't hold that against you." Membre was studying me now, eyeing my head and ears like some kind of crank phrenologist. My freckles, green eyes, and rounded features made me look more Anglo-Irish than anything. American girls had always told me that. Yet they'd also said my walk was too rigid, too precise for an American, so I'd worked on losing that part just the same. At least I didn't have the accent anymore. Still, I knew what was coming. Something about me always gave it away. "You got a shovel head for sure," Membre said and let out a low, rolling chuckle. "Kaspar—that a type of kraut name?"

"Kaspar was a kraut name, sir, yes."

"You born in Germany?"

"Yes, sir."

"Don't tell me you speak that awful language? Good god. Well, I expect we'll need heaps of translating." Membre gave me a single pat on the shoulder that he drew back with a snap as if he'd touched something hot. "Now, no sore feelings, you hear? No time for it. There's plenty to be done and we're as full-strength as we're going to get. Detachment's out scouting trouble spots. Looking into the electrical problem, the dead phone wires. One good note—water will be up again soon. We sure could use a team of GIs, someone to keep guard on things. So. A few posts are still open. Me, I'm heading up Property Control myself, and you'll be pleased to know I already secured billets for the detachment. You're all set up in some of the finest villas in town." Membre added a grin. His narrow teeth were yellow and shiny as if greased, and I caught a whiff of sweet cologne.

"Very well, sir." My legs had gone weak, tired. I couldn't help admire this office suite that might have been mine. It overlooked the square, with wide windows. Blond wood lined the walls as bookshelves and chrome-handled cabinets. The matching desk took up a quarter of the room, and under its glass top was a Third Reich map of Europe, 1942.

Major Membre moved behind the desk and dropped down in the leather chair. He set out a tidy stack of file folders, reports, and carbon forms, his lips forming an O. "You need duty. How old are you anyhow?"

"Twenty-six."

"Just what I thought," Membre said, nodding.

Sure, and he could tell my fortune too.

Membre pointed at a page. "I'm giving you Public Safety. Any experience there?"

"Police? Not exactly. I studied public policy." I didn't mention it was grad school. Let the man figure it out.

"No matter. We need you for this Public Safety slot."

I nodded. I was hugging my thermos and briefcase. All I could think about was getting the heck back outside. Membre fingered more carbons. I said: "In that case? I really should get cracking, sir."

"Of course. How do you mean?"

"I need to find a new police chief. Just like it says in the MG handbook—we get things up and running as soon as possible. Permission to leave, sir?"

"ASAP! Yes."

"One thing I'm wondering about. The locals, they look more spooked than most I've seen. Something rough happen here at the end?"

"Ah, that's just their way. These people, they know a strong master when they see one."

"We're not exactly the Gestapo."

Membre glared. "Of course not. Wait. Where're you going?"

"Back out. Scour the county," I said, stopping in the doorway. "There has to be one cop around here who fits the bill."

"Yes. Get cracking! New men is just what we need."

"Oh, I'm on it, sir."

Get cracking, me and my pressed trousers. Out in the courtyard I jumped into my jeep and stomped on the foot starter and turned the key and steered out the way I came, squeezing the steering wheel tighter, my shock giving way to disgust. If that major had even read his MG backgrounders, he'd know that all the current police were either dead or fled like the rest of those Hitler-licking hacks and goons who'd been running the show here. A few might slither their way back and take a stab at rebirth, but not on my watch. That was the first thing I would tell Munich MG when I got back there and requested a transfer. I'd been assigned my own town and I'd demand one. This snafu was a sucker punch, a low blow.

I cleared Heimgau and headed north on the same country road. At my shoulder I could see, on the far horizon, a jagged wall of marbly white—the Bavarian Alps, her highest peaks smothered in a leaden bank of clouds. The sight should've been wondrous, but my situation got me seeing those mountains, the war, our new occupation, and my new major for what they all were—the massive weight of centuries, dumped right onto me to sort out.

You bet I was out to prove something. It wasn't only that I was a born German. The thing was, I had never been in combat. I had been spared the ordeal. Stateside, college kids with higher IQs were kept in the Army Specialized Training Program, the ASTP. But as the war dragged on, the War Department had to abandon keeping the smart boys at home. In the last year the Army ended up needing far more replacements than planned as the meat grinder chewed up front-line units sent there for the duration, some units suffering 150 percent casualty rates counting replacements. So ASTP recruits were dispatched on the double overseas, right to the replacement depots on the front line. Not me. I was not dispatched. They say I got lucky. I instead got transferred to MG when other young minds got thrown into the Battle of the Hürtgen, the Bulge, the Rhine campaign. Just about every fellow I met through ASTP had died. Meantime, most about every guy I knew from back home had bought it in the ETO or the Pacific, and the few who had survived the front line had fewer limbs and eyes to go around. Others had lost their heads, I heard, including my former first lieutenant. On his first day of combat in the Ardennes he'd stripped naked and curled up in a ball in the cold mud. Our own phosphorus mortar salvos found him there, the scorching white powder searing and basting him right where he lay. My buddy Mike from my old unit had written me about it. Then Mike bought it too. It all horrified me. I felt so relieved I never had to see combat. I knew I would have cracked or ran; that or I should be dead. I had it licked in MG, they said. I tried not to see it that way. I had my own job to do, right here. Occupation was a front line too.

I had driven deep into the woods now. And I was coming to my senses. What if Munich MG accused me of deserting my post? I couldn't telephone them because the phone lines were down, yet what kind of excuse was that? So go get the lines up and running, they'd say. Who better to fix the mess than a German-speaking MG Joe?

I lit up a Lucky, driving with one hand, weighing my only option. I had to turn this jeep around. Orders were orders. The sorry truth was, limping back to Munich might be the only thing worse than losing the Heimgau CO post. Demotion and demerits were the least a man got for shirking duty. Just like an egghead kraut to ditch a raw deal, they'd say.

I steered out of a long curve and let off the gas to turn around.

Something lay along the road up ahead. I saw three lumps, pale and splotchy. But the lumps had limbs. I grasped at the wheel and shifted down, slowing up. My first thought was, they were skinny country pigs. Even after the blow I had just taken, even considering all the horrors I'd dodged by avoiding combat, I could not imagine anything much worse than that.

Two

I STOPPED THE JEEP STARING, gaping. The shreds of civilian clothes—a pant leg, sweater arm, a sock—did little to hide the welts and bruises. It was three men, dumped along the road. Their wrists were tied behind their backs. Only thin red strands kept one man's arm attached. Another man's mouth was open and it bled at the corners, ripped open wider by who knew what. Another had a dark burlap sack over his head. The signs of beating and torture were clear to see. There were burns, busted thumbs and toes, more burns on the feet. Bleeding from ears. Missing ears. Holes that used to be eyes.

A metallic taste hit my tongue. Nausea. I kept my knuckles riveted to the steering wheel and lowered my head, breathing deep breaths. I tried to focus on details, clues. The hooded man lay on his back, naked except for the one brown sock and soiled button-front undershorts. He was much leaner than the others, rail-thin, his limbs like those white-gray birch tree stems, his joints like the knots, his skin gray and yellowed and the blood splotches like peeling bark. His chest was battered, sunken.

The one with the torn mouth was older and yet somehow still had on glasses, the sunlight reflecting off them. The third was the youngest and curled up as if sleeping. He had a mustache, fuzzy and uneven.

I once had a mustache like that, I realized, and a horrid thought rose up in me—the last thing I'd want was to strike out with that weak fuzz on my lip.

A cold strip of sweat hit my brow. My stomach rippled in waves. Vomit gushed hot up my throat and I swallowed it back down, so bitter and burning I had to bang on the wheel.

Get it together, Harry. I needed a mouthwash, but didn't have a canteen so I grabbed my chrome thermos and gulped the luke-warm coffee in there. I knew one thing: These bodies were not here before. This whole road was clear this morning and I would not have missed this. Another thing: The corpses' dark-flowing blood and lack of stench meant they couldn't have been dead longer than a day.

Or were they dead? I switched off the jeep, stepped out and bent over them, one hand ready to cover my nose. I felt neck pulses. The old man had long gone cold, as had the young one. His neck lay twisted at an angle and had to be busted.

I moved over to the leaner man, on my haunches. I felt his neck, just under the ragged bottom edge of his hood. The pulse was faint, the skin lukewarm.

"You," I heard a groan. It came from under the man's hood. It was in English. I could see a spot of the damp fabric suck in and push out, in, out. Then German: "*Sie da ...*"

I pinched two fingers around the bottom of the hood, to pull it back.

"No," the man wheezed. Keep the hood on, he was saying.

"You need help," I muttered. "I can get you help."

"No."

"Who are you? Who did this?" As I spoke my eyes searched his bruised and dented body. I saw a line of numbers tattooed on his inner forearm, at an uneven angle. I had heard about such ID numbers from the concentration camps our troops were discovering. Those SS bastards hadn't even bothered to line the numbers up straight, I saw. Blood rushed to my head, hot with anger.

He had said something else but I'd missed it. I leaned in close, my ear to the spot on his hood. "Can you try saying that again?"

"Abraham," he said.

"Your name?" I said.

I felt him nod, though his head hadn't moved.

"We got to get you help, get you in my jeep."

"No."

"Who did this to you?" I thought I had an idea. The proof was on the man's arm.

He didn't answer me. I touched the numbers.

"No!" he shrieked, his head lifting up, then striking the street with a thud.

"Okay, okay ..."

He gurgled. The fabric sucked in. It stayed there. He rattled, from deep inside.

"Wait, no. Who did this? To all of you?"

He rattled again. Spittle shot through the fabric, making foam. But between the rasps, I thought I heard a morbid chuckle.

"Who did it!?" I shouted. I held his arm. I probably shook it too hard. It didn't fight back. "Just tell me," I whispered.

"They."

"Who's they? Stay with me, man."

"They are you ..."

He went still, stiff. A couple gasps escaped, but they weren't his, not anymore. It was simply biology, trapped air.

I sat on the street, stunned. Features and colors blurred around me, like I was on a tilt-a-whirl at the carnival, but the whole goddamn earth was the ride. I might have been there a while.

They are you. Me? What the hell could that mean?

I peered into the dense forest, all around me. All those lean, pale and mottled birch trunks revealed nothing between them but dim shade and underbrush.

And then I heard it. A rumble.

Was it artillery? An earthquake? The rumble rolled, its pumping rhythm humming in my toes. My nostrils felt a gritty sting. I stood and could see barrels of black smoke surging from the treetops, off to my right.

It was a locomotive. The loco was climbing a ridge, heading for a steep hill.

We didn't have trains this far south. The Army Air Corps had bombed every German train and station, Munich MG had assured me. The rail lines were supposed to be clear and stay that way. I flipped open my briefcase, laid my area map across the wheel and studied the grids, routes, and symbols. The map told me: The train had run parallel to this road before turning for that hill.

Could it have anything to do with these poor stiffs? These corpses would have to wait. I'd have to remove Abraham's hood later. I climbed back in the jeep, started it up, gave it gas, and steered clear of the bodies while keeping one eye on those barrels of smoke. They were rising higher, pumping farther apart. The loco was losing speed up that hill. I could catch up. As I drove I pulled on my helmet and slung binoculars around my neck.

A sign read: "Dollendorf-Traktorwerk, 1 Km" in fading script. A turnoff. I heaved the wheel right and raced up the ridge on a dirt road, shifting down for speed, rattling across ruts, hugging the wheel.

I was no combat Joe. I didn't even have backup. But I drove higher. Fir trees crowded out the birches and cast long, saw-toothed shadows. Then sunlight struck my windshield and the trees receded to reveal a large clearing. I slowed to a stop, taking it all in. Traktorwerk meant this Dollendorf was once a tractor factory, but it looked like a ransacked junkyard now. A garage had shattered windows and a machine shop no doors, its machines long gone. Metal shacks rusted. Wildflowers and heather grew in clumps among the cracking tarmac, rail ballast, stains of oil.

On my map, the rail line passed through this compound. I unclasped my Colt holster and had to use both hands, I was shaking so bad. I lifted the binocs. At the far end of the compound, bordering more trees and a steep rocky hill beyond, stood a wooden rail shelter.

Inside stood freight cars. I counted them. Four.

Crows bolted for the sky. I heard a whoosh-whoosh, boom-boom coming up through the woods, and the earth pounded in rhythm, trembling the trunks and shaking leaves loose. Brakes squealed and white steam hissed, flooding underbrush with its fog. The locomotive had stopped at the trees' edge. It was only the loco, no cars attached. I could see that iron beast, all right. She had to be twice my height. Her boiler, cab, and tender bore thick black sheets of armor plate.

I wheeled the jeep around and bumped up onto the tracks. I was going to block its path. I could jump out if I had to. Yet the loco only waited, the boiler clanging like pots and pans.

I heard shouts, laughs. At the other end of the clearing, a team of five American GIs emerged from the woods with their guns slung low and their shoulders slouching, the look of men reaching the end of a long hike. They saw me, they had to, but they took no notice. They were looking to the trees closest to me.

A man stood there. He was leaning against a birch trunk. He was dressed in plain GI green shirt and trousers and could've been mistaken for a corporal if it wasn't for the silver oak leaf on his lapel, his only insignia. The lieutenant colonel wore no holster or helmet, and he was smiling. He strode on out.

I climbed out the jeep and marched over and the colonel to me. He looked young for that silver leaf. Could he be only 30? I stopped to salute, but the colonel kept coming, still smiling. Was he smirking at my shiny new helmet? I removed it, but had nowhere to stuff it, so I held it at my hip. The colonel came close, within a foot. I said: "Sir, I'm the MG man for Heimgau Town down the road."

"Detachment?" the colonel said with a Southern twang.

"E-166. I'm CO—well, Public Safety now."

"That right?" The colonel grinned. I could smell licorice. He was chewing Blackjack gum. "Looks like we're cousins, son. I'm the CIC agent around here."

CIC meant Counter Intelligence Corps. CIC agents were one of the advance guard. Sure, they were secretive and they got in some units' hair, but the CIC provided plenty of good info. Munich had told me: Until things were up and running, the area CIC agent should be relied upon and given free reign. CIC trumps all. "Good to see you here, sir," I said. "I think we got a problem. I saw corpses down on the main road ..."

The colonel looked over to my jeep. A big GI with a thick, wide face was sitting at the wheel. "Off those tracks. Now!" the colonel shouted at him.

The GI sped my jeep off the tracks and slammed to a halt.

"Stay with me," the colonel said and strolled off. I followed. What else could I do? The colonel smacked gum and waved at the GIs now sitting under the trees as he walked me down the tracks to the rail shelter. I carried my helmet by a strap and it knocked at my thigh. The sun had reached high sky, and my wool shirt itched under my Ike jacket.

"Wait here," the colonel said and headed into the shelter where it was darker. I stood out in the sun, itching, watching. The four freight cars were a mix of types and sizes—gray-green, rusty red, camouflage, yet all were stenciled with Nazi eagles and the words Deutsche Reichsbahn. The colonel heaved open the door of each, checked inside, and then shoved each door shut. I craned my neck but could make out little but the corners of crates and trunks.

GI thick-face was slogging his big wrestler's body up the tracks to us, his gear jangling. He was a sergeant. He and the colonel met where I stood, the sergeant eyeing me like I was Hitler's own brother.

"Ease up, Sergeant," the colonel said. "Our man here is the local MG. Captain, Sergeant Horton."

Sergeant Horton only nodded, no salute. I could overlook it, assuming he'd been a front-line Joe. I faced the colonel. "Sir, about those corpses."

"You're jumping the gun, son. First rule of investigation: verify. They have name tags on them? You don't know who the hell they are, what they are."

"True, sir. I was just about to get on that when I heard your locomotive here."

The colonel had stopped listening. He'd turned to Sergeant Horton. They whispered, Horton nodding along, and I studied the colonel's ruddy skin and sunken cheeks, his bulky jaw with a mouth of thick teeth. Only the strong nose and alert blue-gray eyes could save a mug like that from a life of increasing ugliness, I thought. The man had poise. Yet he wasn't swaggering around like some MG officers did. I knew enough not to get an old hand like this on my bad side. And he was right. Those corpses could have been Bavaria's worst Nazis, for all I knew—except for one, that was. I wouldn't be able to get them in the jeep on my own. I could come back with locals, haul in the bodies, follow up. Improvise when required was the drill.

The locomotive's clang had risen to a hard clatter. "Hear that?" the colonel said to me. "Do that when they're just dying to go. She really is a fine lady. Borsig BR 52, best German engine running."

"And those freight cars?" I pulled out my notepad, flipping it open with a flourish. I couldn't help myself. I had to show CIC that Heimgau MG was no lamb.

"You taking notes. That's what you're doing? For a report or some such?"

"Just doing the job they give me, sir."

The colonel had dropped the smile. He stared down at my brown, non regulation wingtip brogues. "College boy?" he said.

I nodded.

"You're curious. You anticipate. That's good," the colonel said.

"Ready!" someone yelled, and the colonel turned and pumped a fist in the air. A grimy glove waved from the locomotive cab. Black smoke flowed out the stacks, and the three of us stood back to watch the loco pass through the compound, a rolling black wall that shaded us from the sun, its giant black wheels and pistons pounding, punching automatons. It backed onto one sidetrack, and then it went into the rail shelter for coupling to the four freight cars.

Sergeant Horton stood like the colonel, his arms folded and feet wide. He belched and said to the colonel, "What's next move, reckon?"

The colonel spat out his gum and worked it into the dirt with his heel. He turned to me. "Here's the way I see it. You're dying to work all the angles, that right? Despite all this by-the-book? Want to know what can-do really means."

"Who doesn't?"

"And you know German? Like a native."

I nodded again.

"You said CO. But you're not, not anymore. You're nodding like you got a sour deal," the colonel said.

"No. I do the job they give me."

"And you make the most of it. The lowly immigrant makes it into a college, first one in his family line going back to some peasant hut in Old Prussia. That about right?"

"Something like that."

"Listen. In this war I did my time unraveling the German character. It's no different than anyone else's, just a little more tragic, and far more unlucky."

"You can say that for them."

"That country road down below?" the colonel said. "You were almost in the next county, then it's on to Munich. You're not decamping so soon, are you?"

"No, sir."

"Your first day here then? I never saw you before."

"That's right."

"Fine. Now listen here, that major of yours will need some GIs to keep an eye. I'm loaning you Horton's team." The colonel offered a hand. "Name's Spanner. Eugene."

We shook hands. "Kaspar. Harry. Thank you. Use all the help we can get, I'm sure."

The colonel named Spanner laughed. "It's damn unreal, isn't it, Kaspar? Americans taking control in every cursed corner of this fubar snake pit that used to be Germany. A paradox, I say. Here we fight and kill enemy, and we lose plenty friends along the way. Go to a hell of a place that no one's ever been. Then you MG swoop on in and you go and help the enemy."

"It's not like that, sir. We're here to help the refugees, the victims. Children. Germans, they do what we tell them."

"That true? Then be sure to remember that, son." Spanner said this lightly, as if he should be smiling. He was not. His mouth had curled down like he needed to spit. He paused a moment, but it wasn't the type of pause I could wedge a word into.

I might have put it all in my next weekly report, and I could have, but I was no dope. Those freight cars were CIC's domain. They well could have held important documents and plans useful for the war effort, or secret weapons' parts to be studied, or anything that could prevent more of the sick misadventures men had unleashed in these last few years. As for the corpses, this colonel didn't need to hear it, not with that grave stare he was giving me—a stare that was saying, whose side are you on exactly? This is no way to make a name, son.

So, I smiled for the colonel. I stuffed my notebook back in my back pocket. His eyes followed my hand until it returned to my side, and I showed him a thumbs-up, ready for take off. "Will do, sir," I said.

"Good. Well done. Then goodbye for now," Colonel Spanner said and strolled off, adding, "Swell shoes, kid."

I fired up my Zippo with a clank, lit up a Lucky and strolled back to the jeep. Telling myself, I'll have to be more like that colonel when I get back to Heimgau. "Can do," he called it and I'm the same. Always take the straightest line. That was how the front-line types handled it. If I didn't, someone else will make me compromise, set rules for me. Funny thing though—I was thinking all this in German even though these were such American thoughts to me.

The GIs were slinging their guns back on and, led by Sergeant Horton, heading back into the woods the way they had come. I wheeled the jeep around and, as I hit the road back downhill, glanced over my shoulder to see Colonel Spanner climbing up and into that juggernaut of a loco.

I drove fast and hard, the wind blurring my eyes, the ruts knocking the chassis and tossing my briefcase, thermos and helmet around like so much popcorn in the pot.

Down on the main road I turned back the way I had come, heading back for the corpses and on back toward Heimgau. As I neared the bend I slowed, and then I had to squint, just to make myself believe what I now saw.

Three

THE THREE CORPSES WERE GONE. Dark blood stains glistened on the pavement and gravel, coagulating like smashed black cherries. But that was it. For a moment I suspected Abraham himself, as if the lifeless hooded man had been able to recover somehow and haul his dead friends off into the woods. What a frantic notion. I had witnessed the man dying. So I parked on the shoulder and stood in the road, hands on my hips, checking things out. The road was clear either way, and I smelled no exhaust. I paused to listen and heard only the pings and trickles of my overworked jeep. The woods around me were all shadow and murk, a permanent dusk inside there for who knew how far. I entered the woods and stomped around in the underbrush but found nothing, not one clue. I didn't go far though. I'd already lost the corpses and didn't want to leave the jeep, since I had no chain to lock up the steering wheel.

I drove back to Heimgau, making myself chuckle at the insanity this war brought and would bring. MG Joes like me were supposed to cure the slow-acting poisons of madmen, but who'd ever clinched such a deal? I wanted to go back and tell that Colonel Spanner the corpses had disappeared, but the man had his own concerns. I had given him a thumbs-up as if he were the gladiator to be spared, but the truth was he was the Roman tribune with the final say. As far as his operation went, I really had no recourse back there even if I did think the colonel was crossing some sort of line. As our CIC agent, he would see any report I could file. I had to assume that. It was his job to know everything. He could have dossiers on any MG officer.

You know German like a native, he had said to me. Yet he didn't sneer when he said it, or call me Heini or kraut while slapping me on the back. That's what most of them did and I'd grown accustomed to it, sure I did, in the same way a fellow gets used to a case of the pox.

Then I got to thinking about my sudden new post. I was now playing John Law. As horrific as those corpses were, my find did keep me close to the action. I could show the Germans how their new liberators delivered Justice compared to the thugs and rack- eteers who'd been conning them the last twelve years. I definitely needed a leg up. This could be it.

I was back up in Major Membre's new office within a half hour.

"Find anyone?" the major said from his desk as if I'd only popped out to check the mail.

"I came across three corpses. Out where the Heimgauer Strasse hits the woods. Fresh, sir."

I might as well have told him no mail had come. He appeared to be reading, but his eyes had not moved. He turned the page, his mouth formed that O again, and he muttered, "Oh?"

"One passed away right when I got there. I think he'd been in one of the concentration camps."

"Passed away? Oh dear, that's grim. Could he say anything?"

"It didn't make sense, I'm afraid. He gave me a name. So, from here? My first task is to verify, identify—try to find out if any were German locals, soldiers, even Nazis. If any are local civs or had been then it's definitely our jurisdiction."

The major nodded. He turned another page.

"They looked like they were tortured," I added. "Not a pretty sight."

"Dreadful. Well, bring them in and ID them. We'll get some locals to do the lifting."

"That's just the problem, sir. They're not there anymore. The corpses, I mean. I left for help but decided to turn back for them and they were gone."

Membre looked up, grinning. He slapped at the desk. "See, now there you go! That's the way it's going to be here. Could have been anyone, those corpses. Could've been refugees did it."

"Refugees? They're too weak, hungry to do that kind of work."

"Fine, but, the sad fact is we just don't know what these people are capable of, and I mean any of them."

What had I expected? A shiny metal? A shot of CO wisdom? I wanted to leave, but I kept my feet planted. "Also, I met the CIC agent on the way in, sir. A lieutenant colonel name of Spanner."

Membre's head popped up. "Oh? Right. We wouldn't be here nice and safe if it weren't for CIC. That's my feeling."

Did he even have a feeling? He hadn't even asked what Abraham's name was. So I didn't mention the train. Why bother? The major knew nothing about it, I was guessing. He certainly didn't ask. He went back to turning his pages and his face slackened, all serious now like it should've been when I told him about the corpses. His eyes darted along and glittered. "I'm reading up on church matters. Fine church here, they say. Sure was a handsome sight coming in, I tell you that. Just glorious. Bet they have a fine display chamber here somewhere. They all have those here. Know that? I did. Brocade vestments, jeweled chalices and such, maybe even a reliquary. Yes, that really would fortify a man, don't you think?"

I was raised Lutheran and could give a hoot if this was Catholic country. Yet here we were taking over an enemy town and all my new CO wants to do is go tour the old church? He could tour all he wanted. The parish priest, Father Plant, was one of the "brown priests." He had kissed up to the Nazis and even flew the swastika at mass. So it wasn't surprising that the brown Father Plant and his curates and whole rotten retinue had fled the coop weeks ago.

Meanwhile, three poor souls had been tortured to death, and this major was blaming refugees?

I didn't need the CO. I needed to know what made this Heimgau burg tick, and that meant knowing the people. My historical back-grounders, typed by an anonymous German émigré in some faceless MG bureau, had given me a decent start: "Heimgau Town survives as one of many rural townships within the *Alpenvorland,* that green won-derland north of the Bavarian Alps. The town prevails as the *Kreisstadt* (county seat) of the *Landkreis* (surrounding county), which is also named Heimgau. The town houses the offices and courts, churches and schools, and main merchants. Though one must not forget the local artisans. Long ago the area profited from the traffic of a major Roman road. Ever since, through strife, and famine, and scandal, the artisan industry and the handicrafts have thrived here, producing such varied pieces as painted toys and figurines, fine art recreations, furni-ture ... to observers, Heimgau is exactly what it appears to be: smallish and isolated, devout and conservative."

That afternoon I set up an interrogation post in the cellar of City Hall. I was hoping the prospect of thorny questions down in that dank catacomb might help bring out the secrets. I set up a line of empty crates as chairs. I had electricity, so I hung a work lamp above me. Then I called down those few Heimgau officials who hadn't fled or committed suicide, which was easy enough—they had decided to come out of hiding and were waiting patiently inside an upstairs restroom.

They had on natty dark suits and debriefed me with heads lowered. The big Nazis had hightailed it, they confirmed, the police had done the same, all the schools had been closed for months. Only the train station had been bombed. Water, electricity, and phone lines were a mess—it was true. But they weren't concerned, because the *Amerikaner* come well prepared, and they nodded in agreement at that, oh, yes.

"I found corpses. Three. All men. Dumped in the Heimgauer Strasse." I described them. I didn't mention Abraham and his number tattoo. That would only spook them, clam them up for now. "Civilians perhaps? Locals gone missing?"

The men exchanged glances. One shook his head, and another shrugged. All studied their feet with the intensity of men counting money.

I offered each a Lucky and then asked again, losing the tough-mug act. Yet I got the same response, this time with smiles. So much for the magic of Virginia tobacco.

"What about recent records? Local loyalists, resisters? Missing persons?"

More shrugs. Records were destroyed, they said, burned on orders of the SS.

"And the morgue?" Though I had already checked that, it was empty and spotless.

This brought a laugh. "*Herr Kapitän*, surely you know the morgue is now the only place in all of Germany where there are no dead."

"Then what about a fellow named Abraham?"

That wiped the smiles right off. A name like that could not be explained away. The glances returned, and they went back to getting PhDs in studying their feet. One of them had scrunched up his face in thought. His gray hair had receded to the back half of his head in fluffy plumes that made him look like some ancient record keeper, all that was missing were the reading glasses on a chain.

"You," I said to him. "Out with it."

"There's nothing to come out with, sir. There may have been such a man, but it would have been years ago."

"A Jewish man, you mean."

"Yes. There were some here in the county. It's been years. You would need a last name. You would need those records, any records. And without seeing a face, who can know?" He held up his hands as if to say, what good was it? For what?

Without a face. Under that hood. What a thorough idiot I was for not looking. "Right. I get you. I'm on my own," I muttered.

I finished with the town buck passers. I was taking a break out on the square when an unmarked three-quarter ton truck pulled up and unloaded the six CIC GIs from Dollendorf, including Colonel Spanner's big lug sergeant, Sergeant Horton. Children had gathered and they tugged at the GIs' trousers and Horton tossed them licorice and Hershey's. It was good to see someone getting the people to loosen up. If a palooka like that could manage it, so could I.

Colonel Spanner had Horton. I needed my own man, I realized.

Back down in the cellar I read more reports and backgrounders, smoked another butt, and decided on my final interview. It didn't take long to fetch the man. He worked in the building.

The cellar door screeched open. A stocky fellow in blue worker overalls descended the stone stairs, taking blunt steps that would've been a fighter's jabs had those feet been fists.

"Good day, *Herr* Winkl," I said in respectful High German. Uli Winkl was the City Hall *Hausmeister*, a building master being a cross between a building's janitor and a super, depending. For every one of these who was a snoop or a toady, a good many more sang their own tunes.

"*Servus,*" Winkl said, sticking to the Bavarian greeting. He sat on the corner of a crate as if crouching. He had a sturdy face and stout neck that the long shadows of my overhead lamp couldn't narrow. I offered him a Lucky. He shook his head at it, the first German to do so.

I told Winkl about the corpses and the four officials' reaction.

Winkl began to speak. He stopped.

"Well, what is it?"

"Your Abraham, sir. He could have been from here. But in the end, in the last few years, there was no one like that here in town that I know of." Winkl's eyes searched the room.

"There's something else? Take your time."

Winkl began again: "Sir, in the last days, when the SS were still here, some Heimgauers disappeared."

The local SS stuck it out to the end in many towns, always expecting some miracle that would keep them in their showy uniforms, some sacred immunity that would let them play the bully forever. But that was always before our troops passed through.

"No, this is different," I said. "What I saw, it happened later. Their blood was fresh."

"That's all I can tell you. You ask me. I tell you."

So the man was wary. Who wouldn't be? I could play along. "You know what I think? You don't stand for hokum, do you?" I said. Winkl shrugged, waiting for my hokum to end. I continued: "I am the Public Safety Officer for Heimgau, you see. And it's come to my attention that you were a policeman here, before."

"Yes, that is true. But it was well before. Before the Nazis."

"How long have you served City Hall? A good twenty years, counting the cop work? Seen a lot of change here, have you?"

Winkl snorted. "One could say that, ja."

"And you've become a keen judge of how things operate around here."

Winkl eyed me, his lips tightening, face hardening up. "I would not feel comfortable, unlike others, informing like that—"

"It's not informing, and it's not a question of if you decide to or not. Still, I'd prefer that you agree."

Winkl said nothing. He looked down, at his strong hands.

"Go on," I said. "We're just talking here."

"You're not a specialist at this, are you? The Public Safety is new to you."

One smart guy, my man. I had to chuckle. "We don't always get what we want, do we? Look, I'm doing this my own way. I don't want you to spy. This will be just between you and me, a partnership based on trust, not rules. There's no politics here, no ... ideologies. No 'isms' at all. Think of it like this: You're not going to the enemy or to the *Amis* or whatever we are to you. You're going to me."

Winkl's eyebrows raised.

"You come straight to me and only me when you think something's fishy, and I'll do my best to correct it. Promise. What do you say? I'll throw in a carton of Lucky Strike for good measure."

Winkl dared a grin. "And a couple bars of the Hershey's?"

"Done."

"Then I agree."

"Good." So far, so good.

"Tell me something about you," Winkl said. "You are an *Ami*, that's certain, but you are also German, yes? Your accent's too good to be from school lessons."

"My parents are German. I was born here." I stopped there. I didn't want any local buttering me up and especially not on account of my Deutsch. Colonel Spanner himself had warned me of that. "Good? Clear on that?"

"Yes." Winkl looked to his lap.

"Let's just keep this moving, shall we? Now, my directives say I have to ask this: Have you ever been a member of the National Socialist German Workers Party or any other affiliated organization?"

Winkl laughed, shooting spittle. "The pigs threw me in Dachau for weeks back in '37. Morons mistook me for my brother Udo, who was a Communist. Go and put that in your notes."

"Excellent. I mean, you know what I mean." I stood and held out a hand. "*Herr* Winkl, congratulations. I am appointing you Temporary Police Chief of Heimgau."

Winkl's face paled. He shot up, knocking over his crate.

"It's only for a few weeks. You'll help me announce curfews and proclamations till the major finds a full-time *Bürgermeister*. Then we'll find a new chief. Short-time gig is all it is."

Winkl kept shaking his head. He trudged in a circle, in and out of the light, glaring at his toppled crate like he wanted to stomp it to splinters.

Of course, it was not the response I wanted. But then I recalled my backgrounders: Heimgau's geographic isolation had always spared her that influx of outsiders who deluged a town in times of trouble. This time, though, Hitler's fine mess would bring in the newcomers and Heimgauers had to dread it like they had the plagues of centuries before.

"Otherwise?" I added, "I'll have to run things myself until we find someone who's qualified. Say, some German refugee Joe Stalin expelled from the East, or what we in English call a 'Displaced Person.'"

"A what? What's that?" Winkl tried the English word, but only sputtered his P's and S's.

"A Dis-placed Per-son. DP for short. Get used to that word. That's what my authorities are calling all those your Führer brought into Germany and imprisoned here against their will. Maybe you've heard of them. Concentration camp inmates, to be sure, but nearer to Heimgau what we have mostly are men who were being worked to death. Former forced laborers. Slavics, mostly, Russians, Yugoslavs. And not too happy about it either. Many we'll be repatriating—sending back home—but that could take a while and meanwhile? Not too happy."

Winkl's eyes had glazed over with worry. He righted his crate and sat back on it. "If it's like you say. But for a few weeks only."

"Excellent." I handed Winkl a list. "Now, pass these rules on to the townsfolk. Make up some nice big signs for them, post them around. First, though, gather all keys for the jail and the police station—"

The cellar door flew open. Major Membre plowed down the steps. Winkl sprung to attention, his face pale. Membre had a riding crop that he held out as if to strike Winkl.

"What are you doing down here?" Membre said to me.

"Interviews, sir, for Public Safety."

"And you?" Membre shouted at Winkl, who looked to me to interpret.

"He would be the one being interviewed," I said to Membre.

"That man needs to be out manning the courtyard, and p.d.q.. We need new tallies. I've got a proper cameraman out there." That morning Major Membre had instructed Winkl to gather every icon and object of Nazism inside City Hall and pile them up outside for destruction. They already had a great mound of party pins and armbands, SA standards and tin SS daggers, swastika clocks and even kids' play-sets of Himmler, Goering, and Goebbels. Out there, throngs of Heimgauers were battling hunger and jitters and nostalgia to please their new Major-Conqueror in his Nazi Kitsch Destruction Drive. It was one way to get the people back out on the streets. Not to be outdone by their zeal, the major was sure to add tally tables and graphs and glossy photos to his report of the big event. "We're losing the moment," Membre went on. "Don't you see?"

"One moment, sir." I told the major about naming Winkl Temporary Police Chief. There was no one else. So find someone else to play junk collector, I wanted to add.

"That right? Ha!" Membre slapped the crop against his thigh. "You should like that," he said to Winkl as if Winkl understood. "Folks here been kicking you around long enough."

Winkl could only grimace. I dismissed my new chief, and he gave me a hurried half-bow on his way out.

"Hey, lookie there. I think he likes you." Major Membre bounded over and, to my surprise, lit the fresh Lucky hanging from my mouth. "Custodian becomes Police Chief. Rags to riches. It's a swell angle."

"Thanks. I saw the troop truck. What's new up there?"

"That Sergeant Horton is such a front-line ruffian, but he knows the drill. He says that CIC agent of ours will pass through any day, to check in. Spanner's the name? Say, speaking of, let's give his men a poker game tonight after curfew. Set it up, will you?"

"Spanner is the name. Yes, I will." Because I sure have nothing better to do, I wanted to add. I also realized I could bank a few points with CIC Agent Spanner by hosting his men.

"Swell, then." Membre went over to a high cellar window and, gazing out, released a deep and satisfied moan, like that of an aching and grimy man sinking into a hot bath with suds. "Ah, yes. You never asked where my billet is. You know where my billet is? Bet you're just dying to know. Aren't you?"

"Okay. Where's your billet?"

"The castle. There's fine quarters up there, just swell. You'd think it's all old cold stone and dust up there, but no. Oh, no." Membre wagged a finger at the window as if talking to his castle, which I knew from our backgrounders: Hohenheimgau Castle, high above Heimgau Town, had once housed a respected bishopric, including seminary, monastery and chambers. By the 1930s only the small monastery was still operating up there, the few aging monks remaining aloof from local Nazi authority, never blessing yet never challenging while down below in town the brown priest Plant was spiking his many sermons with increasing doses of vitriol. "But there's so much more, more of the church up there, more everything," the major added.

This day, I had to admit, was suddenly a long one and my patience thinning fast. Sure, Major, I was thinking, you got your schön little town, and on top of it, practically crushing it, sits a humongous, stinking, deadly gorilla with the curiously long name of Catastrophic Nazi World War. And the gorilla's latest newborn bastard? Those three dead tortured you could give a hell about.

"This town's like a museum, it really is," Membre droned on. "All of it. A lovely, sumptuous exhibit, chock-full of fine art. This is an artisan town. Did you know that?"

"It says so in the backgrounders."

"The what? It's different when you see it all. It really is, I must tell you. You have to understand ..." Membre paused. He turned from the window showing hard, dark eyes. "Now you listen, Kaspar. These here people here, they brought this on themselves, and we don't owe any of them a damned thing."

Four

We owe these people nothing, my blowhard CO had said. Did he mean poor Abraham too? I wanted to ask him that, but I let it go. We owed people. We even owed the conquered Germans something. We needed to show them a proper alternative to this vile regime they themselves had let destroy their nation, and what better way to kick things off than find and prosecute whoever tortured and killed those three men? This is what they needed to hear, and good: Listen up, sad sacks of Heimgau: You yourselves can and will repair what you were dealt and did deal yourself. Total defeat doesn't have to be a free-fall in a dark well. It could also bring the first grabs of a tough climb up and out of that very well.

First, though, I would have to find a way to communicate with Major Membre on the level, a challenge I feared might just require learning Mandarin Chinese. I certainly had no time for it. Late that first afternoon I met the other six MG officers, a quick introduction of hands shook, and hometowns shared. Wilks, Gerard, Ellis, and Carlson were the names I remembered, Wilks a captain and the rest lieutenants—political affairs, education and culture, quartermaster, and administration, the usual breakdown of posts with a few enlisted clerks on the way.

Then it was on to Colonel Spanner's GIs. As Major Membre ordered, I set up the poker that night in the Imperial Suite of the Heimgauer Hof Hotel. I had hoped Colonel Spanner would show, but he didn't. And as it turned out, getting MG and these GIs to mix wasn't a great move. The MG officers wanted to hear front-line combat tales from the GIs if they had any, but the dogfaces felt more like clamming up and then barking, and a fight almost broke out. After that, the GIs played alone off in a corner, their game somber, all grunts and snickers. At least Major Membre wasn't there to foul things worse, I thought, and so I set out to patch things up. I brought in a record player, got a bottle of rye flowing.

I got Sergeant Horton alone at an open window. Horton was pissing out the window. I didn't reprimand him for it, because he probably expected as much from a rear-line commando like me. After he'd buttoned up, I asked him about the three corpses I found. Any information he could provide would be appreciated. It was a long shot, but wasn't all this?

Horton turned to me, face slack. "Who's asking?"

"We don't need killers in this burg. There's enough to deal with."

Horton laughed. He patted my shoulder. "Flanking maneuver. There's a nice tactic, Cap."

"How you mean?"

"Come on. You just want to know what's in those train cars."

I smiled, swirling my rye. "Hey, who doesn't want to know the score?" I said, going easy, but Horton only wandered off to rejoin his crew.

I could have cared less about the freight cars. So why had I said that? It just came out, bubbled up from somewhere.

At nine p.m. I left the hotel for my billet, my head fuzzy from the rye and smoke. The sun had set and curfew began, bringing a purple sky and dark streets, and I saw that my new Police Chief Winkl had already posted some signs using our MG stencils. "Non-Fraternization Rule Strictly Enforced." "Attention: Curfew in Effect Until Six A.M. Tomorrow." "Violators Punished to Full Extent of Martial Law. Good man, I thought. And just how our Major Membre liked it—laying down the law with big ugly signs. I strolled on, and I turned a corner.

I heard a rattling sound. On up the street, I saw a man lugging along a small cart. I had to follow. It was curfew, after all.

The man crossed Cathedral Square and picked up speed, his stride both graceful and clumsy as the cart's little steel wheels battled the cobblestones.

"Hey, you! Stop there!" I hurried on, following him down a side street.

A narrow alley led me to a small square surrounded by empty shops and a boarded-up pub. The man had found an arched doorway, and now pressed himself up against the dark shadowed door face first, doing his best with just about nothing.

I crossed the square, unfastening my holster. "I see you. Come here. With hands up."

The man turned and, raising his hands, stepped on out. His face was pleasant enough but in the same way that a smile held for a camera was better to glance at than look at too long. Sweat soaked his face, which lent a shine to the scar along his left jowl. It was an actual dueling scar, the true mark of every blue-blooded German fraternity lad. Glossy thin mustache, black hair. He looked well fed, if not pampered, and just shy of middle age. He wore a black leather motoring jacket with fur collar and high boots, all in all looking more like a circus ringleader than the privileged German on the run he probably was.

He shot a smile at me and pleasant wasn't the word anymore. Gold crowns sparkled. His eyes bulged, bloodshot. He stammered in English, "Look here, *mein Herr*, it's really nothing suspicious. If that is what you think."

"That's what you're thinking. I was thinking how you're breaking curfew."

"Yes, yes, of course. First, allow me to ..." He bowed to me, like out of some costume play, and it was all I could do not to roll my eyes. "I am a baron by title, the Baron von Maulendorff," he said. "My family is Heimgau. Like any harmless German, I had hoped to return home, finally, but your Military Government has requisitioned my mansion. So, this curfew is a daunting prospect for me." The so-called baron gestured toward the cart. "But, perhaps you will let me off this one time, for a small largess?"

Fool, I was thinking. Who does he take me for? Who does he take MG for? "Tell you what. Why don't you show me this cart of yours—the whole cart?"

The baron sucked on his shiny teeth. He rolled his toy cart out of the doorway as if it was full of bricks. The thing was a sight up close, with cherry wood and floral carvings and a Bavarian checkered tarp that I tossed aside. I pulled out a beaded gown and a pinstriped suit and set them on the sidewalk. Bottles of Pernod, Hennessy and a dusty Vermouth. At the bottom, between two pillows, lay a porcelain figurine of a court jester. Hand painted, glowing somehow brighter than white. The jester was grasping a flute and scratching at his harlequin smock belly, and the mouth cackled in a grotesque way that made this baron's smile look like a songbird's.

"Just feel its weight. Under the base you find the crossed swords painted in blue. It's correct in every way—a Meissen, to be exact. Seventeen forties. Fine posing, excellent detail."

What did I expect? Silencer pistols? Secret map to some Nazi hidey-hole? I laid the jester back in the cart. "The black market's not my game. Tell you what. Let's trade for something else."

"Ah. But, what else is there?"

"Information."

The baron exchanged glances with imaginary friends—one to his left, another to his right. "Continue, please."

I switched to German: "Yesterday I found three corpses on the Heimgauer Strasse. Not long deceased. They'd been tortured, from the looks of it."

The baron was watching me with softer, wearier eyes. His imaginary friends, long gone. He shook his head and, frowning, began backing up.

"What are you doing? Hold on."

The baron retreated ever faster, shuffling backward. He ran off out across the square.

"Stop! I'll shoot!" Fumbling with my holster I drew my Colt, released the safety and cocked. The baron was sprinting, making for another side alley. I aimed for above his head. I squeezed the trigger.

Click. Nothing. Click. I hadn't even loaded the damn thing.

I ran down that side alley, but only found darkness, another narrow lane that twisted on into others, and more darkness. No one. Nothing but the silence. I returned to the square and remembered the cart, which to my surprise was still there.

Some manner of business had indeed gone down here, Winkl had told me, and now this baron mucky-muck seemed to confirm it. I lifted out the porcelain jester and took another look. It gleamed and it glistened. I had no idea what the thing was worth. I placed a Lucky on my lips and began pushing the baron's cart back to my billet, looking not unlike one of those many sorry refugees who were soon sure to find even a backwater like Heimgau.

When the war was still on, and I was riding southeast across Germany with the rest of the US Army's rear end, I'd had a recurring nightmare of a daydream about the zoos of Central Europe, Germany, Bavaria, whatever city was closest to my route. What had happened to those caged-in animals during all the air raids, artillery barrages, the raging fires? Who was feeding them? Could they ever escape? Such a fate had to be the only thing worse than being in combat. The animals always had it worse. I had to know, even if the answer was that no one fed those poor creatures, their cages had remained locked tight, and they were so starved that only those very firestorms could save them from banging away at their bars until they bled and bled. I knew nothing could save them from eating their young, from gnawing away at their own scorched skin and bones. Ghastly, it was—no, evil was what it was, and not exactly a testament to mankind's progress, but still I needed to know. Telling no one, I went and found a couple local zoos. Either I couldn't get in or I found them empty.

It was like that with these tortured corpses. Dead Abraham was practically shouting at me through that dark hood. He had wanted me to know. So my need to know gnawed at me over the next eight days as each new morning brought MG more crises to manage. The promised refugees began to trickle in, each weighed down by ragged clothes they wore in layers just to keep them in their possession. They pulled carts of scrawny children and the sick and they pushed wheelbarrows, buggies and bicycles laden like pack donkeys. Old men humped rucksacks and women marched in clutching rotting produce and meat scraps found on the way. Then the former forced laborers came and it wasn't pretty. Most were young men who had their best years stolen. For every one that behaved, three had been drunk and violent for weeks and they kicked at the locals and looted even the shops that the locals themselves had already looted. Horton's GIs were crucial here. Somehow they made order out of it and with an ease that impressed all. It helped the locals lose their scared act. They filled the squares now and all doffed their hats to us; although removing hats for us was an MG rule, I told myself these Heimgauers were people who'd do it anyway. We had some successes. We got full water up and running and most electricity. Then trucks and cars both loaned and stolen brought a wave of more refugees, many of them sent by the surrounding counties' MGs who just couldn't take in any more. We turned a former Hitler Youth hostel on the edge of town into a temporary camp. Talk about a mix of peoples, origins, tough luck stories. Whether Displaced Persons, Ethnic German refugees expelled from the East, or those few concentration camp victims who had wandered into Heimgau, all had to be kept together because food stocks were still dwindling. We distributed what rations we had, the DPs and refugees getting first dibs and then the locals. After four days of that, the camp overflowed and we ordered the locals to open their doors and take them in. Something like the opposite of tourism had come to Heimgau.

I had little time to investigate the missing corpses or the Baron von Maulendorff during this time, although locals, when I pressed them, did confirm the baron was indeed an echt baron and still around too. He did have a home here. One evening I raced a jeep out to his family villa beyond the greener edge of town, a surprisingly modest two-story job with a mock tower keep at one corner. A plaque fixed to a pompous gate read, Maulendorff Palace, and above that the standard sign: "Off Limits. Property Requisitioned by United States Military Government." So he had been telling the truth in this respect—he did not have his home anymore. Another afternoon I drove up the road to Dollendorf again and found, as I probably expected, only those broken-down workshops, the old rail line, trees and more trees, and that rocky old hill watching over it all. The rail shelter was empty.

Back in town the hospital was holding on, for now. Soon they'd need medication and more rations. Soon we'd have to get the Red Cross to pass through here. Meanwhile, locals told me the Baron von Maulendorff was popping up everywhere in town—except wherever I was.

On the ninth day, a Friday afternoon, I tried Major Membre in his City Hall office—for the third time that day. To no avail. The major already had a habit of coming in around noon, earliest, and today was looking like a no-show. The only thing worse than a blowhard was a loafer, I thought and started to march right on up to Membre's castle billet. Then I spotted the boy-man major himself making his way through Old Town on foot, cutting a path through a crowd of black marketers on Cathedral Square screaming "Rowss!" and "Gay-hen see!" and whipping at the air with his riding crop. I followed. The major headed down a narrow lane, dim and crooked and one of the oldest in Old Town. Around a few corners I found him watching a group of young boys playing soccer, kicking a brown ball against the walls. I stood behind the major. He was beaming as if he'd just discovered a street paved with gems. The boys had gaunt faces with wide eyes, tattered short pants and frayed collars, lean little arms. Not exactly gems. More like feral cats.

"Sir?" I said.

Membre shot me a double-take but didn't lose the blissful face. "Ah, just look at the babies, just bless their little hearts. I gave them that ball."

"That was good of you." They could use more chow, I really wanted to add.

"Yes, it's really turning out nicely for them. Just look at them. They would make such a fine choir."

The soccer had stopped. The boys stared, only now understanding the importance of two of their chief liberators standing before them. A couple of them ran off. "No, no, no, don't flee," muttered the major. He placed his boot on top of the soccer ball and the boys gathered around him. "I American, I no understand your football," he said in his childlike German, and they laughed and explained the rules to him, and he lowered to his knees to hear better. He waved me over. "Come on and translate, come on."

"I have other business, sir. With you. Those tortured men, for example."

Membre looked at me just as the kids had when they saw the major. He pulled his tunic down tight, marched over to me, and moaned out a sigh. "All right, all right. More sordid tales of rotting corpses, Captain?"

"Not more. Same. And they weren't rotting. They had just bought it, possibly same day. So it's our responsibility." Again, I told him about the Baron von Maulendorff, who just might know something. Though I didn't mention pulling my gun. I hadn't even frisked the man—some Public Safety officer I was. And again the major listened in silence, nodding at random intervals. We should send a few GIs out looking for this slick baron, I insisted. He could not hide long. "And how could he, Major? I see that you've requisitioned his villa."

Major Membre snickered. "Oh, you're a go-getter, I give you that. That's why I made you Public Safety." He pressed a hand to his chest. "So that settles it. I tell you what: What are you doing tonight?" he said with a homey smile that put me back stateside but nowhere I wanted to be. "Nothing, I bet. So why don't you come on up to my billet? What do you say, old boy?"

Five

I ACCEPTED THE MAJOR'S INVITATION. How else to reach a CO who was never in his office, who didn't hear bad news, who'd given me little clue what he wanted here? I could admit I was not the same caste as most would-be MG commanders. Many had been specialists stateside. They taught anthropology, designed Crosley sedans, or headed some school district or electric company board. Others were specialists of another sort. They owed their existence to various states of wealth and power and, being products thereof, came over here to raise their stock back home. The major had to be the latter case, and his All-American roots probably went way back to the Mayflower. I knew men like that didn't use their offices for the big moves. They made their plays in chummy rooms with smart talking and liquor flowing, and so that's just how I would have to play him.

I hiked up to Hohenheimgau Castle and, arriving early, and strolled the main rampart wall with its wondrous view. Beyond the treetops and Old Town's red roofs lay green valleys, a golden horizon. I let the setting spring sun warm my face. I recalled my trusty backgrounders: "Hohenheimgau Castle (ca. 1100) has a dignity not usually afforded to towns of Heimgau's size. Locals call it a gray, mediocre mass (the "block," some call it), but it is intact and supremely located atop Old Town's one hill overlooking the Gothic cathedral below. Old Town with her cathedral is the heart and soul, it is said, and the castle is the head ..."

I had been up at the castle before, on my rounds. But I had only visited the parish offices, checked out Father Plant's address, the monastery. The few officials, curates, and monks there were still in shock that their Father Plant was gone, Nazi and all. The brown father had ordered them to hide out in the county until the surrender, and most were only now returning. In many occupied towns, the church would help keep MG afloat. Here it was a dead end.

Which left my major. Major Membre had the joint all to himself. He had set up his new billet in the newer, rear-side wing of the castle. With its rosy paint, ornate columns, and fenestration and curly wrought iron, this new wing was like an opera house compared to the rest of the castle. Here the sun had already gone under, the sky dimmer. I passed on through a courtyard, where two US Army trucks were parked next to a couple worn German Opels with the plates removed. I entered the foyer and followed a hallway lined with antique paintings—some had been removed, leaving squares of brighter white wall. The air grew warmer and thick with the major's sweet Paris cologne, and it led me into an eighteenth-century-style sitting room. Gold brocade walls glittered in oversized mirrors. Plush tassels dangled from flowing, satiny window treatments. Yet, in one corner stood a black and silver bar in the Art Deco style. The feel was cheap and pretentious, and I thought I smelled vanilla. Would have made a swell bordello, this place.

"You're early."

I flinched. The major stood at my back. "Evening, sir. Uh, I just came that way. How did you—"

"I have my ways. It's a castle, Captain. Full of trap doors, fake walls." The major was grinning and panting slightly through his teeth, and I had the uneasy feeling that he had worked plenty hard to sneak up on me.

"Well?" the major said, holding his arms out to the room. Only now did I notice he was wearing a purple corduroy bathrobe. It had a monogram: R.A.M.

"Nice billet, sir." I made my eyes wonder at the room as if I meant it.

"First thing up here—you can lose the 'sir.' Whiskey? Even got ice."

We drank, the ice cracking and clunking and a rare pleasure, I had to admit. We made small talk. The major had on a ring with a gleaming red head the size of a walnut, and he kept grabbing at it and screwing it down tight to his knuckles. It might have been a nervous tic, but it reminded me of a doctor snapping his rubber gloves. The major asked if I thought his rings were fancy. I nodded, sure, sure. "This one goes way back to my college days," the major said, "from the old fraternity, that kind of business; got that one from the Rotary and this one here's from the Masonic Temple, but don't tell anyone!"

"If you don't mind me asking: What did you do back home?"

Membre grinned again. "Furnishings. Fine furniture, all that goes with it. That's the family business, you see. Membre and Sons." I was expecting a half hour on the Membre family's dominance of the Midwest furnishing business. Yet something made the grin seal up tight and Membre threw back his drink. "So, the Baron von Maulendorff? Why you're really here, right?"

"If it can help, yes."

"Well, I did requisition his mansion, that's right. And now I'm giving it back to him."

"You're what?"

Floorboards creaked, from somewhere beyond the purple major. From behind an orange-red curtain along the wall. I heard a near whisper: "*Herr Kapitän* Kaspar? Is that you? Please listen. I'll come out, but only for the promise that you not harm me."

The baron was here? My head had filled with a black heat, but what could I do? Major Membre was staring at me with pursed lips, in a near pout.

"Oh, all right," I said.

The curtain parted. A cigarette in a silver holder, and then trembling fingers showed. Membre lowered his drink to admire the Baron von Maulendorff as he entered the room. The baron's green velvet smoking jacket was cut in the Bavarian style, with darker stand-up collar and wooden buttons. "Captain Kaspar, let me introduce our very honored guest, the Baron Friedrich-Faustino—"

"Know who he is, Major. I'm the one caught him breaking curfew."

"Very well, Captain. But that's behind us now."

I didn't like where this was going and Maulendorff could see it. He pushed back his longish hair with a flat hand and tried a nervous chuckle. "Yes, well, I must say I understand your anger," he said to me in German.

"Keep it in English—it's the Official Language of Military Government."

"Please, Captain," Membre said.

The baron was sweating again. He wiped at his face with a handkerchief, but the sweat had already soaked his silk yellow ascot, making it look like a soggy crepe. Let him sweat, I thought, and downed my whiskey. I went behind the bar, poured another.

Membre spoke: "Listen, Frankfurt HQ prefers that certain traditional, conservative elements of German society be well treated.

You know that. The clergy are a big help in some towns, as you know. We don't have that luxury here, unfortunately. But we do have a committed Catholic personage here in the baron. So, as long as said individuals were not in the party, which the baron was not, you can consider him vetted."

The baron looked to Membre, who nodded. The baron said, as if reciting a script, "It is our *Stunde Null*, after all—our Hour Zero, where everything restarts from nothing. And with the Bolsheviks, er, Communists in the East, who else can bring stability to a future Germany? Or to an independent Bavaria. God willing."

I nodded, drank, and stared from behind the bar. In their getups, the two looked like a duo from Hollywood's latest screwball comedy. All right, fine. So bring on the big show.

"Still, that is not why I'm here," the baron said.

Membre nodded. "No, it's not. Come along, Captain."

Major Membre left the baron waiting there and led me into what he called his "second office," a spare rectangle of a room with clean white walls and glossy gray floor, its paint job so new I could smell it. The room looked more like a mock Bauhaus workshop than a library. During the day the broad windows gave a splendid view of the stream called the Heimbach that ran along the rear of castle hill, Membre said, stirring his drink with his gem finger (though his glass had a stir stick). Tonight there was no view, no twinkling current. The windows formed huge black squares, sucking any little warmth from the room, and the sterile modern caged light fixtures above cast sharp lines on our faces. The major had a purple love seat and half-opened crates of whiskey and cognac clustered in the middle of the room. On a black steel desk sat two phones.

One of the phones rang, rattling the metal desktop. Membre lunged for it and barked into the receiver: "Heimgau here ... It's late, this better be good ... Ah. Evening, sir. That's fine, just fine. Bibles? Can you be more specific, General—sir." Membre rolling his eyes for me. "Well, what century? More bibles in the 1700s than people think ... Yes, please do that ... Sir. Bye now."

I guessed this helped explain the four heavy trucks out in the courtyard, not to mention all the fine houses the major had slapped with Off-Limits signs. Of course, some MG detachments used their all-powerful status to trade, acquire, and move the goods and spoils of war. Every soldier, every unit did it to a degree, from the lowliest Joe to the shiniest four-star. I couldn't blame them. Some had damn good reasons. Some had been fighting men, and had seen friends die. Other soldiers were Jewish. I wasn't a fool. The trick was in keeping the business civil, discreet. Not like this. Not like a bazaar. The worst of it was, the major had two of the town's five working phone lines – phones that could be used to badger the Red Cross or, at the least, swap some of this plunder for foodstuffs.

"So," Membre began, but the phone rang again. "Heimgau here ... Why yes! Wooden mangers? How nice. Lots of artisan stuff here, we have a long tradition of handiwork ... And clocks? Like cuckoo clocks? Sure, I can get you those ... just send a truck and I'll take care of you ... No, thank you." He set down the receiver, beaming. "That was one of Patton's adjutants."

"Impressive."

"Yes. Oh, yes," Membre said.

Two men with neat gray beards rushed in lugging either ends of a small crate. They were refugees—probably forced laborers from the East—and took little notice of me despite my captain's uniform. They whispered to the major in broken, warbling English and produced a set of silver chalices from the crate. "I just love fine things," Membre said and rambled on about loving fine things till spit gathered at the edges of his mouth, his lips greasy like he'd just eaten a pork sandwich. "It's from the *Schatzkammer* itself—that's the castle's treasure chamber," he told me.

"I know what the word means."

"I know. I know that. Know how much these are worth? These men are about to tell me."

"I don't. Look, sir, I get the picture. What you want to show me. Think I even get why. But—"

Both phones rang. The major's two appointed art experts rubbed their hands together, eyeing me. Membre stared at them, at the phones, at me. "Suddenly it's a rush," he said. "All right, just, wait back there with the baron. Get acquainted. I got a real treat for you. But remember, our baron's Off Limits too," he said and lunged for both phones at once.

Major Membre was feeling generous with his newfound racket, and I guess I should've been flattered. Yet all I wanted was the pack of Lucky Strikes I'd left on that faux deco bar. Then I was out of there.

I marched back through the sitting room. The bar was cleared off. The Baron von Maulendorff was tiptoeing my way. I whirled around. "What? Where are my smokes?"

The baron reached out and pretended to produce my pack from behind my ear like some warmed-over roadhouse magician. I snatched the pack and checked it was still full. And then? I don't know, maybe it was the absurdity of this tin-crown, old-hat aristo that made me not smack that cornball grin off his face (it definitely wasn't his charm). I might've even smiled back. He might have produced another bow. The next thing I knew I was hunkering down with the man in two matching yellow damask chairs. Crystal glasses sat on a silver tray on a gilded table. The baron poured me more whiskey, flailing away now like a hurried maître d'.

"Don't you even want to know what happened to your cart?" I said.

"No. That is yours now."

"Suit yourself." At least the baron hadn't tried to ridicule my handgun skills.

"Listen, we don't have time for chat," the baron said in more direct German. He was close to whispering. "You are a German, yes?"

"No."

The baron's hand pressed on his chest. "Excuse me— German-American. Thus, the sour look? You don't want people to know. It must have been complicated back home."

"It's tough all over, see."

"But not for you here? If you want it that way. That's why your major wants you on-board. You have the fluent language and the ambition to go with it. That's what he is thinking. You come from nothing, am I correct?"

I set down my glass. "Enough about me."

"As you wish. I just want you to know that I respect you. Your Military Government is in a very admirable position, I must say. A long, nasty war brings more than one glorious estate sale, no? And you MG men can be the middlemen for some 'real shiny brass,' as you call it. It's much like your gangster movies. If the US Army was the mob, the Military Government would be the front and the fence. Yes?" The baron only now noticed that I'd set down my glass. "Ah. But of course, the US Army is not the mob, is it?"

"No, it's not. You're talking about the major. I'm not the major."

"No, you're not he. So I'll be direct." The baron stopped to listen, stole a look around. Whispered: "Have you heard about any, shall we say, stray freight trains about?"

"No. Stray how? That's a vague question."

The baron took a quick drink. "I'm taking quite a chance here, understand."

"So don't take it."

"It is said there are more trains. There could be one near here. Many did embark in the last days. All you needed was undamaged tracks and a locomotive."

Colonel Spanner certainly would not like this. Anything Off Limits to me certainly was to this displaced manor swell. So I spoke louder: "You don't want the major to know. I get you. So how you know I won't tell him?"

"You won't. You despise him, if I may be so bold. I would too, if I were you."

The baron had stretched his mouth tight, ready for that smack now. Instead, I lifted my drink and stood and walked around the room as if stretching my legs. I checked the door, the hallway, the curtain from behind which the baron had appeared. Behind it was a door that I opened to find an older, narrower, darker hallway. We were alone. I sat, faced the baron. "You want info. So do I. So I'm going to give you one chance. What about those corpses? The tortured bodies. My mere mention of them made you run from me that night."

The baron held up a finger. "I ran because it was curfew."

"Because I wasn't willing to cut a deal with you. So you go and find a much better deal with someone else. The major. Now your partner, by the looks of it."

"You pulled a pistol on me."

"I drew after you ran. And I didn't shoot, did I? No, I just mention corpses and you ran—"

"My God!" The baron pressed fingers to his lips. "You do, don't you?"

"I do what? Out with it."

"You suspect the major?"

"What? I didn't say that. I just want to get to the bottom of this."

The baron was smarter than he looked. I couldn't imagine one of ours doing what I saw on that road. And yet I had to consider the major a suspect, just like everyone else. If I didn't, it wouldn't be justice I was after. No one should be excluded. That was a Democracy with the big D.

The baron nodded, muttering, "Well, yes, I suppose it is possible." He got up and paced the room. He checked the window,

which I'd forgotten to do. He came back and said: "I do know something happened. One hears things. But I honestly don't know how
it came to pass."

"Then I don't know of any train."

"Please, *Herr* Kaspar, I'm telling you all I know." The baron
stared into the table, his eyes racing, reflecting the glisten of the
gilding. I waited. I had all the time for this, a full pack of Luckies'
worth at least. "I do know this: The major was in town then," he
added.

"How do you know?"

"I saw him. In town. Yes. He was here at least two days before you."

"Two?" The major had told me he'd come in the same day. Or
had he? No, no, it was the detachment that arrived the same day.
Membre never mentioned when he arrived.

We heard footsteps. Coming down the hallway.

The baron spoke fast: "What I would do, I were you? Pursue any
survivors. Gain their trust. Small town, this is. Word gets around;
someone must've seen more, must know more."

"Survivors of what? Is that why all were so spooked when I got
here? This place was a ghost town."

"Spooked, as you call it? The citizens? Oh, perhaps so, yes ..."

The footsteps neared the doorway.

And the baron let out a big fake laugh, slapped me on the knee
for the major to see.

Only it wasn't Major Membre. We heard voices—giggling
female voices. Two Fräuleins entered clinging to each other, smiling
taut smiles. Their skirts were tight, the blouses loose, and their thick
blond curls wavy and curled under, making them look more like
swing-band singers than Bavarian farm girls. They were sisters. I'd
seen them around town already. How could a man miss them?

"Ah, the girls." The baron stood and heaved out another bow.
"Allow me to introduce the esteemed Public Safety Officer of
your town, Captain Kaspar." He added to me in English from
the side of his mouth, "They hope to make their way to Vienna—
to live with their aunt—and all they need are the right papers,"
and the girls nodded along, knowing not the words but surely
the plan. He said to the girls in Heimgau German: "Bärbel and,
what's your name?"

"Brigitta." The sisters giggled again. Lips shined in the light. A
smell like fresh berries had filled the room.

The baron whispered to me: "Lost their parents but not as young as they look."

Major Membre returned. He'd changed into a white seersucker suit with black string tie. He was humming "Mairzy Doats," of all the tunes. His refugee minions dropped off a large picnic basket and hurried off, their eyes lowered, and the major, still humming, laid out the basket's contents on the gold table—three bottles of '37 Mosel Gewürztraminer, Allgäuer cheese, a chain of sausages and two oval loaves of grainy bread. The sisters were clapping and hopping in place.

Even to me it smelled glorious. This was what Germany was supposed to smell like. "Not even we can get chow like this," I muttered.

"I told you. Did I tell you?" Membre grinned. He filled glasses, taking care not to splash any, and did so all over his wrist and cuff. "Why don't you speak some of your *Deutsch* with the girls? It's okay. I told them about you."

Suddenly the smell went a little rancid. "About me? What about me, Major?"

Membre shrugged, the ends of his tie dipping into his wine glass. "Nothing. Nothing at all. I consider you as American as I am."

I turned away to watch Brigitta and Bärbel. They gulped the wine straight from the bottle, tore at bread and inhaled hunks of sausage, gasped at the tastes, and groped at each other's fleshy arms between swallows. It was lusty, like one of those rich and glowing Rubens paintings with a heroic name: Teutonic Virgins Submit To Gluttony Before Battle, or something. Bärbel rubbed the baron's shoulders. Brigitta filled my glass. She gazed into me, cradling the wine bottle low with both hands, her warm green eyes controlling mine. I looked away, trying to recall Colonel Spanner's words, those MG handbooks, my own damn vows. These people were our enemy only a month ago. Swoop on in, take advantage, and they'll return the deed in spades.

I asked Brigitta if maybe she wouldn't be better off filling up the *Herr* Major's glass. Membre seemed to understand. He spat a laugh: "You don't think one of them is for me, do you? I'm CO. My God, man, how would it look?"

"My fair maidens, do you have need of a nest for resting your weary selves so deserving of comfort?" the baron was saying to Bärbel now in elaborate, centuries-old High German. "Verily, you must remove yourselves to my mansion one fine day, consider this my most unconditional invitation ..."

Mansion? A hot rush had filled my head. "No, wait. Wait one minute."

The baron and the Gretchens turned to me. Membre set down his near-empty glass with care as if it was full to the brim. "What is it, Captain? Are you ill?"

I barked at Membre: "You said, 'honored guest'."

Membre raised an eyebrow. "Son, I don't follow you."

"When I first got here, you introduced Maulendorff here as your 'very honored guest.'" What's he honored for?" I stood, my arms cocked taut at my sides.

Membre held a smile. He showed it to the baron and the sisters. He tugged at his string tie and said, "Well, you've forced my hand, haven't you? I was going to post the announcement next week, but I don't see any harm in announcing it to you now." Membre held out his glass to the baron. "Ladies and gentleman, allow me to introduce the new mayor of Heimgau—"

My legs hurtled me to the door and my hands wanted to be fists. So much for the washed-up noble. The major's partner in plunder becomes the mayor? It was balls-out cronyism already, a rotten old game. I kicked a chair out of my way.

"Oh, sit back down, Captain," Membre said. "You should feel honored. I showed you my little side business because I'd like you to play a part. Heck, play quarterback, you want. You have the skills for it. Don't you see that? You know that's why you're here. Why I invited you here. We're cohorts."

Cohorts? In cahoots? Membre could take his skills and choke on them. I turned to them, the doorway at my shoulders. "What about the case? What about that?"

"Case? Ah, yes, your murders," the major said, stroking his lips with two fingers. "Tell you what. Show me some corpses and we'll take it from there. That's a fine start."

The wine in me wanted me to shout at him: There aren't any, you overcooked noodle, I told you that. Then again, maybe Membre knew that—and saw I had no chance. So, I leveled my shoulders and said: "Fine. Sure. I'll get it licked. And, what about Uli Winkl?"

The baron said, "He will remain Temporary Police Chief—"

"Not talking to you, see, so can it. Got no right snaking your way in like this."

The baron sighed. Sipped wine.

"In point of fact, this was my doing, and I'm simply acting on policy," the major said, doing his best to regain his bland MG commander voice. "What I was trying to tell you. He's the kind of man Germany will need."

As the major spoke, I found myself feeling my way back to the chair. That heat had drained from my neck, chest. Despite the booze, smoke and disgust, a cool crisp bite of clarity—of reality— had registered deep within my brain. A local like Winkl could only help me so much, and getting Major Membre on the level was a dud. As is, they had me licked.

Colonel Spanner was the only man who might help me. I simply had not been thinking big enough.

Improvise when required, that was the drill. So play it cool, Harry.

"Pardon me. All right? I guess I'm just a slow learner," I said. I took Brigitta by the hand, leading her to the doorway, Brigitta stroking my hair and neck and dancing around me. "Well, then, thanks for the hospitality, Gentleman." I grabbed a bottle of wine, and me and my very own Victory girl were out the door before Heimgau's very own major baron duo could honor me again.

"You know what we got here, doll?" I said to Brigitta in English. "Too many chiefs and not enough Indians, that's what."

Six

THE NEXT AFTERNOON, a cigar-shaped US Army sedan without markings had parked outside the county courthouse near Cathedral Square. Sergeant Horton leaned against the car, smothering the front fender with his giant frame and chewing on a stick of sausage jerky, its sweet earthy tang piercing the air. So busy chewing that he forgot to stand straight or salute, again. "Cap'n," he said.

"Afternoon. Colonel Spanner, that his vehicle? I need to see him. Only take a minute. Do I have to tell you it's an order?"

Horton's brow folded into fat strips. "Nah." He led me inside the courthouse to a long, corridor-like room so dim we had to squint. The blinds were drawn, leaving only thin lines of daylight. Horton left and shut the door behind him. Letting my eyes adjust, I made out polished dark wood walls and bookshelves and smelled rich old leather. Other details caught my eye. Bullet holes riddled the shelves, leaving splinters and stain peelings. On the farthest wall hung a black flag bearing a Nazi swastika eagle in white. Below the flag, a figure sat at a broad desk.

"That you, Colonel, sir?"

"It is. Captain Kaspar. Get on over here, take a seat."

"Yes, sir." I found a leather chair before the desk. "Why are you sitting in the dark, sir?"

Colonel Spanner didn't answer. I guessed this building didn't have power back yet. In the near darkness, Spanner's face looked less ruddy and firmer, like marble. He said: "First off, just what is this Nazi Justice flag doing here?"

"Winkl must have missed it, sir, he's ..."

"He's your police chief. Used to be *Hausmeister*."

"Right, I didn't have a choice there. Had few options."

"I have no problem with that. I'm not questioning your efforts."

"No, sir, of course not." My chest had tightened. I took a deep breath. "Still, it is my fault—the flag I mean. I should've done a walk-through here. My responsibility. We don't have a legal MGO here, so I'd be the closest thing."

"That's fine." On a chair stood a battered brown Army briefcase, like mine but aged a hundred years, it seemed, the leather cracked and stained. On the desktop lay a few plain tan folders, closed. Spanner touched one. "Now, I took a little tour around town today. Let me stress one thing. Appearances are key, to the locals and to the brass hats in Frankfurt. I cannot be clearer about that. The last thing we want is Investigations Division crawling down here, sniffing around, believe you me. Because I will be right behind them. Might even be in front of them, and you really don't want that."

"Yes, sir. Thank you."

Spanner stared as if waiting for me to continue. In that moment, I entertained the hunch that he really had come here just for me, for my sake.

So I added: "By the way, have you had the pleasure of meeting Major Membre?"

A smile spread across Spanner's face. "You want my reckoning of the man, don't you? All I can say is, the man has plenty to learn. Eager though, in his way. He tried to give me a bottle of absinthe of all things. Boy, I hadn't seen that old rot since my journeys into the bordellos of New Orleans. But, that's not what you mean."

"No."

"Those corpses you saw. You want to know what happened here."

"Yes."

The colonel strode the length of the room. He drew all the blinds open, and I had to squint again. The light came harsh and uniform, reflecting the vast gray wall of the cathedral that blocked all other views. Silhouettes of gargoyles loomed from gutters above, their tongues wagging and their wings sharp against the sky. "And you deserve to know. You do alone," Spanner said. He spoke from the window, his upper body also set in silhouette, like some ancient bust: "You have to understand how it was, before. In the chaos of war. When I rolled in a couple weeks ago, things were far amiss here. Among the locals, there was a storm brewing about how to deal with the arrival of the United States Army. The SS troops stationed here wanted a last stand, but some locals turned rebel. They opposed it. About time for such an uprising, wasn't it?"

I smirked. "About ten years too late."

"Yes. So these local Rebs go knock off a couple top local Nazis. Send the rest fleeing. Secure the post office, take City Hall, this courthouse here. Meantime the SS troops, seeing the writing on the wall, are splitting up over what to do. Some steel themselves for a shoot-out while others go and get smart and think about what comes next." As he spoke, Spanner's accent turned friendlier. He was a family counselor, the country doctor. "Don't have to tell ya, things were getting dicey. The smart SS officers, they don't want to see a nice ole place like this Heimgau destroyed over a war that's been long decided. They do win out. They keep about half their men. The other half head for the hills and who knows where. Now the smart SS hold the town so they can surrender it peaceably."

"To you."

"I was here. Advance team. There was no one else. But I'm in a bind. Our forward combat units had skipped Heimgau altogether. I'm Counter Intelligence. We're squad strength at best. How do I keep order?"

"These enemy troops. The 'smart' SS, as you called them."

"Only answer. Way I figure it, situation like this, there's your good krauts and there's the bad-uns. Good krauts being the smart ones."

I only nodded. The colonel had deployed enemy troops to keep order, and that was supposed to be okay. Okey, I told myself. The colonel had tried to warn me some things would never make sense in peace.

The colonel sighed. "So, these SS, they even provided valuable intelligence. Grand ole dogfaces, some of these SS. They'd served in the East, you see, against the Russkies. That's how I won them over too: I promised a new German army would be formed so we could go on to fight the Russkies together."

Had he crossed the line? Who was to say I would not have done the same thing? Spanner was waiting, demanding a response. I better not patronize or, worse yet, play the toady. He was expecting me to use my head.

"They gave you no problems?" I said.

"Well, now here's the hard part. I did indeed hear about the SS killing a few civs."

"So the bodies I saw were civilians."

Spanner, nodding, returned to his chair. "Listen to me. I could not be everywhere at once. There were shootouts, as you see from these bullet holes here. Other incidents. Up at the castle. Some victims were ... left over from before I got here. The pandemonium rattled these poor Heimgauers all to heck." His eyes had turned a vibrant blue-gray, somber and penitent. "Now, look. The SS must have done the deed, but I was just as responsible, having used some of their kind to keep order. That was my mistake. We make mistakes in war. And I accept it as such. But only unofficially, remember. Only to you."

"They were tortured. Those people were tortured. One was a survivor from one of the Nazis' concentration camps, as far as I could tell."

Spanner's face grew hard. "We—I—didn't do the work on those bodies."

"I didn't say you did, sir."

"No. You did not." Spanner shook his head, his eyes glazing over. "I'll have to take back my GIs soon. I have other matters pressing."

"We'll manage."

"Fine. Do not forget one thing: This is still my op area. All right? Any other questions?"

"Yes. One thing I guess I don't understand. What happened to them?"

"To whom, son?"

"The smart SS. Their officers you dealt with. I mean, officially."

Spanner stood. He walked across the room, leaned against the windowsill and stared out again. "The day before you found me in Dollendorf, we disarmed them and sent them off to POW camps, the SS officers to VIP camps. Ah, as for any local civilians that bought it? They received a Christian burial. Officially, that is."

"I understand, sir."

Spanner stared, not blinking. "Tell me about you for a moment. You're German-born. American citizen?"

I nodded. "Naturalized. Since I was a kid."

"Parents? Other family?"

"My parents have been stateside for seventeen years. I have an older brother, somewhere."

"Doesn't matter sometimes though, does it? The way people can be back home. The fool hysteria. Every German-American's one secret code away from manning a spy submarine, about to land storm troopers on the Empire State Building." Spanner laughed at the thought, warm and fatherly. "You've had a tough time back home? Your family?"

"It's part of the deal, isn't it? That's the way I look at it. Have to look at it. It's part of the war effort. America must be wary. There might be good reason for clamping down."

"Wary, hell. People don't know because they've never been over here. They have never been up on the goddamn line. Clawed their way out of the meat grinder. You haven't. You don't fucking know ..."

Spanner stared off, into a dark corner of the room. Something had taken hold of him. I'd heard of this. Some called it the thousand-yard stare, others the gooney-bird look, but there was nothing funny about it. At the front he must have seen things, done things I could never imagine. Things my buddies in the ATSP must have gone through before they bought it.

"No, sir," I said. "I could never know."

He didn't seem to hear me. His silence went on so long it was like a racket, a droning, revving engine. I stared into my lap. Then I felt his eyes on me. I looked up.

He had turned to me, glaring at me. "Listen up, Kaspar. I want you to know I view you as a valuable asset, what you are. It's not something to be used against you. It can be a plus for you."

"I've heard that lately."

"I'm telling you. You can get things done here. Can't you? Show them what being an American's really all about."

"I think so."

Spanner's eyes had brightened, which took away some of the ugliness. "So you get your first posting, here. You were meant to be Commanding Officer. But then Major Membre gets the hitch. Pushed his papers, the rich civ come looking for medals." That was about right on the money, I figured. I nodded along. The colonel's eyes darkened. "So, you will just have to play things very carefully. With your background, it could still look like you have a grudge or, worse yet, that you're sympathizing."

"I've thought about that."

"I'm sure you have. Because you're a smart egg. No bullshit."

"I see it like I see it."

"We can help each other, down the line. Keep each other informed. I don't want you to spy for me. This isn't about latest directives or politics, isn't combat boys versus the desk brass. I'm talking about a partnership here, one based on bona fide trust."

"Trust," I said and paused as if trying the word out for the first time.

"Just think of me as a friend outside the rigmarole. Do you hear what I'm saying? You can come straight to me and only me, if you think something's fishy, and I'll do my best to fix it. I promise."

It was a bargain, if not a gift. Still, I took my time with it because I had to get the most out of this. I shifted in the chair. I looked out the window. Spanner had owned up nobly. At least two of the tortured dead were probably locals, or had been once, and the torture-murderer could still be in town. But, don't go looking too hell-bent or you could spook the colonel, I told myself. Build up to it, by degrees.

"There is the population's meager food supply," I began. I explained it. Since our detachment had no nutrition officer, I'd gone around Major Membre and written to Frankfurt and then telephoned. But Frankfurt could give nothing, not even new ration tickets—locals were to use their old ones with the swastikas on them. I added, "We also need Red Cross shipments, and a relief team for the refugees and DPs, get the repatriation going."

"Heimgau is on a limb. It's not exactly Munich, Nuremberg. But I'll do my darnedest."

"Great."

"Good ..." The colonel stared down from the window, arms crossed at his chest.

"You confessed to me," I said. "So I'll confess to you. The major, yes, he is a bad egg."

"In what way? You don't mean his little side business—"

"No. That goes on. It's everything else. The reports don't tell it. Can't tell it."

Spanner moved from the window as if someone could be out there, reading his lips. He spoke lower, the first time I'd heard him do so. "These are serious words, son."

"They aim to be. Look, sir, if I may be so bold: You don't need to cover for the major."

Spanner bounded over. "Those are very serious words, those." His right hand pressed down on the desk, his left hand a fist at his side. His face gone to marble again. As he hovered over me, I could imagine him doing a combat interrogation, and it didn't feel like a hayride.

I cleared out the lump in my throat. "They are serious, but I do have to look out for my town. For the detachment. And, so, I have to ask another question. Did you actually see the SS kill those civs? Did you actually see the bodies?"

Spanner blinked. Consulted the table. "No. No ..."

"Actually know, for certain, who killed them?"

"Now that you mention it, no."

"According to you, the 'smart,' cooperating SS were in control by the time those civs got their going over. As far as you could tell. But what I saw, down on that road? Those were fresh corpses, sir. Too new for the shootouts you speak of. Too new for the SS you shipped out to POW camps. But, Major Membre, he was in town at that time. I'm sure of it."

Spanner's knuckles had gone white as he kept pressing into the table, its legs creaking.

Sure, I had taken a chance. But it had to be done. With the groundwork now set, I said: "The bodies were gone when I came back. Where did they go? Do you know?"

"No, I don't know that."

"So, you see what I'm getting at. So how can I give them that burial? They might well pop up somewhere else, and that wouldn't look too good. It's a delicate calm we got here already, what with the refugees flowing in and the people hungry. People unsure about ... our authority."

"Right. I see."

"Do you know who they were?"

Spanner shook his head. He flashed a wild look. "Tell you what. This is what you'll do. Keep a wise eye on the major for me. Things get bad enough, I might be able to pull a few strings. You can't prove what you suspect. Yet. But keep at it. And just remember, you can always come to me, gets too bad here. Like I said."

"A partnership. As you said. That's only why I bring all this up."

"If you need me? Always drop a line to my Munich billet. Hotel Vier Jahreszeiten."

"The Four Seasons. On the Maximilianstrasse."

"Yes. You know it. Good."

I rose. We stood face to face, within inches. Spanner placed a hand on my shoulder. "One other thing," he said. "I've heard tell, certain rumors been floating around. Rumors about trains."

"Trains? Rumors? Sounds like bunk to me," I said. "You mean, freight cars, locomotives what? I don't follow." I added a smile.

"As far as you're concerned. You are a smart man, Captain. Enterprising. And don't believe I'm not appreciative. Good afternoon." With that, Spanner gathered up his folders and his beat-up briefcase and he strode off and out, leaving me staring at those bullet holes and that outlawed Nazi justice flag.

Seven

I DRAGGED THE BLACK FLAG out front to the cobblestones, clanked open my Zippo, and watched the fabric burn. A couple passing locals smiled, marveling not, I guessed, at yet another swastika getting scorched but rather at the odd sight of an Ami wasting a good war trophy. I did feel a twinge of guilt as I stomped out the smoldering tatters, but it wasn't the flag on my mind. The truth was, Colonel Spanner had tricked me a little with his offer. Appealed to the tenacity, the ambition in me. Still, who could beat the deal? I got a direct line to an untouchable, can-do benefactor and all for keeping mum about those freight cars that, I had made myself believe, had only held secret documents or weapons parts. And why not? My first best chance to get a leg up had been a dud on arrival. And Major Membre could choke on his glad-handing sales pitch, and the baron as well. Those two were sure to lay eggs, and I wasn't about to end up just another chicken.

Out on Cathedral Square a refugee girl was eyeballing me, hunched over a bowl of what looked like roots and wild greens. People had been calling her Märtachen—Little Marta. Often Little Marta ran with a chestnut-haired woman I'd seen out calming the frazzled locals, pointing refugees the right way, giving answers from the middle of a crowd. The woman had curves to go with that hair and was a real looker. One time we made eye contact—eyes locked, more like—among the crowds outside the train station and I had started her way thinking, telling myself, a gal in the know like that might just know something, but she only tossed her shoulders and showed me her back. And then she was gone, off beyond the throng. The only one in Heimgau, it seemed, who needed absolutely nothing from us Americans. This time, though, Little Marta was alone. I smiled at her and pretended to tip an imaginary hat. The girl laughed. I strolled on. This afternoon brought out all the Heimgauers. They gathered to gossip, rode bicycles or pushed carts, and a few had cars with stinky sputtering wood-burning engines bolted on the outside. A group of Fräuleins passed, flapping eyelashes, and I put a bounce in my walk.

I walked into City Hall, passing the usual candidates and contenders waiting in the usual lines trading leads and trying out their English on each other, hoping for some of that real sway one day. All but Uli Winkl. Up on my floor, my temporary police chief was waiting alone at my office door wearing the new police uniform I had it cut for him based on MG guidelines—American-style blue jacket and trousers and a simple cap to replace those warlike old jackboots, tight Imperial tunic and peaked helmet. The jacket lacked a button at the belly, nothing a little thread couldn't fix. Still, Winkl was fidgeting with it all and pulling quite a face, and I was feeling a little like a dad who'd sent his boy to school without shoes when it should've felt like I'd gotten him that new baseball glove. You know how many out there would kill to be police chief? I wanted to tell him.

I forced out a smile instead. "Just look at you. Go and turn around, that's good. Look like a real *Ami* bull now—a copper."

"Yes, sir. If you say."

I let us in, dropped into the chair behind my desk, and fingered through papers in my inbox. My office was still a foreign place. On the wall opposite someone had hung an antique map of the Holy Roman Empire—on it, Heimgau was as large as Munich. I had a basic wooden clerk's desk and standard-issue Underwood typewriter, someone's worn Persian rug at my feet and mismatched file cabinets, one oak, one black metal. A smell like mothballs. I really had to get some summer flowers in here, brighten up the place. I cleared my throat for Winkl as the man slouched in the metal chair before my desk. I told him: "Now, about the food situation: Tell people not to worry. I'll get some more grub here if I have to rob it. Same goes for meds. Working on that right now, matter of fact."

"I hope so, sir. Because we can do little about it on our end."

What Winkl meant was, a real mayor would be able to do more. As new *Bürgermeister*, the unqualified and untested Baron von Maulendorff would be little more than Major Membre's lackey, dedicated only to his sponsor and never the people he serves. After twelve years of Nazis, Winkl knew that old drill all too well. That's why he'd shed the police getup back then and didn't need it now, nice new copper threads be damned. He didn't have to say it.

I answered anyway. "That part's out of my hands for now. I told you. In the long run, we'll find a new mayor."

"And a police chief too?"

"Yes. If that's what you want."

Winkl probably didn't believe me any more than I believed Major Membre. This was not going to be easy today, I realized. A darker mood was setting in fast, in both of us. Winkl stared down at his hands and out the window, anything but look at me.

I leafed through the notes on my desk. I grabbed a folder, pulled out papers and moved my pencil down a page as if checking off items. "Well, we just got this in. Really been needing it, too. It's a full list of locals and where they are, a real help to us. There's a few prominent locals unaccounted for. That's where we come in, where you come in as police chief."

Winkl nodded but clutching his new cap with both hands.

No turning back now. I got up, walked over to the door, looked down the empty hallway, both ways, and pressed the door shut. I sat and grasped the edges of my desk, leaning forward. "Tell me what you know, Winkl. Don't shake your head at me. You know who those dead were. It's the only thing you've kept mum about, the only thing anyone around here is mum about."

Winkl set the cap back on his head. He stood. He went to my door, opened it and looked down the hallway each way. Shut the door. He had been muttering all the while in words I could not know. I supposed he was speaking to his brother, Udo, long gone. He'd probably been doing this for years. Then, he sat back down. "You must understand. How can I talk about your own people?"

"Easy. Just open your mouth."

"Why do you care, Captain? About us? About any of it? You alone."

"It's my duty. So stop stalling."

Winkl sighed. He signed a crucifix. He spoke fast, getting it all out: "At the end, when the SS were still here, some Americans came. They were combat soldiers, not like you. Sir, the officer that was here then was here again the other day. He was the one in the courthouse."

Colonel Spanner. "Yes. It's okay. Slow down. Go on."

"The SS was already here, which was frightful enough. They'd put down our local anti-Nazis, locked up the leaders who'd survived."

"How many?"

"Two. I don't know who else."

"Where?"

"Up at the castle, sir."

This was just as Colonel Spanner had said. "And then?"

Winkl held out his palms, shrugging.

The bottom desk drawer held a bottle of Bushmills and two glasses. I poured a glass and pushed it across the desk. "Remember, this is just between you and me."

"Like you promised? On that first day."

"Like I promised. I want to focus on the two. Why lock them up, keep them in the castle?"

Winkl stared at the glass of whiskey. "Some of us had rebelled. Townsfolk. I had helped out, too, but I was able to hide. Others were not."

"I understand that. Good for you for standing up. But then what? The two—"

"I told you! Locked up, they were, after good civilians were butchered. So you see, that's what you get for standing up."

I poured a shot and threw it back. Letting it burn. Glaring at my ceiling of yellow-stained plaster, anything but look at Winkl. That was why Heimgau was so tired. Why no one wanted to speak up for the past. You finally take that stand, look what you get. I went to the window and opened it. Out on the square, a crowd of DPs was selling brown rotting apples. I could smell them from here.

Winkl spoke much lower, almost in a whisper. "Sir, he's a powerful man, your major, much more powerful than you."

I whipped around. "What exactly do you mean by that?"

"Well, your rank, it is lower."

"That's not what you mean. Spit it out."

Another of Winkl's grimaces had spread across his face, this one closer to that sorry smirk all the defeated shared among one another. "Why, you are a German, too. It's clear to me. So it is clear to them, is it not?"

I had a good long sigh myself. Breathing in those rotting apples' aroma. Winkl was calling it like he saw it, and why shouldn't he? I was the one who'd demanded it. So who was the one breaking eggs now? I stomped back over to my desk and sat. "To hell with rank. Names, where a man was born. All right? I want you to go on, Winkl. Tell me about the two, up there. Did anyone hear the torture? Did anyone see it?"

"No. Not that I know of."

"Major Membre was here by then, is that right? Up at the castle, when the two were still locked up? He was here before it all ended."

Winkl threw back his whiskey. He nodded. He began to speak, but stopped. I moved to pour him another belt. Winkl waved me off and said, "Old *Herr* Buchholz, he had persuaded some of our most loyal Heimgauers to take a stand. Close to him, leading us, was his son Gerd, a carefree boy."

"The young one. With a fuzzy mustache?"

"He had a poor mustache, yes." Winkl added a sad chuckle. He went on to describe the two. They matched the corpses on the road. He had slumped in his chair. "We haven't seen their brave souls since. Just like my brother in Dachau. And I tell you, that is all I know."

"There was a third. From a concentration camp, I believe. Maybe he broke out at some point. Could it have been your brother Udo?"

Winkl's eyes widened. "Did he look like me?"

How could I tell him about the hood? "It was hard to say. This man had lost plenty of weight. He was taller than you."

"Udo looked like me. He had a build like me, and he was shorter. In any case, we got a death notice years ago. Influenza." Winkl chuckled at that, more grim than sad now.

"I'm sorry. That was a long shot."

Silence found us. Somewhere out the window we could hear a baby crying, then a bell tolling. Winkl dabbed at his eyes with his handkerchief. "I don't know if it's the American or the Prussian in you, but it's unrelenting the way you are."

"I'm not Prussian. We came from Holstein. Near Kiel."

"*Ach*, you're a Northerner, same thing," Winkl said.

"Says you. Listen, I appreciate your honesty. You're a courageous man."

"You mean it? Then let me be directly honest." Now Winkl leaned into the desk, grasping at it with his thick white knuckles. "You won't let it happen again, will you?"

"No. You can forget that. You can try to, anyway."

"Then give me your word. Again. Because things are different. Because, now you know what happened."

"Yes. All right. You have it."

We drank another, on my good word.

"I hope your word sticks. I hope so for me, and for you, dear Harry," Winkl said, addressing me by my first name for the first time.

The whiskey still warm in me, I shuffled the papers on my desk and stared down at one. Pretending. My so-called list of locals had been anything but. It was a standard roster of detachment personnel in quadruplicate. I was getting creative, just as Colonel Spanner had prescribed.

"Joachim Buchholz, he was once the mayor, back in the days when I was a policeman," Winkl was saying. He stood between his chair and the door, unsure if he could leave.

I nodded, as if my lists already told me this. "Before you go? What about other survivors? The family of the killed, I mean. Any around?"

"Should not your special lists tell you that?"

"They're, uh, incomplete."

Winkl had taken two steps forward, staring down at me. Nodding. It wasn't the kind of nod that carried a smile.

"What is it, Winkl? Don't tell me Hitler's alive and in town, too."

"God no. I'd know what to do with that crackpot Austrian."

"You'd like something? How about some coffee, the real stuff? No problem."

"Yes, but no. Not now."

"So, tell me."

"Old Joachim Buchholz also had a wife, who has gone missing." Winkl paused, snickering. "You might want to add all this to your list."

"Yes, yes. I will." I reached for my notebook and scribbled.

"Also, there is a daughter. Gerd's big sister. She is here now."

"Daughter, in town," I said as I scribbled. "What is it? You're still looking at me like that."

"You might have seen her about. Sometimes with the Displaced Person-girl, Märtachen."

"Maybe. What's the name?"

"Katarina."

"Last name? A married name?"

"No, she's not. Not anymore." Winkl's head had cocked at me, as if I really should know who she was, like a boy who should know a top ballplayer.

"What? What is it?"

"You must be careful with her," Winkl said.

"Sure, I will. How you mean? You know what, never mind. I'll find out myself. Where can I find her?"

Eight

Six a.m., the next morning. A Sunday. Months ago American bombers had swooped down on Heimgau's train station before flying off to juicier ducks, leaving her roof with more holes than cover. Yet she was far from KO'd. Even at this hour traders, traffickers and greenhorn speculators filled the main hall, too busy dealing to be bothered by the heaps of charred bricks and twisted iron and shattered glass, the gritty dust with flies swarming around as big as bullets. This was the black market that regular civilians knew. This was about supplementing the rationing of only 1500 calories on most days—calorie levels far below those of 1940 or even 1943 when the war was raging. Blankets, silverware and coffee from town were traded for cabbage, potatoes and meats from the country and back again, a swap that sounded quaint compared to Major Membre's fine plunder scheme but was not without its own gougers, hoodlums and bad eggs. It too was illegal, technically.

I had come in here on my own. I wore a simple tankers' windbreaker with no insignia and carried no sidearm. Wanton beams of dusk shined down and the din of bartering echoed as I approached the throng, moving along a field of hats—Fedoras and fake sables, faded caps, Tyroleans with feathers glowing in the light and cone-shaped Bavarian farmers' hats tied with rope. Jackets covered satchels, cloaks shielded suitcases held together with strings and straps. A lookout eyed me, an old man with white beard and a U-shaped pipe. A peasant, in any other age but this. I showed him my upturned hands, old man lookout nodded okay, and I found a spot next to a shrapnel-scarred sign that read: DEPARTURES, FEBRUARY, 1945. TEMPORARY!

I stood there and focused on the faces under all those hats. I knew her face. In case anyone else here needed refreshing, I had a thin German-language newspaper called the *Bavarian State News*, fresh off our MG presses. On the last page was a studio still of Katarina Buchholz singing with hands clutched at her heart, the photo so fetching I had to remind myself they were talking about a successful actress in Nazi Germany. The story read: "Hitler's Movie Stars: What's Their Fate? Here's our own Katarina Buchholz. Is Bavaria's high-society darling of the stage and screen one more victim of the senseless war that Hitler, his party brutes and the Prussian war machine unleashed with your blessing? Bavarians: you share the blame! …"

I saw her, deep within the mob. She seemed to be holding four, five debates at once, calling and gesturing and twirling as if dancing. Workman's overalls hung off her, leather gloves capped her hands and her chestnut hair was stuffed under a wool cap, but a few strands had eased out, shining as bronze. Soft dimpled chin, those high cheekbones and full lips. Talk about a looker actress. She was saving this whole sorry train station scene, like some lone smiling cherub in a dark Bosch painting of fear and misery and want. A lock of that hair had fallen over one eye. She touched a finger to the lock and lifted it back in place.

She pushed through the crowd, coming right for me.

She got in my face, poking at my shoulder. "Why do you follow me?" she said in English. "I've done nothing suspect. I know nothing. So why?"

All the faces had turned, snickering—finally, someone was scolding an *Ami* officer.

"Maybe you should lay off the lip, sister."

"Perhaps you should answer my question."

The crowd circled us, chattering away in German and *Ost-Deutsch*, Russian, Polish, Czech. I hadn't expected an audience. She was in her element. I switched to German: "They say you trade here."

"Trade? They?" Katarina's hands found her hips and she flashed a grin at the crowd. "I was hoping to catch a train, that is all. Yes, I truly enjoy rail travel." All laughed. "So, what can I do for you?" she added.

What could she do for me? She was speaking to me like I was just another German. I went flush in the face. I really hadn't thought this out. "You think I'm a soft touch," I blurted.

She shrugged. "Prove that you are not this."

A hawker stumbled our way calling her name. She pushed him away. She glared at me, waiting for an answer. Prove it how? What the hell did she want?

I grabbed her arm, led her away far down the platform and found us a bench of cold iron out in open daylight. We sat overlooking stretches of littered, rusting tracks. Out there vagabond gimps hobbled among burnt-out rail cars.

Katarina Buchholz had gone quiet, arms close to her sides, out of her element now. The curtain down. "So, you come alone," she said.

"I like to be discreet. It's S.O.P." What was I saying? I hated our acronyms and abbreviations, especially the army gobbledegook.

"S.O.P.? Explain please."

"Uh, Standard Operating Procedure. For me it is. I didn't want to scare you off, or anyone for that matter. People need to eat."

"I see. Is this too S.O.P.?"

"I don't follow."

"Your sympathy."

"You tell me." I placed two Luckies between us. "And let's quit the small talk."

She snatched up the smokes.

I said: "You're the daughter of Joachim Buchholz, correct?"

Her eyes pinched. She threw the Luckies in my lap and stood.

I pulled her back down. "Look, I'm trying to help. All right? Just give me a chance here."

But something had made Katarina freeze. She pressed her fingernails into my forearm and peered over my shoulder, her eyes narrowing.

Inside the station, Major Membre was working his way through the crowd, shouldering men out of the way and barking in broken German.

"I'll take care of him. Wait here."

She whispered: "Garden plots outside of town. Number 10A. This afternoon," and she jumped off the platform.

"Wait."

"No. And come alone," she said and ran out across the tracks, slipping past the unaware gimps and vanishing beyond the rail car carcasses.

I pushed back through the crowd and found Major Membre buying, for a few Pall Malls, what looked like a fake Fabergé egg. He had a runny nose that really needed wiping. He kept yawning. I stood next to him. It took him a good minute to notice me there, and he didn't so much as start.

"What are you doing here?" he said.

"Public Safety, sir. Reconning the black market."

The major pursed his lips, his eyes leaky and pink-rimmed. "Ah, yes. Of course you are."

In that moment, I had realized the major could easily conclude I suspected him of things far worse than any black market. The man might even infer that I was reconning for Colonel Spanner. Which might have been yet another reason why the major had offered me a part in his racket—to gauge how easily I could be bought off. Call me guarded, call me wary, but I had to consider every angle.

That afternoon I navigated the last reaches of Heimgau's medieval wall. It led me to the train tracks leading away from Old Town, out behind castle hill. Here stood Heimgau's once precious garden plots, each with a garden hut like a miniature log cabin. Most plots were squares of barren dirt, the huts moldy and gray. 10A was looking much the same, though I noticed, as I neared, that its hut had cleaner, browner wood. The windows were boarded up. A short iron fence lined the plot. I lifted the gate latch, took five steps up the path. At the small green door, I knocked three times, hard. I heard latches unlocking and hoped they were latches, but I'd brought my Colt just in case. The door opened a crack and stayed that way, all dark. I unfastened my holster, raised my voice: "On orders of the United States Military Government, open up and identify."

"Why should I?" Katarina Buchholz asked from the dark.

She wanted to put on another show, apparently. I could play along. "Because I say so. Now open wide or I'll kick my way in."

"I have a choice?"

"No, you don't."

"Send your men away first," she said, louder. "Now."

It had stopped sounding like a show. She was scared I had GIs watching, ready to charge the place. "Look. It's just me, I promise. There's no one to wave off. Just me." She said nothing. I stared into the darkness. "Listen to me, very carefully. All right? I saw your father. Your brother. What happened to them."

The door opened halfway. Half her face emerged, just the contours.

"But, you came after," she said. "You weren't there during that ... incident. This is what I hear."

"You heard right."

The door opened. I placed a foot in the single room and a musty smell like old attic filled my nose. The light was dim. On a table stood binoculars and a gas lamp, which illuminated a high rocking chair and a small bench painted with Alpine flowers. On the table was also a photo frame, face down.

The room filled with light. Katarina stood at the window holding a shutter board over her head as if prepared to fling it at me. In the corners I could now see suitcases and crates stacked three high and canvas sacks and boxes, some of them GI rations. She had a secret general store going in here, about what I expected. You want to find her? Follow the food, Winkl had said.

She set the shutter against the wall. Her hair was down, in a loose ponytail. She sat on the flowery bench, crossing her legs, then placed a hand on the rocker and began rocking it, back and forth. With her other hand she ran fingers through her hair, and I could smell it—roasted almonds, fresh from the fire, all warm and sugared sweet. After weeks of facing grubby refugees, stone-faced locals and starving children I found it overpoweringly sensual, and had to look away. She said in German: "You covered for me back there. At the train station. When your major came."

"Sure, I covered for you. I told you. It's just me here."

She cocked her head at me. "Why? You want to deal somehow? Is that what you're doing? But if I'm to work with you, ever, I must know your loyalties are good."

"I'm not looking to deal. I told you, it's about an investigation."

She sputtered a laugh.

It brought a hot rush to my face. "Look, doll, you can lose the tough mug with me. I thought you'd want to hear more about your father. Your little brother. I didn't like how I found him. All of them. And I want you to know I plan on doing something about it."

She stared at the table, her face hard. Maybe I was finally getting to her.

"There was a third man with them," I added. "A Jew, I think. Know of anyone named Abraham? Anyone your father or brother knew?"

Her head shot up. Her eyes searched the dark corners of the room as if trying to recall.

"No? Nothing?"

She held up her hands. "So many Jews are named Abraham. No. I do not. Not anymore."

"No one knows him, no one at all. Which just makes me wonder."

"Me? How can I know? I also just returned."

"You knew of your father, brother."

"Only that they were killed."

"How did you know that?"

"Call me clever," Katarina said, pointing her index finger at her head like it was a loaded Luger. "The war was ending. The SS were here. And now my father and brother are gone ..." She turned and gazed out the window. I could see the light softening her cheeks. I could stare a while at that, could let her think all she wanted.

She turned to me. "I wish to move into my parents' old home. Hopefully your major hasn't ransacked that too. Can you see to this?"

"I don't know. What's the address?"

"Cathedral Square Seventeen, second floor. Right on the square."

"I know the building. Nice roost. I'll try and see that it's secure." I studied the room again. "I'd make sure this stuff isn't restricted before you unload it, rationing rules are getting tighter every day—"

"Please. This is not for me. This is not some commodity! It is for the children, for the elderly. Whoever needs it."

So she wasn't just a dealer? My face flushed. "Oh. Well, I can appreciate that. I'll have you know, it's not all cops and robbers with me. I'm working on scoring more for them."

Her eyes shimmered. She shot up and stepped forward. "How? Tell me how?"

"I helped score a heap of C-Rations last week, for the children. There's that."

"And? What else, Captain? What else can you score?"

"Said I'm working on it. There's ... there's Red Cross coming. Medicine. Sulfa tablets. Small load of morphine if we're lucky."

"Liar," she said, but I'd gotten her grinning. "Not even you can get that right now. Where is it? Tell me."

I hadn't meant to say it, but I'd wanted those eyes shimmering again and it had to be meds, the most impossible goods of all. "I don't have it yet. Still, it's coming. I put in for it, I got a source, well, not really a source really but a certain benefactor—"

"No, no, no," she said, shaking her head. "You're doing it all wrong. Never reveal how much inventory you have—especially if you don't have it yet." She crossed arms across her chest. "Besides, you've been talking to von Maulendorff."

"Talking? Maybe I listened. But I'm not hearing."

"You should hear this: During the war, von Maulendorff never lifted a finger. After the assassination attempt on Hitler failed and the arrests came, the baron stood back and let old friends die. He could have vouched for them, could've warned them, but he only hid out in Karlsbad the rest of the war—at a spa!—right until the last man was hanging from the Nazi judges' meat hook. Understand? It wasn't his problem. He didn't want to lose business."

"Like I said. I trust him about as much as I trust the major."

"He is in business with your major, correct?"

I shrugged.

"Yes? No? You don't think it matters? I tell you it does. One never knows what that first trade will lead to, does one? Do you?"

She had switched her attack yet again, and I was feeling a little punch-drunk. I backed up, feeling for the door. "Seems I'm getting nowhere here. If they're not deaf, they're dumb. So, anything you know, you let me know and I'll use it."

"And, that's really why you came?" she said.

"Yes."

"The only reason?"

"Well, apparently now I'm scoring meds for you."

"And, that's it?" she said, taking a step toward me.

"Yes. No." I stepped around her and grabbed the photo frame. I saw a lanky old man, his long face bright, yet the color of charcoal where the eyes sat. It was her father, Joachim Buchholz. I recognized him. Attached to his arm, smiling, was a black-haired woman with a wide face and high cheekbones like Katarina's.

She turned her back to me.

"Your mother. I take it she's missing, right? Maybe I can find her. Now that I know what she looks like."

She snatched the frame out of my hand. "I know nothing that will help you. Nothing that can change any of it. But, let's promise each other something, shall we? We'll promise to tell each other about any good thing, especially if it can help someone. Promise, Captain?"

"Swell. Give me a ring when you have something."

She grinned again, but this grin was different—a curl at one corner of her mouth. Her tongue might as well have been in her cheek.

"I'm no soft touch," I said, "I told you."

"No, perhaps not. But I'd guess you're relatively new at this, eh *Mein Kapitän?*"

New at what? Why did everyone keep saying that? It wasn't like the old hands had done much good with the world, had they? I ignored her and turned for the door, kept going with my back to her. Actresses didn't like to be ignored, I knew that much.

I reached the door. But she was at my heels.

"Don't worry, you'll learn this," she continued.

I stomped out. I found the path.

"Thank you for my home back, Captain!" she yelled after me. "Give me a ring when you have something!"

I snagged my belt on the gate latch, which made my Colt flip out of my unclasped holster and bounce into the dirt. "*Scheisse.*" I snatched up the gun and re-holstered it, dirt and all. Pushed through the gate, saying nothing. Don't look back.

"And do not worry too much! You will get the hang of it!"

Nine

ALMOST CURFEW, NEAR DARK. I kept peering over my shoulder as I crossed Old Town, lurking in doorways, listening to the alleys I passed. It wasn't these verboten streets that worried me. Sergeant Horton and his team of CIC GIs had left town, and Major Membre now had us using Yugoslav Displaced Persons of dubious origin as curfew guards. He even had them wearing our OD uniforms. I had to suspect most were in the major's pocket.

I found the yellow-washed, eighteenth century building with its rows of ornately framed windows overlooking Cathedral Square. Tucked down deep in my briefcase were two packets of sulfa tablets, two vials of morphine and a syringe.

It had been a few days since Katarina Buchholz had led me to her stocked garden hut, more days in which I made little ground in my investigation, hampered as I was by constantly picking up Major Membre's slack in the face of each new county crisis. Then, just this morning, a Red Cross truck had rolled into town with medications and food parcels, just as Colonel Spanner had promised that afternoon in the courthouse. After the truck unloaded, I offered our detachment's young medical clerk all manner of booty for two vials. The fellow could have anything in my villa, including the baron's cart with the expensive Meissen porcelain. But the clerk had more than enough booty. He only made me promise my grab was for a good cause. So I promised him. We were alone in the hospital storage room, whispering. "I need to hear that," the clerk had told me, "because I don't know how much of these meds will make it to the patients."

"Who's it go to? The major?"

"Who the heck else, Captain?"

"He sells it? Taking it himself?"

"Runs the gamut, I figure."

Katarina's building once housed some of Heimgau's finest citizens. Now it sheltered refugees of all stripes and a few headstrong yet cooperative Heimgauers, sometimes ten or more people to one room. I realized I didn't know which floor so I sat on the foyer steps, lit a Lucky and let the vapors of Virginia tobacco curl around the banister and drift up the stairs.

I heard footsteps. They bounded down the stairs. The refugee girl Little Marta jumped to a stop before me. A wiry thing, no more than eight years old, she had on a tattered pullover and clutched a worn long-haired teddy bear missing one arm and an ear. "Cigarette?" she peeped in German, "Or perhaps it's chocolate you have."

I winked. "Little Marta, right? That's a nice name: *Märtachen*."

"Yes, sounds like *Märchen*, no? A fairy tale." Little Marta frowned at her comment; no fairy tales around here, her frown was saying.

She told me the Buchholz flat was on the fourth floor. I started up the steps but had to stop. Little Marta had squared her narrow shoulders, like a toy soldier. I smiled but she only stared back, her small gaunt face hard and defiant. I reached to pat her teddy bear. She pulled back, glaring at me.

"Whoa. All right. I just wanted to give him a present. That all right?"

"It's a she. The name is Sally."

"Right, Sally. Here, Sally ..."

I pulled two Hershey's and my pack of Luckies from my pockets. Keeping herself between me and Sally, Little Marta bent her other arm to take the goods. I set them in her little cradle of an arm.

"Sally says, 'thank you, sir'."

On the fourth floor I found a door with a tarnished brass plaque reading "Familie Buchholz." I knocked. The door flew open, Katarina. I held up my briefcase.

Katarina rolled her eyes. "It's about time you came."

"I didn't know I had an appointment."

Katarina pulled me inside whispering, "Voice down." She led me through the dark room, forcing me to step over dark figures sleeping on the floor. The air heavy and pungent. I looked back to see Little Marta following, tiptoeing around the people without looking as if she could see in the dark. We reached another room, the air just as stifling. One of the dark figures rose to hug and hold Little Marta as Katarina and I passed on through.

"Where is it?" Katarina said.

"Where's what?"

"The medicines."

"Ah. I got sulfas, and some morphine, but small amounts only. I couldn't get penicillin, too rare, but I got a syringe. I feel like some dope fiend dealer, sneaking around like this."

Katarina released a curt laugh. "We'll only need that morphine."

She rushed me through a kitchen, down a hall and into a bedroom. The odor turned more sour than stifling here. On the bed, next to an open window, lay a woman naked except for long white underpants like bloomers and a towel across her breasts. Her skin was so white it glowed blue in the moonlight. Her thin muscles stretched like strings. Wads of blood-soaked linen filled a small pot at her side, and on a night table stood a bottle of clear brandy. Katarina closed the door. The woman opened her eyes and nodded, and Katarina unclasped my briefcase. She found the morphine vial and syringe and readied them.

"Your mother? That's your mother."

Katarina nodded. "It's worse at night, much worse the last couple days." She slid the needle into a blue vein, which forced me to look away. Her mother groaned, her eyes shut.

Katarina frowned at the syringe, now empty. "It's *Tuberkulose*," she whispered.

"Tuberculosis? She has TB?"

"Yes. I'm afraid your penicillin won't help her, in any case."

"I'm sorry."

Katarina gave half a shrug. "I just want her to die comfortably now."

"Die?"

Katarina gave me a curious look, as if I'd just guessed her favorite color. "Of course. It won't be long."

"What about the hospital? It's reopened. We reopened it."

Katarina shook her head. "I will have nothing to do with your occupation hospital."

What could I say to that? She had returned home to find half her family dead, her mother dying, and a raving *Ami* major in charge of the whole mess. No wonder she was so guarded.

"So that's how you knew. Your mother knew they were dead."

Katarina nodded. I watched her stroke her mother's forehead. Her mother moaned and rolled over, facing the brandy. Katarina poured her mother a glass, tipped it to her mouth, whispered in her ear and her mother rocked, and rocked, and then stopped, heaving a great sigh. Katarina pulled the duvet to her mother's shoulders. She grabbed the bottle. "Now what about you? You got any cigarettes, Joe?"

Katarina led me into the kitchen, her hand warmer from handling her mother. In the corner stood a pantry cabinet on wheels, which I helped her push aside. Concealed behind was a narrow old door. Stairs rose up to a ceiling door, which delivered us onto a compact roof courtyard walled in on all sides. In the middle stood a waist-high grill made of stones. "Have a seat," she said, nodding at the red corduroy sofa along one wall. She made the fire and sat next to me on the sofa. "It does grow quite warm up here," she said in English, "when the fire burns." She pointed a finger and moved it in a circle. "See? The thick walls around us keep it so." Loosening her overcoat, she revealed a delicate white blouse.

I was feeling a little warm, too. I tried a joke to cool me down. "Haven't you heard the directives? The lighting of bonfires is restricted."

She ignored it. "I love it here. Few of the refugees know of this. Sometimes I sleep here."

I could sleep here, I was thinking. I had to get ahold of myself. I sat up straight. "How long has your mother been ill?"

"One year? It's become worse now. It's not only the lungs; she's developed a need for morphine. It makes the pain leave her. All the pain."

"How does she get morphine? How do you get morphine?"

"How do I? How do you?" Katarina pulled two glasses from under the sofa and stood them on a crate before us. "In any case, when my mother passes? I'm going back to Munich."

"Munich's Off Limits. Besides, it's too mucked up, too crowded for any more refugees."

Katarina shrugged.

"Permits are impossible to score. I can't even get you one. Look, it will get better here. I got you morphine, got it right here without a problem."

"Yes, but what made you really come? Could it be to spite our new mayor?"

"Spite? I told you, I do what I want."

"Ah, yes, your so-called S.O.P. But, did you tell your major you take from his inventory?"

My face was growing too hot and it wasn't this fire. Maybe I had her all wrong. Maybe the spite was all hers. She was only drawing me in just to torment one of us *Amis*. That was it, sure, she had her own brand of torture. I poured a glass, drank. "It's not his inventory. Why should I tell him?"

"And why should he tell you?" Katarina snickered. "Complicated, isn't it? Still, wouldn't you rather make a profit on your medicines?"

"Who said I wasn't? Who said I wasn't going to charge you?"

Katarina laughed, exposing her white teeth and pink tongue. Moving closer, she filled her glass, held it over her open mouth and, throwing her head back, emptied the glass without it touching her lips. "You won't because you aren't like that. I do see it, you know."

Her hot, sweet breath had passed over me. I stared into the fire, my hands as fists that pressed at my knees. "You don't have to do this," I was mumbling, "as *Kompensation*, I mean. If that's what you do mean."

"Please. If that was the case, you'd be on your way home by now."

"Tell me about Little Marta," I said.

Katarina blew out a rope of smoke and sat upright, studying me. "You want to know?"

"Of course."

"Little Marta is Jewish, of course. She's so young, she grew up in a *KZ*—a concentration camp."

"That's tough."

"You do not know tough. Have you ever seen one?"

"No," I had to admit. I'd made the effort to find those bombed-out zoos, but I'd never bothered to see a concentration camp. "She got a mother?"

Katarina looked away, shaking her head.

I drank, finished it off. "How she get here?"

"Wandered in with a pack of ethnic German Poles. Not exactly what one expects. But what is? In this aftermath, this so-called 'peace,' allegiances are never what one thinks, are they?"

"No. I'm learning that real quick."

Katarina moved closer. I felt all of her now, her knees and her shoulders framing me up. "Captain, what can I call you?"

"Harry. Just Harry."

"Call me Katarina then. Only privately, of course. I wouldn't want to break your regulations—'absolutely no fraternization between occupier and occupied.'" She wagged a finger at me.

"'Occupier'? I prefer 'liberator.' You?"

"Liberated."

We laughed. Touched glasses. I poured another brandy. Her eyes had locked on me. She slipped a hand around my waist. I felt her breasts against me, her sweet hot breath again. The fire painting her creamy cheekbones with oranges, yellows, pinks. She placed her head on my shoulder and I pulled her head to mine, gently, though marked by an intent that was not so natural, as if I was watching this scene from the midnight sky above. Seeing it play out, as if it was being revealed to me. My mouth found hers and I couldn't pull away. Not a chance. I slid the overcoat from her blouse, the blouse from her shoulders. I stroked her knee, her warming thigh.

Ten

I LAY AWAKE IN THE DARK. I'd been having a foul and agonizing dream. In it I was driving my jeep on that road to Heimgau, my route lined with all those trees, but the tortured, half-naked corpses that were Abraham and old and young Buchholz showed at every bend I steered into, then more new corpses with each new bend, and the faster I drove and steered into more turns, more corpses would appear, skinnier and paler, piling up like all those trees cut down, the trunks of too many men and women and children to count, my relentless twisting road consumed by ever higher piles of corpses and the horror persisted until I somehow shook myself awake and back to reality where, if I just kept at it, I told myself once again, I could go to battle for those corpses just like a dogface had stormed the Normandy beaches or charged the Siegfried Line.

I stared around my villa bedroom. The moonlight made crazy distortions on the walls with their dark wood paneling that had been slathered over the centuries with a shiny tar-like stain as if candied. This was a true Kammer, or bedroom chamber, complete with timbered ceiling and a decorative tile kiln in one corner for heat. The feel was cozy and alluring, but also cave-like at night.

Katarina lay next to me. Not such a cave with her in here. It was June now, almost a month since the surrender. A few days had passed since I'd brought her the medicine. Since then we had met at times arranged and improvised, when she could get away. Among Heimgauers it already had become an open secret that *Fräulein* Buchholz and the *Herr* Captain were involved.

Here in the dark, she moaned herself out of sleep and rolled over to me, nuzzling her knee between my legs. She kissed me on the ear. I lay still.

"What is it?" she said. "The dream is come back?"

"Yeah." It had already woken me once that night and I'd told her about it, joking, darkly, that she should be the one having the nightmare. She had agreed, and she wasn't joking.

I found her hand and squeezed it. "Do you know what my real name is?" I said. "It's Heinrich."

"I think I like Harry better." She lay on her back like I was, both of us staring at the ceiling timbers so dark they glistened blue from the moonlight.

"But I wasn't always Harry."

"No, it wasn't." I told her about it. My family got to America in 1928. I was nine. The first couple years we spent in New York City around other immigrant Germans, and I had to learn English on my own. My dad was a baker, mom a seamstress. Manfred and Elise. All they knew of Amerika came from Karl May westerns, silent films, and letters from relatives. Yet the Great War and its aftermath had left them penniless, so they saved for a boat over and never looked back.

"It wasn't easy at first. Pop's big curly mustache gave him away. He spoke no English."

We settled in Manchester, New Hampshire. I took to English and learned to suppress my accent by mimicking radio plays and shows. Sometimes people thought I was born Irish or Scottish. My looks helped there. I did have those freckles.

"What did your parents think of this?" Katarina said.

"Oh, it amused them, to a point. My father? He always told me the Americans are a good people." I let out a sigh.

"But?"

"But, he also said I'd never be as good as them—in their eyes—because I am an immigrant. He said this matter-of-fact. It was simply the luck of the draw, our draw."

The Great Depression wasn't kind to us. My father lost his bakery job to a local relative of the owner who needed work. Scraping by, dad got odd jobs cooking and baking for WPA construction projects coming out of the New Deal. What was the New Deal? A creative mix of policies and regulations that could do good things for the little guy, even inspire them. This was a new thing for Americans. Many wanted their government to go away. The fat cats wanted government for the people to sit down and shut up, let the barons and the corporations set the tone. They still do. "War's not even over and there's some who want to let people fend for themselves, no matter that the odds are stacked."

"So, you are like *our* New Deal? You personally."

"The soldiers did their work—now it's time to do mine. Don't look at me like that. I'm not naïve. Born yesterday. Stop looking at me like that. Out with it, Kat."

"Your Major Membre is not a New Deal."

"No. He definitely is not."

I didn't elaborate. I hadn't told her: I had to consider the major an accomplice, a suspect even. I hadn't told her about a certain CIC agent named Colonel Spanner either. What the man offered was my affair. She would see the result.

She stroked my hair. "You have no accent in English," she said. "You sound like an American when you speak it. I can tell."

"Thanks."

"You would be a good actor." She chuckled.

"You should know."

"Did you ever come back here? I mean, before the war?"

"To Germany? No, but my parents came over for a summer. This was thirty-six. They took an early boat back home, horrified at what was happening here. Many of our relatives were in the SS or SA. Uncle Hansi in the Gestapo, cousin Roland the SS. Letters made it worse. My father looked like he'd lost a lung after he read my uncle—his brother—boasting about taking the Hitler Oath. Pop told me, 'I'm never going back. From now on, we disown them. *Schluss.*'"

"And then?"

"What else? Pearl Harbor. Everything changed. America was at war with Germany. And our so-called neighbors, they knew the Kaspars had visited Germany. They called us spies behind our backs. Huns. Heinies."

My parents had always helped out at a German Saturday school; it was closed down. That was only the start. People turned scared, suspicious, paranoid. The authorities weren't much better. Anyone was a threat.

"They set up these tribunals called the Alien Control Boards. My father was hauled before one. Questioned by the FBI. Roughed up once or twice. Neighbors had denounced us, it turned out. This was about forty-two, forty-three. We had German friends who were taken away. Father of one family was sent to a camp in Texas without a real trial, evidence, nothing. Houses were abandoned. I heard of houses looted. Property seized. Some families even repatriated back here, in exchange for Americans in Germany. It's still going on. My mother, she lived in constant fear. Pop, he stayed upbeat. By then he was baking pastries again, his love. He knew all the German immigrants, many of them Jewish by the way. Ran a route delivering pastries to elderly Germans. He'd always read the German-American papers. He'd belonged to plenty of groups, just like any German-American—or any American, for that matter. Musical society. Nature hiking club. But the local FBI gang wouldn't quit. Accused him of passing secrets through his pastries of all things, of going off hiking just to spy on military installations."

"And you?"

"I worked harder, got my head in the books, the typical hard-working immigrant, found my way into graduate school. I enrolled for the draft. I was going to show those Fed heavies. One thing led to another—boot camp, ASTP. I should have been sent to fight, but I get sent to OCS, MG School ... funny old world we have got now. I can just imagine Vati und Mutti showing up here like any other German refugees. And if they did find a roof? As MG I could go and confiscate it—a Property Control requisition." I looked to her, found her eyes. "God, you know I've never told anyone all this?"

"I like that you tell me. How are things now? With your parents."

"As of the last letters, things have settled down. They stay away from all things German now. Pop even quit delivering his pastries."

Katarina kissed me on the cheek, on my eyelid, my lips. I kissed her. Then I let go, and lay back. I said: "I can tell you. I have a brother. Max. Max was older than me. He was an actor, like you."

"Was?"

"Max traveled back over here on his own, in thirty-nine. He never came back. It was always tougher for Max in America. He was caught between two places. You know? Rock and a hard place. He was an Alien, not Naturalized like me. He tried New York, but Germans were streaming in by then, pros with tons of stage and film experience. It wasn't only that. Max argued with pop about America. They fought. Max didn't believe in the hope, in the promise that a guy could get ahead here—back home, I mean. Pop never talked to him again. No letters came, went."

"There were opportunities for actors here, with all the German Jews leaving."

"Sure. Ever hear of him?" I said. "Max Kaspar? He might have used a stage name."

Katarina pressed her hand to her mouth.

"What?"

"That's your brother?" she said. "*He* was your brother?"

"You knew him?"

"Not quite. I knew of him. You are certainly the more serious brother."

"Sure. It's not the first time I heard it."

"I saw him at a party or two. I don't think he found the roles or the success he wanted, but he was one of those who really seemed to love life. Such a small, strange world this is. I'm so sorry, Harry. The last thing I heard, your brother had been conscripted into the army. But so many had. He could be alive. He could be ..."

"Don't tell me: The Russian Front."

"I'm sorry."

"So you said. Don't be. It's not worth it."

"I take it you don't think much of him."

"Thinking's got little to do with it. At some point the Feds learned about Max being back over here. It only made things worse for us. They hauled Pop back in again. Kept him for days without due process. So maybe I don't talk about Max too much."

"Did you ever hear from him?"

"No. Early on there was news. One aunt wrote, word was Max was making his mark on some regional stage. He had a girlfriend, a singer. After that? War smothers a lot. We did get word that he was called up. Then another aunt got a letter through to us that they had received a Missing-In-Action notice."

Katarina nodded. "You could go up north sometime. Find your relatives."

"Absolutely not. I don't know them and most are dead from air raids, combat, what have you. Anyway, they're in the British Zone."

"You have your place here. You want to show Max."

"No. I aim to prove him wrong."

Eleven

THE NEXT DAY WINKL RUSHED into my office with sad news to report, in confidence: Katarina's mother had died.

I tried all Katarina's haunts, the train station, the family garden plot. The squares, the cellars. Not even little Marta knew where Kat had gone. I cornered Kat's black market friends, offering all manner of goods and then threats. They would've been happy to tell me for a small reward, but no one had a clue. The next day was a Saturday. I resorted to driving out into the county and asking farmers, stray refugees, anyone I found, and they must have wondered at the power of a Bavarian girl to snag a Joe. It concerns an important investigation, I told them, growing a little hot under the collar, or maybe you know something I don't, is that it? Sunday, I wanted to try to enter Munich for the day, but had no orders, nor leave, nor the faintest clue where I would go to find her there.

On Monday morning, first thing, I found a message on top of my inbox pile: "See Me p.d.q.—Maj. Membre."

Major Membre had kept the mayor's office for himself, one floor above mine. I knocked on his door and heard: "Come in, before I give you one merry wrath of ..." The same old song and dance. I entered. I saluted.

Major Membre sat behind the desk, arms folded on his chest. He grasped at the watch on his wrist like a commando in a war picture. "Now, Captain, what does p.d.q. mean?"

"Pretty damned quick."

"Correct. And when I say p.d.q., I mean p.d.q. At ease."

I unlocked my knees, spread my feet apart, but my bitter glare on my mug wasn't going anywhere. After my weekend, I was in no mood for his big show.

Membre peered at me. "I know you'd like to have my job. Do things your own way. You're trying to usurp me. Oh, don't I know it."

"Usurp hell. I'm trying to help this town."

"Are you? So what is your duty anyhow?"

"How do you mean?"

"Your responsibility. Your role here."

"Public Safety."

"Is it? It's not as if a man would know, would he?"

"Sir, just what are you talking about?"

Knocking. At the door. Major Membre grinned at me. "Come in!"

Uli Winkl entered along with the other town officials we'd appointed, a lineup of eight dark suits. They bowed and grimaced. Their Baron Mayor von Maulendorff was not with them. Membre went back around to his desk and sat. To his office, he'd added a tapestry, velvet curtains, and a pair of pewter candelabra. He cleared his throat, once, twice. His face had gone as pale as that porcelain he loved so much, and sweat rolled down it. His nose was running again. He pressed a hanky to it, his hand shaking. He rearranged files and carbons on his desk, looked up and said: "Two locals and an unknown were murdered here. This much we know. First tortured, to be exact, and then murdered. It happened around the day I arrived." No one was translating this for them. I was probably the only one who understood. "Tortured means, someone was looking for something. What was it? Information? Valuables? I want to know exactly what. So I'm launching a formal investigation."

"That's Public Safety's role," I said.

"Silence, Captain Kaspar. I want this to be, shall we say, impartial. That's why I'm running this one myself. Bring the Criminal Investigation Division down here if I have to."

I must have been snarling and I let it show. Let the bastard see it. Let them all see. "You sure about that? Bring the CID? Here? Who knows what they could find."

Membre's eyebrows rose. He'd gotten the message: There was his plunder racket, for starters. Our eyes had locked. Then the major let a smile spread across his face. He could handle CID, his smug mug was telling me, all it took were a few tokens of Heimgau MG appreciation. Sure thing. Grease the wheels with gold juice. A Stradivarius violin, fine porcelain, a couple looker sisters.

Still no one was translating. That part of the show had all been for me. His eyes still fixed on me, the major pulled a notepad from a desk drawer and a silver Parker pen. "Translate, Kaspar. Now! Who knows anything?" he said as I interpreted, repeating the part about the corpses, the torture, the major's own "true" and "impartial" investigation. The men listened with their old stone faces. The major went on: "We and you know the identities of two of the dead. Ex-mayor, his son. The captain here believes the third man to be a former concentration camp inmate, possibly a Jew. Who can tell me more?"

No one spoke.

I said: "His name might be Abraham. He spoke the name, in any case."

"What?" Membre barked.

"It's the victim's name, sir." I repeated it in German.

"Yes, fine." Membre added: "At any rate, the corpses are gone. Vanished. Who knows where they went?"

They waited for me to interpret. Still no one spoke. I felt Winkl's eyes on me.

The major snarled: "So you know nothing, is that it? Any of you? You do nothing. All of you? Any of you?" He was snarling at me too. Even still, no one spoke. Membre stood. "No? None of you? Then you know what I should do? I should fire every one of you right now."

I didn't translate it. I wouldn't.

Winkl glared at his peers. He said in German: "We must protest this treatment."

Membre bounded over to Winkl and shouted like a drill instructor: "What's that, you say? Something about protest? You have no right to protest now, not after what you've done to this decadent, diseased, decaying continent. I assure you, all of you here, that you are far too unworthy, as a town, county, state, country, a nation, a race. Now get out of here. All of you!" He pointed toward the door, stabbing at the air.

The men filed out and down the hall, mute, slouching.

Winkl stayed behind, standing firm in the middle of the room.

I said to the major, "You mention a formal investigation. This is a criminal matter, sir. Do you want the police chief here, or not?"

"No. He's to leave. *Gehen heraus!*"

Winkl shot out the doorway, his eyes wide with rage and fear.

Membre went back to his chair and slumped with exhaustion as if he'd just run up a flight of stairs. His mouth stayed open for the extra breathing, which posed a clear hazard with his nose still running. Otherwise, I would have wanted to slap his mouth shut.

"And me, sir?" I said.

"Stay. Please—there, I said it. All right? You can tell me what you do know."

"Know? I know about as much as you. And I guess that's not too very much."

The GIs had a saying: Sooner or later a Joe's gonna get shit on from a great height. So Major Membre was flexing some muscles. I knew it had to come. This way no one could dare touch the major. He could even clear his name with this if he was guilty in any way. But what was the major's game? Was he fishing for information? Seeking favor again? Or was it simply a direct threat? Maybe he even wanted to implicate me somehow, turn the tables on things gone foul. I couldn't rule that out. At least the major didn't seem to know much about Katarina. That seemed one good sign.

And as it turned out, my good major was just getting started. The next morning he had me lead him through every nook and cranny of Old Town. The major already had all the villas. Now he wanted to know which houses and apartments were confiscated, where the Displaced Persons lived, what refugees lived where. Along the way the major scowled at the locals, his blond eyebrows twitching, sweating. June was really heating up, into the high eighties, and the hot afternoon turned into one hell of a humid evening. It went on into the next day. When I wasn't stuck with the major I searched the town for Katarina, forgetting meals and sleep. Locals were now asking me where she'd gone, even the seedier black market types who stayed clear of me. The baron kept a low profile too, but we did pass each other once on a square. I wanted to stomp on by. He grabbed at my elbow. "I tried to talk to him, tried to talk the major out of it, captain, I really tried," he said.

"All right, all right, let it go for now," I said and shook his arm free.

The next morning I had to draft the major's other new directives, which included the order to have every dwelling posted with a list of the occupants—Germans, refugees, Displaced Persons or otherwise. "For the purpose," Membre dictated to me in his office, "that occupants may only overnight away from their posted homes with permission of Military Government. Current curfew remains in effect also. Any violators will be punished by eviction or military jail." The major snickered at that. "This is the way to keep track of these Neanderthals. You never know when they're going to pull a fast one on you."

"Yes, you never know." I left without being dismissed.

Major Membre really had me locked out cold. If only it had stopped there.

Two days later, a Thursday. Out on the Stefansplatz I found myself standing deep within the biggest crowd I'd seen in Heimgau. Heimgauers, refugees and Displaced Persons swarmed, pressing at my shoulders and ribs, emitting odors of sweat and smoky stale wool. Before us, in front of City Hall, a long, low cart was set up as a stage. On its railing hung American flags and German ones of various origin—black-white-red with Prussian eagle and cross, the black-red-gold of the Weimar Republic, the simple black-white-red of the Imperial German Reich. A Yugoslav guarded each corner of the cart stage, before which an oompa band of locals, German Czechs and POWs played "Rosamunde" ("The Beer Barrel Polka," to us Americans). At the front of the crowd stood hordes of children, all the *Kinder* of the county, it seemed, many dressed in newer jackets, caps, and short pants that the major had somehow procured for them.

Uli Winkl was working his way through the crowd to me. "Largest rally I've seen since, well, you know when," he said. "And this band is shit."

Major Membre was up on stage throwing the children candy. He wore his dress tunic, with jodhpurs and tall and shiny brown boots. Ellis, Koch, Wilks, and Carlson from the detachment were up there chatting and smoking. Baron Mayor von Maulendorff stood behind them in a simple gray suit cut Loden-style with stand-up collar, wood buttons and Tyrolean hat to match. He kept his head lowered as if praying. "You better pray," I grumbled to myself. I kept my dark green flyboy sunglasses on, as if that alone was going to protect me or even hide me.

"Why don't you go up?" Winkl said.

"Can't. I'm spying. Yeah, that's it—surveillance. Wouldn't want anyone to get out of hand."

"Ah. So you know why the major calls us here?"

"Me? Of course not. Why would I know a damn thing?"

Membre whacked his riding crop on the tuba and the band stopped in fits and starts, bursts of air. The major moved to the edge of the stage, his pink face glowing pale in the sun. No one clapped. Someone near me said, "Are we allowed to clap? Do they want us to clap?"

Membre began talking, but no one could hear. They'd forgotten the microphone, the fools. The baron mayor had to shout a translation:

"Citizens, I hold this public meeting today in the interests of policy—
of ours, and yours ... The Military Government's new Denazification
program enters its first phase. All German citizens will be required to
fill out a background questionnaire, called a *Fragebogen*, from which
we will classify each individual into groupings that describe their
level of support for the Nazi regime ..."

Membre kept speaking, but the baron waved for him to stop
and leaned on the railing to catch his breath. Membre glared at him.
Chuckles rolled through the crowd.

Membre spoke again; the baron shouted: "Make no mistake, you
could lose your job, be tried by a tribunal, or jailed, or hanged. Do
not fear this process. We offer sane and rational American planning.
A technocrat's justice, you say? Hogwash. Fiddlesticks! You Germans
out there deserve to be punished, and you will be."

The refugees and Displaced Persons snickered, whispered.
Heimgauers glared, tight-lipped. "They deserve it for all they've
done!" one DP shouted. Another shouted: "Bastards are lucky to
get off so lightly!"

Then, hushes. Whispers and hisses shot through the crowd, passed
and shared by Heimgauers and outsiders alike. The Yugoslavs were
escorting four men in Bavarian-style suits like the baron's onto the stage
and they positioned the four men at the front. The four stood awk-
wardly still, mouths tight, their hands flat like marionettes at the ready.

Winkl gasped, "No, it can't be."

"What is it?"

"You don't know?"

"You see a memo in my hand?"

"The baron mayor knows these men. He had the Yugoslav
guards round them up from the refugee camps. It was on the major's
orders, you see." Winkl shook his head, his thick fingers pressed to
his forehead. "I thought they were to be kicked out. Purged."

Up on stage, Membre stood next to the first of the four, a wiry
little man with narrow face, waist, and shiny mustache. The man
gave a terse bow. The baron waved hands for quiet but the hisses
thickened. Membre slapped at the tuba and the player let out a high
burst, then another until the crowd silenced. The major shouted and
the baron: "This is the Doctor Hammerstein! Doctor Hammerstein
is your new deputy mayor!"

Winkl glared at me. "You really didn't see their dossiers?" I
only glared back, to show him I'd been kept in the dark too. "That

whiny pig Hammerstein was a Hitler Youth leader, in Saxony," Winkl added.

Membre stood behind the two men in the center. Both were pudgy and red in the face with four chins between them. The baron shouted, his voice straining now: "Kappel and Verbitska! Expert innkeepers! They've been licensed to run the Heimgauer Hof inn."

Boos here and there. "German Czechs, those two, ran a casino in Karlsbad. Hid our baron mayor from the Red Army." Winkl's voice had turned hard and gravely.

The boos and hisses grew louder, killing the chatter.

The last man had a square jaw, shiny hair shaved high and parted down the middle, and that square and infamous Schickelgruber mustache that had all but disappeared from the rest of the earth by about 1942. Winkl said: "Jenke. Convict turned SA thug, then a bootlicking party man." He spat. "Choice Golden Pheasant, that one."

"Mister Jenke will become the new police chief, for both town and county ..." Baron von Maulendorff stopped interpreting, his mouth stuck wide open. Even he looked surprised at this one. He moved to the front of the stage and stared at the major, daring him to say it again.

"Gestapo pig, MG pig!" yelled a man and people near the front rushed forward, shaking fists and elbowing children out of the way and scattering the band and the cart rolled and pitched, forcing all aboard to grasp at the railing. The crowd rocked the cart. The Yugoslavs pointed their carbines. The crowd pulled back.

I had frozen up. How could I dare look at Winkl? I had promised him it wouldn't happen again. I turned and began to say, "I'm sorry—"

"No!" he shouted. "The two go hand in hand, do they not? Democracy and incompetence. And all that comes with it. The corruption. The cronyism. This is how so many felt before, they'd had it up to here. Up to here! And in their rage, you know what they did? They voted Nazi Party. Even I felt that way then, so much that it got me wanting to vote Nazi. Did you know that? So not even I will pass your Denazification. But my brother? He never bought it. He fought harder. Abandoned the Socialists for the extreme Reds."

People had started hearing Winkl despite the tumult around us. They stepped back, giving us room, a local scolding a victor at a mandated public event—who'd ever seen such a thing?

"Go on, get it all out," I said.

He spat on the cobblestones, a yellow gob of it. "The pursuit of personal gain over everything? It's every man for himself? Well, then your democracy is nothing new, is it? You think it's special? It's just as doomed as the rest."

I stood there, and I took it. But Winkl would see. I was going to fix this like I should have in the beginning. Yet, right now? I had nothing but a joke.

"Well, at least you get to be janitor again," I said.

Winkl had always liked dark jokes. Not this time. He threw his police chief cap into the crowd, where the grinding throng sucked it down and their stomping feet were sure to mash it to shreds. "You want my opinion, I give it to you. I'm not the janitor any more. You are." Then he pushed his way free and was gone.

That evening I stayed late in my office, in the near dark with only a desk lamp on. I was sucking on Luckies and entangling my lamp's light within coils and gnarls of smoke. I sipped on whiskey. I recalled a proverb I had seen chiseled on the main gateway of Heimgau's medieval city wall, from the days of the plague:

> When a Curse Comes Due,
> The Symptoms Swell Faster
> Than a Mountain's Stream

So Major Membre, the Dopehead Plunder King, was locking us all out with his ironclad new regime. Improvise when the situation required? Get creative? The man could write a book on it: Oligarchy for Covetous Blowhards.

I had overheard the impromptu jokes bursting from the crowd as I stormed off from the square in shame that afternoon: "Major Membre wakes, shits, eats, sleeps, and threatens arrest, not necessarily in that order." Or this gem: "Every night before bed, the pious major never forgets to demand that God show his Denazification certificate." It shouldn't have been too hard to come up with them. They were rehashing the same quips once reserved for Nazis hacks and Gestapo goons.

For his part, the baron had closed the gala with a little cheerleading, a short happy speech in which he called his new officials "The Old Bavarians," though none were too old or born

Bavarian. The man was one heck of a hokum artist. For a bargain the baron was putting up men he owed favors, men who'd support his cherished separatist Catholic politics and grateful enough to help protect his and the major's trading business. It had to happen now or never, before the Denazification kicked in.

Maybe one of these cronies had even killed those three, in concert with Major Membre even.

Of course, this was where my investigation had been heading all along—right to the major.

I smoked and stared into the hot white of the lamp, letting my eyes blur and muddy up from the smoke-light muck. I couldn't know who Major Membre knew in Frankfurt. He might even have friends in Washington. After all, the man had nabbed a CO posting right from under me. Meanwhile, the major's so-called investigation would help cover him and his big brass balls, even puff him up with friends he surely had in CID to boot. Who did I know? Me, a German-American. I had nix. I had ended up supervisor of a one-man rural police department now staffed by an ex-con ex-Nazi.

Craftier means were needed here. The trick was in isolating Membre first, then removing him. Like a cancer. Colonel Spanner was the only field surgeon I knew. Contact me at the Four Seasons in Munich, the colonel had said, and he was sure to respond. You can always come to me, he'd promised.

I didn't need to prove the major had tortured and murdered three civilians. I only had to blow the golden whistle that had been given to me.

Major Membre had really given me no choice. And I had waited too long as it was. So I sat up straight at my desk and wrote a letter addressed to the Hotel Vier Jahreszeiten, Munich:

Lt. Col. Spanner: Greetings from Kreisstadt Heimgau.

I am still a man you can rely on, so I'd like to report on how dire the situation has become here under Major Robertson Membre.

It appears certain that the major's unfortunate command style and forceful behavior toward the civilian population will adversely affect the high standing MG enjoys and in doing so will severely threaten the proper conduct of our plans here.

The major has lacked judgment, and intelligence, and practicality. In point of fact, he rewards gift giving, flattery, and empty promises. He thrives on reciprocity. The MG officer who's lulled into confidence by surface obsequiousness from unscrupulous local operators is forgetting an essential fact: no occupied people trusts or wishes to help the power that occupies it.

Colonel, you said I deserved your help. May I now collect my due? Perhaps you could tug on a few strings? After all, as you once said: Appearance is key.

I appreciate our partnership and I look forward to working with you.

With utmost respect,

H. Kaspar

Captain, Det. E-166, LK Heimgau

Twelve

AT 7:30 P.M. THE FOLLOWING SATURDAY, the sun was setting over high-peaked Old Town rooftops. Jeeps and staff cars clogged the small plaza before the Heimgauer Hof. The hotel had been made up like an Alpine villa, with flower troughs at the windows and Bavarian flag waving on the roof. Boy GIs and teen lieutenants from who knew where huddled at the main steps, joking and smoking while locals waited at a darkened side door hoping for a night's work.

I leaned against a lamppost across the way, eyeing the scene. Major Membre had set up a special officers' club in the hotel and was about to break it in with a Bavaria-wide to-do. The major, ever the glad-hander, had seen it fit to invite even me. I had vowed to avoid it. Yet the night before I had that nightmare again, with those corpses piling up at every turn, and without Katarina there next to me when I woke, it was tough to take. Saturday afternoon I had cracked open a pint of Johnnie Walker. The whiskey was smooth. I could get used to it. I'd taken it out back under the shade of a linden tree. Deliberating. Dissecting. Grasping things.

So, Major Membre had taken over the investigation. Fine. That didn't mean I wouldn't pursue it. I'd be my own private dick now, sure, that was me—a shamus doing a pro bono. And then Mister Johnnie Walker helped me realize that calling on Colonel Spanner and solving this case belonged to the exact same fight. Two sides of a gold coin. Of course, I was going to that party. I should be watching Major Membre's racket much closer, see if it led me back to those corpses. CIC would want to know. The vice and the violence went hand in hand. What was blatant plundering without a little blood? After all, wasn't the term called "pillage, rape, and murder"? My Heimgau had two out of the three at the least.

Right up those main steps and into the Heimgauer Hof I went. Like some front-line GI on the assault I had to keep moving, keep probing, never make myself the target. I made my way through the lobby, past the front desk, past the black GI porters and bored guards. I heard laughs, hollers, singing, and babbling and the droning on of a hundred drunks. A dance hall. A band was playing "Flyin' Home." I peeked in and saw slick heads of hair and elbows swinging. I smelled fresh Virginia tobacco and the bouquet of real peacetime beer. They even had a few USO girls helping couples dance. Not a bad canteen here, I had to admit.

I found a chair just inside the entry, lit a Lucky, and got my bearings. The band had the stage at the opposite end and to the left stood a bar. To the right, on a long table, piles of hors d'oeuvres and tiny sandwiches, salads of all colors and what looked, incredibly, like the remains of a massive smoked salmon on ice. That salmon sent my mood south. I imagined smuggling out the rest inside my jacket and delivering it to those poor souls waiting hopelessly at that side door.

In the farthest corner, to the right of the band, was another door. It led to a cellar. A sign there read: "VIP Casino and Cabaret: Membre's Only. Real clever, Major. I stumbled on through, for the cellar door. The MP guard there saluted and to my surprise he let me through, closing the door behind me. The landing was dark and I used it for cover as I considered the cellar below, with its vaulted stone ceiling that sweated like a moldy wine barrel. The scene looked medieval. The cellar radiated from candlelight and the ceiling glimmered as if the candle flames had hardened the ceiling's musty slime into crystals. Tapestries and fiery red drapes lined the walls and a long table ran almost the length of the cellar, all decked out with linen, silver, wine goblets, tankards and platters of food scraps. Lush aromas of lager, meat, and cologne mixing with the smoke, mold and ancient things. A giant golden candelabra stood there. Valuables were arranged on one end—porcelains, weapons, jewels, age-old books, religious objects. Major Membre sat at the table among high-ranking officers and dapper civilians. Fräuleins rode a lap here, massaged a shoulder there. Brigitta was there. On the far end, a makeshift stage was draped off by red, white, and blue. The VIPs jabbered on like boys over a game of jacks. The major had a wood-and-ivory pipe in his mouth—a prop, the sort of thing a movie producer or a mogul might employ to look educated. He wore the latest-issue summer tunic with open collar and was talking through a constant grin, though his eyes would glaze over whenever he had to listen. These were such civilian eyes, it seemed to me, those of the salesmen and salary men, the mark of a man under pressure to perform. A man always on call. No wonder the man liked his dope.

I gripped the railing and made my way down. A Fräulein clutching ceramic tankards of beer passed—Bärbel, sister of Brigitta—and I grabbed myself a tankard. At the table I was seeing pinstripes and smart lapels of the type I hadn't seen since I left stateside. A couple VIPs were staring my way. I tugged at my tie, smoothed out my tunic.

Major Membre came over grinning. "Captain Kaspar, warm welcome!"

"Evening."

"You're just in time," the major said, close to me, feeling me out with his eyes. "You want to stay for this? You're welcome to it. I always said you're welcome."

Three times now you said it. "Yes," I heard myself say. Major Membre wanted me to see this, flexing those muscles again. So why not watch the man show off his barrel chest? Maybe someone will come along and kick sand in it.

"Swell, just swell." The major slapped me on the back, led me over to the table and sat me in the middle of the bunch. "You behave yourself now, Captain," he said, loud enough for all to hear, "and I'll get you the best kraut coozie in the joint, but only after I'm finished with her."

All laughed. Major Membre took a seat across from me, boasting of "my good Captain Kaspar." To my surprise again, the major didn't tell them I was born a German. I met the civilians. One was a senator from Ohio, oldest of the bunch; some Congressional committee had sent him to study "local conditions." He had mottled red cheeks, a cigarette holder. He spewed patronizing phrases like "I can assure you" and "my good man" and proclaimed that FDR himself had copied his own "proliferous" (a word he insisted was real) use of the cigarette holder. "That's what really got the man elected," he could assure us. There was a writer for Colliers doing a tour of Major German cities that apparently included a side trip to this whistle-stop. All said, this writer was a real go-getter, for a writer. I met two majors, two lieutenant colonels, a general from quartermaster and another from Army Air Corps. One officer wore dress OD with no identifying insignia, what I took to be the major's man inside the Criminal Investigation

Division. Some came from the region, though most were just in from Karlsruhe or Frankfurt. Most had still been stateside when the war ended. All spoke with that self-assurance only confidants can muster. These were men who knew a good bandwagon when they saw one and damn well knew how to ride it. I held my tankard with both hands, twisting it and wanting to grind it into the table. And noticed: Instead of an Alpine scene or the logo of some bombed-out brewery, the tankard bore a coat of arms specially created for the major's MG command and town.

Major Membre clanged a spoon against his tankard and he rose waiting for voices to cease. He tugged at the hem of his tunic, flattening his stomach.

"Gentlemen, and ladies," he began, winking at Bärbel (to snorts and chuckles). "I invited you here for more than a party. Consider yourselves members of a secret society." His voice grew fuller, like one of those optimistic, know-it-all radio announcers I could never stomach. "Now, most of us have been involved in profitable 'trade,' some since before the war ended, a few since before the war." He flashed a smile to a colonel whose lapels bore the insignia of Supply Section. "And we've had much success, have we not?"

Flushed smiling faces nodded to him and each other.

"Gentlemen, I wish to establish an exclusive network for the new United States Zone of Occupation. A real and live market, one that will involve only the highest quality goods." The major picked up a gold music box imbedded with gems and cracked the lid to let out a chime. "Take a look at these fine pieces. They're the spoils of war. Touch them, feel them."

The VIPs passed the objects around the table. I recognized a gilded china plate from the major's office.

"Why do I propose this? Fortune has shined on me here. Heimgau has been around since Roman times. In the Holy Roman Empire, Heimgau was an Imperial Free City. Baroque Period, she thrived as a bishop's seat. You see what I'm getting at, oh yes. A place like Heimgau breeds artisans and their wondrous handwork, breeds and breeds them like so many jackrabbits. And with such a heritage comes an almost unlimited supply of merchandise. Modern, antique, ancient even. The best thing is, it's our own domain. Let those distinguished and coddled MFAA teams chase down their grand old museum pieces and arts treasures the Nazis stole. Let them have the glory. And let them play decoy for us. Because all those gleaming goods carry with them what those high and mighty Monuments Men call 'provenance,' which means it is all traceable. We have something far better. Here, anonymity plus commodity equals advantage." Membre paused and scanned the faces, waiting for silence. He was in his element, the speaker at a hometown Rotary Club. "Gentlemen, look around at your friends here." The VIPs glanced at each other, smirking and smiling. "See what I see? We have every good man we need, and then some. Supply, transport, tactical, security, CID. Not to mention us in MG, who, I must say, are the real ones in charge in the days to come. It's occupation time now. When's the last time you saw an MG officer take a boot in the bee-hind from the combat brass?"

"Doesn't happen," said a major. "Ike don't let it happen, General Clay don't, not since everyone's going home. MG's the outfit now."

"He's right," Membre said, "I'm talking about opportunity, what every conquering army has practiced since wars and empires began. I'm talking about the best and biggest market of all: the US of A. The Big PX."

Colliers writer cleared his throat. "Let's get to it. What's in it for us?"

"Controlled market. Monopoly, if you will. One fellow supplies it, another partner sells it, another good fellow stores it, his partner gets it home. Everyone gets a cut down the line."

"My good men, if I may pontificate," said a fatherly voice. It was the Ohio Senator. "I know Robertson perhaps better than any of you, and I assure you he's worth his word."

"We can work with you, Major, sure we can," blurted a colonel. Heads nodded. "Can-do, Robbie!" crowed another colonel, and the others began in excitedly and at once, agreeing, praising, jabbering and hollering.

Colliers waved a hand, then both hands. "One moment. If I may?"

Membre waved for quiet. Voices hushed.

"Thank you," Colliers said. "I only have one question. How safe is this Heimgau?"

"The safest. I command a force of reliable DP guards. Displaced Persons. Hardened men, these ones, they're Yugoslavs with grit."

Colliers sniffed. "What about political stability? How is the local administration—how is Denazification affecting it? That can cause problems. MP, CID, CIC agents even. There's a million ways to get burned on this and, with due respect, you gentlemen can't stop all of them."

One of Membre's eyelids was twitching. He quashed it with a broad grin. "Politically, we are lining up dependable and acceptable people as we speak. Take my new mayor for example: The Baron Friedrich-Faustino von Maulendorff."

"I know of this Maulendorff fellow," said a General. "Politically, the man's untouchable as far as Frankfurt is concerned. From the old school but knows how to play our game."

Membre nodded. "What is more, the baron has his own men in place all down the line."

The crowd went on with the agreeing and praising. I drank down another tankard, tore into my pack of Luckies. Meanwhile the Fräuleins were putting out most of the candles, which created a sensual light. Voices quieted. And Major Membre was watching me, a half smile distorting his face in the murkier light.

A spotlight burst from the dark end of the cellar and shot across our heads, illuminating the red, white, and blue of the stage at the other end. We heard the crackling of a phonograph, and then the long slow notes of a piano and melodies of a flute. The curtains parted.

A soft ankle and calf, a shiny thigh. Hoots and catcalls reached a crescendo as the spotlight traveled up the body, revealing heaving breasts and white shoulders. As the light reached her face, all the mouths dropped, silent.

It was Katarina. She let loose a pout. Her eyes twinkled, inhaling the light. She hovered at the edge of the stage, staring us down in thigh-high mesh nylons, black short pants, and bustier.

I stared back. My stomach rolled, pinched. I grabbed my tankard and held it in front of my mouth. Could she see me? These lights were damn bright.

A US officer's cap sat tilted on her head, barely holding in her hair. She sang in German, a Kurt Weill song I knew, "Nanna's Lied," about a streetwalker reflecting on hard years spent toiling on the *Liebesmarkt*, the market of love. It was a dramatic song, one my brother Max had loved. Some here could understand the words but most certainly could not. Neither camp gave a shit about the tale. Her voice stupefied them. I stopped listening to the words. I gave in to the beauty of the sounds, how she reached so deep and conjured such silky rich power from her lungs. I watched her movements, fluid and feeling. I knew how wonderful that skin felt, how firm yet smooth.

The somber and sad melody swam, haunting and consuming. She sauntered to the front of the stage and rocked back and forth, taunting us. Heads cocked back in wonder while others' swung slowly with the music, aware and unaware. The senator loosened his bow tie.

The music stopped. They cheered, clapped, hollered. "Encore!" "Bravo!" "*Zugabe!*"

"Goot even-ink, meina Herrrr-en," Katarina purred, adding a faux Dietrich rumble to her voice. She pranced down steps off the stage and made her way around the table, stroking necks and heads with a riding crop—Major Membre's riding crop, no doubt.

"Dame's more dangerous than ten of our tanks!" blurted Colliers to nervous laughs.

She stopped at me. My tankard came down. I grimaced, a sick smile stuck on me. She gave me a kiss on the ear. And moved on.

"Atta boy, Kaspar!" one of the generals roared and all joined in, barking, cackling, congratulating.

She disappeared behind the curtain. The spotlight went out. All fell silent. "Man, oh man alive," someone muttered. They tittered, drank, hooted. The light fired back on, to a screechy recording of "You're in the Army Now." The curtain parted.

Katarina was straddling a steamer trunk, clad in a tight-fitting WAC uniform and an Uncle Sam top hat on her head.

The getup would come off, I was sure of it. My head whirled, my stomach swirled. I got the cold sweats. I couldn't breathe. No air or windows and no way out.

"This ain't cabaret," I growled, "it's a meat show, a lousy goddamn meat show!"

"Who said anything about a cabaret?" someone joked and the laughs crashed over me, howling in my ears. I bolted up the stairs, grabbing at railing and knocking my shins on steps.

"Where ya going, tiger?" Major Membre yelled after me. "You're gonna miss the best part!"

Thirteen

THE NEXT MORNING, A SUNDAY, I headed back into Old Town doing my best to ignore my hangover headache, the dry furry rasp on my tongue. I first tried Katarina's family place. Little Marta was there. Had she seen Katarina yet? I offered chocolate and cigarettes and offered to get Sally a new arm and an ear, but Little Marta only shook her head harder. She wouldn't let me get Sally fixed up, but I gave her the goods anyway. I went and tried the equally hungover Heimgauer Hof. The drowsy new owner, Verbitska, met me at the front desk. No, there was no one under that name.

I roamed around until I ended up at Cathedral Square. The square was empty. A few pigeons circled me, picking between cobblestones with their beaks. From here the gothic cathedral stretched on like some giant stone coffin. Its drastically slanted roof with mosaic of blue, white and black zigzags imitated the pattern atop St. Stephen's in Vienna. At the front rose one single towering spire, so high that the sun's rays danced brightly at its tip and I had to wince. I walked up the front steps, pushed open a small door built into the two massive front doors. Inside it was chilling cold with a faint smell of mold, yet the chill stilled my hangover. I approached the pews. A hunchbacked cleaning lady passed and gave me a hard stare because, I guessed, I hadn't signed the cross. A protestant, I wasn't sure how. I showed her my American smile instead. She trudged off into the confessionals.

I sat in a back pew taking it in. Shafts of sunlight through the stained glass made colors dance around, but the stone walls and stark altar were bare and marred by holes and grotesque shapes—the previous spring, the elegant old woodworking had been removed for fear of looters. And now, with their brown Father Plant surely off to reinvent himself in some other far-flung parish if not Catholic country, this was still a body in limbo on yet another Sunday. I stared. Heard nothing here. The silence a vacuum. My eyes closed ...

I woke. I was lying on the pew. How long had it been? I popped up.

Katarina stood behind me. Her hair was pinned up, and she wore a loose blouse that showed off her shoulders in the Spanish style. She was sweating, damp at her clavicle and cleavage. "Come here," I said.

Katarina slid into the pew and kissed me on the cheek. I kissed hers without thinking and then pulled back. Fighting the urge to touch her hair.

Her eyes glistened. "How are you this morning? After last night?"

"Me, I'm great. Everything's jake. How was the meat show? Everything come off?"

"The what? Oh, that. It did if you must know."

She grabbed my hands and held them out, like someone about to part for a long time.

"What's the hurry?" I said.

"Nothing. We have time." She squeezed at my hands, pulled me forward. "I had to perform. To get a permit, to secure permanent residence."

"In Munich."

She nodded. Her eyes welled.

"I'm sorry about your mother. I never got to tell you."

"She's better now, where she is. I really think it is true."

The hazy colored light twinkled in her hair. Our legs had intertwined down on the pew bench. She smiled down at that and, slipping one foot out of a shoe, slid her toes against my shin. I began to harden. Her face opened wide. She wrapped her legs around my waist and pulled herself onto my lap.

"What about that cleaning lady?" I said.

"I paid her to stay away, to lock up the doors for us ..."

My mouth joined hers, my tongue searching, finding. I lowered her down, flat on the pew. She slapped hands around my neck and pulled me down to her, and we tugged at each other's hair, and her sweat came rolling back, like tears right from her hair, and it tasted sweet.

Afterward, we sat on the pew, in a grim silence. Something had gotten off track. My grip on her had turned to clamps. My clamps had held her down and forced her around the other way and pressed her head to the back of the pew, so hard that her face bore a red mark from the pressure. My clamps had spread her open and I had entered her with deep, spiteful thrusts. She had to grab onto the pew's edge with white knuckles, and it had made her sweat and pant and not in a way a girl liked. Somewhere along the way we had made love, but I had gotten too rough with her. It scared me more than her. I had never been like that with a girl. Now she pushed back her damp hair, and glared into her lap, and faced away from me. Eventually she let me hold her by the shoulders. Kiss her on the cheek to make the red go away. I could tell she had not loathed it all, but it wasn't a kink I wanted to keep repeating even if she had liked it. I wasn't one of her damn Wehrmacht officer lovers, some oafish rough-houser in bed.

"That was not like you. Why don't you love me for love's sake?" she said.

"I don't know what got into me, darling," I told her, and it made me feel even more like a heel. My new modus operandi would only help her justify leaving for Munich. I couldn't get that out of my head, and now I was the one looking away, the shame fighting the anger but losing out. I said: "So, he cut you the paperwork?"

"Major Membre? Yes."

"What else did you have to do?"

"Nothing. Oh, please. Who do you think I am?"

"Not that you wouldn't. Am I right? It's no different now than before. You moved in elite circles. I never asked you about it because I'm too damned nice, or awed, head over heels, something. So I'm going to ask you now. Or don't you remember? Maybe the booze was too rich at Reich Marshal Goering's balls?"

"That's not fair," Katarina whispered.

"Isn't it? It's just my *Ami* innocence, that it? So what's the answer? You weren't a Golden Pheasant's girl, no. You only cuddled up to them."

"What's happening to you?" She turned away and slumped down on her end of the pew, her eyes wet. I made my way down and slumped next to her, listening to her sob, the sobs echoing. Why couldn't I ease up? I only felt like more of a heel, attacking her like this, lecturing her as if in some War Department recruiting film— Why America Fights, by Harry Kaspar. Was I just sore she'd left me hanging, or was it something more?

It was the ambition rising up in me. There was a twisted pride that came with it and it had gotten hurt.

"My name will come up in the records," she said. "This is the thing. The regime had its black markets too, especially among the party high society. When censorship increased and the roles became too stifling, I gave up my acting. I developed a side business. It was to help my parents and their friends at first."

I pulled a Lucky and my Zippo, almost forgetting I was in a church. Slid them back in my pocket.

"The air raids came day and night. Then it was survival. There I was, a somewhat famous actress, and I had many contacts— Wehrmacht, the party, the ministries, aristocracy." She gave me a long, hard look. "I was more than a messenger, you understand. I served the resistance in other ways."

"Resistance?"

She nodded. "Of sorts, yes. I used the bedroom to gain information. Influence fates. I did that. But later, I used my wiles to stay off the meat hook." She rose and we sat side-by-side as if riding a bus. "I wanted to help more. But I lived in such fear someone would give me away. And now? It is ironic, no? Who is left to verify my resistance activities? No one."

"A forger. There must be a few good ones here among all the artisans."

"I know many forgers. And a false *Fragebogen* won't work, not with your major. This is why I had to secure that pass to Munich, as a way out. To buy time, as you say."

"Then I'll call somebody. I know people."

"No. Too risky. You can't trust people. You can't trust anyone here."

"I can." I wanted to tell her all about Colonel Spanner. I would, someday, when we were all in the clear. In the meantime? Katarina had said it herself: Never reveal your inventory.

She had turned away, thinking, already in Munich.

"Wait," I blurted. "You said, Munich's a 'way out.' What kind of way out?"

She held up her hands, a sad smile. "A refuge. For protection. You see, it's become personal now."

"Personal how?"

"You don't know?" Katarina sat up. "You haven't been to City Hall?"

"It's Sunday. I got hangover leave."

"This morning Major Membre began evicting the refugees, the DPs, everyone."

"No. Has to be a rumor. I was just at your place, saw Little Marta." I shook my head. It ached again. "Christ, how long was I asleep anyway?"

"Perhaps too long. My eyes saw it happen. The Yugoslav guards are evicting everyone from my building, from other buildings." She twisted her mouth in disgust. "The guards claim the occupants disobeyed the major's new curfew orders. This is an outright lie, and they were told to say it. So I went to City Hall, went straight to Major Membre—"

"To his office?"

"I had to stick up for them. For Little Marta. She's out on the street with the rest of them."

Katarina meant this as hard as it hit. I grasped at the pew before me with both hands, wanting to rip it in two like spent typing paper. "Where are they all going?"

"The camps on the edge of town. He will fill them up till they bulge. The major says a refugee relief team is coming. Who knows? Some will probably end up in this church, on these hard pews."

"What did you say to him?"

"I pleaded with him to stop the evictions. But he grew nastier, his arguments more petty." She bowed her head. "And, I might have been a little harsh. I scolded him."

"You scolded him. In front of others."

"A couple of your officers were there. New Police Chief Jenke. Winkl, in the hallway. I called the major a coward. He said, 'I'm after you, Frow-line' in his horrible German. He threatened to 'look into my past.' He demanded everyone out of his office except me."

"What then? What then?"

She whispered: "He said, he'd help me erase my so-called 'Nazi past,' if only I'd—"

"That settles it. That son of a bitch."

"It's no matter, Harry. I can go to Munich, blend in there much longer. That was my home for much of the war. I do want to help there. Find any survivors."

I stood but had to lean on the pew. I closed my eyes. My head swirled again, my stomach. I really should've eaten something.

She held my hand. "Can you visit? At least. Say that much."

I nodded. I pulled her close. "I'm going to take you to my place," I said.

Then I remembered Major Membre and how I'd just love to bust his fat jaw. The adrenalin pumped in me, devouring my hangover. "Listen. Go to my villa. They won't nab you there. Stay there no matter what. I'll be there soon enough."

"Absolutely not. I'm coming with you—"

"No! Go there and stay put."

My shouting made her step back. I left her standing at the pew, biting her lip as I stomped out the cathedral door and across the square.

Fourteen

I CHARGED UP THE STAIRS to Major Membre's office, burst through the door, and kicked a chair from my path—and stopped in shock.

Major Membre had his back to me. He stood before a short, frail man who was holding a paint palette and more narrow brushes than he had fingers. Next to him stood a canvas on an easel, the canvas so wide it blocked the windows and so tall it touched the ceiling beams.

I had to blink. Was this real?

The major turned to me, but trying to keep his pose—feet planted far apart, one out forcefully before the other and one arm outstretched, the fingers gesticulating as if ready to bestow mercy or pronounce sentence. He had on a red cape with white fur fringe, a gold brocade vest, a jeweled sword, and gold chain with more jewels hanging from that. It was a papal court costume, the same getup I'd seen in the town museum. The major's other arm cradled a gold brocade headpiece that matched the vest. On his fat head, balancing atop his thick boy-hair, tottered a spiked Prussian helmet with plumes.

The bastard was having a portrait painted? I snorted a laugh at him.

Membre laughed back. "Well, if it ain't ole Harry Kaspar, the town drunk. How can I—"

"Shut your yap. Just listen."

Membre looked both ways, as if many others were there. Portrait painter already had his coat on; the major waved him out the door. "Well? What's this about?"

"I know what you're doing. I'm not going to put up with it."

Membre smirked. Jewels jangling, he moved before his desk and met me face to face. The fur and brocade smelled sour, like wet dog fur. "Captain, you are well out of line. This is your commanding officer you're talking to."

"Me out of line? Strictness is one thing. Germans are one thing. But threatening harmless women, kicking refugees onto the streets is another. Who are you to make things worse for those people? Don't you think they've seen enough?"

Membre chuckled, his potbelly shimmying. "Fancy yourself the expert, eh? After little over a month. Still, you can't deny that Fräulein Buchholz has a past."

"This is about far more than her. You know it."

"I know that a relief team is coming." The major glanced at his inbox. "Just got the memo. First it's a Red Cross truck, now it's a real team. Yes, fortune does smile on our Heimgau."

Colonel Spanner must have made it happen. And this blowhard thought it was his doing. He would only take that morphine on top of the rest. He was probably stoned right now, and who knew what sick things he did when good and hopped up? I never liked the way he gathered those stray children around him like all those shiny treasures he coveted. He had the whole castle to himself for it ...

"I'm simply clearing houses in preparation," the major added. "They'll be heading to the camp outside of town. And from there? Repatriation. It's the policy now. Send the foreigners home."

"Is it? Whose policy? Camp's already bulging, crowded like the ones we liberated them from. You could've left them where they were. But you want what's inside those houses, furniture, art, the goods in them. You need what's inside them. Don't you, Major? You promised your new partners a hell of a lot last night."

The major shook his head, clucking his tongue. "I feel sorry for you. I do. I've given you all manner of opportunity. Complete freedom. Yet you continue to box yourself in."

"Freedom? Opportunity? Why don't you call it what it really is?"

"Ah, now look who talks. Don't think I don't know."

"Know what?"

"The sulfas, the morphine. Good god, man!" Membre was shouting now.

I pulled back. Of course he had found out. Nothing got by the man. "I returned the sulfas," I said. "The morphine helped a woman. She had tuberculosis."

"So put her in a sanatorium." Membre forced out a laugh. "You don't give a good nickel for some woman. Not even when it is someone's mother. Truth is, she tempted you in just the right way. Isn't that so? She being that Katarina Buchholz. So don't kid yourself. You took the fastest route to that Gretchen's gash."

"She's not a Gretchen," I sputtered.

Membre shrugged again. "That all? You finished?" I said nothing. "Good. Now I do have some interesting news if you care to know. It's about my investigation. I might be getting much closer to figuring out who did their dirty deeds on those corpses."

"You bastard," I muttered. The black heat boiling away in my brain. I lunged and pinned the major to the desk, grasping at the fur of his cape. The helmet tumbled to the floor. I released my grip, stepping back.

Membre's eyes shined, like black marbles.

"You talk some fine talk about morphine," I said. "You're stoned. I see it."

"Go to hell. You don't know what you see." Membre stepped forward and produced his riding crop from his cape. Slowly, he rested the tip of the crop on my shoulder.

My fists had balled up. I snorted again. "Why don't you just use your sword?"

"How far you think you can take this? Eh? Think about it. You have no idea."

I said nothing. Heard nothing. My thoughts spun and my chest heaved, red-hot. I clenched the riding crop. Membre held the other end. I said: "Major, I should really knock you down so you don't get up. I should ..."

"How far?" Membre repeated.

And this time I heard him. I gazed around, stupidly, at all those golden crucifixes and jeweled relic chests lining the shelves behind his desk. I let go.

Membre lowered the crop. "Wise move."

"I'll come back. We will. Maybe next time you won't be standing so well."

"We?" Membre shook his head, snickering. He smoothed his hair. He went behind his desk and settled back in the leather chair, which squeaked like a fart. "Oh, I wouldn't do that, Captain. You see, I always want to know everything about the officers in my detachment and I know all about you. Your family. Suspect Aliens, that's what they are, right? They could catch one merry wrath of hell."

"Then I got nothing to lose, do I?" I wanted to charge him again, but the room reeked of sweat and the major's sweet cologne and I needed fresh air. I was drooling. I wiped it away. I stepped back. I was backing out.

"You want it both ways, don't you? The all-American. The kraut. But both ways doesn't work in life, does it?"

I bounded down the hallway, found the stairs.

Membre laughed. He shouted after me: "Tread lightly from now on! Very lightly! Think about it. I'm untouchable, and you? My God, I'm as untouchable as you are to a local krauthead!"

Fifteen

I COULDN'T SHAKE THE SIGHT of Major Membre doped up in his make-believe Prussian papal costume. Incongruous it was, this crass melding of Church and State, and yet the proud and sturdy pose was familiar. It reminded me of all the majestic Otto von Bismarck statues I'd seen traveling across Germany, practically every Old Town square north of Bavaria had one. Old man Bismarck, my father had told me, had united Germany back in 1871, but the uniter was also a stubborn and cagey despot who cloaked himself in democracy and the Grand Manner. Bismarck ruled for a long, long time. In the end, his grave legacy had produced a leader like Hitler. And now look where his people had landed—exhausted, disillusioned, all out of luck.

All the more reason to send that SOS letter. I was glad I sent it. It would settle this, all right.

The next morning, Katarina's last kiss had seemed rushed and her embrace rigid, but I told myself it was only her way of dealing with yet another miserable farewell all made possible by yet another gruesome little tyrant. That evening I could still smell her, sweet and warm in the folds of my sheets. By now she was somewhere deep inside Munich. Certainly she had a plan—she always had a plan—but not knowing it left me in a lather and I tried to sleep, but I tossed and turned until my sheets had twisted into a corkscrew, all damp from my sweat. I sat up and found myself staring at the antique tapestry someone had once hung to brighten this dim bedroom chamber. On the weaves of thick fabric, a contingent of European trader merchants, their sailing ship looming, offered gold trinkets to native elders in loincloths and headdresses. I could just make out the figures in the dark. The lead merchant was a plump dandy dressed fancier than even the native chiefs. It might as well be Major Membre up there, I thought; all the merchants needed were US Army uniforms and the native elders the Bavarian garb. And as

I stared, this timeless tapestry made me contemplate just how things had played out with Major Membre's trade network.

Major Membre's cellar powwow at the Heimgauer Hof had sealed a deal. Heimgau was to become the central source in the American Zone of Occupation. The major's partners would keep on thriving, and he'd reap so much in-take he wouldn't know what to do with it all. He'd pass a generous cut to Baron von Maulendorff, of course. Yet something did not add up, and it hadn't occurred to me until now. They had so many orders to fill, but where did they score all the goods? Sure, there were always far more untraceable personal treasures to be grabbed than there were fancy museum pieces. But how many, really, were worth the effort? Could all the requisitioned houses in Heimgau county give them enough? And how did they store it? The main stocks were supposed to be up at the castle, in cellars and storerooms and chambers, but just how much could those hold?

Something else I didn't get. The major was employing more artisans like that portrait painter, not just locals but well-skilled refugees and expellees from the farthest reaches of war-torn Europe. I had heard Von Maulendorff say they needed the artisans for "refurbishing." Yet how much spruce-up could a crew do? A whole lot, it seemed, since the artisans had been working well past curfew, seven nights a week, many in those chambers I didn't know so well.

I turned over and found my alarm clock. One a.m. I kicked off my twisted bedding, pulled on my trousers, threw on a lightweight but dark civilian coat from the closet—the previous owners'. A motoring cap was in there. I put that on.

The night carried an unexpected chill for summer, but the march up to the castle warmed me up. I met no guards in the main courtyard, so I continued on through an archway that led to the second, smaller courtyard. Hearing footsteps coming my way, I stopped inside the archway and listened. It was a jaunty shuffle, not the paced gait of a bored guard. I peeked out.

A small, wiry man had stopped before the archway. He lit a match to the cigarette in his mouth, but the wind blew it out. He scooted into the archway to try again, and his flame lit me up against the wall.

The man's eyes narrowed. Then he smiled. "Prosim, prosim," he said, holding his flame for me.

"I don't speak what you're speaking there," I said in German.

"It's Czech," squeaked the man.

"Right. I don't speak Czech."

"Of course not, good sir," the Czech said, his German quaint and clumsy. He had thick eyebrows. He wore a dusty worker's cap. He struck another match, cupping the flame. "Would you like a light? This would give me pleasure. Please."

I had an unlit Lucky between my lips. "Gladly."

The Czech bowed slightly as he lit me, looking up at me, our faces glowing. The Czech held his cigarette straight up. "This is tonight's payment. My training wage. I only smoke half."

"Good thinking. You're new here? Excuse me for not remembering. So many work here now."

"Yes. A great number do now. And all do such fine work."

"Why, yes we do. And I'm sure you do too."

The Czech smiled. "Oh, that I do, sir."

I rested a hand on the Czech's shoulder. "Tell me, what is it you work on again?" I tapped my forehead. "With so many here now I simply forget."

The Czech took a deep breath. "Well, sir, what I do best is my handwork."

"Handwork, did you say?"

"That's right and all from scratch," added the Czech.

From scratch? I played it casual. "That's swell, friend. What are you working on now? From scratch, I mean."

The Czech blurted something I couldn't understand. He plucked the cigarette from his mouth. He frowned at it and smacked himself on the side of the head.

"What is it?"

"Stupid! I am stupid. I tell myself, I only smoke half yet I almost smoke it all! So stupid. My wife, she gets so angry for such things." The Czech stood on one leg and pressed the cigarette's lit end to the sole of his boot. "She is all I have, my Hana, she is all I have now."

I held out two Lucky Strikes. "Here, that'll make your gal happy."

"Oh, I couldn't."

"Sure you can. Tell you what, you heading down the hill? I'm going that way. You could tell me about your work, how you find things here in Heimgau, all of it." I patted my front pocket. "I have whiskey to keep us warm."

"Whiskey?" The Czech placed a hand at his heart. "Ah, I couldn't."

We began our stroll down the hill, a full moon following us up above the branches.

The Czech walked fast to keep up. "I am a Czech-German refugee, from near Pilsen. You know Pilsen?" I nodded. "I'm just lucky they found me."

That made me slow a few paces. Don't rush this, Harry. "So it worked out nicely for you."

"Oh, yes. The Americans' Military Government is very thorough, even more than the Germans. All refugees must register a domicile, along with a profession. But you know all that. That's probably how they found you, too."

"Sure is." I handed the Czech the flask. He walked along with it.

"The baron mayor gave me the tryout," the Czech said. "He was very precise. He told me, build a little statue of the Virgin Mary from scratch, but make it look very old, and of gold, and slightly smoke-damaged. I got right to it. Carved the mold myself, poured the plaster, painted with faded tones. Much effort. Then I weathered her: I sanded the sharpest edges, applied a special wash and—this is key—I put her in a smoker for a whole day, so the finish cracks just so." He smiled.

"Nice touch. Got you the job?"

"Oh, yes. I was told their major kept my Maria himself."

"That's quite a compliment."

We strode step in step as if promenading, sipping the whiskey.

"I'm amazed at the mock artifacts we produce," the Czech said. "Though I must admit, I've never witnessed a twenty-four-hour operation. The skill level of our artisans is quite admirable."

"Yes. They all deserve a drink. Here's to 'em."

"Here is to them, sir." The Czech drank, wiped his mouth. "There's this one old Heimgau craftsman, fills furniture orders. Copies antique chairs, buffets, saw him do an Empire desk styled after Napoleon's own. Another Heimgauer, he specializes in porcelains."

I halted, the moon hiding behind a tree trunk. "Figurines?"

"Right," the Czech said, waiting for me and my flask to catch up. "In the Meissen fashion. Courtiers, nymphs, harlequins, valuable pieces, surely, though not my favorite." I let the Czech hold the flask again. "We're from all over, aren't we?" he went on. "There's that Pole who tarnishes silver and another replicates weapons, and this man-and-wife team from Danzig who do obscure paintings. Know them?" I nodded. "Monk from Austria reproduces medieval texts, aye, and he's a master, that one." Another nod.

I was almost feeling sorry for the little guy. If I was Major Membre or the baron in disguise, my talkative Czech would already be sent packing if not digging his own grave right now. And if his Hana could hear him? I shuddered to think it.

"So, you feel you're rewarded well enough?" I said.

The Czech eyed me. "You're not a Socialist, are you? A labor man? We're told to stay away from the likes of you."

I eyed him back. "You're not, are you?"

The Czech looked away. "How could I admit something like that? The baron and the major are paying so well."

"Indeed. So? You're getting by."

"I'm rewarded. We craftsmen get something, no matter the product. But we're told it will get better for us. Some who've been here from the start have been promised confiscated houses. You have a house, I bet." I nodded, sure. "I look forward to one of those. Hana and I, we share a musty cellar, with three other families."

"See anything else? Jobs, say, of a different nature?"

"Some claim *Fragebogen* and other documents are falsified. I don't want to know of it."

"Of course not. Me, I always wondered what all the others do, all those less-skilled workers around."

"The scrubs and drunks? The apprentices? What else? They hammer together the wooden crates, the palettes. Gigantic things, those. But then the Americans have such grand trucks and trains and airplanes. Now that's the way to haul the stuff out, I say."

"It sure is. It's impressive."

We strode on, arms swinging. I shook the flask—our whiskey was running low. The Czech grew quiet as we walked on. At the bottom of the hill, we entered the yellow cast of a streetlight.

The Czech halted, flat-footed. He peered at me in the light. Looking down, he had seen my American brogues and olive-drab Army trousers.

"What's the matter, friend?" I said.

"You're not an artist? What are you?"

"It doesn't matter."

The Czech was shaking his head like he had ants in his hair. He started to run.

"My friend, listen, that's really not a good idea."

The Czech stopped. Turned. He made his way back, his head low and his face ashen.

I offered a handshake, in which I left two more Luckies. I added a smile. "I thank you for our little talk. I really do. And you shouldn't worry yourself over it."

"I shouldn't?" The Czech spoke to the ground, fidgeting with his fingers.

"No. You're new. You didn't know. Here's the thing you should know: You might see me around. And when you do, remember that you never saw me up here. And I never saw you." The Czech nodded as I spoke. I handed him the flask. He drank with both hands. Handed back the flask, empty. "All right? Good man. Look, there will be no interrogation later. That's what I want you to know. Just as long as you never, ever, never, tell anyone what you told me, and that means even your dear Hana."

"No. Never, ever. Not even my dear Hana."

"Good. And remember, if you see me on the street? Never saw me. All right? Now go."

The Czech nodded again. "Never saw you," he said and bolted into the darkness.

I slogged my way back across Old Town, my hands deep in my pockets. I recalled what my father, adapting General Clausewitz's famous axiom, had said about crooked businessmen: "Fraud is simply a continuation of trade by other means."

Everyone was a crook or a lug or a fool. My fine billet house, I had learned, had last belonged to our absconded brown priest's dead Nazi brother, sent to fight on the crumbling East Prussian Front in the final months. Good riddance. All the more reason I should take over the place. I marched inside and upstairs to the study. I grabbed the baron's Meissen jester and was about to heave it against a wall. Instead, I took a careful look at the thing. The porcelain shone and glistened like the deepest pearl. Those tiny buttons forming perfect little orbs. Such elegant detail. No, this one was no fake. This one had come from before, I told myself. I set my jester back on its shelf.

It seemed the major just couldn't get enough of a good thing, so much so that he was willing to risk it all just to keep on getting it. It sounded like his style. The only thing I didn't understand was, what exactly did any of this have to do with those torture-murders?

I had to be patient, and trust that it was all coming together. Major Membre was the one digging himself the hole now, and I wouldn't be the sorry shamus much longer.

And with that thought I went to bed, sleeping better than I had in weeks.

Sixteen

FOUR DAYS LATER I WAS HUNKERED down at my villa, waiting and pining and starting to wonder just how patient I would have to be. It was a Saturday afternoon. June had brought perfect summer days. I lay slung in a hammock I'd made from camouflage netting. I swung in the hammock hoping, once again, to stave off the doubt plaguing me. It had been days since I sent that letter to Colonel Spanner, but I'd heard nothing from him. It would've taken no time for the colonel to dash off a telegraph, memo, letter or even a runner with a note, even if only to say he appreciated my concern and would get back to me at the earliest. And yet, nothing? What could it mean? In my darkest moments, I wondered if Major Membre's growing influence had reached even Colonel Spanner.

I swung some more, and forced out a sigh. No wonder I was so worked up. This was not just about my investigation. This would gain me my CO spot back if I played it right. Was it too conniving of me? Sure, I could admit it. The urge to solve those torture-murders shared the same drivetrain with my need to prove myself as the American. This was about success. So perhaps the colonel had seen right through my motives, didn't want to reward some inter-detachment dispute, and this was my punishment. This waiting. I sighed again, stuck here in this damn hanging net, thinking of heading back into town with more questions for the baron's new ex-Nazi cronies. Over the last few days I'd taken each aside and interrogated all, but I'd done it by plying them with Luckies and whiskey and slavish manners. Sticking to a game they knew. None of the four had been anywhere near Heimgau during the torture-murders, I learned. And my cross-questioning of locals backed it up. But they had to know something. So what if I now leaned on those cronies a little? Wave some Denazification papers in their face, or even my Colt? I had never played it that way, but maybe it was the only way to force a break …

I heard someone over on my villa patio. I turned in the hammock.

Lieutenant Colonel Eugene Spanner of the CIC filled the patio doorway with his angular posture. He strode straight out across the yard to me, ignoring the paths and making those seventy yards more like forty. He was wearing his simple khaki tie, shirt, and trousers and only the silver oak leaves for insignia, just as I remembered him.

I hadn't expected to be found curled up in a hammock. I moved to dismount and salute and almost toppled out.

"As you were. You're fine up there." Spanner held out a hand.

I shook the hand, still swaying. "Afternoon, sir."

"No 'sirs' today, Kaspar." Spanner winked at me, his eyes that same wet and rich leaden color. Summer had given him flushed cheeks and dry, cracking lips. He sat in the wooden chair below the hammock, the chair I needed to climb in and out of my berth.

I sat up, slowly so that I didn't roll right out and into the colonel's lap. "Still working out the kinks," I mumbled.

Spanner smiled. He leaned back, which pressed the rear chair legs into the soft grass. "Say we talk a little? Talk about that letter you sent me."

I decided to play it safe. "Maybe I shouldn't have sent you that. I mean, with all due respect to the major, who is my commander—"

"Bullshit due respect." Spanner glared. "Know what a sphincter is, Kaspar? A sphincter is an asshole. I submit to you, here and now, that Major Robertson Membre is a bloated sphincter spewing conceit, avarice, and hate. You see? Your CO shoots it out without end."

I showed him a smirk.

"I pity every German, Yankee, refugee or otherwise who's had to tolerate the major. And this isn't just about Heimgau. It's about your Fräulein. Katherine, that her name?"

"Katarina. How did you know about her?"

"She delivered your letter to the front desk, did she not?"

She had. I had asked her to. It was the quickest way.

"I happened to be in the lobby," Spanner added.

"Did you meet her? She see you?"

"No. I just observed. Lovely. Bet she's a tough gal, too. Good head on her." Spanner's face went blank a moment, then hardened. "So. You and our major do not get along. You are like oil and water. And why do you think that is? Because you stand so far above that man it hurts to have to serve him. You don't stand for the bullshit, do you?"

I sat steady in the hammock, perfectly balanced. "No."

"You ain't lazy, stubborn."

"No."

"Hell, you're more American than most Americans I've seen around here."

I nodded. Call it what you will, Colonel.

"Damn straight, Captain. But Major Membre came and screwed the pooch, didn't he?"

"I told you. He hasn't made anyone's life easier. Only his own."

Spanner reached and grasped the hammock, pulling me to him. If he wanted he could have rolled me on out. "Son, you are not willing to give in to the Major Membres of this world. There's damn few of your breed. You do things your way, regardless of consequences. I respect that. That's why you're perfect for what I want to propose. And if you accept it—if you act on this—you will have realized what it means to act."

"Propose? I'm not sure I follow, sir."

"Forget the 'sir.' I know you. Know what's like to be the outsider. The alien who's never good enough. Whose motives are always questioned by little men thinking they're better. I told you that."

"You did. I respect it."

"I know from here," Spanner said, pressing a hand to his chest. "This here simple exterior, it disguises a noble upbringing. A Southern gentleman of long lineage, I am the closest thing to an aristocrat as can be found in our young nation. Was a day when noblemen were knights, the cavalry. Now they ride polished desks instead of proud horses. Now they're pussyfooters like the major's baron. I never stood for fighting this war from a desk. You must understand why. I was a sickly, shy boy, Captain, the youngest of four competing Georgia squires. I overcame my weakness by competing, always slugging back, and discovering thereby that anything is possible if you're willing to do what others will not dare, simply will not dare." He chuckled, his head rearing back. "The hard charger, if you will. I got myself sent over here as fast as I could. North Africa, Sicily, Italy and onward, up Southern France, the holy shit I've seen and done and they made me do, you do not even want to hear. It would give you nightmares that shiver your heart. And this was only the start." The colonel pressed hand to chest again. "You are much like me, like this, here. Truly. You just haven't had the chance to discover how much so."

"I'm listening."

"I knew you would, son. Knew you would." Spanner yanked on the hammock, forcing me out with a great leap. I landed on both feet. "Nice landing," he said. "Look at you. You got more of an edge to you now, I can see it. Sharpened up. Good and ready to do this."

I wanted to smile, but held off. "I feel it. I'm always watching my back, day and night. Sometimes I think I get a feel for how a GI must have felt like up on the line."

Spanner's face opened up, flat and slow, his eyes dull stones. "You have no goddamn earthly idea what it feels like up on the line. Do not ever say that you do. Ever."

His glare made me lower my head. "Understood."

"Yes? So? Let's get to it, then."

Parked in front of my villa was that cigar-shaped and unmarked US Army sedan, a smooth Detroit cruiser under all that matte green paint with a polished chromium dashboard and curtains for the rear windows. The colonel drove me through Old Town, me in the back seat.

"You might not like where we're headed, but just let things play out."

"All right." I stretched out. The leather seat was a sofa. I felt the soft curtains and the sparkling knobs and handles, more chrome than I'd seen in a long time. If Membre had been driving me, I would've been sickened. Yet, like this? After the colonel had confided in me so? Spanner hummed. The engine thrummed. We swallowed streets whole, forcing Heimgauers onto sidewalks and around streetlights. Spanner slowed. I slid open the curtains. A group of refugees was crossing our way, workers and artisans just down from the castle. My little Czech friend skipped by, passing the fender.

The Czech froze. He'd seen me in back. He scampered off, pushing through the crowd.

Spanner drove on, unaware. I said nothing about the bogus goods. Let things play out, the colonel had said, and so I did. We rode in silence a while. I told Spanner about the major's portrait and blessed Bismarck costume. Spanner shook his head, sickened. "Not surprised. I found out a thing or two about your major. If he ain't the scion of the Membre Home Furnishings empire. Joined every fraternal organization known to American Civilization. By the time the war was won, he makes himself an Army Reserve mucky-muck, with some amount of pull, no doubt. And well before that? He was in a Catholic seminary. Didn't make the grade, it seems."

I snorted, disgusted. Spanner was eyeing me in the rearview mirror. We had cleared town, out among the green hills and open valleys and the cab filled with a calming light. It made me think of the first day I met him, with those train cars. "I went back to Dollendorf once, to that old tractor factory," I said. "It's been pretty quiet up there. I checked it all out."

"You did, did you?" Spanner smiled. He sped up for the next turn, pressing me to the door.

I saw the overblown gate, the plaque reading, "Maulendorff Palace," and above it the sign: "Off Limits." That modest box of a mansion with its two stories and mock-tower keep filled my window as Spanner wheeled into the courtyard, our thick tires crunching gravel. In the full sunlight I could make out all the cracks in the building, the flaking stucco and fallen stones. It went well with the boarded-up windows and overgrown greenery, like some Austro-Hungarian outpost in Transylvania. It might as well have been the year 1645 here.

The colonel was eyeing me in the mirror again.

I held up a hand. "I'm holding my tongue."

"Good man." The colonel jerked the parking brake, sprang from the sedan, and bounded up the front steps. I followed. The front door cracked open and the Baron Mayor von Maulendorff peeked out, his green velvet smoking jacket buttoned to the neck. One eye was puffy and bruising, all yellowed and purpled, and a cheek showed fresh scrapes. The baron lifted a water bottle to the eye. I looked to Spanner.

"Had to show him who's boss," Spanner said. "Afternoon, Baron Mayor," the colonel added in southern-tinged German and added a mocking bow. The baron bowed anyway, but it made him wince and hold his ribs, and yet he also bowed to me, who had never bowed in his life, and I wasn't about to start now. The baron stretched out a hand instead. I shook it.

Spanner smiled at me. "Captain, you should know something before we continue. The baron mayor is my man now."

"Right. Yes, sir." I looked to the baron, but he kept his head lowered.

The baron ushered us inside. Whole rooms were empty, furnished only with shafts of dusty daylight. This mansion was all but cleaned out. He led us upstairs to a meeting chamber lined with windows and more shafts of light. Once upon a time the room must have had a fine long table running down the center, but now only a mishmash of chairs and crates stood at random. The colonel chose the one lavish chair, a modern brown leather wing model that wrapped around him. I grabbed a stool. And I kept holding my tongue. I broke open a fresh pack of Lucky Strikes and offered one to the colonel.

"I don't smoke," the colonel said. He grabbed my pack and tossed it to the baron.

The baron stood over a tarnished silver platter set on an old packing crate, a makeshift bar that held two bottles, three glasses and a tin ashtray. He placed the cigarette pack on the tray with fingertips, like it was a loaded grenade. "Scotch or gin is all I have. Neat only, I'm afraid," he said in his Oxford-accented English.

"None for me," Spanner said.

"Bourbon," I said. "Double."

The baron poured. Spanner stretched his legs and laid his head back. "Baron, why don't you tell the captain here what you told me."

The baron handed me the double bourbon. He pulled over a wooden chair that creaked, and cleared his throat. "So. I offer the colonel a tremendous opportunity, one cultivated during my long period underground—"

"Stop," said Spanner. "You mean 'taking the cure' in old Bohemia. We all know what you were during the war, so let's cut to the chase."

"Yes, yes." The baron lit one of my Luckies, taking his time. "You see, your colonel controls one of the trains that was 'liberated.'"

I looked to Spanner. "The one I saw in Dollendorf?"

Spanner nodded. "Yes. The rumors are true."

The baron looked at me with eyes screwed up and forehead pinched—a look that seemed to be saying, I told you about trains in confidence that night at the castle so please, please don't bring it up. Or did he know I'd found out about the bogus goods racket? In which case his pucker face could be saying, if you tell Colonel Spanner about that, my goose is cooked and well done, too. Yet had the baron even wanted to know about the artisans' fake pieces? He was so good at looking the other way, his eyeballs could probably revolve in full circles, like ball bearings. I didn't know what to say. A part of me wanted to hope our absurd baron was more rube noble than wily Machiavelli. This was supposed to be about the major, last time I checked. Yet now the major's top toady was the colonel boy? I gulped my whiskey, tasting only fire, and wiped my stinging lips. "Very well," I said.

The baron sighed in relief. "The colonel, he plans to run his train across the American Zone and onward into Switzerland. I have friends in Zurich. They are interested in acquiring."

Spanner glared at the baron. "Your goddamn bankers. They'll want to jew us down."

"Please?" said the baron.

Spanner looked to me and shook his head. I shook my head and sipped some more. I was grasping one part of this visit. The colonel had come to lean on the baron, to score the best deal, and I was another mean face.

Spanner said: "What's your take from the laundry, Maulendorff?"

"Please? Again, I don't understand—"

"Your cut. Graft. Fee. Much you want?"

"Yes, well." The baron brought his hands together, forming a triangle. "Colonel, you located the train. I have my Swiss contacts, which you yourself do not have." The baron faced me. "The Swiss do not ask embarrassing questions, you see."

"Get on with it," Spanner said.

"So, this makes me the middleman, does it not? I expect a reasonable portion of the treasure, or profits thereof." The baron smiled, his teeth jutting out like they wanted to chatter. "Say, only twenty-five percent."

Spanner held up a hand. "You'll go down, under certain conditions. Spit 'em out."

The baron rocked on his chair, which squeaked in rhythm. "Yes, there is something. It concerns a political matter, one significant to the future of my Bavarian state."

Spanner sighed. "I don't meddle in kraut politics. Helping out Nazis could make trouble down the road."

"All I ask is that which I have here may continue. I owed these men favors, yes, but they are not doing so poorly, are they?" He looked to me, his eyebrows twitching. I managed a shrug. The baron lifted his water bottle back to his face. "I'm an avowed monarchist, good sirs. I aim to bring back my Prince Rupprecht to Bavaria, and with him a level of sovereignty and civility that the Freistaat Bayern has not for some time enjoyed."

Spanner laughed. "I tell ya, you Bavarians are worse than Texans with your cursed pride, your Free State of Bavaria."

"No one can turn back the clock," I added.

"By then it won't matter to you. Wooing the prince will take time. I only ask that you allow me to stay, no matter what happens. My colleagues could remain immune from your Denazification authorities. Surely you understand this, men like you. Surely? People need a second chance. Myself, I could not have survived without a few friends."

Spanner smiled, faintly. He ran his finger along an eyebrow.

"And, yes, this would greatly compensate for any lesser take," the baron added.

The colonel rose and ambled over to the row of windows, the sunlight gleaming his hair white. The baron glancing sideways at me. I swirled my bourbon. Sipped. The baron was made of stronger steel than he looked, I'd give him that much. I could have brought up the major's bogus goods racket at any moment. Yet I held out. Never let them know your inventory.

"Captain? How you read this?" Spanner said.

"Well, as you know, MG keeps hearing that the War Department policy makers do appreciate the stable 'decentralization' of Germany that state monarchies offer. It could be possible. For the time being."

Spanner grinned his big teeth, a full American smile. "Baron Mayor, I can't help but say I'm honored by your proposal. All of it. You get ten percent."

"Very well. Most excellent, Colonel." The baron cracked a smile, which made him wince from the black eye, which made him grimace from the pain in his ribs. "Sirs, this moment is not lost on me."

"Of course it ain't," Colonel Spanner said. "One day soon we'll discuss our treasure train in detail. See, I never sold to neutrals like those Swiss before. And you can tell me more about your prince. Monarchy's such a mighty-fine antique. But right now? Me and Captain Kaspar here have a fair amount of dealing to get to."

Our ride back was like some harebrained rum run. Colonel Spanner drove hard and fast, shouldering the steering wheel one way, then the other, a blur of trees and fields, and he whooped as we caught our breath for the next turn and I couldn't get a word in even if I dared try. He shouted that his roaring beast of a sedan could make it across the whole US Zone in an hour on any good flat road. My wobbly legs confirmed it as I climbed on out back at my villa. I led the colonel into the study and offered him a blue chenille chair. I liked this room. It had a three-foot copper globe standing in one corner, a high ceiling fan turning, windows with thick Venetian blinds and a view of the ivy-laced wall of the neighboring villa. I fixed myself another bourbon and offered the colonel a scotch, which the colonel accepted, and then I took a seat in the other blue chair, our two chairs sharing either side of a copper-top table. Spanner watched me and chewed gum, kneading it with his molars yet barely shifting his horse-like jaw. Last time his gum was licorice. This time it was mint and medicinal in its intensity, overpowering the aroma of my bourbon.

"You're gonna help me with this," Spanner said.

"Help how?"

"You can make a new future. For you and your Fräulein, if you want that."

"Katarina?"

"Maybe I could cut her a passable *Fragebogen*. Top of that? You get a share of the loot."

"That's not what I'd do this for."

"Membre took away your CO posting. I'm giving you the chance—the only chance—to have it the way you wanted."

"You can do that?"

Spanner nodded. "I want someone who can work alone and keep it sub rosa. Too many men can't handle that once they catch the gleam of gold in their eye."

I snorted another disgusted laugh. "The major, he told me he's launching his own investigation, can you believe it? Says he's making progress. But nothing's changed."

Spanner shot up, his knees clanging the table. "What?"

"Nothing's changed."

"No, not that."

"Investigation? He launched his own investigation. He won't get anywhere. He doesn't want that. It's just a bluff. He just wants to block my tackle."

Spanner stared off, into a corner and so forcefully that I had to turn around to check and make sure no one was there. He was like a sad widower, induced by a séance. His hands had clawed at his sides. He had stopped chewing; he might have swallowed his gum.

"Can you prove it? That Membre did it? Can you pin it on him?" I added.

"I cannot provide that kind of justice," Spanner said, mechanically as if reading a cue card. "You might as well forget about that coming from me. But I can help you make sure, good and sure, that it never happens again."

I nodded. I had questions, like what did Swiss bankers want with a US-held train, for starters? And what would the colonel think of the major's (and possibly the baron's) bogus goods racket—that one detail I hadn't told Spanner about? I would get around to that, I told myself. These things had to be done in stages. Consider the angles, get your duckies in a row, make it count.

Spanner had lowered himself back into his chair. His stare had come back around to me.

"Let me ask you something," I said. "Am I obligated if I hear your plan?"

"I'll give you vague details only. Cargo, you don't need to know about. No precise dates, destinations, times. That way you won't feel you know too much."

I sucked down bourbon but didn't taste it. "All right. Shoot."

Spanner said: "Those four freight cars you saw your first day? They are still near here, sitting tight. I still have that locomotive. That's where you'll be. I want you to ride it."

"I don't know how to drive a locomotive."

"You won't drive it. You represent the Military Government across the neighboring counties. But only to the French Zone. I'll provide the driver, a coal man. Horton will be there."

"You won't be there?"

Spanner shook his head. "Captain, son, think about it. Things look normal with an MG man on board. But a colonel in Counter Intelligence Corps? People watch me, friend and foe. No, I'll be busy keeping folks looking the other way."

"You want this quiet. The least amount of men. You don't like too many chiefs."

"Right. You'll have lots of time," Spanner said. "Whole day for a four-hour train ride."

"And, Major Membre knows nothing?"

"Absolutely nothing. And he won't. We're doing this on our own—me, you, the baron."

I stared at the globe in the corner. My cheeks had grown warm and it wasn't the drink. This all was being handed to me on a platter, yet it wasn't how I imagined it. Still, wasn't this something like the next best thing? If the result was the same? Even if I had just promised the baron support that I would never honor? I heaved myself out of the chair, my thoughts in knots. "I think I've heard too much, for now."

"Nah, I think you've heard just enough." Spanner's good mood had returned and his Georgia twang kicked in stronger. "Look at you. You're all flustered, that's what you are. You want this more than a frog wants wings. But don't give me an answer right now."

I stood over at the globe. I spun it and watched it go. Major Membre gets pushed out. The murderer and torturer might never be nabbed, but it never happens again. Not on my watch. I could start over. We could. I pressed at the globe, halting its spin. "Improvise when required," I blurted.

Spanner smiled. "That's right. Bigger the risk, bigger the payoff."

"All right, sure. But, why me?"

"Told you. I need you, as MG and Public Safety at that, to get us through checkpoints inside the American Zone. CIC's jurisdiction has shifted, what with the Russkies getting all itchy on the borders east of us. The CIC focus is east now. Your word goes anywhere inside."

"I understand that much, sir. But why not someone else?"

"I told you why," Spanner said. "I need a man who can live up to what I expect."

"And what comes after? Where do I stand?"

"Where you think?"

I knew the detachment's protocols better than anyone. If the CO was reposted or out of action, one Captain Harry Kaspar was next in line.

"What if there's another replacement?"

"There won't be," Spanner said.

I sat. I grabbed at my glass and held it in my lap. "I need some time. Mull it over."

"Understood. I need to smooth the edges in any case. I got an idea: Get the hell outta this village."

"Out?"

"Put in for leave. For Munich. See your Fräulein. It'll go through and pronto. Major doesn't want you around. You know how to play it."

I had eased deep into my chair, legs outstretched. I tried not to think too hard. I should have been asking plenty questions right about then. Never mind the Swiss. What was in those freight cars exactly? And how long have you known Major Membre, Colonel? Did the baron come to you, or vice versa? I should've been asking about plenty more things. But I only tried not to think. I lit a Lucky, the nicotine numbing me. I blew a long barrel that reached the high ceiling fan. It churned my smoke and scattered it into particles.

Spanner leaned across the little table and his breath of scotch and mint came reeking. "Here's what you need to know. If I do not hear from you within a week from today? We're on. Follow me? It's a go."

I nodded, yes. We drank. I swallowed hard. The bourbon was giving me heartburn. I ground out my stub in the ashtray.

Spanner emptied his glass and sat up, eyeing me. "I don't have to warn you. Do not tell a soul about any of this. Because I will know."

"Not a chance, sir. I wouldn't want to spoil my chance, would I?"

"Atta boy." Spanner rose and, like he always did, he ended up at the window where he separated the closed blinds with a fingernail and peered out. "One more thing. I know about the little sideline swindle they're running."

My heart skipped, raced. "Swindle?"

"The counterfeit racket. Mock loot. Why do you think the baron earned that new decoration of his?" Spanner pointed to his eye, meaning the baron's black shiner. "You did know about it, didn't you?"

"I just found out," I blurted, "was going to tell you, but I didn't know if you knew, and I didn't know if I was supposed to know, that you did know. If you did know. Sir."

"All right, never mind. It's not your doing." The colonel came back over and stood behind his chair, leaning over it, grasping either wing as if he wanted to lift it above his head. That or crush it. "You want me to keep my end of the bargain, don't you? Isn't that why you wrote to me? Isn't it? Tell me."

"Yes. And I want to keep my end."

"Good. Then keep your head down for now, because here I come."

Seventeen

Somehow the steep spires of Munich City Hall still rose high above the Marienplatz, the ravaged heart of Old Town. Old Munich's busiest street ran through the square, "Off Limits" to any traffic not US military. Trucks and jeeps, staff cars, and motorcycles rushed by in a whirlwind of gritty ash and grime, stench and stone dust that bit at my nostrils, a constant reminder of the incalculable tons of this busted, bombed-out city yet to be cleared and already cleared, piled up, scoured in vain. I got dropped off here and continued on foot, navigating the rambling rubble heaps strewn in every direction. Skeletal building fronts loomed at random as if ready to topple. I passed the ruins of the Frauenkirche, the National Theater. One charred column was all that remained of the Bavarian State Opera. And on and on, an unending testament to centuries of beauty and reason betrayed from within by dogma and hate and smashed from above in protest.

"Choking on its own puke," Colonel Spanner had said of Munich. So CIC agent Eugene Spanner was no Jimmy Stewart. I had realized that much. This wasn't Hollywood and didn't I know it. Justice was a compromise, the colonel had said. This was the way it was done in the real world and how a man gets ahead to boot. So maybe I had not asked enough questions. Maybe I hadn't taken a stand with both feet. I could make myself live with that. So why did I feel like I needed a cold shower? All I knew was, it wasn't the sandpaper air.

Spanner spoke to me on the inside, challenging me to go for broke. Everything he said I could do if I pushed it became possible. The power of it wanted to drop my jaw. Take this leave, for example. I had requested a few days off in Munich, and here I was free to roam. Past the Odeonsplatz I walked, heading north, down narrower lanes that zigged and zagged through the rubble heaps. Second and third stories of buildings hung half-exposed like cross sections in an architecture textbook, showing mosaic floors, floral wallpaper, hutches, and family photos, all of it useless now. I caught a rough smell like rotten eggs, ammonia. At my feet liquids seeped from pipes, broken somewhere, gurgling at bricks and wood and gobs of who knew what, releasing their oils and stains. Further on I reached the district of Schwabing, once the home of artists and performers, thinkers and radicals and one two-bit rabble-rouser calling himself Adolf Hitler. I turned onto the Barerstrasse. Here most streets looked salvageable, a few unharmed. Streetcars hustled by, clanging and creaking and crammed with people. Up ahead, a group of stocky Fraus was staring down a monstrous pile of rubble. A truck pulled up and they attacked the heap with shovels, boards, bare hands. One caught me watching. "Don't you worry, *Ami*," she yelled over, "We'll have your mess cleared in no time!"

The colonel had said I was more American than most he knew. Is that all being American meant? Knowing how to cut a deal in your favor? To beat the other guy out of a good gig? The Baron von Maulendorff had sold out Major Membre to Colonel Spanner, apparently. So wasn't I doing the same thing?

I strolled on and turned onto a street of bustling shops and pubs, the Schellingstrasse. Number 35 wasn't like the rest of the neighborhood. The building was scorched from fire. The windows had been boarded up a long time and a main door was nailed shut, the nail heads leaving rusty trails. I was sorry to see it. This was the address Katarina had sent me.

Around the corner I found the building's inner courtyard. Across the yard stood red double doors, on which a black stencil read: "Off Limits: Schwabinger Volkstheater und Kabarett." It was some kind of community theater. Above the red doors I saw fading letters, barely legible: "Wiesenberg u. Söhne: Fleischerhandwerk." A butcher's. This cabaret was once a slaughterhouse.

I went to the red doors and listened. Nothing. I knocked with a knuckle and waited. No answer. I went in. A haze of musty diluted tobacco stung my eyes and I had to squint. The room was dark, with dingy windows up high and candles on small cafe tables here and there.

"Whom do you search?" asked a male voice in an English pulsing with Munich accent. I saw the reflection of eyeglasses, over in a corner.

"You mean, who am I looking for?"

"Yes, that's it. The American-style English is quite odd, is it not?"

This fouled-up city had me edgy and I didn't like the smug tone, the defiance in this man's voice. "Says who?" I grunted.

The man only shrugged at me.

"Looking for a woman," I said in German. "Name of Buchholz."

"Ah. Of course. She is here, Captain," the man said, sticking to English. "There, behind the curtain."

The curtain was US Army blankets dyed black. I felt my way through more curtains and reached a larger room that I spied on through a tear in the blankets. They'd made a theater out of beer hall benches and church pews, a stage cobbled together from plywood and sandstone blocks. A line of dim light bulbs hung along the edge of the stage.

A sliver of fear cut at me. Munich was the big city. Katarina had left Heimgau behind. Sure, she'd sent me her address, but what if she didn't really want me here anymore?

I felt a draft. I pushed on through the blankets. A door was cracked open over in the corner, letting in dusty cool air. The door opened to the street. I peered out, but the street was empty. Was it her? She'd made a quick exit? I sprinted back through to the front room. *Herr* Eyeglasses was gone. "*Jemand da?*" I yelled, "Anyone there?" but only got echoes.

Moron. Goof. Why had I hesitated? I ended up back out in the courtyard, kicking at pebbles and planning my next move.

A straight arm stopped me.

"That was you there?" Katarina said. Her hand had recoiled as if to slap me.

I grabbed at her shoulders. "You in trouble?"

"Me? Of course not. But you never know, you know?" She wiggled loose. "What if I had a pistol, or I hit you on the head?"

"Probably do me some good." I grabbed her, pulling her close. She fought it a second, and then let out a full laugh. I kissed the laugh.

"So, welcome to Munich!" she said, sounding like a bubbly tour guide.

I stayed with Katarina in her dressing room-bedroom above the theater, reached through another courtyard door, up squeaking stairs and past wardrobe and storage. A lumpy daybed sofa clogged half the room. Armoires, mirrors and racks of costumes surrounded us. The only window was painted over. She wouldn't let me get intimate until I'd proved I could be kind, she said.

A guy never had it so good.

Billeting with a Fräulein was still illegal under MG law, so I wore civvies to avoid any run-ins. A pack of Chesterfields bought me the nappy wool trousers, shirt patched on elbows, corduroy jacket and leather cap I wore on the street while Katarina did her trading. We hit the black markets on the squares and in the beer hall near the train station. We met contacts on shaded corners, knocked on doors in code, argued out deals in cellars—coffee for cigarettes there, the cigarettes for an iffy slab of pork here, the pork for a bag of gray potatoes there. Katarina scored a loaf of rare farmer's bread, fresh and moist. She gave it to an old woman who was huddled under a tree crying.

Lunch was cheese smelling of mold on a bread dry like sawdust. That was the clincher. I was going to the Munich PX, get us some rations. Katarina refused. In the afternoon she helped Munich's women clear debris. *Trümmerfrauen*, people called them—the rubble women. "Who else is going to do it but us gals?" Kat said.

The next morning, hunger woke us early and we lay on our sides facing each other. My two-day stubble chafed. My head ached. I had to yawn again, and my stomach wanted to cry uncle. "Boot camp was easier than this. At least you got hot chow."

"I assure you, this is nothing," Katarina said. "You were not here for the bombings."

"Why don't I just hit the PX? Could go this morning. Just a tin of coffee, how's that? Can't you enjoy just one luxury?"

She moved closer, smiling. "I have it." She nuzzled me, her forehead onto my pillow. Then she pulled away, and sat up. "But do you know what? You were right to say what you said, about me."

"What? No." I sat up. "I wasn't right to treat you like that either."

"Such things happen. You were upset somehow. Perhaps I deserve some of it."

"Look, so you had some good times during the war and bad times. You don't have to go nailing yourself to the cross, sister."

It was too late for that. Katarina turned to the edge of the bed, speaking away from me. "I danced, you see, and I sang, and I drank champagne—"

"And you helped the resistance. So I don't know what you're beating yourself up for. Your parents are dead. Your brother. Okay. That's not your fault. You're not responsible."

"I never said I was, Harry."

"I wonder what you think. You've never asked me how the investigation is going. Not once."

"I know how it's going. And I don't hold a grudge."

"No? Well, maybe I do."

What if I told her, only her, about Colonel Spanner coming to the rescue? A breakthrough in the case was even possible. Still, I had promised. No one must know. I pushed out of bed and made for the painted window. "This room's too somber, sure, needs some light. I could scrape this paint off in no time."

I scratched out a line in the window paint, enough to squint out at the courtyard. All I saw were craggy, mud-caked cobblestones. Katarina was staring at me, her head to one side. She got out of bed, pulled her hair back and left the room. She returned lugging a silver washbasin and splashed her face with ice-cold water.

"Today? I begin to show you things," she said.

"Most of the theater troupe are Jewish," Katarina told me as we headed out onto the Schellingstrasse. Bike bells jingled and shop doors squeaked, open and shut. "German-Jewish, actually."

"You founded this troupe? You've been here less than three weeks."

"Oh, no. You know the troupe's founder. You met him."

"Guy with the glasses." I slowed, my fists rammed in my pockets. "You're seeing him. I shoulda known."

"Oh, please. You mean like you and your farm girl? What was her name, Brigitta?"

I had only walked Brigitta home that night when the baron and major pushed her on me, but I could let Kat think the worst if she was looking for a fight. "I wouldn't know," I muttered.

A US Army paddy wagon lumbered by. A huge speaker was attached to its roof releasing commands in earnest, American-accented German.

Katarina yanked me by the lapels. "His name is Emil Wiesenberg. He's a Munich-born Jew. Emil was the youngest son of one Ignatz Wiesenberg, a butcher. So don't get all daft and rattled on me, Harry. It's not flattering."

"I'm not."

"I can see that."

We walked on, crossed a square. Okay, so maybe I got a little rattled.

"That building where you're living was burned," I said.

"Yes, but your Army Air Corps did not bomb it. Emil's so-called friends and neighbors gutted it long ago, on the night of November ninth, nineteen thirty-eight."

"The Night of Broken Glass. I read about that, back home."

"I met Emil later, when he was in hiding. This was during the war. He and his family had joined a group of Jews we were trying to smuggle out. They were caught before we could. They never fingered us, said they were hiding out on their own. They ended up in various camps. His family was shipped to Dachau and, as far as he can find out, Buchenwald and an underground armaments factory called Dora. His greater family, I mean."

"The extended family, we call it."

"Yes. There were twenty of them."

"None have come home?"

Katarina stared at me a moment. She shook her head, and her eyes welled up.

She led me through tree-lined streets and into the vast English Garden. We found Emil Wiesenberg on a bench, gazing at sunlit treetops after what I guessed had been a hard morning of trading. Out in the daylight the man looked fit for a former concentration camp inmate, though he was still too lean. His hard cheekbones matched his strong chin, and his brown eyes darted and sparkled behind those glasses. Yet at 29 years old, he looked 40. His black hair had thinned, leaving fuzzy clumpy patches.

Emil stood as if to shake hands, but he didn't.

I smiled. "Morning."

Emil smiled. "So, you are this captain who plunders the heart of Katarina," he said in English. The intonation was unclear. Was plunder a good or bad thing to him?

We looked to Katarina, who stood back, grimacing like a kid who had to find a toilet.

The three of us strolled the paths of the English Garden, Emil and I in front and Katarina trailing. We talked, but also yielded to long silences. Birds chirped. Branches crackled underfoot. Bells tolled. Germans could stay silent for hours on end, strolling, gazing, contemplating. I had lost that. I never felt more American than during the silences. I needed interruptions just to think.

"The knees are shaky, and my joints ache in the cold weather," Emil told me. "Blows to my head have silenced the hearing in one ear and the prolonged lack of sleep? Well, that's where I get these purple bags under my eyes, which I don't believe I ever will lose."

We left Emil so he could do more trading. "He suffers from fits of diarrhea and migraine headaches," Katarina told me. "And nightmares. One is the same. It comes every night."

Back home, she showed me Emil's nightmare. He had scribbled it on the back of a ration card book: Out on the roll call ground the Kapo named Henk kicks my mother at the back of her legs, forcing her to her knees. She faces me, with Henk behind her. She looks at me wearily, it is true, but also lovingly and proud, as if knowing I must and will survive. A single shot from behind explodes her shaven forehead, splattering warm blood on my trembling legs.

She lies at my feet, yet I dare not touch her. Henk screams that if I whimper, I die.

So it goes. Every time I fall asleep, the bastards murder my mother.

On my third night in Munich, Emil and I drank whiskey in the empty cabaret, feet resting on chairs, a bottle on the table between us. Only a couple candles provided all the light. Our faces seemed to float in the darkness, like illuminated masks. We could have been anywhere—in a cave, around a campfire, down in the cellar of some bombed-out building on some godforsaken front line.

"Coming back here, after, one gets an odd feeling," Emil said. "Time has stood still, yet everything has changed. I keep the family property here. I don't live here. It's only a convenient place to perform. Me, I prefer the brotherhood of the Deutsches Museum camp, where all us Jews stay. It's a special deal, compliments of UNRRA"— the United Nations Rehabilitation and Relief Administration. He was smiling. He drank. I drank. "Now, Katarina, she tells me you're what they call the Public Safety officer in lovely little Heimgau. Ironic, no? Considering what you can achieve there, what you can obtain with such a status. It's the perfect front." He chuckled.

"So I hear."

Chuckling made Emil wheeze and fight a screeching cough, bending forward until his face flushed red-hot and his temples bulged. I offered him the bottle, but he waved it off.

"I like you, Captain," he said when he'd recovered. "Therefore I will tell you the truth behind our cabaret troupe. It's an excuse, you see. Sure, some are actors, and there are relative outsiders like

Katarina who contribute by performing, but this is all excuse and alibi—another way to congregate at all times and for any reason."

"You're a fence. That's what we call it."

"A fence, yes. That's clever. But it's more than that. I help run a ring called The Survivors. Not such an original name, but what can you do? We're a Jewish ring, just starting up. We had hoped to leave Germany by now, but we are forced to wait out our 'processing.'"

"Where you heading?"

"Palestine. We hope to settle in Palestine. This is why you have to endure my English that I practice. Meanwhile, we score. We prepare using the black market and we always buy up. Provisions, clothings, medicine, informations. We work with the DP gangs, Germans, does not matter, whoever can pay or trade for the materials we receive from the Red Cross and UNRRA relief people. It's faultless and foolproof. As so-called 'United Nations Nationals,' we Jews enjoy special status. We're immune from German police authority and your officials ignore us. So we exploit that status."

Of course, this made me think of Abraham, and what a man like that must have seen and done once he busted out or however he had gotten free. He might have become this fellow.

"I found one of yours just outside my town. He had the numbers on his arm."

"Yes? There are so many."

"He passed away on me, unfortunately."

"Ah. I'm sorry."

"No, I am. You probably don't want to talk about things like that."

"Not now. I'm enjoying this evening too much. Here's to it." Emil reached for the bottle, drank, and handed the rest to me.

"Here's to it. No wonder Katarina like'sh you," I said, fighting a slur from the whiskey. "I tell you, you guys sure got chutzpah."

"Chutzpah? I don't know what this word means, Captain. But if you ever have some good action for my chutzpah, you please do let me know. Maybe we make a deal."

"Will do."

Emil took a last drink and went quiet. He had pulled back from the light. Grim shadows filled his sunken features. Like this, he could have been back in his concentration camp cell block. He seemed to be, inside his head. He had that thousand-yard stare.

I let him stay there as long as he liked. "It's a goddamn shame," he said eventually.

"What is?"

"I can tell you. Katarina wished that I wait, but you deserve it. Because you made such a great effort."

"What is it?"

"The man you found, before he died? It was Abraham—Abraham Beckstein. I'm sure of it. He was my cousin."

Eighteen

EMIL HAD FLOORED ME WITH HIS NEWS. When I told Katarina about it, she was still mad at Emil the next morning, but what could she do? Emil had a right to tell. Abraham Beckstein was how Kat knew Emil. SS trucks had hauled Abraham and his family away from Heimgau years ago. She had thought him long dead. This was why, among other good reasons she had, that Kat was so wary of me when I first came asking. When she was back in Munich, her old acquaintance Emil Wiesenberg, another cheater of death, told her what he knew about his cousin. Abraham had escaped from an SS death march across Czechoslovakia in the last days. Emil had seen Abraham passing through Munich. Abraham wasn't looking for a family reunion. He was heading back to Heimgau, hell bent. He had his own agenda. Emil didn't know what it was or why, and Abraham wasn't telling, not yet. Emil could only guess that Abraham was returning to take revenge on the sicko beasts who had condemned them all. There was plenty of that going on. Emil had tried to talk his cousin out of going back, to no avail. Right as the war ended, Abraham had gotten a message to Emil in Munich saying that Heimgau was chaos, but he was helping a few trusty locals, including onetime mayor Buchholz, take over the town. The next thing Emil heard, and only recently from Kat, a US captain might have found his cousin dying along a road.

"I can still get to the bottom of it," I reminded Kat, but she didn't answer me. She headed out for more trading, more humping bricks.

That afternoon, Emil worked the sidewalk outside his theater in a burgundy smoking jacket and white ascot, shoving leaflets into the hands of passersby. I'd just gone to the Munich PX for that can of coffee. I strolled up and took a leaflet. "Cabaret! No Cover!" it read.

"Subtle."

"Thanks, Mister." At some point in our whiskey session the night before, Emil had taken to calling me Mister. "I'm glad you came back," he said. "You must see something."

He pushed open the courtyard door. Inside stood a US Army motorcycle, its matte green paint as smooth as new. Emil followed me in. I handed the can of coffee to Emil and circled the machine as if it was a sleeping bear. "Wowee. Just off the boat. A Harley-Davidson. Ridden Excelsiors and Indians, but nothing this strong. Stateside, I was a courier, you see."

"Katarina told me you were a student at university."

"I was, but some students had to work. What do you think?"

"It's formidable. It could be worth a great deal."

The bike reminded me of home as much as any letter or package. It had a second saddle on the back fender. I grasped the left-side throttle, stroked the gas tank. Mounted on the right fork was a leather rifle holster, empty. "Wait. Who's here?" I glared up at Katarina's window.

"No one. The holster was empty. Someone only left the bike." Seeing my mood shift, Emil went and shut the courtyard door as a precaution. "I thought to trade it after I suck out the petrol of course, but then I discover it belongs to you."

"Me?"

"Look in the saddlebag."

There I found goggles, gloves, a fur-lined cap and an envelope marked "ATTN: Cpt. H. Kaspar." The note inside read:

Don't consider this gift a token of my appreciation. A motorbike affords you anonymity and mobility. I don't want you stuck on a kraut train or in some motor pool jalopy when you should be working for me. Enjoy your leave.

It came with a regulation permit and trip tickets too. I felt like whistling a tune. I couldn't help feeling relief. It was Friday, June 29th. One week had passed. I had not contacted Colonel Spanner, which meant that the colonel and I had a deal. Strings will be pulled, Major Membre will discover his limits and not a day too soon. That morning I had been itching to get back to Heimgau, I had to admit. I wouldn't mind seeing Major Membre squirm a little under Colonel Spanner's big thumb. There was no escaping the colonel, his reach. Even I was feeling it. I hadn't told the colonel where I was staying in Munich and yet the man knew where to leave this fine motorbike? It did give me a chill, but nothing a mug of my new hot fresh Joe and a ride on this bike wouldn't fix.

I smiled at Emil but he'd already gone inside. I shot up the stairs to Katarina.

She sat on the bed sofa, sewing. I beamed at her, held out my hands like a dancer in a musical after the finale. She said nothing. Maybe my gesture wasn't the best choice. Draped across her lay a fabric of fluffy orange and white folds, resembling a cancan skirt. She poked the needle and pulled it out. At her feet was a stack of records, theater playbills and movie posters. One poster read "The Mountain Cavalier," costarring Katarina Buchholz.

"What you doing there? That a cabaret getup?"

Still she said nothing. I picked up a record: "Lili Marleen," as sung by Katarina Buchholz. On the cover, a sketch of a woman singing under a lamppost: Lili Marleen is the most popular soldier's song, sung by Bavaria's popular actress and songbird! All over Europe and the East, our valiant German soldiers never tire of humming it and whistling it, and darling Katarina Buchholz has to sing it at least twice wherever she appears ...

And I was just stupid enough to think a joke was in order: "If you guys woulda just quit when you were ahead," I quipped, "you mighta gone down as Germany's Betty Grable."

Katarina sewed on, poking and pulling. I placed the record exactly where it was in the pile. Sat on the edge of the bed. Without looking at me, Katarina reached into the pile and produced a soldier's magazine pinup—she in a bathing suit, her lips retouched bright red. She sneered at me, her eyes bloodshot, the rims pink. She sewed on. Forced the needle in, then out with a yank.

I went over to the painted window and scraped off more of that paint, for a better look. "So, guess you saw the bike? Think of the picnics we can have. Hit Garmisch, the Chiemsee ..."

She glared at me, driving in the needle without looking. "I want to know," she said.

"Okay. Know what?"

"Who you are. Who are you?"

"What?"

"A motorcycle? Such indulgence? You don't trade for something like that. It's a—how do you say?—A bonus. A special extra. You're doing a job for someone, a special job."

"I see. I get you. You read the letter."

She sewed faster, harder, practically stabbing herself.

"Keep that up you're going to get hurt." I came back and pushed the fabric off her lap, took the needle from her and stuck it in the sofa arm. "Look, I didn't ask for the bike."

"No, but you want to keep it now that you have it, don't you?"

I pretended to think this over. Frowned for her. "I can't just give it back."

"Of course not. Patrons, fat cats, they don't like their lackeys to hesitate. It insults them."

"Hey, who you calling a lackey?"

Katarina's voice rose: "I don't forget what you told me: 'I know people.'" She snapped fingers in my face. "See there, I knew it. I knew it."

I looked away, rolling my eyes. "Aren't you just like a Jane?" I said, but she stood over me, hands on her hips. I sighed. "I can't talk about it. But it's for you, what I'm doing. It's for Heimgau."

"I remember Heimgau. I remember we had a deal, from that first day. You were going to tell me about any good thing."

"Is that what this is about? You want in on a score? Don't want to be left out? I see. And I thought you wanted to help. Thought you wanted me to solve a murder."

"I thought you wanted to solve it," she said.

"What? Of course I do. Just what are you getting at?" I shot up to my feet. "Wait one moment. You don't think I had anything to do with that, what happened to Abraham Beckstein?"

She studied me, eyes narrowing, her crow's-feet clenching up. "Do you think that you did? Perhaps not even you know for sure."

"What does that mean? That's just nonsense you're talking."

"Listen to me. All right? There's one thing you must not forget. It's always about the trade. The black economy. That is where you will find the truth."

This was getting nowhere. Every time I pressed down the pedal, she let off the gas. She knew how to play drama all right.

"Even when you don't want to find the truth," she went on, "even when it's bad for you."

Bad for me? Who did she think she was? I had that GI bike now. I could just speed off out of here. I shot up and searched the room for my knapsack, but couldn't remember where I'd left it. It wasn't on her dressing table or wardrobe racks, wasn't on the door or the sofa. Along one wall stood matching armoires. Opening them, I found exotic trusses, pads and wigs, small chests that held jars and tins, stage makeup. The Bakelite grip of a Sauer 38 pistol protruded from a powder mitt. "I'm going to ignore that right there," I said, getting down on all fours to peek under the furniture.

"Harry, I must tell you something," she said, her voice slowing.

I heard the pain in her voice and had to look. Her face had slackened, and the delicate meat of her chin trembled. I dropped back down on the sofa bed.

She sat down, her hands limp in her lap. "I loved someone once. A Luftwaffe pilot from the Rhineland. A big producer's son. His name was Christian. Christian was shot down in the Battle of Britain. This was 1941. After that I took various lovers, staff officers and ministry officials mostly. Most are dead or perhaps a couple are prisoners now."

"I'm sorry."

"*Ach.* Who isn't. I just wanted you to know."

I didn't feel much like that good coffee now. I rubbed at the back of my aching neck. We traded a couple sighs.

"I can't find my knapsack," I said.

"You would not find it. I hid it on top of the armoire."

"All right." I took her hands, held them in my lap. "Listen to me. I'm trying to help."

"I know, you are. I just don't want you to get hurt."

"Hurt? How could I? It's almost over. This war I'm fighting, it's almost done."

She only nodded, slowly. She might as well have been shaking her head.

I stayed that night. She let me make love to her and we did, quietly, gently. My rough way with her had not come back and I wasn't about to let it.

Early the next morning, Katarina shook me awake. She had pulled on a silk robe. I crept out of bed and kissed her on the cheek as she pinned up her hair. "Get dressed, we're heading out," she said. "You have seen where Emil and Abraham have ended up. But you must see what I have seen. You must see where they were."

In another world, in another time, two motorbikes racing along on a summer morning had to be as good as it got. A happy tour. Yet here, in this aftermath of total war? Emil led the way on a Wehrmacht

BMW that was burly and beat-up and repainted matte black like some wild boar. I trailed on my spotless US Army Harley with Katarina in the spring saddle hugging my ribs. A narrow two-laner had carried us north of Munich. Here the land was flat and dark and raw, like a land after the flood, revealing vast untended tracts of dusky soil and a drab grass far too brown for late June. A dirtscape. We passed a man digging with a stick, then a woman, then another, and more poor souls prodding and poking for any roots fit to boil, any seeds with promise. The faster we sped, the vaster this grim plain spread. High above stretched the sky that, though laden with charcoal thunder clouds, seemed to brighten at its highest center, demanding that I squint. It was, after all, summertime.

On the horizon a long wall of gray revealed itself, and a line of what appeared to be trees planted at perfect distances from each other. As we barreled onward I could see they were not trees. These were watchtowers. We turned right and the wall included lines of electric barbwire fences, ditches, a canal. More watch towers. We parked before a monstrous brick gatehouse. The iron gate was left open, pushed far back. In its place stood a chair and a table for the one guard, a GI corporal. I strode up, gave my name and detachment, and the corporal said, lifting a clipboard, "Don't see you on the list, sir, but, can you excuse me a moment, sir?"

"Sure. Yes. Carry on."

Emil and Katarina joined me at the table. As we waited I had to breathe deep, my lungs were so tight from those thunderclouds and their smothering humidity. The open gate read, wrought in iron: "Arbeit Macht Frei"—Work Will Set You Free. I could see that inside the compound the earth was harder, paler, mixed with gravel and pounded flat. I heard little in there. A shuffle of footsteps. The steady cracks of wood being chopped. I craned my neck for a better look. To the right was a large main building shaped like a right-angled C. To the left, rows and rows of wooden barracks. An odor of charred wood lingered, but then the wind shifted and I caught a bitter-sour stench that I hadn't smelled in months.

Katarina tore a Lucky in two and placed a half in each nostril. Emil had wandered off. Down along the fence, he was talking to a gaunt man in US Army work fatigue shirt and trousers. They gestured at me.

"It's all right, you can come in, seeing how you came all this way for a look-see. Sir?"

"Huh?"

It was the corporal, back at his table. "The look-see. Dachau camp."

"Right. What we're here for," I said.

"The Fräulein can't come in, sir. Off Limits for her. There's another locals' tour later today, she wants in."

Katarina whispered to me, "It's no problem. Emil can still go in with you."

"No problem? Of course it's a problem." I pulled at her elbow and placed her in front of me. "Corporal, do you know who this lady is?"

The GI stared. "She's a German."

"It's okay, Harry," Katarina said, yanking out her Lucky nostril plugs. "I've been inside."

The corporal had lost interest. He sat and wrote on one of his five clipboards. Emil strolled back to us, buttoning up his natty whipcord jacket.

"You don't have to go back in there," I told him. "Not for me."

· Emil smiled. "This is not the first time, Mister. Some days I return to answer questions for your doctors and psychiatrists, and for your Legal Branch—there are so many of those. Although I would not call this much of a reunion."

"No. Good." I had out my handkerchief and my Luckies to smoke or split in half or both. "I'll be fine. It's not like it's a surprise. I've seen the pictures in the papers."

"Yes."

"Those pictures might look a little different next time," said the corporal without glancing up.

I followed Emil in through the gate. We roamed the roll call grounds, and we inspected the barracks that Emil called cell blocks. Their wood was gray and soft. Inside, crammed-in tiers of bunks showed rusty nails, splinters, unknowable stains. A wall stencil read: "Your Lice, Your Death" in old German script.

The next few cellblocks had been burned down, leaving huge rectangles of black ground.

"I know what you are thinking," Emil said. "People want to think it. But there was no battle, no revolt. Your medics had these burned down to kill the typhus."

We walked on. A group of doctors passed. One waved at Emil, and he waved back. Emil told me, "When your soldiers came, there were sixty-thousand still here. Most of the last SS had fled the day before."

"Still here? Where the heck were the rest—where were you?"

"This is another story. I was with a group the SS marched south days before, there were seven thousand or so of us—the so-called 'healthy ones.' It was a death march, like Abraham's. Eventually, some guards fled, but others shot at us and each other for whatever reason. We ran as best we could, into the woods and hills, barns. I did this. But first, I found Henk."

"The SS Kapo. The one in your nightmare."

Emil nodded. The stench had thickened and I held my hand-kerchief to my nose. We rounded the last cellblocks to find a trench as long as a football field and wide as a tall man's height. At the far end, men wearing Army olive drab and red-cross armbands milled around. A camera stood on its tripod. Beyond, along the barbwire fence, stood freight cars with their sliding doors wide open. All empty inside.

"Many survived," Emil said to me. "This is true. Others lived for a time, for weeks, some of them, but they were too weak and sick to be let go on their own. So they wandered here, as I did outside in the woods, all of us like so many zombies. Sometime after Henk I found myself on the big shoulders of a big GI and he took me to a Red Cross truck." Emil's voice cracked. He fell silent. He added, "And so, some of us return to provide informations. As you see over there, the worst only appears just now. Go on, see for yourself."

I approached the edge of the trench. Looked down. They looked something like corpses but didn't look real, what was left of them. They were coated white with lime and stacked many high. I pressed the handkerchief to my nose and mouth, holding my breath as long as I could. Looked as long as I could. I made out the thin, hard white bodies, the legs and arms bowed. Mouths gaped. Some eyes open, all dark. These were women and men, but no children? I peered hoping to find no children.

I turned away, stumbled off. Between the cell blocks I saw long carts stacked high with striped fatigues and smocks, all mangy and stiff and faded. Yellow, red, green, and pink triangles I saw. I must have counted ten, fifteen carts of the clothing.

Emil was yards down the trench, hugging a medic. They were smiling, the medic hugging him back. I'll just wait here, I told myself, but the truth was I didn't have a choice. My lungs had squeezed up and my eyes burned even though I held the handkerchief tighter. I crouched, closed my eyes. My legs went weak anyway and began to wobble. My head spun.

Emil was jogging back over to me. I screamed at him: "They're still here? What for? Just laying there? It's almost July, could've leveled this hell hole in a day."

Emil held me steady, speaking low. "It's exactly because there were so many. Many had to be dug up. All must be recorded. It takes time, something like archeology. Now come on."

Emil walked me along. In the farthest corner of the compound, across a canal and inside a small wood, he showed me a squat red brick building. Inside stood rows of brick and iron ovens, the bricks blackened all around the doors. This was the Dachau oven house. On the way back we passed another trench, "just discovered," Emil told me. GIs were marching German civilians along the trench and forcing them to look down. "This is the locals' tour. Probably citizens of Dachau Town, from just down the road." They wore gloves and cashmere overcoats, their hats, nice and boxed, looking much like the fine folks back home, I thought, though their faces had gone ashen and their lips clenched so tight they had no lips. A pretty woman sprinted on by as if in a race. A grandfather had dropped on all fours, vomiting.

"At least that old donkey sees it now," said Emil. "This camp has been here since thirty-four."

We walked along train tracks to the main building. A sign read: "Working Quarters," and a GI stood guard. Emil placed a hand on my arm. "I must talk to some of your doctors, so I leave you here, Mister. I'll meet you out at the motorcycles."

"What do you mean here? Inside there?"

"Yes. You'll find it. Just keep going." Emil walked off.

The GI guard saluted. I saluted, stepped inside. The walls were white, the floors polished concrete and it was cool in here, giving no smell. I followed a long corridor, passing offices and rooms with high tables, what looked like operating rooms. The corridor widened as the floor slanted downward. I pushed through a door and found myself in a type of long warehouse. The roof was much higher here. Tall sliding doors at the opposite end stood half open, revealing more waiting, emptied freight cars. It was darker where I stood in here and I looked around, squinting. Giant rambling heaps lined the walls on either side of me, blocking windows and almost reaching the rafters. The colors and textures varied. I walked along the heaps. The first pile appeared to be clumps of straw, or animal pelts. I stepped closer.

It was hair—shorn human hair. Black, blonde, red. Curly, straight, long and short.

I wanted to crouch again but kept moving, kept looking.

The next pile was prosthetic arms and hands, legs and feet. Large, medium, small.

Then, suitcases and travel bags, still bearing the owners' names in white chalk.

Next, toys. Dolls and tiny teacups, airplanes and trucks, dreidels.

At the end stood a pile of metal ware, place settings and such all mixed together, most well tarnished and some made of tin. Votives, bowls and jugs with handles so worn they glistened. Battered old goblets, candlesticks, and menorahs, naturally.

And another tear rolled down my cheek, splashing on my wrist. I ran and stomped outside, my elbows cocked and my fists set like some hell-bent Marine.

Outside the camp, Emil stood between our two motorcycles and drank from a canteen. He pointed to the road. Katarina was a quarter-mile down talking to refugees with a cart. A skinny dog and three puppies circled the scene, sniffing each other and wagging their tails.

"Always getting her nose in things, that girl," Emil said.

My limbs were heavy, tired. I had sat on the ground and slouched, my hands limp in my lap. "She's good, I'll give her that. She made short work out of me," I muttered.

"Say again?"

"Forget it. Just forget it. Maybe I better take a finger or two of that hooch."

"Of course." Emil handed down the canteen.

The sky had cleared in the center, leaving clouds only along the horizon. Emil sat in his saddle and leaned back in the sun. He pulled off his jacket and unbuttoned his shirt, his skin glowing white, his cheekbones, knuckles, and the knobs of his collarbone wanting to poke through his skin. Meanwhile, I stayed down on the ground and scratched at the dirt like some lonesome boy in a sandbox as if some answer to my feelings lay just beneath the surface. Unknowingly, I was drawing a rough layout of the camp.

"You killed him," I said. "You killed Henk. Good for you. But, still he lives in your head."

"That's correct."

Just like that, Dachau stopped plaguing me. Heimgau replaced it. I had to be dead honest with myself. I had started wanting Major Membre's head on a platter more than I was hoping to make a clear-cut example out of the torture-murderer of Heimgau. The major seemed to be—had to be—my culprit, but did I really know it? Did I really want to understand, really grasp what had happened? One very can-do colonel named Spanner had showed me not to muck things up too much with pondering like I was doing now. The only thing to understand was action, he was saying. Yet here came Kat to remind me I shouldn't let brains and drive defeat heart and soul, otherwise I'd be just another sucker for power like the rest of them. I didn't know if that was what she meant to show me, but that was the way I saw it.

We passed the canteen. The whiskey was smoother. I was coming around. I stood. "Funny thing. I'm the *Ami* here. Your big liberator. I should be the one taking her in there."

Emil looked at me, cupping a hand over his eyes.

"I'm just realizing something," I added. "When I was heading into Germany with the army? We never passed a concentration camp. Not a one. And I never even thought of visiting one. It didn't even occur to me. Tricky thing, sympathy. I've been to more zoos here. I wanted to throw up back in there, but I couldn't."

"The tears can be worse. They weigh on you. You were gone awhile."

"Yeah. That GI guard calmed me down, lit me up. We were watching a crew of SS POWs pass by. And you know what this Joe says? 'Sir,' he says, 'you wanna go take one of them Heini bastards aside and give em a good licking, go right ahead. Makes me feel bet-ter …' And you know, that was the first time I didn't take offense to that—to the word Heini."

"I don't blame Germans," Emil said. "I don't even blame Nazis. I blame people who want to live at the expense of others."

"I'll try and remember that."

"You will. That's your real name—Heinrich?"

"Yeah."

Emil nodded. He handed me the canteen but I waved it away.

"In any case. I didn't take the GI up on his offer." I knew why. Emil probably knew. I was scared I would not be able to stop what I started.

We heard far away shouts, popping sounds. A black plume was rising from the compound—another cellblock being torched. A bitter grit tickled our noses.

"We buy weapons," Emil said in German.

"Come again?"

"We buy weapons."

"Your racket, you mean. Should I be hearing this?"

"Yes."

"You deal in weapons?"

"Not deal. We buy them, and we keep them. Rifles, handguns, mortars if we can find them, German or American, it doesn't matter. Any and all ammunition. It's all very illegal."

"Very illegal? It's the most illegal, more illegal than meds." I raised the canteen. "Well, good for you. Keep at it."

"Thanks. Bread and produce, GI coffee and chocolate, this is all very well, but it only buys so much, you know?"

"I do. I mean, I can imagine." I broke open a fresh pack of Lucky Strikes. Down the road, the refugees were laughing with Katarina, who was lifting a jug to her mouth with both hands. The dogs slept in a pile at her feet. I lit up. "I'll do what I can for you. If I can."

"Fine." Emil patted me on the shoulder.

I hopped on my saddle. "Now come on, let's grab Kat before she trades for those pups."

As if hearing me, Katarina turned and made her way back up the road. Emil and I waited for her, slumped in our saddles like weary cowboys admiring a carefree young prairie wife, just watching her walk and watching the refugees watch her walk.

"I'm sorry, I have to get back," I told her.

"Well, did you tell him?" she said to Emil. "It doesn't look like you told him."

"He told me," I said. "They're looking for goods they can fight with."

"Not that," Katarina said.

Emil nodded. He turned to me. "Your house, in Heimgau. Your requisitioned billet? It last belonged to a Nazi who's dead as you know—the brother of that brown priest, Father Plant. But before that, it belonged to the family Beckstein. To Abraham."

Nineteen

KATARINA AND EMIL AND DACHAU had really done a number on me, really shook me, and it stayed with me. I wasn't that itching to get back to Heimgau anymore, back to my haunted billet. I'd known the villa had belonged to a dead Nazi, so be it. But I finally got my third man identified, and it turned out that me and one Abraham Beckstein had shared the same roof. It only reminded me that I really knew so little about what had gone down in Heimgau. I made it back early the next day. Even the clouds from Dachau had followed me to Heimgau and stayed, hovering low and dense, bringing a cold that sunk the temperature almost twenty degrees even though this was the first Wednesday in July.

I walked to City Hall. A rain had passed through Old Town and the wet cobbled lanes smelled like charcoal. Then the wind picked up and sent a chill up my trousers and shirt, where it clung in the folds, and I had to huddle in a doorway.

I heard footsteps. Shuffling steps. Major Membre himself came my way, sauntering along, hands flapping and head rolling. I moved to salute, but the major didn't break stride. He moseyed right on by and said over his shoulder: "Captain, there you are. I knew you'd show." Then he halted. He turned and faced me, scratching at his temple as if he'd just remembered something. His face was bloated and crimson, his eyeballs the same color. The morning light revealed a patchy blonde beard forming. "You were on leave? Yes, that's where you were. You were on leave."

"I was, sir. Just heading back to the office now."

We were alone here and I was relieved for the major, given his appearance. His uniform was rumpled and soiled, his shirt unbuttoned. He didn't smell bad, but then I wasn't standing so close. He stared at me and closed one eye to do so, swaying now. "Cap-a-tain," he said, "I wonder ... I think ... I know I haven't given you much good duty. I know, I do, I know that. But that will change." He lost his train of thought. He staggered a little. He held up a finger, and I saw that those normally neat pink fingers looked jaundiced, with grime under his nails. "Yes, well, carry on, on to City Hall, onward and upward you go," he said, clenching his hand in a salute as if it was the first time he'd ever done so.

"Yes, sir, will do."

"And, do be sure to check your inbox."

"Yes, sir."

I watched the major stumble around the next corner. Sure, I had wanted to see the major squirm. This was far beyond that. A rash skid right off the road is what it was. I lit up and walked on and recounted the vices that may have contributed to it. There was his binging on absinthe, and his juicy new morphine allotment. An ample dose of opium suited the major, its beatific and benumbing calm just the thing for those damning burdens of responsibility, those delusions of grandeur, his bankrupt dreams of priesthood, and I couldn't forget his odd way with children. A thick-witted and devious despot, your average dipso or dope fiend—those I could handle. But Major Membre was looking distraught, almost brain-sick.

I made my return to City Hall, asked around. No one had seen Major Membre in three, four days. The major had reported ill, was the word, but the medical clerk hadn't seen or tended to him. I got into my office, shut the door, and tried to tackle my overflowing inbox, get at all the memos and requests, orders, and reports—yet the words and lists only blurred, made no sense. Despite the weather my office was warm, too warm. I cracked a window, but still I was hot. I looked for the radiator and realized I didn't even have one. Was the heat broken? I wanted Winkl, who was back to being janitor again, but I didn't know where to find him now. I stood to go open the door, look for someone to find him.

At that moment, I remembered the last thing the major had said: *Check your inbox.*

I sat back at my desk, erect, as if trying to look normal for some suspecting fellow not actually there. I sifted back through my inbox piles, my usual crisp focus taking over. I recognized the usual paperwork. One envelope stood out. It was blank on the outside and letter size, tied off with red string. I opened it. It contained one page. It was from CID, from Criminal Investigation Division.

"Wanted Report," it read at the top in bold capital letters. I'd seen a couple of these bulletins, for GIs on the lam mostly, of which there had been thousands upon thousands, especially after the slaughter-battles men like that had seen in the Hürtgen and the Bulge. Some GIs had simply walked away while others turned to crime because they had nothing else. Few had made it this far south yet. Why follow the war when the trick was to escape it? But this report was also stamped "Confidential" in red at the top. I'd never seen one like this, not lowly me. A middle section contained boxes for various physical traits, such as Hair, Eyes, Complexion, Characteristics, with sub-boxes for further defining traits that could be circled or described in the briefest shorthand. The bottom section had a heading: "Particulars of Crime or Reason for Which Wanted."

My eyes were darting around the page, checking, cross-referencing, discovering. My nerves had tensed up like steel cables, torquing up my muscles into clamps on my bones, squeezing, wanting to crush them.

The top left had a box for a small ID-sized photo and to the right names and aliases.

His real name was Virgil Eugene Tercel. Aliases included Virgil Jones, Terence Eugene, Gene Smith. His Civil Occupation was left blank. The various characteristics matched him, such as the ruddy, pocked complexion, protruding jaw and large teeth and nose, and those gray eyes. Apparently he had shrapnel scars on his back and legs and a bullet scar somewhere under his hair. Other battles had left him with a deformed left thumb, and he was missing the middle left finger. I had not even noticed this. It did not mention him having Southern speech. The list of crimes, typed in abbreviations so they all fit, included desertion, fraternization, treason, looting, theft, extortion, racketeering, rape, and murder ... separate sheets with the details had been attached at one point, but the left corner of this one page bore only a ragged staple hole where there must have been many of these attachments, and who knew how many paper-clipped too, all gone now, possibly destroyed.

I had to assume that someone in Frankfurt or Munich or even Washington had gotten this one page to Major Membre, in a hushed and frantic hurry.

The sweat itched under my hair. It rolled down my face, neck, down along my spine. Wide wet drops of it blotted my neat stacks of quadruplicate forms under my elbows. My eyes moved back to the photo, one last time. Of course it was him. He wore a civilian jacket and tie in the photo, smiling right into the camera. He looked younger, with a glimmer in his eyes, and I wondered if this was him before the war. Before North Africa, Sicily, Italy, and on up Southern France, all the holy shit he had seen and done and they made him do, he had said it himself. I wondered when he had started veering off, carving out his own route. He might have been this way since North Africa even. And that was the cruelest notion of all. Your regular deserter had one trick: They escaped from war. They did not run toward it, chase after it, feed off its blood.

Three scribbles filled the right margin. It was Major Membre's handwriting. These read:

Spanner was never in CIC. Never!
Spanner knows them. Checkmate
Help me, Harry Kaspar

My throat wanted to swell up like from an allergic bee sting. I let my mouth hang open just to get any air down there, drool and all. And I had thought the major was just babbling, trying to mimic everyday reality by having me check my inbox. But, who was "them"? Friends up high? The major's cohorts? Abraham and the Buchholz men? I gasped, choking on the air. These were like a child's scrawl, an imagination getting away from itself after too many hours left alone. But Major Membre was not playing, not any more. He had gotten curious about Spanner, and used his contacts to find the truth. Maybe now he wished he hadn't.

I burst out my door and, so that no one saw me, took the service stairs out. It was late afternoon now, but the sky still gray and dim. The fresh air helped. Major Membre had changed his billet from the castle to the Heimgauer Hof, and had a crew remodeling an old wing on the far side of the inn. Today it was mayhem back there. Bricks were dumped and toppled and cracked like a thousand bowling pins struck; mallets drubbed and hammers knocked; picks clanged and shovels scraped. Hazes of dust and grit rose and fell back into it all.

As I neared the square before the inn, I saw a man leaning against a streetlight. He was dressed like no local I'd ever seen in his pale custard yellow suit, possibly a zoot suit with its wide padded shoulders and hat brim so wide it looked like a serving platter. He held a newspaper high and close to his face, as if he were far-sighted or half-witted, that or some dum dum private dick. Either a goon, or a goof.

I lit up and walked the edge of the square, flanking the man for a frontal look. He had a mint green pocket square, brown and white two-tone shoes, and not a zoot suit at all, I realized, rather a swanky summer suit. The zooty cut was an optical illusion—this lug was so large he looked gargantuan in his custard getup. I couldn't get a look at the man's face behind the newspaper. I passed him, and then doubled back. The newspaper was in German.

The man lowered the page, showing his meaty brow and those eyes a little too close together. I started a moment but had to play it cool despite the sweat chilling my skin under my summer wool. I tossed my butt, marched over. "Horton? That you?"

Sergeant Horton stared, a homemade toothpick between his teeth.

"Thought it was you. Long time," I said and offered my hand.

Playing the calm operator. After all, we were more or less partners now.

Horton kept staring. "Captain Kaspar. How do."

"Just fine. So what gives?"

"Not a lot, Cap'n."

"That newspaper there. Didn't know you read German."

Horton blinked, but that was it. Old stone face. The construction racket had eased, leaving only a shout here and there, a truck engine revving. Horton gazed off as if listening for something.

"Still working for the colonel?" I added.

"Yeah."

"So, the colonel around? He come with you? I was hoping to hear from him."

"No, not today." Horton blinked again. "Where you headin' to?"

"Major Membre's, believe it or not. Thought I'd visit him in his new suite."

Horton smirked and held it, as if waiting for someone to take a photo, but a mug like this one wouldn't make the cut. "Why would you want to do that?"

"Seems like as good a time as any."

"Word is, you two haven't always seen eye to eye."

"No. I don't know. So maybe I'll try and patch things up a little, you know, smoke the peace pipe."

"Bury the hatchet. Heh. You want to bury that hatchet."

"That's it. Things'll be changing around here and, well, it's just better that way."

"Sure. Sure." Grunting, Horton heaved himself from the light post. He walked around me and the post as if he had a rope and was tying me up. Then he stopped, tipped his hat back like a gumshoe in the pictures and said: "Me, I'm just passing through, see, heading to the mountains for the fresh air, and I have only been here about ten minutes, no more. But I'll see ya again."

And he wandered off.

"All right." I turned and faced the three-story, block-sized inn. Plain white bedding hung from the windows, airing out despite a threat of dust.

I started up the main steps, thinking how this was going to play out. I'd make the major a stiff drink if he needed it, get him into a chair. I'd get right to it. I'd say that we had to do something about this Virgil Eugene Tercel, even if it endangered all that the major had.

Deputy Mayor Hammerstein exited the inn, humming and skipping down the steps. I slowed for the usual bow, for a nod, but Hammerstein just breezed on by swaggering his narrow shoulders, his shiny little mustache. I glared, ready to dress Hammerstein down, this cheap stooge for Major Membre, but then I saw lipstick on the back of the man's thin neck. The man was giddy. He'd put up his own Fräulein in the inn, I recalled. So let it go, for now.

Inside I passed the front desk with its brass bell and fusty old guest ledger and pine hutch of cheap fading porcelain birds. An old man in a cardigan puttered around in a back room. Amazing, how this country hotel had been restored to its former quaint obsolescence. The lobby's main elevator was out of order so I went down a side hallway and found the employees lift, a constantly circling chain of wooden booths without doors, like so many oversized coffins. Each floor had two portals—one for up and one for down. At just the right moment you stepped—jumped, really—into a booth heading up or down and then out again as your floor passed. *Paternoster*, or the Lord's Prayer, the Germans called these elevators. Most dangerous for rowdy kids and slow elderly, deadly if you entangled a limb between moving booth and elevator shaft.

A booth passed up beyond the ceiling and into the shaft, and another; the next booth showed, its floor met mine, I stepped in and rose into the darkness, the coffin-like booth twitching and rumbling all the while. Light again—third-floor passing. I stepped out, turned corners and found the main hallway with its deep-piled rug and copper sconces. I knew the way. The major's new billet was the Imperial Suite, the same room where I'd thrown that poker game for the detachment and Horton's GIs. It seemed so long ago now.

I approached the suite door and knocked with one knuckle. No one came. I leaned on the knob, and the door swung open. I peeked in. "Hello. Hello? Major, sir?"

In the center of the room stood an Empire-style table, a vase of red roses on it. I strode on in. "Major Membre, sir?" Nothing. I passed through to the study. It smelled sweet like the major's Paris cologne. I kept going. The master bedroom door was wide open, a rectangle of dusty gray light. I went in.

My eyes swelled, my head seemed to shrink. At first I only saw the fine details—slimy blue veins on slippery red meat—then I saw the whole room yet nothing in focus. Just the red, the white of bone, the pink of flesh, the glaze of it all.

It was a corpse, a chopped-up corpse. Who was it? What was it? Man, woman?

"It can't be, can't be ..."

Boom, booming. The construction had started again outside. I couldn't breathe. I whirled around, taking it all in. Blood stained the walls, carpets, and sheets in splatters and pools, pools and splatters, sparkling with specks of construction dust from the open windows that looked out on the old wing. Now I was freezing, like in a butcher's shop, but no butcher could make sense of this mess. What had they used? An axe? They made no attempt to be neat. I saw a flash of brocade, folds of red fabric, a wisp of white fur. I stepped forward, and again. My mouth opened to scream, but it didn't scream; my pounding heart had risen up my throat, clogging it. I stepped back. Focus, Harry. Make some sense of this, any sense.

There was no smell. This was fresh. Bubbles rose from slits and holes. Fresh wouldn't smell, especially if it was cold and drafty from windows left open—especially if someone remembered to leave the stomach intact, which it appeared to be, as best as I could make out. Someone knew what they were doing. He meant this. For keeps.

All right. So it's happened. Get yourself together. You're Public Safety.

The gold brocade, the white fur—it was the papal costume. Grimacing, my mouth as dry as bark dust, I tiptoed forward, peering around for a sign. Any clues? Tiptoeing, tiptoeing. My toes met something hard, under more gold brocade. I lifted the fabric: The face of Major Membre, eyes open blank. A red footprint across his lips.

I wheezed and gasped and stumbled back, slipped on the slime all around and fell. I crawled out and backed down the hallway, feeling my way along the walls. Gasping more, hyperventilating, I found the *Paternoster*. The booth rising was only halfway up, but I dove in landing in a ball on the floor as the booth wobbled on upward. All dark now. The booth came around the top of the shaft, peaking up here, ready to plummet. Splinters of light flashed on thick flat belts and mighty, oily gears. I squeezed my eyes shut, head spinning. Next thing I knew I was passing more floors, but going up again. How? The place only had three floors. Had I blacked out? I was stuck in this chain of coffins, this goddamn runaway amusement ride. "Help!" I screamed, "Help!" I passed the third floor and heard others screaming, saw blood on the hallway wallpaper. From my hands? I passed the mighty gears again and back down. Third floor again—still the screaming, and servants rushing by. First floor came—halfway down I jumped out and hit my forehead on the frame; my feet dangled under the next booth coming down, I pulled them free and the booth passed. People rushed me, tugging at me and screaming in German and English, neither of which I seemed to understand like one of those nightmares where everyone talks but it's all gibberish, baby talk, pidgin twaddle, and my screams came out like smothered moans.

I pushed at them shouting, "It wasn't me!" I scrambled through the lobby for the front steps. Daylight hit my eyes, twirling me around. I was dizzy, spinning again, my head pounding. I couldn't hear at all. I tumbled down and the sky dimmed and even the sun went black.

When I came to, I was kissing cobblestone. Face down on the square. My hands and chest were warm and moist. My mouth burned and my teeth felt as if stripped by Turpentine. I'd vomited. I lay in my own vomit. Hands grabbed at me, pulling me up. A boom of voices pounded my ears. "The man's in shock!" someone said in German. A crowd of civs stood over me. I saw Police Chief Jenke and two new recruits, then a couple Joes from the detachment. They propped me against the steps and I sat up, staring down my front. Blood had mixed with my vomit—the major's blood, in splatters and splotches from my chest to my toes.

"He killed him," I muttered, "somebody killed him I mean."

Glances exchanged. Hands patted me on the shoulder, carefully.

"It wasn't me, Jesus, it was not me!" I shouted, gasping again.

Uli Winkl was there now shouting, "Give the poor devil air!"

Lt. Carlson had pushed his way through. He crouched next to me and said, speaking low, "It must have happened right before you arrived." I nodded, uh-huh. That was it. "So, this is important: Did you see anyone on your way in? Anything suspicious. Investigators will need to know."

I started to breathe better and, as I did, I understood how this was playing out. How it would have to play out. It was the only way and always had been. It was as sharp as the vomit burn on my tongue.

"Hammerstein," I heard myself say. "I saw that bastard Hammerstein, hustling right out of here down these very steps. Passed right by me without saying a word, too. Can you believe the gall? So that was strange, yeah, real fishy. And I remember he was humming, humming like some damned crazy man just escaped ..."

Twenty

CRIMINAL INVESTIGATION DIVISION had come later that evening after dark. There were two CID men, both with those bland, unmoved faces of midlevel officers treading along in a sea of authority and protocols. They had hidden me and kept me under watch for two days. The first day, they gave me my own suite room in the otherwise crowded hospital. The second day I spent in an old town Heimgau cellar bar called the Amerika Klub. Certain Displaced Persons and ethnic German refugees had opened the tiny "AK" as a way to convert their black market margins into insurance for an uncertain future. Here the target catch was sightseeing American officers with holes burning in their pockets. The lure, stateside swank. Walls were mirrored, pillars paneled with black Vitrolite glass, the bar polished chromium. There was even a neon Miller Beer sign though the Champagne of Beers could not be had unless you knew a guy, and the only German brews going were thinned-out near-beers on account of the grain shortages. So it was all hard juice and overpriced. Latch a Fräulein on a chump's arm and they had a sure thing going. Socko.

It was late afternoon, pushing evening. Since early morning my two CID men had detained me in a dark corner of the AK, in a low and wide velvet club chair that faced the door. A smoking stand stood at my knees, stabbed with so many of my butts it looked like a porcupine. They had requisitioned the AK just for yours truly. They had picked it, they told me, because it was central, easy to watch over, and comfortable for all concerned. I'd told myself I would never set foot in this shifty hole, and yet here I was. They even brought along two MPs to stand at the door, just for me.

How dare they keep me locked away like some enemy general or turncoat spy. It was just like the Alien Control Board had done to my father back home. CID said it was for my sake since the murderer may still be out there and I was next in command. Now that's a load of bull, I wanted to shout. Yet I did no shouting. I kept quiet. and I bit my tongue so much I practically chewed it right down.

Glasses had accumulated on one side of me and magazines and newspapers on the other, few of which I'd read. On the chair arm lay the new MG-run newspaper—the *Münchner Zeitung*, open to page two. The headline read:

MG DET. COMMANDER BRUTALLY MURDERED IN HEIMGAU

...investigations indicate that an East Prussian refugee, Lothar Hammerstein, a former Nazi Party member and Sudetenland Hitler Youth leader, murdered Maj. Membre to cover up revelations of his past not entered in his Nazi background questionnaire. Hammerstein fled and was apprehended trying to enter Munich...

Then, the CID men told me I was free to go. They took their MPs and they drove away.

I stayed down in the AK a little while. I had gotten used this flashy yet dim dungeon of mine. It let me think. I wondered if the man born as Virgil Eugene Tercel and now calling himself Lt. Colonel Eugene Spanner even knew I was down here. I was sure that he did. He seemed to know it all.

The door burst open flashing sunlight. The man himself strode in wearing a brown pinstripe double-breasted suit. There he was, my very own sham CIC agent. His eyes found mine. I raised my Lucky in salute.

"Captain," Spanner said, his voice solemn. He sat on the arm of the chair next to me. "So. How you faring? You look like heck."

About time you showed, I wanted to say. I've been waiting for this. But my throat was tight, my chin like stone. I sucked on my cigarette. "I'll make it."

"You're cooling off down here."

"Yeah, that's it. On ice."

Spanner patted my knee, with his right hand. "All right, now, all right. Let's get a drink, kid." We settled into a corner booth. "They keep you here the whole day?"

I nodded.

"The air is foul in here," Spanner said.

I shrugged. I blew more smoke and flicked into the ashtray.

Spanner looked around. At the bar a GI waiter in a white vest was polishing a glass with a cloth, chatting up the authorized Fräulein whose legs had wound around a bar stool.

Spanner barked at him: "Boy! One bourbon, one scotch. Top shelf and neat."

GI waiter jumped. "Pronto, sir." And a bartender appeared, snapping fingers.

"I don't drink it neat," I said.

"I drink it neat. Only way to taste the fine likker."

As we waited Spanner tapped on the table, again with his right hand. I wanted a look at his deformed left hand, but he kept it to his side or in his pocket. He probably always had. I smoked, saying nothing, and the colonel didn't push it. Of course, he was no colonel, but right now I had to think of him that way, just in case he could read my thoughts. I could give away no tell, not a one.

"Sirs." GI waiter set down the drinks and a dish of cashews and hurried off.

I moved to lift my drink. Spanner grabbed my wrist and squeezed. "Now. Why the mopey pose, huh? What are you trying to pull?"

"Pull?"

Spanner kept squeezing, turning. He was using his left hand. I glared back at him and let the pain burn. I could see the missing middle finger, with just enough stub to make it look like a full finger when fisted. The thumb was withered but tapered, like a claw. It had clamped on me.

"Do not fuck with me," he shrieked, his temple veins pulsing red. This made GI waiter and bartender disappear in back, and the Fräulein unwound her legs and scooted for the door, snatching cigarette butts on the way. Spanner loosened his grip. "You're brooding, okay. But it's time to regroup now, don't you think? Turn the corner some? Spooked is one thing but cold feet is another, of that I can assure you." He let go.

I rubbed at my wrist, at the dent left by his claw-thumb. He could've punctured me with it, his nail was long enough. I didn't need to see his left hand anymore. I gulped down half my glass, eyeing the room, anything but look at that hand. To my surprise, the top shelf bourbon was fine neat, rich and silky and hinting of smoke. I took another drink. "Brooding? Let's call it rattled. Playacting it, see. It only happened two days ago, sir. So appearance is key. Right?"

Spanner sat back, nodding. "All right, all right." He tasted his scotch and licked at his lips. "How did the interviews go?"

"Oh, rough, sir. Real rough."

Spanner fought a grin, or maybe it was a grimace. His knee wanted to bounce, and he pressed it down. "What they ask?"

"Ask? How's the coffee? Would I rather have a drink or maybe a hot plate of hearty grub? I jawed on, they listened—like wolves. Yeah. Real buncha bulls, CID really take it out of a man. One even slipped me a five-spot, asked me if I had any SS daggers to sell."

It was a grin now and Spanner let it fly. "Ha! Don't say. Really put the screws on you?"

"Yeah, and I was one rat fink." I was snickering. I made myself snicker. "I guess they're just not the toughs that everyone makes them out to be."

And Spanner nodded along to my words, his knee slowing down.

This was all the confirmation I needed. I had no way of knowing just who was in his pocket. After all, his CID Wanted Report had been made to go away, Major Membre had found out. So I had to keep playing along, even when the CID questioned me, even when it all made my stomach roll and want to choke up my own gut right into my lap.

It burned under my skin though. I just couldn't let it ride. I had to test him a little.

"See, they want the real hatchet man like they want the dose," I added. "They seem to collect Nazis, so a cretin like Hammerstein made it pretty much cut and dried."

"That's their game now, collecting Nazis. Denazification, where the glory is. War crimes are the next big thing."

"You know what that newspaper article doesn't say? Way the major died. He was chopped into chunks. A real demo job. But I guess you know that, huh?"

Spanner shrugged. "Membre had a heap of skeletons in his closet. I told you that. People probably had it in for him. If you ask me, this was the result of some sordid lover's quarrel, but his lover being no lady, if you know what I mean. I mean if it wasn't Hammerstein ..."

"You mean, did I offer them any alternatives? No. Any clues would've been too weak, even if they had felt more like snooping. In the room they did find tanker coveralls, gloves and booties, a head sock."

"Kept hisself real clean, that Hammerstein."

"Right. Spotless."

Spanner stretched out. He unbuttoned his jacket and found his reflection in the mirrors. "Mirrors or no, this is still a cave. You know ole Horton has a stake in this here honkey-tonk? He thinks Heimgau's going to become a travel destination for us Yanks. What he done called it too, the big goof—a 'travel destination.'" Spanner's possibly fake Georgia accent sang now, but his smile had changed. It had become a scowl to me, full of those mighty teeth. He slid a stick of his licorice gum between his teeth. Blackjack. He offered me a butterscotch candy from his pocket, but I declined and he popped that in his mouth too. He chewed and smacked and hummed, sucking on the gum and clacking the candy against his teeth. "We're all trading up. Damn, if I haven't gone and moved again. Four Seasons was top-notch, but I need my privacy. Still in Munich. But it's the Nymphenburg Palace now and boy is it dandy."

I lifted my glass in toast.

"Yep, ole Schloss Nymphenburg has been req-quee-sitioned." Spanner chuckled, outstretching his arms along the booth. I couldn't believe I had once felt awkward in this man's presence, like the poor kid stuck with a rich relative. And I'd even gone so far as to consider the colonel noble, honorable? The more he droned on, the more he proved obnoxious, conceited, patronizing. His Gone With the Wind accent was less authentic than my American English, I was sure of it. You want the world? Play up what worked for you.

"How did you get in here?" I said. "I heard the CID doesn't care for CIC agents."

"I showed them my CIC card. Doesn't matter if they care or not." Spanner called for two warmed brandies. I hated brandy. He threw back his scotch with one hand and hoisted the brandy snifter with the other. He swirled the copper liquid, smiling at the legs on the glass. "So, it's settled. You are in," he said. He didn't say it like a question.

"I am in. I am all in."

There, I said it. I was waiting days to say it. What else could I say?

"That's grand. And you're just in time too, because I've ironed out the last bugs." Spanner leaned over and rubbed at my shoulder with his broad right thumb, his lead eyes giving off a little spark. Within this moment the man seemed to care, about something. "You feel bitter. Because of what's happened. Little bit ashamed. Is that it?"

"No. I will never be that." I lifted the glass and drank, letting the brandy burn.

Spanner clinked his glass against mine. "Our train, guess where she is? She's hidden up in Dollendorf. Been there all along."

"What? I was up there. I told you. Nothing but rusty old warehouses. Refugees won't even camp there."

"Behind Dollendorf, I should have said. You see, about the time my granddaddies were fighting Yankees at Bull Run, that place was part of a mining operation."

"A mine? There's no mine. Wait … There's a hill behind, on through the woods. A rocky hill."

"That's exactly right. This Dollendorf used to be a salt mining village, but it went belly up before the last century was out. After the Great War they tried to build tractors there but laid an egg, so folks think it's nothing more than an abandoned tractor shop. But, out from the rear side of the rail shelter? Train tracks keep on going straight into the forest. Pretty well covered by underbrush, yet they still do run through and into that rocky hill—or into a tunnel in the hill, I should say. Follow me? Your rocky hill is what they call a salt dome."

"A salt mine? Inside there?"

"Yes, Captain, we got ourselves a big ole mine tunnel that no one's been in for at least fifty years." Spanner held a finger to his lips. "Now let's do stay quiet about it, shall we?"

I nodded. I held up my glass and swirled it, so I could think. Ask all the right questions, Harry. Information was key from here on out. "Should I see these freight cars?"

"It can't hurt," Spanner said. "Tell you what. I'll have Horton show you one of these days. He'll come find you."

"Great. What about your locomotive?"

"As I said. You'll ride it. Get us westward to the French Zone, through any checkpoints. CIC doesn't have much authority over transport anymore, but for MG? Should be a breeze."

"'Like shooting fish in a barrel,' you said." I lit up a Lucky, sat up and took another drink. My mind was buzzing, coming back to life. "What about the diversion?"

"That's in the East, of course, seeing how it's a diversion. I got it all figured. A Red Army patrol crosses over Bavaria's international border, seizes two German border officials and a ranking US officer. Wounding a GI for proper effect, mind you. The hostages get taken back to the Russian Zone into Czechoslovakia."

"Only the Red Army aren't Russians. They're yours."

Spanner wagged a finger. "Oh, they are Russkies, I can assure you. After a fashion, speak the tongue. They just ain't Red Army. They're Russian DPs—confederates of mine. Next morning, one German hostage gets released after being questioned at length about precise strength, armament, and location of US Zone troops by

Moscow mucky-mucks the Germans and US officers will believe to be Red Army staff officers. Russians also send back with the freed German a message warning they'll move across the border in force if demands for further info on US forces are not met. So there you are. Such incidents are happening, mind you, but nothing this severe. It should provoke Tactical to transfer troops eastward to shore up that border stretch, leaving the harmless points out west near the Frog Zone thinner than they already are."

"Sounds like so much hoopla just for one stray train."

Spanner smiled. "Suckers need the hoopla."

I made my shoulders shrug. "Well, it sounds like a joyride for me."

"Yes. And, you'll have ample notice. Though you will not see me beforehand."

I fought another sudden urge to run right out and keep running, back to my villa and jump on my motorbike, but even that was the colonel's. I went back to swirling my drink. I lifted a cashew and stared at it. Tossed it toward the bar.

"So, keep laying low for now," Spanner added. "Just don't get in the way. Right?"

"Right. Of course not. Thanks for the motorbike, by the way."

"I told you: There's nothing to thank." Spanner sat back again. He whistled through teeth. "So you pin the tail on Hammerstein. That was brilliant, I got to say."

"He had a girlfriend there, in the Hof. He had lipstick on his collar. I didn't tell them that."

"And they didn't ask. Who cares? Probably some hick whore. Yes, son, that sure was brilliant. Now you got all the more reason to clean house."

"Clean house?"

"You are certain to be named CO."

He was right. I was getting what I wanted. So show it. I smiled, nice and big with lots of teeth—a jumbo, smug, turd-eating grin that Eugene Spanner aka Virgil Tercel could lick all he wanted. "Which reminds me," I said. "All this time on my hands, I been thinking. That VIP party of Major Membre's, at the Hof? I didn't see you there. But then, you probably didn't need to be."

Spanner set down his drink.

I continued. "You're involved with that plunder network they've built up, I'm guessing. And you didn't like Major Membre and Company getting too high and mighty. Why else give the baron a black eye like that?"

"Well deduced, son. I told you we think alike. Yes. Let's say, I'm a benefactor. The silent partner. But let's not call it plunder, shall we? The war's over. We can go back to killing for money, instead of for some fucking flags owned by old men and blessed by priests."

"All right. So what happens to it now? I take it over. That's your plan."

"I told you, you are next in command. You inherit all that comes with it. We'll see about the why and the how."

"And, you get a better straw man." I couldn't help saying it. I gave Spanner a long hard look when I said it, holding it as long as I dared. Then, to cement the effect: "The price isn't so bad, either, is it? One dipso dope fiend major done for, and one sorry kraut to blame it on."

Spanner brushed lint off a trouser leg, shaking his head. He spoke low, and slowly, leaving equal pause between words. "Listen. I want you to listen. Do not get any hopped-up ideas. You asked me to rein in the major, and I did."

"I was thinking more like a transfer for him. Promotion, need be. Section Eight even. But what's the difference? That's what you're saying."

Spanner nodded. "They're hauling Hammerstein up to Frankfurt for the official MP firing squad. So that makes two dead men. But you are alive. We call the shots. And that's what matters." He tried a smile. "Though you been cooped up in here too long, I'd say. You should get outside. It's high summer out there, hot and fine. All right? CID and the Legal boys have all gone by now. You are free to go."

I couldn't lose the hard look. I set my glass on the table, but it slammed down.

Spanner's eyes narrowed. "Son, it is far too late to bear regrets. Play scoutmaster. This could be reopened. You wanted that CO spot. You threatened Major Membre. You wanted strings pulled, hatchets lowered. You even sent a letter about it."

He attached another smile. He stood.

I stood, did my jumbo smug grin again and placed a hand on Spanner's bony shoulder. Then I forced out a sleazy booming laugh that made Major Membre's cocksure bellow seem like a newborn's titter. "Hell, sir! Don't you worry so much. I'm not going true blue on you. I was just thinking out loud. Calling out the score. I did come to you, right?"

"Right, yes. Good. Amen, said the preacher man."

"Amen." I choked down the last of my brandy. "And thank you, Colonel. Thank you for paving my way."

Twenty-One

I HAD PLANNED MY PERFORMANCE in the Amerika Klub to keep Spanner believing I was none the wiser. His lackey Captain Kaspar still assumed he was in the Army, still supposed he was just a CIC operator making his big play. As for the CID, I couldn't assume what they knew and did not. Whom they trusted. They might not know Spanner was involved, but I had to suspect someone was pulling the wool over their eyes at the least. At the worst, they'd been bought and paid for.

By the time Spanner released me from the AK, the clouds had returned and it rained and rained. The next day, two actual agents from Counter Intelligence Corps showed up at my billet. One was Jewish-American, the other German-Jewish and now American. Both sounded well educated, and more so than Spanner, I could see now. They were passing through, they said, and wanted to introduce themselves to the local MG Public Safety man. They showed CIC ID cards of the type Spanner carried, presumably—I had never even thought to ask him for a look. They asked if I was doing okay, considering what had happened to my CO, yet trusted that CID would get to the bottom of it. These were the real CIC agents pinpointed for the area and for much of the region south of Munich as it turned out. They apologized for not coming around sooner as they had bypassed this county along with our advancing troops. In the preceding months of war and peace, they had surely performed splendid feats, persuading trigger-happy German units to surrender, hunting down sly Nazis, sniffing out dungeons and concentration camps. In the days to come, as they told it to me, they would do a thorough job tracking down war criminals still on the lam and monitoring suspicious communists. One smoked a pipe. The other wore a non regulation wool cap. As CIC agents, they, of course, wore no officer insignia, unlike Spanner, who'd made sure to show off that silver oak leaf for me. I had known this about CIC agents, that they shunned rank, but I had let myself overlook that too. I guessed they were captains. Just for kicks, I asked them if they had ever heard of an agent named Spanner. They only shrugged at the name.

The day after that, on a Friday, a telegraph from Frankfurt named me Acting CO of Heimgau detachment. And the rain kept coming, on through the weekend. Come Tuesday the rain was still streaming down, the downpour making two sounds inside my requisitioned villa—a thousand taps at the roof, and that constant rush down the gutters.

I hadn't left my villa much. I was having trouble seeing the point.

I had put myself here, right in this spot. Spanner had been prepared to remove Major Membre for me and remove the major he did. I was the one who'd misjudged the man. I thought I was being the persistent one, but I was really only a desperate chump and the so-called colonel's brazen accomplice at that. Some might call me brilliant—the consummate Machiavellian vigilante criminal. I wasn't seeing it that way, not at all.

I heard a pounding on my front door. Reaching the foyer, I heard shouting: "Open up, Captain, open up if you please." It was Uli Winkl.

I opened my door to the hiss of rain and the humid air that smelled like mud itself. Winkl was shaking water beads off his Loden-cloth raincoat. "So, you are here," he said in his new English.

"Sure I'm in," I said. I hadn't reported to City Hall. I had, however, relayed my one major order as the new CO through the detachment's other captain, Wilks: All available local domiciles and premises were to be again made available as an extra shelter for all refugees, whether Displaced Persons or ethnic Germans. It was noble enough of me, but only went so far. The castle didn't count because its vast rooms still held the Baron Mayor von Maulendorff's bloated stocks. As for the baron's surviving monkeys? Police Chief Jenke, and the innkeepers? They remained in place. It was part of the deal, this hand I'd dealt myself.

"I was worried you had left," Winkl said.

"Left where? I'm CO now. What? Don't tell me you forgive me."

"I meant what I said that day."

"As you should."

"But this is not about that. Or, perhaps it is," Winkl said.

I had shut the door behind him. He stayed in the foyer, his squishing wet boots planted wide apart.

"Well? What is it?" I said.

"I've come to fetch you."

"Fetch? Sounds ominous. Better get warm first. Dry off."

"No. We really should leave. It's urgent, you see, and we have a long drive. In secret. I think it best if we take your motorcycle for this, so you don't have to use your motor pool and leave a record."

He meant my Army Harley that Spanner surely had stolen, permits and trip tickets and all. "Hold on. What's urgent? What's secret?"

"That is all I can say now. He's waiting for us so we must go."

"Who's waiting, Winkl?"

Winkl kept his eyes steady on me. "Von Maulendorff."

"I don't think I heard you so well. I thought you just said, Maulendorff."

"*Herr* Kaspar, please do not be difficult. I promised I'd bring you."

"Oh, you can break a promise to him. They come cheap in his book."

"Sir, please, he says he must tell you something, immediately."

"I don't need this. Not now. Get me?" I wandered off, back down the hall.

I didn't need Winkl and certainly not my baron mayor. I needed to figure my way out of this surefire trap I'd set for myself.

Winkl followed me, which left streaks of brown water on my marble floor—on the Beckstein family's floor. I faced him. "A janitor tracking mud. This must be serious."

"This is no time for humor," Winkl said.

"I'll deal with civil matters when I'm good and ready."

"This doesn't concern town administration. It concerns you. He has faith in you, as I do. As I still do."

"Ever occur to you that your baron mayor might be pulling a fast one on you? On us. He was in Major Membre's pocket, but that got a little cold didn't it? Sure. Freezing even. So now he's looking to cozy up in mine."

Winkl was shaking his head. "If the baron wanted to pull a fast one on you, why would he come to me? I have no power. I trust him and, odd as it may sound, I believe you can trust him too."

"Trust," I said as if recalling the title of a movie I'd forgotten.

Winkl seemed to complete my thoughts. "Maulendorff is a survivor. This does not make him evil," he said, and began marching back down the hallway to the foyer. Shaking his head again. One of these days he was going to pull a muscle doing that.

And there I was, following him. I grabbed my rubber riding coat, gloves, and goggles on the way out.

Baron Mayor von Maulendorff was waiting over 40 kilometers south within the foothills of the Bavarian Alps. The rain had given way to wind. Mud and washouts clogged roads. I dumped the Harley once and threatened to turn back, but Winkl insisted. The baron's summer home sat at the end of a twisting high road passable only because thick overlapping fir boughs sheltered it from the weather. It was a one-story, one third-sized copy of his Heimgau mansion. The front door knocker, a brass Bavarian lion head. Winkl banged it and stared at me.

"Why you looking at me like that?" I said.

"Sometimes, it's hard to tell when you Americans are ready for anything."

"Oh, so now I'm an American suddenly?"

Deadbolts clanked, the door swung open with a whoosh of warm air. "Ah, there you are, gentlemen." Maulendorff stepped back to let us in wearing a wide-brimmed hat with hunting jacket and striped tie, looking more like a renowned botanist than our cagey middleman of a mayor. He removed the hat and held it to his chest as if at a funeral. "Do come in. How very nice. Please, do have a seat in the study, just straight ahead, I'll take your coats and be right in, please, please."

I said nothing. He gave me an antsy pat on my back—too antsy for my liking.

The study was small but grand in a provincial way, the walls cluttered with trophy game heads and horns, shields and flags. I smelled freshly cut firewood. A fire crackled in a stone fireplace—a fire in July, and it made me shake my head in disgust at all the pageantry that was ever created. I took a green wing chair with black fringe, only because I assumed it was the baron's favorite. Winkl chose a cushion on the fireplace hearth and stared at the floor. Above us hung a candelabrum of black wrought iron; the thing was heavy and sprawling and its candles were missing, which made it look like a giant looming spider.

The baron came back and gave a nervous chuckle that could've been a horn screeching. He sat on a satiny yellow settee, the fire reflecting carrot orange on his pasty face. We sat across from each other, facing each other, only a lush brown animal rug between us. Winkl, excluded now, stoked the fire.

The baron smiled and his jowl scar shined. "Captain Kaspar. How very nice."

"So you said."

"I say, that's some sturdy motorcycle you ride. A Harley-Davidson, I suspect?"

"Sure."

The baron wiped at his neck. "So. I want to express my condolences. I'm sorry you were the one to find Major Membre, how ghastly, so horrible—"

"Forget about it. I see your black eye's gone."

"Yes." The baron smiled again. Chuckled again. "Strange, is it not? You and I, here like this …"

I turned to Winkl: "You know what? Suddenly I don't like being here, don't like being treated like one of his caste or what have you and having my ass kissed in just the right way."

Winkl only frowned.

"You did not come for a social visit," the baron said. "All very well, but …" He took a deep breath. "I should also appreciate some understanding on your part. No, I demand it for what I am about to tell you. Yes. I demand it."

"You got it." I checked my watch. "You got a full sixty seconds of understanding."

"Do keep in mind, I am very distraught." Eyes wide, the baron looked around at the shields, stuffed heads, iron chandelier and timbered ceiling as if noticing the power and sinew of it all for the first time. Tears swelled at the rims of his eyes. From his breast pocket, he produced an envelope. "My world crashed with this letter, *Mein Herr*. You must be prepared to believe that if you believe anything I will tell you."

"So try me."

"You are aware of my monarchist leanings. This, it's a touchy, tricky calling." As the baron unfolded the letter, the corners of his mouth curled downward as if a fishhook hung from each. "About a week ago, this missive arrived from Northern Italy by special emissary of his majesty, Prince Rupprecht of Bavaria."

"Correction: his ex-majesty."

"Yes, that is correct. Since 1918. Here." The baron held out the letter.

"I don't want to read it. Just tell me."

The baron sighed and lay the letter across his thighs. "In this letter, Prince Rupprecht says he wants nothing to do with me or my movement. Nothing."

"That's your problem."

"I wish it were so. Unfortunately, it has everything to do with you. Everything." The baron drew closer, barely on the edge of the settee. "Especially, because, I was also seeking a train like the train Colonel Spanner holds. This train that involves the both of us now. Me and you."

I turned again. Winkl was staring into the crackling fire. "You shouldn't be talking about this," I whispered to the baron.

Maulendorff didn't whisper. "Well, I'm afraid I must. So why don't you listen now, eh? Instead of sulking? Because what I have learned about this train affects you most directly."

At least I'd gotten the baron talking like a man. "Okay, okay," I whispered, "but give it to me straight. Can't you just give it to me straight?"

"Indeed." The baron sat back, put a hand to his chest. "As middleman, my intentions for the train started out innocent enough. I had my contacts in Zurich. *Herr* Engels from the—which bank is not important—was committed. I had a goal. My share provided more than I needed personally, so I had planned to put a portion of it to a higher use." I sniffed at that and the baron shot back: "Ah, I see you think me admitting fault is a pathetic sight? Well, it is. I must digress: You see, more than one monarchist group had been striving for the prince's attentions, and my little circle has not been the most attractive."

"Like I said: straight."

"Fine, then. A few weeks ago I sent an emissary to the prince. I offered His Highness most of my share of the train treasure, without divulging its origin, mind you. Because at that time I did not know its exact origin. This was stupid of me, so amateurish, to make such a blind offering ..." The baron stopped to rub his soft wet eyelids, then he stroked them as if wringing out every last drop. Across the room, on a roll-top desk, stood a decanter of clear schnapps. Winkl fetched the baron a glassful and then retreated to the hearth and the baron gulped it down with a grimace, as if it was warm cod liver oil. "So many compete for the prince," the baron went on, "pretenders surely, but... I assumed the money would help, and Colonel Spanner, well, he said he was behind me. You heard him, did you not?"

"I also saw he gave you a good whipping. So your prince rejected you. There's others. Not the end of the world."

"Oh, no, no, you misunderstand. The rejection, this I have learned to accept as fate. But it seems I've not only misjudged the prince, but the whole enterprise." The baron paused yet again.

"You must be ready," Winkl said to me.

His stoking had made this room an oven, and yet my arms and legs had tightened up when they should've felt sluggish from the warmth. "I am ready. Haven't I been ready?"

"The prince's letter condemned me and my movement," the baron said. "Because the issue is not my checkered past, but a much graver one. It concerns the contents of your train."

"The contents?"

"*Herr* Kaspar, I come from a certain—how does one say?— social stratum. A standing. From the prince's retinue in Italy to my circle here in town, from my wartime friends in Karlsbad and the military and even certain Golden Pheasants in the party, we are all aristocracy. Regardless of affiliation, most of us come from the same noble stock, or at least we pretend to be. Call this silly. Call this out of date. We are what we are. In any case. When I set up the train job I overlooked this completely, obvious as it is."

"So pretend it's not obvious."

"Word gets around among us. Yet the ones at the top of the heap often find out before the ones fighting to climb it—men like me. Prince Rupprecht sits much higher."

A hot rush hit me. I was already sweating. It made me itch, right under my hair.

"The prince knew where the train originated," the baron continued. "So he was appalled at my offer, enraged and insulted. I claimed I had little idea, but to no avail. I was the fool. I should have known, but I did not want to know. You see? Things looked too good for me."

I shot up, fists balled. "Know what? Spit it out."

"*Ach*, this is wrong, so wrong." The baron rose and, patting his greased hair, circled the room and ended up at the fireplace, speaking into the flames, oblivious to its searing heat. "It's really too much of a burden to place on the captain," he said to Winkl, who stared dumbfounded, so the baron moved on, rubbing at his hands. "Especially since the man is on the job himself, and not only that, I mean, our good captain was practically there from the start, and people have died, haven't they? And he could have done something about it, oh yes, what a burden, such a tragic twist of—"

I lunged. I knocked the baron to the animal rug.

"Desist!" he wailed, squirming on his back. "Don't hit me, don't hit me!"

I sat on the baron, right on his chest. I held him by his oily neck with one hand and raised a fist. "Listen up, you. You're going to tell me exactly what I'm dealing with here, Maulendorff, or this time I will shoot you—and in the back if I have to."

I dismounted and the baron rolled away, gasping. We stayed on the animal rug, the Baron with his back to the settee and my back against my chair. The sweat rolling down our faces.

"Quit huffing and puffing. I wasn't choking you," I said. "Look, I'm sorry. I'm no thug."

"I know that. I'll tell you the truth: Colonel Spanner's train of four freight cars does not carry the prized museum art, overpriced known antique pieces or central bank gold of top Nazis as I had let myself assume. As you might have. Or perhaps, since your justifications differ from mine, you let yourself assume it was something like top secret Nazi plans or weapons parts? And why not let Colonel Spanner grab it before the other party, eh? Expensive, rare art. Rocket blueprints. Why not?" The baron lowered his chin to his chest, directing his grimace at me, zeroing on in. "Those four freight cars? They hold the fine heirlooms and personal effects, assets and savings, of European Jews. Bourgeoisie, most of them. All of it looted. Stolen. From the heaps of personal belongings in the concentration camps to the plundered homes of Europe. There is much quality art here, do not misunderstand. Only no one hears of this plunder, do they? Because most of it has no provenance or listing, clout or cachet. This is not the glory the Monuments Men in your MFAA art units seek, or even know about. Thus, it may be all the more valuable, for it remains untraceable."

I probably hadn't blinked. My sweat had cooled. It made me shiver.

"You understand, yes? You see?" the baron said. "This finery was passed down, for generations, only to be snatched from trembling hands—from those who had dreamed of these, their cherished pieces at night, and which of their fine young children would receive each. The treasured belongings of a household. Of a family. Now, it is perhaps the largest remaining yield of a most vicious human harvest.

I hear you have seen Dachau. This is everything that did not end up in those monstrous storeroom heaps there. Much more stayed at home. Let me remind you, Himmler's SS-state-within-a-state had taken great care to extract Jewish wealth. The most valuable products were plundered from homes and gathered from his camps as part of an elaborate laundering operation. There were foreign banks. In Switzerland, this scheme bore the code name 'Melmer,' but it had other code names elsewhere. Portugal, Sweden, England—the US? Few know. Even fewer know that, near the end, those hoards that had not made it west were loaded in special trains and pointed toward Berlin. They said it was Bormann's idea. Bormann believed this could help buy the Führer's safety. Other trains, with so-called 'unknown' goods, were sent south. This was such a train. It had enjoyed special priority on our rail lines, but the Red Army overran its route. For two weeks it sat in a depot, its masters on the run. Then, competing claimants within the SD and the SS canceled each other out until someone brought the train into Bavaria. Now, some three months later, it is to be liquidated by a certain Colonel Eugene Spanner." The baron pulled himself up, eye to eye with me now. "Captain, I tell you, this train was stocked through rape and murder, tears and blood, and fueled by greed. This is not even the spoils of war. No museum collections or catalogued art. No gold bars. This is a sacking of unthinkable evil, a rolling museum of the deep cruelty that is possible between us all."

"And me, I'm the delivery man." I had slumped. My hands lay limp on the fur rug. "Dachau. Heimgau. Same damn thing."

"Not quite so. Opportunistic, certainly. But you have not killed anyone, have you?"

My chin wobbled like a spent top. My eyes burned hot and I squinted them shut. The tears swelled and trickled out.

"Captain?"

The baron was frowning at Winkl, who'd joined him up on the settee. "Really, Prince Rupprecht must think I was in on it all along," the baron was saying, the first thing he'd said in minutes.

I didn't respond. I hadn't responded in some time. For a long while I just gaped at the ceiling. Now I sat sunk in my chair and stared at the roaring fire, my cheeks burning and my right hand clenching a glass of herbal hunter's liquor I sipped on at intervals unknown to me.

"It is good for the stomach," the baron had said of his thick and minty brown hooch.

I had seen Spanner's freight cars again. Sergeant Horton had showed up at my villa to take me on a jeep ride up to Dollendorf as promised. I had played the jolly new Acting CO for him; I didn't even mention Major Membre, and that thick mug Horton probably could've cared less if I had. Those freight cars were hidden deep inside that rocky hill, all right. Horton unlocked and rolled each door open just as Spanner had done that first time. Horton hadn't kept those doors open long yet it still had looked so harmless to me—stacks of crates, mostly. That's what I was thinking, even then, only two days ago. Stacks of crates had nothing to do with Major Membre, or with torture, or murder, certainly not mass murder or concentration camps. Those were different animals. How could anyone make a buck from extermination and the reaping of its spoils? Anyone could, when properly motivated. I saw that now.

"And here I was thinking you were the crony," I told the baron. "I make you look like a goddamn nun."

In the evening we ate tiny servings of Kuchen und Kaffee in the kitchen, a stark white room with open cupboards. The coffee was weak, but the cake filled with a rich poppy seed sauce. Winkl was out tending to the fire. The baron smiled as he ate and talked. "The first legal elections will come one day and I need a real political party. Have you heard of the new Christian Social Union? CSU. Solid Catholic center base. Yes, I'm giving up my wish for monarchy. Ah, but there was a time... Not twenty years ago, I managed to get His Majesty one-on-one at a party in Bayreuth, to discuss dachshund breeding—"

"Stop. Hold up. I want you to tell me more."

"You know dachshunds? As I say, I once had quite a passion for longhairs."

"No. More about Colonel Spanner. The train. Everything. I have to know everything."

The baron frowned at his plate. He picked at the last of his cake. "Well, you know as much as I. You probably figured out more. Colonel Spanner required a 'respectable' straw man, a man with contacts, and there was Major Membre obtaining his command. Major Membre was to be the obedient pawn, but our proud major developed other notions. The fool. He challenged Colonel Spanner. And, with time, our mighty colonel began to see Major Membre as the threat to his operation instead of the answer."

"I helped him see it. Without me, maybe he wouldn't have seen it so fast." I pushed my plate away. It was all I could do not to fling it.

"Sadly, yes, you are his answer." The baron held up hands. "I am through, *Herr Kapitän*. I must tell you. I went to see the colonel in Munich. I divested myself of my share. So he deals directly with Zurich now. If he knew I was telling you any of this, I would be dead."

"So why me? Why come to me?"

"You know why. You and he are two sides of the same medal."

"The same coin, we say. What, some kind of depraved doppelgänger? The evil twin? I don't buy it." I tried to smile at that. It felt sick and greasy on my face, like a toxic goo. The kitchen had a window looking out onto a veranda. I went and gazed out into the night. The rain had ceased, the veranda slate all shiny bluish-white from the full moon. "How do you get out of this so easily?" I said.

"Me, easily? The colonel did thrash me, don't forget." The baron shrugged. "Now, I pose no threat. One hopes. The beast can gain nothing more from me. He was never going to give me ten percent. So I gave it up before it was too late. Still, I've taken a holiday up here, just in case."

"Your plan C."

"Yes. But for you, on your own, it is not so easy, I'm afraid."

"Right. Now it might be a guy's funeral. And yours too ..."

The baron pulled back as if yanked by a cable. He shot up, knocking over his chair.

"Easy! Don't get the wrong idea. Pick that up. And sit back down, will you?"

The baron righted his chair and sat, hands limp in his lap, faced drained of blood.

"Good," I continued. "Now, listen up. Are you listening?"

"Yes," he whispered. "I'm afraid so."

"Here's what you need to know. You're not going to like it. The man we call Lieutenant Colonel Spanner is not a colonel at all. He's not even in my Army. He probably hasn't been for a long time. He was once. He fought in the war."

"Thus, his hand," the baron muttered.

"You noticed?"

"I have an eye. But I did not ask. I did not want to know."

"That makes two of us. I didn't even see it. The man saw nasty things. Did nastier things. What exactly, we probably don't want to know."

The baron had closed his eyes, squeezing them shut. "Dear God. He's a deserter of the rarest kind. The very worst kind. The one who went to war and did not find it horrible enough. Well, then I can assure you that Spanner is certainly not his real name."

"I can assure you that it's not."

The baron saw his coffee cup. He grasped at it and sucked down the last of his coffee as if it was the last ever made in the world. "I stand corrected. For you, the trick must be to get out of the colonel's way."

"Or, get the colonel out of the way myself. He's got me. He's involved me too deep in all this. It's incrimination, see. If I don't play by his rules, he might have a way of framing me. I can't know what high friends he has bought or blackmailed or what. On top of that? I'll end up like Major Membre. It's only a matter of when."

Saying these words gave me a chill, sure, but I'd already made up my mind. The problem was, I had no clue how to do what had to be done.

"It's the choice that is no choice," said the baron.

I returned to the table. The baron stared at me, his face slack. I sat with him in silence, the fire crackling in the other room. I said: "Do you know the name of Beckstein? Abraham Beckstein?"

"The first name I do not recall, but the surname? Well, there were the Berlin Becksteins, in Grunewald, and the Becksteins in Hamburg."

"*Were.*"

"Sadly, yes."

"There *were* Becksteins in Heimgau, too."

"Yes! You are right. I remember." The baron slumped. "But I fear they are gone also."

"There was a son. Abraham. He escaped from a camp. I think he came back to Heimgau because he must have learned about the train. Maybe the SS had made him work on this Melmer program. We might never know. But I think he was after that train and Spanner found out."

"Oh, dear. That certainly makes sense. But, I didn't know."

"I know, relax, I believe you. You know what else I found out? I'm living in the Beckstein's house before the Nazis nabbed it. It's my billet. Katarina told me."

"Yes, of course. That would be the very Strasse. I'm sorry."

"Don't be."

"In any case: She knows everything, that girl, always one step ahead."

"Yes. Yes, she does ..."

My mind was racing, revving. I thought things out, right there. Brainstormed. The baron was watching me, waiting. I didn't notice him anymore. I must have sat there twenty minutes, transfixed.

One idea persisted, taunting me, no matter how still I sat. If I was going to go after him, somebody might as well get something out of it. Somebody who deserved it.

I looked up so quickly the baron flinched.

"That porcelain jester of yours," I said. "The Meissen you left in your cart that evening I chased you down. Is that one real?"

The baron nodded. "I looted my own house, I told you that. That's what we Germans do now to survive—we loot our own houses. In any case the artisans and their work came later. The forged, finer chattel, this was Major Membre's idea."

"I wouldn't be able to tell if such goods were faked, would I? Not if one of your artisans did the job."

The baron pressed a hand to his chest. "I should think not. They are the best around."

I wagged a finger. "Now, be honest. About this train. You really didn't know until the prince told you?"

"I told you," the baron said. "I never dealt with such goods during the war. I dealt in black market foodstuffs, set up high-class *Kompensation*. Caviar and rare venison, Absinthe, morphine—and mistresses, if you must know. I was more or less a glorified caterer."

I shook my head. "Right, and, suddenly now you just up and quit altogether."

The baron's lips had drawn tight.

"Maybe you don't get out of this so easily," I said. "You want a new start? Your Year Zero, where everything restarts from nothing? You're going to have to earn it."

"Earn it? God help me."

"With any luck. Now listen. You and Membre's bogus goods— are you still producing?"

The baron released a nervous snort. "Producing? Well, Major Membre, he had us stop selling. He did not want the colonel angry about it."

"I'm not talking about selling. Talking about production. Come on, you can tell me. After all, I am stepping into Major Membre's shoes."

"Yes, yes, okay. The artisans have nothing else. So they keep doing what they do. Even without pay they keep doing it. It's what they do."

"How much is there? Your inventory."

"We have our warehouse, up at the castle, the monastery. That's near full."

"Full how? In crates?"

"Yes. Stacked high."

"Good." I could go and smile now. It felt fine and loose. The goo had dissolved.

The baron's chin had dropped away, right down his shirt. "That's a right dead set look you have there," he said, frowning, and I saw it wasn't going to be easy to rope in the baron. Landing his commitment would take the right balance of flattery and argument, stroking and pleading, just as his touchy caste required. There were things I could not tell him yet. Still, I had all evening, plenty more of his hunter's hooch around, and two packs of Lucky Strikes in my pockets alone.

I pulled the minty brown stuff down from the cupboard and set it on the table. We stood over it. Two glasses appeared, from the baron. I nodded for him, good work, baby steps are what you take. I poured. We lifted the glasses, touched them. Sipped.

"Now, how easy would it be to mock up a little stencil?" I asked him. "Have it say, oh, I don't know, the words 'Top Secret'—in German. Or 'Melmer?' 'On Strict Orders of the SS-Reichsführer,' stuff like that, making it look real official-like. Theoretically, that is."

The baron's eyes had been looking a little bloodshot. Now, as he thought this out, they lost most of the red and gained a lot of sparkle. "Theoretically? A stencil? *Ach*, well, that ruse there by itself, that would be child's play—a 'piece a cake,' as you *Amis* say."

And we laughed, just the two of us, for as long as we dared.

Twenty-Two

Two days later, the July sun was back. Through the Munich checkpoints and into Schwabing I drove my Harley. Little Marta rode in my rear spring saddle, bouncing on it and grasping the loop handlebar and grinning at me in the rear view mirror. On down the Schellingstrasse to number 35 we drove, and I steered into Katarina's courtyard. I tooted the horn.

Katarina appeared in the doorway wearing a floral apron over a simple blue dress. Seeing Little Marta, she rushed over and lifted the girl off, kissing her on each cheek. "It's good to see you," Katarina said to her in German, "so good to see you well."

Little Marta laughed. "Likewise, *Frau* Buchholz."

"My, but you are so big now." Katarina stood Little Marta up straight, smoothed the girl's pageboy bangs and Peter Pan collar. They freed Sally the teddy bear from my saddlebag. The bear was heavier than I'd thought; carrying Sally across Central Europe had only made Little Marta stronger. "So, go inside now, Katarina told her. "Ask for a Herr Wiesenberg. He might have half a treat or two, but you must remember to be polite."

Little Marta curtsied. I tossed her a Lucky for Emil and she ran off. Katarina and I watched Little Marta push through the double doors clutching Sally. Kat's hands found her hips, clamping down. "Well. Here you are. How long is your leave?"

"Two days. Self-appointed. Nice to see you, too."

"Much has happened. I do not see you. I have not heard from you."

"They kept me cooped up. It was nasty, Kat. I don't have words for it. Major Membre ... he didn't deserve it."

"I don't mean that. You, I mean. You take your good time coming here."

"Maybe I needed the time."

"To sulk, yes? You are brooding. Is that what you're doing?"

"No. Not anymore I'm not." I touched her cheek, and she let me. She kissed me hard on the lips. I said: "Let's go for a stroll, take Little Marta. Our little gal's good cover."

I pulled on my civvies and we headed out with Little Marta between us, grasping our hands, Sally the bear riding along in a little rucksack Kat had for Marta. A few blocks away, a small carnival had found a home on a lot cleared of rubble. Little Marta jumped up and down and we let her run ahead, taking it all in. They had wooden pee wee rides powered by hand and foot—paddlewheel canoes on strings and pedal-cars on cables, a carousel propelled by a donkey. No electricity needed here. "Floh-Zirkus," read a sign, a Flea Circus, and another read "Wild Treasures," but it was only used stuffed animals I saw, all nappy-furred bears and one-eyed monkeys. They had none of those good old carnival smells either (hot sugared almonds, cotton candy, sweetened popcorn), but Little Marta didn't seem to know or care. She made straight for the carousel. I caught up and sat her on a giraffe. A man with no teeth slapped the donkey, the carousel took off and ole no-teeth played an accordion.

A row of stray sandstone blocks served as adult seating. I sat Katarina down, her eyes searching me and her face tight, a mask of itself. "Emil has found out some things," she said. "Abraham Beckstein was searching for a train. That was why he came back. And, I must tell you about your Colonel Spanner. He is not who he says he is, in no way."

"I know. I know all about it." I told her what I had learned about the man calling himself Lieutenant Colonel Spanner, CIC agent. Major Membre had proved a sort of hero in the end. In his way. I told her about the train, told her everything, exactly what was in it and why, and what I was supposed to do with it. I had set myself up for the rawest of deals. It didn't make me look good. I could be implicated, framed even. Going over his head was one vast teeming minefield, because I couldn't know who he had in his pocket. The sadistic deserter had become a sadistic, double-dealing operator of unknowable means. I told her about the baron's role. I didn't have to tell her what it all meant. "I had it wrong from the beginning," I told her. "I shouldn't just have been asking about corpses, torture. About Abraham. I should've been asking about Colonel Spanner. That train. Follow the money, not the victims. I'm sorry, Kat."

As I spoke she stared straight ahead, not blinking, her knuckles white on her knees. Every time Little Marta passed on the peewee giraffe, Katarina forced out a smile. "Don't say that, I could've done this or that," she said. "You would've gotten nowhere. No Heimgauer—no German—was just going to offer you that information. Germans have learned to know nothing at all, even when the evidence is right in front of them."

"It was right in front of me. Me, an *Ami*. So what does that make me?"

Her look softened. "You haven't heard the rumors about you. No, of course, you haven't. And how could you? Who was going to tell you to your face? You're their conqueror—"

"To hell with that. You tell me. To my face."

Little Marta passed again, waving. We waved.

Katarina said: "Some were saying you were an enforcer planted and run by this Colonel Spanner. To keep an eye on what he'd reaped. You could launch a putsch, if necessary."

So even the hapless natives knew me better than I did myself? I spat out a grim laugh. A Lucky butt hung from my fingers. I let it drop and ground it into the ashen dirt with my boot.

"You mustn't take it the wrong way. None of this surprises or even upsets Heimgauers, you see. So many factions vied for primacy during the Nazi regime, over these last twelve years. This was the daily rule. And now, you Americans come and you are *All-Powerful*. But we are smarter than you think in our looking-the-other-way manner. We are cautious for good reason. We know the Major Membres of this world are never, ever acting alone. Others operate them."

"He's not just a bad apple. That's what you're saying."

"The bad apple is only a scapegoat covering for the real criminals high above. You can't have bad apples without that tree. You *Amis*, you don't think your trees can get rotten because you're the victor here, but maybe you are not so much the liberator as you think."

"And you? What did you think?"

"I told you, I knew you were different. Not at first, but I learned that you were."

Little Marta passed. We broke into smiles for her.

"You stayed clear of me long enough," I said. "God, and here I was thinking it was only because I was in the same unit as Major Membre."

"You showed me what you are. What you can be. You wanted truth."

I was shaking my head. "Truth, sure, but I wasn't listening. All I heard was Major Membre and his jawing on. I couldn't get past

that. Back of my mind, he had to have done it all. And to think—
I'm supposed to be the one teaching you."

"I showed you," Katarina said.

Our hands had found each other's. Little Marta saw it as she
passed around.

Katarina dropped my hand. She jerked up and marched toward
the carousel. She froze halfway there, her back to me. Clenching
at the folds of her dress. She kicked at the dirt. And she stalked on
back, spat at my feet and kept on going by me.

"Hey. Wait ..."

She swung at the air as if swinging a club. I grabbed her by the
arm and pulled her back. "I'll pretend that wasn't a left hook. What?
What is it?"

"You. Here! I thought it was impossible to take revenge. A lost
cause. And now you give me the chance? Now, of all times. You, of
all people. Like this?"

"Hey. Better late than never, sister."

"But do you know what you get yourself into? Do you?"

"Yes. I do."

She pushed at my chest, but I held her there, squeezing her
shoulders to me. Little Marta passed again, frowning now as she saw
us. We couldn't help but frown back.

"How could you?" Katarina said. "You never fought in the war."

On the way back Katarina was still steaming so I sat her down on the
edge of a shrapnel-scarred fountain among the ruins of the university.
She sat with legs far apart and hands hanging off her knees, like a dogface after a long firefight. Little Marta sat the same way and giggled
about it. That made Kat come around, and she dipped her fingers in
the water and stirred back and forth to make little waves. Little Marta
did the same. They did it 'til Kat was ready for more of me.

"Colonel Spanner, a heartless man like that, he figures I would
not do a thing," she said in English so Little Marta wouldn't
understand. "Even if I found out. This is the kind of man he is."

Little Marta had gone back to stirring the fountain water. I
spoke in English: "I can't let Colonel Spanner have that train. We
can't. You know that, right?"

Katarina nodded.

Little Marta had stopped stirring, her head perked up. Katarina
stirred again to keep her busy.

"I have a plan," I said, "the makings of one, anyhow."

Little Marta nudged Katarina. A couple professors were strolling by, eyeing us as if we were students they should know. We lowered our heads until the profs passed.

I told her my plan, how it could work. She nodded along, pursing her lips, and she didn't laugh at it or even speak the whole time I told her.

When I was done, she led me and Little Marta onward, across the broad Ludwigstrasse and past the rubble of the State Library. She walked ahead a while with hands clasped behind her back, now like some field marshal on the eve of a great battle. She turned to me. "This will not work without Emil's help," she said as we caught up. "I can help here. But what about the baron?"

"He's in. If he balks, I'll make him."

We walked faster, squeezing Little Marta's hands and lifting her over curbs. Rounding a corner, we found a tree line punctuated by trailheads. Beyond lay Munich's famed English Garden. Little Marta ran ahead and picked a trail. Inside the wood, the air was cooler.

"I've seen inside those freight cars," I told Katarina in English. "It was only about a week ago, and I got a good look. The baron got a better look, plus the man has an eye. There's a mishmash of crates, trunks, suitcases. Mostly crates. I think I can get the crates, but you'll have to score plenty of trunks and suitcases."

"Emil can. In Dachau he can."

Little Marta waited for us against a tree trunk, her heavy one-eared Sally staring from her rucksack. Woods surrounded us now, a sky of green leaves with sparkles of golden light. Katarina was glowing from it. Despite our plotting, or maybe because of it, I wanted to kiss her here.

"It requires precise timing and dependable manpower," Katarina said. "Nothing a little *Kompensation* wouldn't fix there. But the key is Colonel Spanner suspecting nothing. He must believe nothing has changed."

"Don't call him a colonel. He's not one. But nothing has changed, as far as he can tell. I'm acting CO. Just how he wants it. His new crony boy."

The next morning, Katarina and I met Emil Wiesenberg at the Jewish Displaced Persons camp on the grounds of the Deutsches Museum. The museum occupied a narrow island on the Isar River, just skirting Old Town, and Emil met us in the middle of the bridge. He led me and Katarina on over and along a path that snaked along the river island's shore. Through the trees we could make out the museum's red sandstone buildings that resembled a parliament or a university and once in a while, when the path veered inland, we got a closer look at the camp itself, at the crowds trading, boys playing chess, women hanging washing, old men painting. Gaunt faces staring from windows. We sat on a low stone wall at a far end of the island where the muddy Isar River rushed by. Behind us, among the trees, a woman in a white dress wandered barefoot playing a saxophone. She was trying to, in any case—her high notes warbled and her lows sputtered.

"That is Lucy," Emil said. "I know what you're thinking: Lucy's nuts. She's really not. She says, 'I play every day, simply because I can.' And so she does."

Katarina nudged me. "Tell him."

I cleared my throat. "That's not nuts. Want nuts? I've got nuts for you."

I told Emil about the train, about my plan, about everything except where the train was. As Emil listened, he stared into the Isar's stream, at the brown water churning and shifting and surging. His temples pulsed. He coughed once. He stubbed out his cigarette and started another.

"This is the other stash," Katarina added, "the one you never hear about."

"Yes, yes," Emil said. "These are our relics, one could say. Our reminders. I'm not surprised by what's in your train, Mister. I have wondered where the family treasures and heirlooms would turn up, there were so many. I've imagined the exclusive antique shops fifty, sixty years from now, filled with these items, but you cannot tell them from the general estate pieces—from pieces of those who died old and warm in their beds." He fell silent, his hands clenched in his lap. He coughed again. Stubbed out his new cigarette and started another. I let him. A man like that wants to stub out a new butt, let him. I picked it up for him.

Lucy's saxophone honked and shrilled on, in and out of the rush of the river.

"I am honored by your coming to me. So, yes. We will help. We will do it. The plan must run through my ring."

Emil turned and faced us. We stood, in a triangle. Eyeballing each other, as if holding up glasses to toast.

"You'll be pretty active setting this up. What if word gets out?" I said.

"About my gang? It won't, Mister. We're always up to one job or another. Everyone knows that, so no one will be the wiser. And the wiser? They don't stay so wise for long."

Twenty-Three

FOR THE NEXT DAY AND A HALF, Emil met people. Katarina, Emil, and I met too, at locations intended to throw off Spanner in case he was getting smart to our ways. As we watched a soccer game in a stadium south of Old Town (1860 Munich vs. Bayern Munich, 4-1), Emil told us he was putting together just the right mix of brains and skill, lugs, and lumpers. As we huddled in a pub inside the sprawling Hirschgarten Park, choking back *Einfachbier*, that thin ersatz beer caused by shortages of hops and barley, Emil reported he had the trucks and paid off the decoys. Afterward, we strolled the Hirschgarten arguing details, and Katarina pointed out that we were only a few trees and a fence removed from Spanner's new home in the Nymphenburg Palace, which bordered the park. How the man had pulled off that one, I didn't want to know.

"We better get back," I said. "I should be in Heimgau to wait for the call."

That evening, Little Marta and I bundled up and mounted my motorcycle. We kissed Katarina good-bye. I held Kat close, her face in my neck and chest. The ride back was cool and windy and Marta held on tight the whole way. I didn't stop once.

Back in Heimgau I sat on my hands as Acting CO, as best as I could. I did negotiate, quietly with neighboring county detachments to score more food and medicine for my hurting burg. Yet for the most part? Lived like a lord. Polished my brass. And those few days brought the grimmest interlude I could imagine. Toe the line and do nothing, yet act like you care? How do all those stooges in power sleep at night? It must be their baby blankets.

After five days of it, I got my call in a white envelope with no return address and postmarked Munich. Inside was one typed page, which told me to meet the train in Dollendorf at 0700 hours on Friday, August 3rd.

One week away. My first thought was to find Katarina in Munich. I left Captain Wilks in charge, headed north, and rode the Harley hard and fast, swerving into corners, passing all vehicles and columns and the endless lines of refugees.

Once in Munich, I headed straight to the Nymphenburg Palace.

The palace itself was a grand baroque copy, yet another mock Versailles to please yet another show-off king, in this case a direct ancestor of the baron's beloved Crown Prince Rupprecht. I parked in its sweeping C-shaped courtyard. A gate of black iron blocked the entrance arch. The Yugoslav DP sentry saw me and unslung his rifle. "You!" sentry grunted, "Go wait behind in garden!" and he waved me on through, eyeing my back.

Behind the palace I sat on the terrace steps for five minutes. No one came to me. The last thing I wanted to do was appear a threat so I put on my dark flyboy sunglasses and strolled around, making myself as casual as could be. I wandered the planned garden's symmetrical, landscaped pathways. Hard dirt and scorched scrubs had long replaced flowers and topiaries in the beds and plots, but the gardens still looked vast and tranquilizing, stretching on to the horizon. I was the American tourist. I perused statues and fountains, ponds and bridges over canals, all of it so well sheltered by a perimeter tree line that the city's grimy stench invaded only with a good wind.

As I was admiring a statue of Neptune, Sergeant Horton ambled up in a blue pinstriped suit that was far too classy for his meaty face. Of course, he wasn't a sergeant, and probably never had been. Spanner had probably busted him out of some stockade long ago, and Horton played the grateful muscle ever since.

"Well, if it ain't Horton and all dolled up again. What are you, some kind of aristocrat?"

"You like?" Horton tugged on a lapel and smiled. Then he frowned. "You came on the wrong day, Captain. The colonel's got important meet'uns."

"Oh, I'd just like a quick chat. No hurt in that, is there?"

Horton looked around, one way, then the other—what for I could only guess—and it made him grunt. He was one of those people who didn't seem to notice they were grunting, belching, whatever. "Well, reckon not," he said and directed me to a path that led into a stretch of colorless orchards, all the fruit trees black and withered, more victims of the air raids and wild fires the raids had unleashed. I pushed onward alone, crossing a tiny canal bridge, and the dead orchards gave way to a clearing. From all directions, more paths like mine emptied into this plot and for good reason. In the center stood the Amalienburg, a secluded mini palace.

There Spanner reclined in a wooden fold-up chair, his eyes hidden behind his own flyboy sunglasses so it was impossible to tell if the bastard saw me or not. His skin glowed pale. Only those large teeth bleaching in the sun showed he was enjoying himself.

No turning back, Harry. I swallowed hard and strolled up, half-smiling, a butt on my lips. Keep it light as ever. Never show your inventory.

Sensing me, or perhaps seeing me, Spanner cocked his head my way but didn't appear surprised. He looked indifferent as if tanning was more important. He stood, lazily.

I put out a hand for shaking. He offered his right hand. I shook it, two pumps—not too servile or too hostile.

"Captain. To what do I owe the pleasure?"

"In Munich, thought I'd stop by. You know, catch up."

"I see. Then what are we doing out here frying in the sun?"

The Amalienburg was the size of a suburban bungalow, but a thousand times grander. Spanner led me inside to its circular, lavishly overdone, Chamber of Mirrors. Glossy sky blue walls and silver gilding twisted and danced among myriad mirrors, in which the opposite walls emerged and scattered, flowing on in a stream of twinkling forever.

"It's rococo style. A masterpiece," Spanner said, rocking on his heels. "Yep, it sure has an intricate charm. Renting her out for a steal."

I had pulled off my sunglasses. Spanner kept his on, and in the mirrors I saw droves of those dark green lenses, as if the colonel was multiplying himself into an army as we spoke. I fought off the shiver it gave me. I turned to him and grinned, as wide and long as I could. I put my hand on his shoulder. I said: "You tortured those three men I found in the road. Then you killed them."

The colonel faced me, his lenses now reflecting a thousand mirrors. "Who's asking?"

"Me. No one else. Just catching up, like I said." I kept the grin going. "Sure, there was a little civil war going on when you rolled into Heimgau. But the rest of it? It was your big play. Those men you held up at the castle might know where those four freight cars ended up near their town. That's what you're thinking. You're calling your-self CIC so you need the info, the whys and wherefores. The full torture treatment doesn't help you, though. Oh, they try—they'll tell you anything so you'll stop—but they can't give you anything you can run with because they don't know. Meanwhile, last minute, those 'good' SS officers running the town for you are getting des-perate about what's going to happen to them, what with no more war to play in, so they go and tip you off about the train. They had it all along, I'm guessing. At some point, though, a onetime local Jew named Abraham has the tough luck to come back into town. He knew about the train. So, you kill him too, along with your new SS partners, because no one can know. All have to go, one day only, the final closeout sale. Because, Americans, we don't torture, and we certainly don't double-cross."

"This is good. Keep going."

"Enter Military Government. The occupation. Major Membre is perfect cover for what you'd done. Now here's a man with a consumption problem—just your kind of CO, right?"

Spanner shrugged.

"Maybe you had something big on him, blackmail him if need be. Perfect cover too—with Membre here, your efforts get paved right over. Locals aren't a problem either; they're conquered and aren't talking. But the major, oh our major, he turns into the crazy little tyrant and fast. Napoleon with a kink. All of which threatens those appearances that are so key to you. Maybe you even lay the blackmail on him, but it doesn't phase our very own megalomaniac, no, not him." I held up a finger. "Still, none of that is why you erased Major Membre from the board."

"You wanted the major out. You are implicated."

I had been expecting this part. I made myself laugh. "Implicated? Who's talking implicated? I know what I have done. Hell, I wrote you that letter. Way I see it, we're limited partners now. So why not come clean, now that we're working together, put it all out there, you know?"

"Sure. Understand."

I slapped Spanner on the shoulder. "Hey. Don't I even get a drink?"

"Sorry. No time."

I shrugged it off. "So, a lot must have happened right before I got here. You had your crew keep those civs up at the castle until right

after Major Membre arrived, so as to make the major look bad—
implicated, if you will. And the major, he's too hopped up on his
castle treasures to care who you're holding there. Figures it was Nazis.
Leave it at that. Why question the area CIC agent? You even repainted
your torture room up there, all nice and clean in gray and smelling
like paint instead of blood and retching, and lo and behold it ends
up being the major's so-called second office. Still, he has no clue. And
later, he doesn't want to know. He's got such a swell throne."

Spanner's lips had constricted and pulled back from his big teeth,
as if dissolving, and he grinned now too. "War will do that. A little
chaos, mayhem, suddenly once discordant interests find harmony."
He pulled off the sunglasses, and I wished he still had them on. "You
got it all figured," he said. "You have been using your noodle."

"Hey. Use it or lose it, I say. That's why you never came around
town, stayed in the open for long. You didn't want Heimgauers seeing the *Ami* mucky muck who took the ball from the SS and kept
on running with it. Didn't want them spooked or fingering you for
that matter while things were still hot. Same reason you holed up in
the courthouse till I found you that Sunday afternoon—let me find
you, I should say. And left as soon as you came, once you gave me
the answers I needed." I made myself shrug again, the casual Yank
operator. "Now, all along Major Membre hardly knows you. You're
the silent benefactor. But later, the major develops a kink you don't
like so well. His investigation. It's heading straight for you at top
speed. Membre can't believe what he's seeing. He wants it, mind
you, but he hesitates. Not sure how to proceed with this beast. He
could trump you with it or get dumped on all the same."

"What exactly does he know?"

"*Did know.* He found out that you are not CIC. You're not even
in the Army. You left the front lines months ago, if not years. Any
old part of the ETO you pick is your territory. Sure, lots of Joes go
AWOL, desert for good, on the lam, get a racket going. But they
weren't thinking big enough. Why Paris and Brussels when the front
is what you know? You were never an officer, though they might have
thrown you a field commission for all your sweat and blood. You
saw horrible shit up on the line, I'm guessing. Things I'll never know
and couldn't take and I won't ask. Whatever you went through, it
only prepared you better for when it came to busting up other Joes."

As I spoke, Spanner squeezed his deformed left hand into a fist,
ratcheting it down, ever smaller but denser. He stepped toward me.

"Don't you ever, ever tell me what made me. Never do that. Didn't you hear me the first time?"

"No, and I should have. It's simple. You had a way, some way, of keeping clear of CID. Never tell when the real CIC might show, but maybe you had someone letting you know that too. Meanwhile, Military Government in general is gaining more pull all the time. So, what's a Joe to do?"

Spanner nodded. "How do you think I found out about the major's investigation?"

"Yours truly." I pointed to my chest, stabbing at it. "He was using up all my energy and my effort, the major. Me, I was eager to prove something, on account of who I am. Where I come from."

Spanner shrugged again. We were having ourselves a real fine shrugging contest, the more sad truths, the better the shrugs got.

Spanner said: "There's no proof. Never was."

"No. You're right. I checked Membre's files, reports, everything. You, or Horton, got all that out of him before you took him to the butcher's."

"This isn't about cold feet. You're still on the train job. Correct?"

"Of course. I'm just learning the ropes here, seeing how I'm your new CO. Wouldn't want to make the same mistakes. Want to know just where I stand." I moved to a window, giving my sick grin a break. "You never pulled any strings to get the Red Cross here, with their food and meds. They showed up on their own accord."

"If anything, it was the major who made it happen. As for you, you believed what you wanted to believe. It was better for you that way. I knew they'd show eventually."

"I know you're in a hurry. But help me with one more thing. Those corpses? Where did they go?"

Another contest-winning shrug. "I don't manage every detail. You figure it out."

"You were mopping up the last of your tracks. So I can guess where they came from. You dropped them along the road that first day."

"Not me. Horton, goddamn Horton. He had himself a three-quarter-ton truck and he took them along—killing two chores with one stone. Said he got rid of them. Along the road? That was sloppy. Lazy. And don't think I didn't kick the sergeant around for it after I found out from you. Up there. It was foolish. Might as well put up a billboard."

"Someone took them away," I said. "You don't know where they disappeared to?"

"No. That part I do not know. I really don't. All this newfound knowledge of yours, I was thinking you were going to tell me."

"What can I say? You know me all too well."

I had turned to Spanner. Our grins had faded to grimaces.

He moved to a window, just behind me. I stood with him and we stared out at the lines of skinny and bare black trees.

"Not much fruit in your orchard," I said.

"Any left wouldn't be worth saving. Look: The major, he was an imbecile. Thought he had friends. But you must not think—you must have. So you keep playing it smart, Captain."

"Oh, I will, sir."

"You have to be prepared to take this all the way. Whatever the assault demands. It might be a meat grinder. Are you ready, soldier? Are you steeled? The hard charger?"

"You bet I am."

"But you don't fucking know. Do you? No. You don't know till you spent the night in an OP foxhole, the krauts in their holes just feet away, taunting you, some of the sick fuckers slinking over to slit throats in the night ... And then, you learn how to know." Spanner added a smirk, his lips surged back over his teeth and he said nothing more about that or any of it. Subject over. He didn't even show me the other rooms. Back in the foyer, he turned to me. "Okay? We done here? You got what you wanted ..." And his words trailed off.

He peered out the doorway. A man in a gray double-breasted suit was approaching from within the dead trees, toting a shiny black briefcase. The man's hair was bright white, his face was pink and he might have been an albino.

"Swiss," I said.

"Right again. You're on one hell of a streak." Spanner turned to me. "You edgy, kid? What? That it?"

"Maybe a little. Maybe I just want to do this job right."

"That's fine. Come to see your Fräulein one more time?"

"Why I'm here. Just for the night. Acting COs don't get much leave. By the way, she knows nothing about this and never will."

"About what parts of this?"

"All of it. Her family buying it like that, from us. The Jew. The train. Membre. All of it. War's war, right? And it's too damn bad. That's my policy."

"Then there's no problem. Go on, git. Nice piece of ass like that, keeps the nerves steady."

Spanner had said that before, and just to get rid of me. Go and grab some Gretchen and get out of my face.

"Yeah, that's a damn good idea," I said, and I strolled off.

I took a different path out, way wide of the Swiss, and before I reached the front gate, I'd gone over our ten-minute meeting three times.

Spanner had just admitted all of it, but he'd done it with the same feeling others used to tell a man the time of day. It was why he had shown me his deformed hand back in Heimgau.

He didn't seem to care what I knew now. It was academic to him.

And he didn't even bother to say good luck for the train job.

I marched past the sentry, grinding my teeth. The least Spanner could've done was suspect me, or threaten me. At least that was respect. But indifference?

As I mounted the Harley and pulled on my goggles, I imagined Spanner hovering like a ghost in those stunning mirrors. The image stayed with me. Spinning in my head. My heart seemed to skip a beat and then started in again, racing.

"Like a ghost," I muttered, "like a ghost."

The truth was, I was that ghost. To Spanner, I didn't exist anymore. I was a goner, a dead man for sure and stiff already, my throat slit in the night. Who knew what Spanner planned for me? Maybe he'll dump me in the road, sure, wouldn't that be fitting? Or out on train tracks somewhere remote, where the next train would come and chew me up good. I imagined Spanner out in the sun, chuckling about it, even boasting about it to albino bankers …

My mind ran away from me. These were like those middle-of-the-night horrors, the sham kind that hit a man at three a.m. as rash elaborate worries I couldn't do a thing about yet I lay there anyway and went over them, again, again, hoping those three hours awake had only been one. Only problem was, these horrors were no sham and I had so little time left. My odds were zilch. So I had an idea, despite what he said. This was what it must have been like to be a replacement arriving on the line for the first time, hearing the screams and shrieks between the shelling and tracer fire, knowing you were done for.

I pulled off my goggles, ripped open my overcoat. I wanted to head back in and take out Spanner right then. I wore my Colt. I had a US Army pocket knife stuffed down a sock. Yet I couldn't pull myself from the saddle. Paralyzed by it all, the bleak certainty of it. The baron could falter or cave, Swiss don't talk, and I was to be silenced under six feet of Bavarian soil and worms. Any way I looked at it, that cursed plunder was his. I slumped in the saddle. Get it together, Harry. The only thing to fear is fear.

I banged on the handlebars. I fired up my bike and shot off for Schwabing as fast as I could, charging down the clogged streets, kicking up pebbles and dust and people jumped from my path scolding me, just another crazy *Ami* buckeroo. At Schellingstrasse 35, I found no one. Katarina was out and Emil was out and I'd just have to hunker down. I sat tight by inhaling six Luckies and a half bottle of whiskey, and still I was shaking.

Twenty-Four

Wednesday, august 1st. evening. I went and led the way, remembering to step around any crunchy underbrush and crouching whenever we passed through a clearing. My fingers cramped tight around binoculars. Dusk had hit us and all had gone dim. The trees were iron pillars, our trail a winding black alley, and the humid summer air lacked smell, save a hint of charcoal. Checking behind me, I watched the Baron Mayor von Maulendorff play catch-up in his floppy felt mountaineer's hat, knee-high socks with knickers and suede jacket with more pockets than I cared to count. Flanking the baron were the sisters Bärbel and Brigitta, who kept their heads down and tried not to giggle because in their ears the baron kept whispering lewd jokes a decade or five old.

The trees thinned out up ahead. The baron pointed that way and the giggles ceased. We squatted at a thick oak trunk, the baron wheezing and leaning on his alpenstock, wiping at the back of his neck. Brigitta panted and Bärbel huffed.

"I know it's a tough hike," I whispered, "and I know you want a smoke." Brigitta pouted at her sister, who pouted back. I added: "Tell you what, I'll throw in another pack of Chesterfields for when you can. And the good baron here, he will now spring for your train tickets to Vienna." The baron shook his head, but Brigitta's eyes sparkled and Bärbel cooed. "Won't you, Freddy?"

"Yes, fine, all right, yes," the baron said in English, losing the wheeze. "But you must be sure to secure them the papers, Harry. They are quite worried about it."

"They can quit worrying. They do their job, they're home free."

The girls had on shabby smocks, splitting boots bundled with rags, babushka kerchiefs. Yet underneath? Puckered-up skirts and taut skimpy bodices embellished with wanton reds, ripe greens, tiny flirty flowers and all-time low necklines. I'd had the sisters wear their traditional dirndl dresses, which, according to a trend of high style that I could not fathom, had been all the rage in Hollywood and thus America. Pin-ups wore them and every GI wanted to see them come off.

The baron peered around the trunk, getting our bearings. "The road up must be over here to the right. And before us, the brighter path through the trees there, that would be it."

"Listening, gals?" I said. Brigitta nodded. "Baron's talking about the abandoned tractor factory. You should see a sign, a rail sign: Dollendorf—Traktorwerk it should say. Once you're there, find the tracks and stay on them, you'll pass through a rail shed at the far end. It heads back into the woods. Just follow those tracks, and be sure to make it loud at that point."

The baron shook his head again, this time in wonder. "It's brilliant," he said in English. "A salt mine? A whole shaft inside that hill? The exterior woodwork must have rotted away long, long ago. I never knew. Although it's bound to be in the family ledgers somewhere. We probably owned it. Yes. In a just world I would have claim to this train as it sits on my property, my very property—"

"Stop. They don't need to hear that, not even in English. What if someone questions them?" I pulled the canvas rucksack off my back and tugged it open. "Now, gals, let's go over this again. So. You got your meager sawdust bread and turnips in here, for effect, and the three bottles of absinthe, of course, your canteen of water." Pulling out a vial, I held it between my thumb and forefinger to show a white powder that twinkled. "Now. This here's what we call a Mickey Finn."

The sisters frowned.

"It's a strong narcotic," the baron added.

"Chloral hydrate, to be exact. A sedative. Other words, knockout drops. They knock a man out. Freddy, over to you—you're the expert here."

"It goes in the absinthe," the baron said. "Half a vial each drink is good, then mix water in the absinthe, so he really won't notice a thing. Here's two vials. You should only need one. Okay? Good." He cleared his throat. "Now, darlings, he might want to frisk you. That means, you must stick these vials somewhere safe."

Bärbel pursed her lips tight. Brigitta sighed.

"It's the only way," I said. "When you get there—if he doesn't find you first, you'll see he's got a little campsite set up along the train tracks. Pup tent, folding chair, fire going with a bucket on a tripod for boiling, you know, much like in a Western picture."

The baron nodded along. "Like a Karl May cowboy tale. All that's missing is a horse."

"And the good guy. Listen. He's been there over a day at least"—ever since Colonel Spanner left for the Czech border—"and he's sure to be lonely by now. And thirsty. I visited him just this morning, made sure. Probably be sitting in his canvas chair, maybe leaning on his gun too, but don't worry; that's so he won't fall on his face asleep. He'll tell you he's a deserter. That's what he's supposed to do—play dum-dum. Got me? Good. Now, what do you tell him?"

Brigitta spoke. "We are also deserters. Runaways. Our parents are dead and we want to get to Vienna, to relatives—which we do—and we are sick and tired of waiting it out so we're going to hike the way ourselves, we are, right on through the passes into the Austrian Zone. Break into climbers' huts if we have to. Refugees try it all the time. But, we lost our way already. We don't even know which way." Her chin had compressed. Her eyes welled up. She was a natural.

"That's it, good. And, you followed the tracks hoping a train might come along you could hop. Right? And you play up the poor-me bit."

"What if he recognizes us, from town?"

"He won't, but don't lie, just go with it."

"Yes. And the rest of it." They bowed their heads, held each other's hands.

"You might not have to do anything if you get my meaning. Just get him drinking. Loosey-goosey. Two drinks should do it. But one of you's going to have to nuzzle and smother him a little so the other can pour in the Mickey. Can you do that? Can you?" The sisters locked eyes. They nodded together. "Swell. Just, make sure he's comfortable, so he takes that second drink, to make damn sure."

Brigitta's face had hardened, and she crossed her arms. "Where will you two be?"

"Here. We can't get too close, not till you're sure, absolutely sure, that he's good and crapped out. And that no one else is around."

"Then you two run your darling little selves straight back here," said the baron.

"And we'll take over." I shot a glance at the baron, and whispered in English, "This just better work."

"It will. Certain of my lady friends—ladies of the night, that is—have used the very same mix on all manners of undesirable customers: your party pigs, nasty generals, smitten aristocrats."

The baron grimaced, perhaps having realized the allusion lay too near Katarina. "And it worked for the Gestapo, did it not? Just look at their success rate."

"All right, all right. All we do now is, we hole up till full dark."

I unrolled a bedroll and spread it out, and there we four sat. Flies and bees buzzed us and we took turns swatting and missing. As the last light thinned, the mosquitoes took over, whirring in our ears and we slapped at each other, sighing. I wanted a smoke. The baron wanted a drink. I wanted a drink; the baron wanted a smoke. The sisters had to pee, and then they were hungry. We gnawed on sausage and bread. We swatted. Slapped and sighed. I wanted a smoke ...

The sky had gone black and the trees retreated into the blackness as evening descended. As our eyes adjusted, the tree trunks reappeared as bluish pillars, reflecting the light of a full moon. The baron's eyes glinted with it. The girls' blond curls gleamed. It was time.

The baron smiled for the girls, rocking on his haunches. "Now, nubile sirens, go and make your good lord baron proud."

Bärbel snorted at him. Brigitta glared at me. I crouched close to her. "Do you think you can do it? You have to be sure."

Brigitta stood, her face blank. Then she stroked a lock of hair, and put on a smile with it, and she curled the lock around a finger. "I am sure. I got you out the door, did I not?"

I gave Brigitta a hug. She yanked her sister to her feet, grabbed the rucksack and a blanket, and the two marched off on through the trees.

The baron and I leaned against the tree, shoulder to shoulder, saying nothing. A plane's engine droned, far away overhead, the third plane we'd heard. "Sounds like another recon craft," I said. Probably making fast for Spanner's border diversion.

More waiting, less insects. I yawned. I might have fallen asleep. Trees became clearer, their ornate bark etched with purple and white moonlight, and the leaves shined like silver fishing lures. It was full night now. We had heard no shouting or gunshots—a good sign.

The baron's head bobbed, half asleep. "Ah, nubility," he murmured, "sweet, sweet nubility."

We heard cracks and crunches. We lowered to the rocky ground. I drew my Colt. More cracks and crunches, then gasps and giggles, whispers. Two silhouettes appeared and growing fast—the sisters were running back to us, tripping and laughing and trying not to laugh. Their kerchiefs were off. Hair bounced and whirled. They dropped to their knees at the tree, gasping. "Oh my, oh my," Brigitta was saying, "Vienna, here we come." Bärbel pushed hair out of her face and beamed at me, her eyes wild. "I think he's dead!" she blurted.

The baron started, white-faced. "Please, do not even joke about this."

"The giant shit slob, he peed in his pants," Bärbel said through more giggles. "Yes, it's true, he has died of peeing his pants, an acute case of terminal urination ..."

"You're stoned, sister." I grabbed Brigitta. "Give it to me straight."

"We had to do it twice—both the vials—but it worked, the silly stuff, it did, and he curls up like the biggest baby I've ever seen there in his tiny tent, which is the tiniest tent I have really ever seen." She burst out laughing.

"Keep quiet! And no one else was there? You're sure?"

"No. Yes. No one. Absolutely not."

Bärbel was on all fours. "Pup tent, doggie tent, woof woof," she jabbered, "woof, woof, woooof." She began to sway, back and forth. Her eyes closed. She fell hard into Brigitta.

Brigitta made a tisk-tisk sound. "Stupid cabbagehead, she took a good swig of your potion. Maybe two."

"Sweet, sweet nubility." The baron rolled Bärbel onto the bedroll, stroking her hair. "For you, little one, lovely Vienna is waiting."

Sergeant Horton lay just as the sisters described—all conked out and curled up, his crotch soiled and damp and who knew what else, his tiny tent smelling like a field latrine for a regiment. His fingers still clutching Bärbel's babushka. He wore an outfit not unlike the baron's, suede and knickers and all, though with a feathered Tyrolean hat instead of the floppy mountaineer style. Looking like this he might've been Maulendorff's idiot brother, son, something.

The baron peeked in at Horton and had to hold his nose. "Odd, I've never seen this much side effect. My God, that's such a load of side effect."

I grabbed the baron by his shoulders, turned him around. "This is it. Head back down the road and wave the all-clear."

I added a little bow for him, the first I'd ever done. The baron smiled. He bowed fully, bent at the waist and extending one arm holding his hat, and he trotted off into the woods.

Outside the tent, with the fire's embers still popping, I grabbed Horton's tommy gun and took a seat in his folding chair. I had about ten minutes to myself. The old salt mine loomed behind me, a black hole in the trees. And the ten minutes felt like sixty. So far, so good, I told myself. Chloral hydrate blocked sound, vibration, anything. A double dose like that would put even big Horton down a good ten hours or more. Yet we had a long way to go. I did. This was only the first inning of a ball game.

I heard a rumble. I ran down the rail line to the edge of the woods and hunkered down inside the rail shelter. Out in the clearing, the full moon was making those shoddy warehouses glow as if just painted and the rails glistened, two slick lines stretching out from my feet. The rumble had become roars. Headlights bounced off trees and shot my way as our trucks lumbered up the road and into the clearing they came.

I waved the first truck onto the rail line—driving on the rails left fewer tire tracks—and on through the rail shelter and into the woods the truck rolled, its tires pounding the rail ties. Men jumped out, pointing machine guns, waving more headlights our way. The rest of the trucks drove on the rails till the workshops, then they steered around and backed in among the buildings to halt in the dark, waiting their turn. All told, I counted seven large Willys and three smaller Phaenomen trucks, each sporting Red Crosses and the white stencil letters UNRRA—the United Nations Rehabilitation and Relief Administration.

A relief convoy. The perfect cover. Jews running care supplies were all but untouchable.

I now saw silhouettes along the tree line—our guards keeping watch out there. I ran back down the rails. A guard stood before the pup tent, his face rubbed dark with coal. He nodded in salute to me. Beyond I could see the salt mine's earthen walls flickering orange and yellow from torches, like some primeval caveman's lair. I jogged along the rails into the mine. The first truck, a big Willys, was backing up in front of the four freight cars. It halted, hushed whoops sounded out and roughly thirty men and a few women piled out the back and laid down wide plywood boards before the freight cars, to avoid making excess tracks. Others were mounting what looked like a theater curtain over the mine's entrance, to block the light.

"The Survivors," said a voice. I turned around. Emil, face rubbed with coal, wore black leather and watch cap and had a Schmeisser gun slung on his shoulder. He looked a foot taller like this and I wouldn't have recognized him if he wasn't wearing his glasses.

"Am I glad to see you."

"And I you, Mister."

"We did it, we conked him out and real good too," I said but Emil had stopped listening. He was watching his crew. He walked toward them shouting directions.

I followed and wandered among them. A stout woman with a bald head passed lugging a welding torch. One man was missing thumbs. Another had a deep dent in his forehead and an eye patch. Boys without teeth. So many limps and scars I saw.

Another truck had emptied hoists on wheels, hand dollies, and a small lift truck. A blue-orange flame illuminated the front freight car, and the welding woman went to work. Sparks popped and steamed dead on the plywood. After three minutes—I timed it— one padlock was cut. Emil heaved open the door and I pushed my way through for a look.

Crates marked "Top Secret" and "Melmer" were stacked in neat blocks, the gaps filled in with piles of trunks and suitcases and bags.

We stared. Someone grunted. There was no time for eulogies. We worked hard and fast heaving the crates and cases and bags into the Willys, groaning and whispering and panting as one, four or five languages clashing and blending, heave ho, heave ho. As we labored a sprightly old man Emil called the Pigeon hurried to mark and record the stocks, climbing on the truck and train and up ladders and hopping in and out of the way, a pencil behind each ear and a clipboard around his neck; he tapped and poked and guessed at the weights, hunched over bags, and stooped inside the crates and made sure someone recorded the names painted on the cases and bags. An assistant sketched the arrangement of crates and larger trunks, much like on a movie storyboard.

The Pigeon was standing over a heavy canvas bag. He opened and closed it, opened and closed it. Tears spilled down his cheeks. Others around had bowed their heads. Inside, I saw, were marble-sized lumps of silver and gold.

"Melted tooth fillings," Emil whispered in my ear.

"I can't count this. How can I count all this?" the Pigeon said.

"It's okay. You don't have to," Emil said.

The first freight car filled two, three trucks. And again, and again ...

And in his pup tent, Horton slept on.

Emil ran up to me beaming. He wagged a thumb at the last truck, which was packed full. Brigitta and Bärbel sat up front, sleeping on each other's shoulders. "Guns are not everything. You know what we also never had?" Emil said. "Never had enough warm clothes. Never. And bread and medicine. And of course safe passage, that's what we really need."

The truck fired up, the driver waved from the cab, and the last of the convoy was off and away.

Still it was dark. I headed back into the mine. The plywood and hoists, hand dollies, and lift trucks sat waiting. Only the Pigeon had stayed behind, slumped against the earthen wall with his eyes closed. I peeked back in the pup tent—still Horton slept. I dropped back in the chair there, my shoulders aching and arms trembling, but I was fighting sleep, and soon my eyes closed too ...

More rumbles. My eyes popped open and I stumbled to my feet. Someone was jogging up to me—the Baron von Maulendorff. The sight of him in his silly getup made me break into a big corny grin. The baron grinned and ran right up and hugged me. He stepped back, as if he'd punched me. "Good to see you too," I said.

The baron caught his breath, leaning on his knees. "So, we're still here. And our patient?"

"Still sleeping in his own piss."

Headlights flashed—the first of the Baron's Willys trucks loomed from within the woods. The baron waved the truck on through along the rails and we followed it into the mine. A mixed refugee crowd of Displaced Persons and ethnic Germans were jumping out the back, arms hanging loose as they sized up the freight cars. The baron shook hands with the Pigeon, who showed the baron his clipboard and storyboards. The baron, much impressed, told the Pigeon he should be working in motion pictures and the Pigeon said he had, before; he'd worked with everyone in Berlin and they probably knew the same people, they decided. This made me think of my brother, but I forced the thought from my head. We had too much to do.

An ambulance drove up, squeaked to a stop and delivered more refugees, and then it backed out with a whine. Another Willys pulled in, this one whining loud, loaded down with cargo. I found the baron, eyeing it. "It's all there? In the spec crates?"

"As you wished. All we had, and then some. Rocks and iron to fill space here and there, back in the corners. Crates are all stenciled and I got your Emil's bags, suitcases, trunks."

"Nice work." Back to guarding the pup tent, I watched the baron help the refugees load the freight cars. The Pigeon moved among them, waving his clipboard and holding up storyboards here and there. Men scribbled names on the suitcases with thick yellow pencils.

One Willys truck emptied, and another ...

A jeep raced in, its skinny tires whirring across the rail ties. It was Emil with the welding woman. They drove straight on through. I called a guard to the tent and jogged after them.

In the mine the refugees were standing around crates, shrugging and rubbing their faces. The loading had stopped, a truck waiting half full. In the last freight car—the last one to be filled, the baron was arguing with the Pigeon over a storyboard. It was his production here, the baron shouted, and what he said goes. Emil grabbed the baron by the shoulder.

"Who the devil you think you are, man?" the baron barked at Emil, "get back over there and start lumping it like I paid you to do."

The Pigeon stood back.

"Freddy, this is Emil Wiesenberg," I said. "Emil, Baron Friedrich-Faustino von Maulendorff."

"The cousin of Abraham Beckstein?" the baron said. We nodded. The baron went flush and rubbed his hands together, bowing. "Apologies, sir. It's nice to finally meet you."

"And you," Emil said. "But I'm afraid you must be faster." He looked to me. "We have to be out of here within two hours. The sun will come up."

"Well, I don't know how I can," the baron said. "These refugee fellows, they only work so hard, you know. The sad fact is, they don't have as much stake in this as you—as we do."

Emil held up two fingers, then one. "Less than two hours. That's it."

The baron threw up his hands. "Very well." He marched back toward the truck, climbed onto a crate and stood and clapped his hands. "Listen to me, all of you here!" he shouted in the most common German he had.

The refugees gathered around. A few grumbled and snickered.

"You're doing a bang-up job, you really are. But, can't we do better? What we got here, anyway? Four freight cars? And only one left? That's not much, boys. Ask me, that's nothing but woman's work!"

"Oh, it's so heavy!" someone yelled in a high-pitched voice. They laughed. The baron laughed with them. Yet a gray-haired man at the front shouted: "This ain't funny. My arms are just howling!" Others yelled, waving fists. The baron waved at them to hear him out. "Very well, I tell you what: Get it loaded within an hour and a half and I'll double the payoff!"

The refugees cheered. They hugged and shook hands, and got back to heaving. The baron jumped down and looked to Emil, but Emil had already strode off, though Emil was nodding, I saw, and I thought I heard him chuckle.

"That'll keep their mouths good and shut, too," the baron told me.

An hour and a half later, the bald woman was re-welding the last padlock. A teenage-boy sanded and polished the precise weld lines, his tongue hanging out. The baron had left with the last of his trucks, and two thick men were sloshing buckets of water along the rail ties to clear all the tires' dirt and tracks. The horizon now showed hints of sapphire. Out in the clearing, I found Emil helping men mount a heavy textured roller to the back of one last truck. This would smooth out the road up—the same one I'd raced up that first day in my jeep.

"Good morning," Emil said. "Your baron mayor did well. Now it's your turn."

"Don't tell me—this here is the easy part," I tried to joke, but my chest was heaving with fatigue and emotion and my voice went and broke. I put out a hand. Emil held it, grasping it steady. I told him: "I'll try not to muck up all your work."

Emil smiled. He pulled me close and grabbed at the back of my head with both hands as if to break my neck. I felt something wet on my forehead. He had kissed me there.

He pulled back, facing me. He had a look in his eye that made me shudder a little inside, and my pulse started racing. He pulled out a long object, in a hard sheath. He held it out flat for me with both hands, like some medieval squire offering a gilded scroll on a velvet pillow. I almost thought he was going to go down on one knee. I stepped closer. I lifted the thing from his hands, grasped the rounded and grooved grip of firm leather washers, and drew it out.

This was medieval, all right. It was an M3 fighting knife, carried by paratroopers, Rangers and frontline GIs alike. I had not held one since basic training. The stiff fiber OD sheath with its steel throat and web strap were scratched, nicked, faded. The matte-finished blade did not shine by design, but the sharpened edge surely made up for the apparent dullness.

"Much better than your little pocket knife," Emil said. "But you must know how to use it. Do you know how?"

"Yes, I said. I do. And I thank you."

Twenty-Five

THURSDAY, AUGUST 2ND: the eve of the train job. Another summer downpour had come and gone, and I stood on my front steps to survey the puddles in my villa courtyard. For once, this unseasonable rain-soaked ground was making me smile. It might even help keep me alive a little longer. It was better than relying on my Colt or the GI combat knife Emil had bestowed on me. I wasn't feeling too thankful for that knife, not at all.

I had told Emil I knew how to use the thing. Who was I kidding? I had lied. I didn't want him to worry.

A blue-and-white BMW 327 lumbered up my courtyard driveway, the sleek coupe overloaded with a wood-burning engine mounted to its trunk in a tangle of makeshift tubes and, on the roof rack, bundles of kindling and one bicycle. Emitting a vile cloud, the sorry *Sportwagen* clanked and sputtered to a halt, its front tires hopping. Then I saw Katarina waving from the passenger seat.

Katarina? Here? Talk about unseasonable. My smile went tumbling down the steps. I walked out to them.

The baron von Maulendorff bounded out flapping his tweed driving cap at the smoke, fighting a cough. "Dashing, yes? If it wasn't for this damnable wood-burner, a most unsightly necessity of wartime. Shameful. Is this how they will remember Germany in these days?"

"You should be so lucky."

The baron held out a hand for raindrops. "Such shit-weather again?"

"It's not so bad. Weather hides our tracks."

Katarina was waiting for the smoke to clear. She stepped out wearing a pale yellow raincoat and a light orange scarf. She eyed me with a blank and wan face. I came down the steps and kissed her.

"You had such a long night," she said. "Did you sleep today?"

"I'm fine. You?"

She nodded. I stepped back to consider Kat and the baron standing here together, something I never could have expected. They stood closer for me, like siblings forced to make up. Something about it made me a little homesick. "I just realized something," I said. "Freddy here, he reminds me a little of my brother Max. Though Maxie didn't have title or this man's luck. But, yeah. You got the same silly style, same ridiculous outlook."

"That's a compliment?" Katarina said.

The baron smiled, poised in a half bow. "I believe it is. So, your brother must be alive."

I shrugged. I'd probably never know.

The baron's smile withered. His eyes had welled up.

I shook his hand, using both my hands. "You did well, man."

"I thank you."

"No. I should be the one thanking you."

"In any case. We will meet again."

"Of course we will."

The baron pulled his hand from mine and hauled the bicycle down from the roof rack. He grasped the handlebars and mounted the saddle, wobbling so much it seemed he was the first fellow ever to ride on two wheels. He rode a circle around us to find his balance.

"One more thing," I said to him, pivoting around. "Could you get a message to Winkl? Have him come by and gather all my porcelain, silver, whatever's worth something. Consider it a fund, for Little Marta. And her bear Sally."

"Consider it done, *Mein Lieber Herr*." The baron added a wave and he pedaled off, out my villa courtyard and on down the lane.

I took Katarina inside to the study, sat her down at the copper-top table and placed a sandwich of bread and cheese before her. She inhaled it in two bites. Chewing, she said, "Now. Emil's sources confirm there was just an incident on the Czech-Bavarian border. An American officer, two German border police were killed."

"Spanner wanted a diversion. Sounds like a bona fide international incident. I figure it can only help us." Even more US troops could relocate east to the stretches of Bavaria that bordered Soviet-occupied Czechoslovakia. It wouldn't do the rest of the world a favor. Still, was it that surprising that a con man of a killer would help set the tone for the next war? I could imagine the chaos, the resolve, the outright hate that a shocking new fear like this would generate. Most GIs here now were not war-weary combat Joes, but boys sent over well after the fight, so, of course, they'd want to prove themselves against the Reds. Of course, Spanner had counted on that. I only hoped that he was staying out there on the eastern border like he claimed.

"Has your route changed?" she asked.

"No. It's northwesterly all the way, to the north edge of the French Zone—near Kempten im Allgäu, South of the Danube. I have papers for the checkpoints."

"And you end up where? Let's go over it."

"Main line spurs off. There's a village, Aschendorf. There's woods along it. Inside the woods, at the end of the spur there, is the warehouse."

"Good."

"Kat, why the car? And riding together? It's not normal. Someone could be watching."

"And deduce what? That the baron has a woodburner?"

"Which he just left you."

"I can pick you up at this warehouse," she said. "I even have a full can of gas if I need it."

"No. Nothing doing. Absolutely not."

"No one said you could not get a lift. Why would Spanner care? Don't shake your head at me. I don't care. I will be there. You need a—how do you say?—a bailout."

"A backup ..."

Katarina held my hand. "Where's Little Marta?"

"Upstairs, sleeping."

"Good girl."

"She's better off at Winkl's now, but she just won't go. And I sure as heck don't have the heart to make her."

"I will keep her close to me."

"All right," I said.

"Good. So, then, you will let me meet you?"

I was coming around. She didn't need my okay. There was little I could do about it now and certainly not from aboard a speeding train of plunder. I threw up my hands anyway. "No. I told you. Not unless you want to bring a coffin."

"Do not speak like that."

It was too late. My words had made a rush of panic fill my head, hot and cold and white. "Don't you get it? I could be dead by then."

"Listen to me. You must get a hold of yourself before you lose the will."

"I am. I'm fine."

I looked at my watch again, for what seemed like the thirtieth time. It was six o'clock in the evening, one minute later than the last time I looked. Katarina hadn't looked at her watch once. It was like she had a timer built into her head.

She hugged her arms and rubbed at them. "My God, it comes so fast, doesn't it? It's as if you go away to war. It's just like Christian, you know he ... I'm sorry; I should not have said that."

"No, you should have. Because that's exactly what I'm doing."

The next morning: Friday, August 3rd, 4: 30 a.m. Katarina stood over me in bed, pulling on a light sweater, her raincoat and scarf. "I'm going to wake Little Marta, go trading. It's best we keep to our routines."

"Okay." I sat up. I clutched her hands in mine. I should have told her I loved her, but I didn't want to curse us further. Start adding true love to the mix, a guy was certain to die.

She seemed to sense it. "We will see each other again," she whispered to me. We kissed. She backed out of the bedroom, her chin tightening up. We watched each other till we couldn't anymore.

I lay in bed and listened for her leaving, but she made no part of the house creak like it did whenever I went down the stairs and out, not even the door. Eventually, I heard the car sputter away outside.

The next thing I knew it was 6:30 a.m., and I was dressed and ready. I wore tall combat paratrooper boots of russet leather I'd once bought off a GI rotating home, and slid the M3 fighting knife inside the top of the upper, along my shin. I left the hem of my trousers untucked, to help hide it.

Out in the villa courtyard, still in the dark, I fired up the Harley. His motorcycle.

Dawn broke as I pulled away from Heimgau on the two-lane road heading west. Forget about Kat and Little Marta, I told myself. Forget Freddy Maulendorff. As I drove on, the engine heat pulsed up through my hips, filling my empty stomach with nausea. Behind me a sole steeple poked above the tree line, a black spear against more of those untimely August clouds. Heimgau cathedral. I wondered if this was the last time I'd see it, then I killed the thought. Forget Heimgau.

I sped on and passed the turnoff for Dollendorf, kept on going. I entered a valley and turned onto a steep little cow farmer road and drove uphill, climbing until I saw a mossy stone cross. A plaque on it read, HEIMGAU REMEMBERS ITS LOVING SONS, in honor of a rifle unit lost in a place with a French name, 1917. Beyond, at the tree line, stood a little hikers hut.

The opposite trailhead. This was it. I turned off my engine. I unclasped my holster, slowly. Move deliberately, Emil had told me. This shows them you are careful and calm.

I pushed the Harley well into the trees, placed the keys in the saddlebag and covered the bike with branches and thicket, never rushing it. Then I hiked into the woods heading due east, the branches above me still trickling from rain.

I heard steam pulsing, clanging, and belching. Up ahead, beyond the trees, I could make out a black mass—the locomotive.

A barrel poked me in the back. I hoisted my hands to the sky. Firm hands frisked me. They left my Colt in its holster. They felt the fighting knife down my boot. They let it be. I had my US Army pocket knife in the inside pouch of my Ike jacket. They let that go too, but I wondered if they had even felt it there against my papers and cigarette pack in my front breast pockets. It was supposed to be the decoy, but that would have been too easy. Easy was a cruel fantasy.

"You walk straight ahead, you walk with head down," a voice instructed me in poor German, which I did for about three minutes, and as I approached the edge of the woods the barrel left my back. "Good-bye for now ..."

The Borsig BR 52 stood before me, a black wall, its iron wheels up to my chin. No one came to me and I didn't know where to go, so I pretended to inspect the train as if I was an expert. Black-blue grease coated the bolts and rods. Massive armor plates protected the front boiler, looking like giant horse blinders. The cab was like a tank itself and that coal tender? More menacing than any tank. The four freight cars trailed the Borsig and stretched on back to the mine. Beads of rain coated the train, mud puddles blotched the open ground. Horton's campsite had been cleared, I saw, even his campfire. Erased. The rail line had been repaired here and there with new ties, and spikes, and stretches of rail. I hadn't noticed this at night.

I had come in from the back way, from the opposite side of the mine, which meant I wouldn't be seeing the main clearing until we headed out. How would it look in the daylight? Would they see the footprints, our giant truck tracks?

The damn loco wouldn't stop vomiting its vapor and soot smoke. It stung my nose and bloated my sinuses and I had to sneeze, cough. "What gives?" I shouted. "Anyone here?"

The cab window slid open. A blackened, bearded face stared out, the engineer, who said something I thought might be Polish. I shouted back: "What's that? Don't speak Polish."

The engineer nodded down the tracks, toward the rest of the train. "You follow!" he shouted back in German. "In wagon at end!"

I walked along the freight cars. The Nazi eagle insignia had been painted over, but the words Deutsche Reichsbahn remained. The doors sported those thick square padlocks. They looked fine, I told myself. The Survivors did a fine job. Keep it together, Harry.

Hooked to the end of the freight cars stood a rusty red passenger car, lower and shorter than the rest. It had a row of windows so stained I could barely see light through them.

A hand popped out the doorway at the rear. It began waving me onward. As I mounted the steps at the rear, the hand reached out and pulled me on up.

"Wilkommen, Fedora!" said the same voice from the woods. The man was grimy black from coal dust. His flat face had deep wrinkles, thick stubble. He wore GI fatigues, no insignia.

"Morning. Ushanka, is it?" I said, feeling a little ridiculous because our code names were hat styles. This Ushanka was the locomotive stoker.

"Yes. You were almost late. Late no good." Ushanka wagged a finger at me.

"But I wasn't late, was I? Big difference." I looked around the passenger car. Benches and dividers at the rear had been torn out to allow for bedrolls and provisions, a cooking stove, boxes of ammo. The interior paint was flaking and marred and stained with who knew what. Then I saw dark red smear stains and knew exactly what.

We heard grunting, heavy creaking footsteps. "That's Papacha coming now," Ushanka said. "Your comrade."

Sergeant Horton trudged up the aisle from the front. He had his tommy gun. In his big hands it looked like a kid's potato gun. He wore GI dress with corporal insignia, the fatigues so new I could see the folds. On his belt, a non-reg hunting knife and a black German Luger holster. He looked pale, too pale. He rubbed at his eyes.

"Morning." I tried a smile, but my face felt slow, paralyzed. I might have smiled. I hoped I'd smiled. "How dee-do?"

"Not so swell." Horton placed the tommy on a crate and slumped down on a bedroll, facing a corner window.

Ushanka smiled gapped teeth and said to me, "You like bread, Fedora? Cheese, vodka, what you like?"

"No. Let's just get a move on."

"He's right, goddamn it," Horton barked, "and stop with them fool code names." He lay his head back and moaned, rubbing his forehead.

Ushanka shrugged. "Okay, Joe. We wait for good steam. About ten minutes." He sat on a box of ammo and slapped his hands on his knees.

"Then what the fuck you doing here?" Horton sat up, his brow fat and red. "Get back in that cab and get shovelin, jackass. We's gonna need all the stokin you can take."

Ushanka sighed. He ambled down the stairs and out of the cab.

Horton stared at me. His eyes were puffy, his eyeballs darker. He grinned and held the grin. "Aren't we, Kaspar? All the stokin' he can take."

"Sure. Sure thing."

Horton dropped the grin. "Sure, sure," he repeated, and stared out his corner window.

I pulled a crate to the opposite corner window, for sitting. Stared out. All I saw were trees, a mix of firs and oaks. I'd be seeing plenty trees from here on out, if I was good and lucky.

"Oh, I wanted to tell you," I said. "I'm having someone pick me up near that warehouse, at the end of the line." I added a chuckle. "Funny thing. We didn't talk about that. The ride home."

Horton shrugged. "Don't see no problem with it."

"No, I didn't think you would."

The engine's steam thumped harder, faster. Our car rumbled, the floorboards shuddered, and the train began to roll. We passed through the woods and rail shelter, the tracks clicking along. As we passed the warehouses and workshops of Dollendorf out in the open light now, I saw that just enough rain had fallen to muddy the ground. It had to be impossible to tell trucks had been here. At the moment, it was.

"Man, I love the rain," I blurted.

"Hate the dang rain."

Branches brushed the car, scraping and squealing and spraying water. Back into the woods we rode, all dim and thick with trunks. I huddled at my window. Turning every so slowly away from Horton, I pushed back the flap of my holster and felt for the butt of my Colt.

Twenty-Six

HORTON CLEARED HIS THROAT with a piercing rasp, then spat out the window. "That stoker and driver up front, I don't like em," he said, eyeing me again. We sat at our opposite corner windows, watching the rail line that stretched on and on from the rear of our passenger car, carving a gorge through our dark world of dense woods. After clearing County Heimgau we had slowed for one roadblock, a bush-league black market check. I knew the MG louie on duty there and didn't even have to show papers. And we rode onward. Horton spat again. "Russkies. Why trust em? Never hustled with em before."

I could only nod. Already I was feeling the strain. The locomotive expelled billows of black smoke that thickened the air, the floorboards throbbed and swayed under my feet, and my stomach rolled. A cold sweat clung to my forehead, upper lip, chest. I'd stopped fingering the butt of my Colt. It was there and wasn't going anywhere.

"Guess, that's way Colonel likes it—keeps everyone on their toes." Horton was sucking on one of his homemade toothpicks, plunging and twisting it far back inside his mouth. "Your most lazy, no-good bum can turn the most bloodthirsty, that's what the colonel says. Or even your weak-kneed know-it-all." He opened the chamber of his tommy gun, slapped it shut. "Kaspar? With me Cap'n?"

"Here," I grunted, pushing wet hair from my eyes. "Just a little car sickness, I guess."

Horton twirled the toothpick with his tongue. The tracks thumped. We'd crossed a road. He said: "Every time we been over a bridge, crossed a road, crick, anything, there's not one US patrol. Nuthin'."

"All quiet on the western front. Just like the colonel wanted. With the Sovs acting up in the east, what's the point guarding the west? Guard against what?"

"The French? Owe us their shirts. Swiss? Got guns that go 'cuckoo, cuckoo.'" Horton laughed at that, holding his gut like some jolly glutton in a silent picture.

And we chugged on, crossing the road south to Garmisch-Partenkirchen, on through junctions for the Starnberger See and Landsberg up north, the counties passing like so many fallow fields.

The rain came, driving through the loco smoke and pelting our faces at the windows. My ears popped, and my nausea seemed to pass. The train lurched over a steep hill.

"I don't like slowing, don't like slowing for nuthin' and nobody." Horton popped his head out a side window. The locomotive whistle shrieked and I stuck my head out, same side. We were passing an ancient one-room train station, where a German rail official waved us along. Up front Ushanka, the stoker, leaned out the cab window, giving a thumbs-up.

Horton slapped his knee. "Hot dang. Easy as pie." Then, he fell silent. Staring out the window, the tommy gun between his legs. He drank from a small silver flask, which he kept close to his chest and didn't share. I tore open a fresh pack of Lucky Strikes. We listened to the clicks of the tracks.

Horton squinted his eyes shut. He looked over to me. "I got a girl. Over near Garmisch. Her name's Gisela, and if she knew what I was in for today, she would not like it, not one bit. Frown at me like she does. Call me a *blöder Lump*. But what can I do? It's the job." He took another drink.

"I know what you mean."

Horton shifted his squat and faced me, the green of trees rushing by behind him. "Better than patching tire tubes. Kansas City, that was the drill. Hell. Wrastlin' dang tire irons, smell of that glue and scraping up the rubber. Here's what I done: when I got the call-up I gone down to the station and socked my boss Mr. Potter right across the jaw, flattened him for good measure. Told him, that's for all the riding you give me." He formed a fist. He punched into his open hand. Smack.

I showed Horton a grin. "You told him."

We gained speed and the wheels shimmied and clattered—the rails were worn out here. Our cab darkened. We'd entered deeper woods. Horton, still facing me, stroked the barrel of the tommy gun between his legs as if it was hair on a doll's head. He drew his hunting knife from its sheath. The blade was jagged and rusty. He turned it and let it catch the light as if he'd never held a knife in his hands before.

I stabbed out my Lucky on the floor and felt for the butt of my Colt.

"Hey, Kaspar. You wanna know why I look so sluggy this morning? So dang dopey? Why I feel so goddang fubar?"

"What? Hardly noticed. You tie one on, what?"

"No, not like I do. And that's just the problem." Horton scooted forward, leaning on his tommy. "See, I think someone mighta knocked me out. Slipped me the Mickey."

I swallowed. Talked around the lump in my throat. "That's nuts. When, last night?"

"Nope, night before. And I still feel sluggy, too. Something happened. Two kraut sisters ran into me at my camp-out, said they was hiking to Vienna, finally gonna do it. We had a few laughs and drank some nasty green swill. And then? All kaput, Cap'n. I tell you, musta been out ten, twelve hours. All too kaput for normal. I was one real mess when I woke and I still am."

I made my eyes big. "Now wait a sec. You think somebody had a crack at it? At our boxcars?"

Horton grasped both hands around the tommy barrel, twisting. He smiled. "That's just the thing. Boxcars look the same, far as I can tell. Padlocks are locked. Far as I can tell. Colonel never left me a key so I couldn't a checked inside."

"You did check around though? This could be serious, Sergeant. Real serious. Maybe somebody tried. Jesus. Maybe somebody's going to try again?"

"There was trucks up there. More than just a one. Out of the warehouses, at least. Had to be. And the rest of it? All a little too clean—spanking new, in fact, if you know what I mean. No trace of a thing. No leaves, branches, ruts, weasel holes, nothing, like a garage floor been swept." Horton's eyes seemed to pull closer together. "Now. How do you explain all that?"

"Explain it? Me?"

Horton scooted forward. The tommy gun rested level on his thigh now, the barrel pointing between my legs. "You. On account of you're the only one who would have tried, on account a you're the only one who knew about that salt mine. You and maybe that baron. But he's not that greedy, is he? Or dumb. Or trusted. Nope."

My back had pressed to the window, the draft gushing down my shirt. "Well, I can't explain it. Mean, how could I?" I laughed. Grinned. Horton grinned too and aimed the tommy higher.

I waved hands. "Whoa there, wait, wait—you think I did it? Come on, why would I be so stupid as to try anything?"

"Maybe you went and thought, why not? Sure. Because the colonel going to go and rub me out anyways? Me, meaning you." Horton lowered his eyes to the floor and his tommy with them. "But the colonel finds anything rotten? I'm a dead man too."

Of course, I was a dead man. Who was I kidding? I said nothing. I let his words settle in, under the weight of my thoughts, but the words didn't lose their barb. I didn't know what was worse—the crush or the cut of it. I was falling, plummeting down a giant iron funnel, the walls narrowing. Yet I still had to try. I still had to fight it.

The brakes had grabbed. We tottered and held on. We were slowing again and fast. Horton rushed to the window.

I shouted to him. "If it's another checkpoint? You need me. And I need you."

Horton glared back. "First, gimme your rod. And do it nice-like."

I handed over my Colt, butt first. What else could I do? Trust seemed the only weapon I had at the moment. We poked our heads out. Up ahead was a crossing and a white building that was square and stout, like a bunker or a jail. Everything was painted a fresh white. Road markers and fences, the two thick metal barricade bars blocking the tracks. A broad sign read:

ALL VEHICLES HALT
TRANSPORT CHECKPOINT

We pulled back in, facing each other. "This is the real deal now," I said. "We get through this one, we're home free."

"Yeah? Don't be so sure."

Brakes screeched. Full stop. We looked out. Three armored cars had pulled up. A line of soldiers stood ready wearing starched new tunics, bright yellow scarves, and silver helmets.

"Silver helmets?" Horton said. "Look like a goddang football team."

"Worse. They're Constabulary Corps—MG's new occupation police. Real elite troop if you like that kind of show."

"I heard about them. A show's one thing. They got teeth?"

I nodded. "Can't wait to bite, too. Worse than rear-line MPs. Never got to mix it up with krauts or combat GIs so they're aiming for the next best fight—AWOLs up to dirty tricks, deserters running rackets, thieves, and murderers on the run."

Whistles sounded. The constabulary troop advanced in step aiming glossy black M-3 submachine guns. Horton's face had scrunched up. "Hate those little grease guns. Only thing worse than a copper? Copper for hire."

"The company cop, that's right. MG goons were exactly the kind of snag the colonel was worried about. They're not on any take, and they play it by the book too. That's why I'm here. So. You going to let me earn my keep, or maybe you'd like a try?"

Horton unhooked the hunting knife and German holster from his belt. He set them down. He handed back my Colt. "I'll be right behind you."

I tugged my Ike jacket down straight and pulled my side cap tight. Strode down the stairs. The silver helmets stood at attention all down the line—milk-faced teens, most of them. I snapped a salute. A lieutenant was marching over to me, all riding pants and thin mustache. He stomped his shiny brown boots together, saluted. I said: "At ease. Real spit and polish, Lieutenant. I can't tell if you boys are cops or cavalry."

"Thank you, sir." The lieutenant glanced down at my paratrooper boots.

"I'm Public Safety myself, County Heimgau, and Acting CO now." I wagged a thumb at the freight cars. "We have here a confidential shipment—"

"We'll get to that. Sir, your men up front—the driver and coal man, they don't speak English. They're Russians, it seems."

Horton had followed me. He'd pushed his shaggy hair back and pulled on a side cap, let his face go slack. The change amazed me. He looked like the cheery slothful clerk he might have well become had he not inherited a fierce temper, habitual bloodlust, and deep hatred for authority. He even saluted.

"Worse yet, they don't have authorization," added the lieutenant, glancing at Horton now.

"I got that, got it right here." I reached into my front pocket, unfolded papers.

The lieutenant held my papers out in front of him like a scroll he was about to read aloud. He checked the carbons underneath. Meanwhile, two of the armored cars directed their cannons at the train.

The lieutenant looked up. "Heimgau? That where that major was killed?"

I nodded. "I served under the man." I raised my chin, in mock respect.

"That's rough, sir. The fight's never over here."

"No. Not ever."

The lieutenant read on and handed back my papers. "This is transport authorization, but these are CIC orders, sir, supplementary trip permits for the zone frontier. That means beyond the border only." He stole another glance at Horton. "This is an internal checkpoint, you understand."

"I know that. But you asked for them, didn't you? So why the runaround?" I took a step forward.

The lieutenant glanced at his watch, for no reason but nerves. "Sir? I don't follow you."

"Huh?" I barked at him: "You don't follow? What's the big idea?" Another step forward.

The lieutenant stepped back, feeling for his mustache, glancing at his men and armored cars.

Glaring, I patted my other pocket and pulled more papers. "Of course I got my MG paperwork ... trip ticket, permit, cargo clearance et cetera, drafted and signed by yours truly if you'll notice."

The lieutenant read. He stabbed at a page. "Ah. There now. These are fine, fine. See, MG orders take precedence." He handed back the papers, beaming. "Why didn't you say so, sir? All you had to do was say it—"

"Because you did not ask. You were imprecise. Get me? You did not do your job, and you're lucky I don't take your name. Just watch out from now on, hear? People die for less. For Christ's sake." I placed a Lucky in my mouth and talked around it. "It's all right. You're a young kid. Kid, I'm detachment CO, did I say that? Got the paper for that too, up in the train if you need it."

"No, no. That's fine, sir. Everything's fine. Confidential is confidential. Please, carry on." The lieutenant saluted. He waved toward the white bunker, whistles sounded, and the silver helmets pivoted and headed off single file. "Enjoy the rest of your trip, sir."

The train charged on, full speed. Horton watched me from back at his corner window. After the checkpoint, he had told me I did a nice put-on. I had thanked him. He didn't take my Colt back. Now he stared at me with a hangdog look. His thick brow had twice the weight. He scooted over my way.

"How long have you been a deserter?" I said. "A year or more?"

Horton nodded.

"Colonel Spanner kept you going."

Horton's eyes glazed over. "He's no fucking colonel." He scooted closer, his big hands loose in his lap. I said: "You killed Major Membre, didn't you? That's why I saw you that day out on the square."

"Spanner did the deed this time," Horton said. "I was the muscle and the lookout. He was still up there in that suite when you waltzed in there. Holed up. Said he had good cover behind a hutch."

A shiver hit me. Spanner had to have been seconds from lowering the hatchet on me too. "Guess I should be glad there was no friendly fire."

"You should be. The colonel did quite the job on that major, considering his gimpy hand."

"That the usual way?"

"It's our way. I helped the colonel torture those three you found, and kill them too."

"I know."

"You did something to this train, didn't you, Cap?"

"No."

Horton wiped at the glaze in his eyes. He stared at the floorboards a while. He looked up. "Whenever I do a job like that, I don't feel a thing. Only that same empty feeling I always got in the morning on the way to work. Same with those three corpses you found."

"You dumped them out along the Heimgauer Strasse."

"Yup."

"Why not in the woods? It was so someone could find them easily, pick them up. Wasn't it? You got a small fee for that, I'm guessing. Little dump job on the side you had going."

"Yup, sure."

"A local hire you?" I said.

"That's it."

"Who?"

Horton said nothing. He couldn't answer. His chest was heaving, and tears welled in his eyes. His tommy gun lay at his feet. He let it stay there.

He let me be. He left me with my Colt, my racing thoughts, everything. I sat under my corner window, weighing just how to take out the sergeant before it was too late.

He made his way back to his window. I stayed in my corner, eyeballing him. He sat with his shoulders towards me, his forearms resting on the sill, his chin on his arms. Hard to tell if the big man was sleeping or looking out. His tommy gun lay five feet from him.

What if I just kicked him off? Aim my Colt, get his hands up. Walk him to the door ...

I drew the Colt. I aimed at the center of his back and took a step forward. And another.

Horton swung around, lunged, and grasped at my wrist, directing the Colt away. He pressed his hunting knife to my throat.

"Whoa, wait, hold on." I backed a step and the knife moved with me, into my flesh, a cold sting. His putrid parched breath hit me.

Then he eased off my wrist and to my amazement, I was able to bring the Colt back around, pointing it at his chest. His knife was still at my throat.

He snickered. "Shoot," he hissed, "shoot."

I'm dead anyway, I thought. I squeezed the trigger.

Nothing. I squeezed again. Still nothing.

Horton laughed. He drew the knife back and stroked the air sideways with it. "You dang idiot."

I stared at my Colt, searching for some logical reason why I had the grip safety on.

Horton karate-chopped my wrist. The gun flew away and spun across the floor.

I sputtered: "You were scaring me, see, with all your crazy talk and I thought you were going to take me out. But I had the safety on, didn't I? Didn't I?"

Horton lowered his knife. "Dang idiot, you probably had it on since you got here."

"I ..."

We both paused. We had both heard it. The clicking of the rails was sounding farther apart. The train was losing speed again.

"You can't kill me," I said. "Not yet."

The brakes squealed. The train lurched and slowed.

Twenty-Seven

Horton stuffed my colt into his belt. "Why're we stopping? Too early for another checkpoint," he said, the veins in his thick neck bulging like waking snakes.

"I don't know," I muttered. I was still shocked that I had let him snatch my Colt back. "I need my gun."

"No! You made me mad," he said, a whine creeping into his voice, and for a moment I knew what it was like to be his girl Gisela. He snatched up his tommy too.

We peered out windows, front and back. We had reached a higher, denser stretch of wood. Thick tree trunks lined the rail bank. The locomotive's smoke and steam had settled around us and locked us in, a gray, humid fog that crept into our cabin.

I felt for the fighting knife under my trouser leg, and eased out the grip a little.

"Nothing around here, far's I can tell," Horton said, "no crossings, switches, nuthin'."

He came at me. He grabbed me by the throat. "You know about this? Do you? Do, tell me now."

"I swear to you. I wish to God that I did."

The train jerked to a full halt, more steam spurted out. Horton cocked the tommy gun. "Stay here," he barked and bounded down the steps.

I squinted out the window, but he was already lost in the swirling steam fog. The locomotive hissing and clanging. I thought I heard boots crunching out on the gravel.

I pulled the fighting knife from its sheath, which popped out and hit the floor with a slap. I crouched, holding the knife grip with both hands, the blade out in front of me. I crept toward the steps.

I heard boots clanging, on the rail car steps.

Horton plodded back up into the car. His face looked heftier, paler, a doughier version of itself like a papier mâché. His hands

214

hung at his sides. He didn't have his tommy gun. He didn't look at me, didn't see me.

A figure followed him up. It was Colonel Spanner. He flashed his big white teeth. I lowered the knife and stood.

Spanner had Horton's tommy gun slung on his shoulder. He wore his nondescript uniform but under a stiff, rubberized GI rain coat.

"Colonel," I said. A charge of purest fear had shot through me, like hot sterling metal injected right up my asshole and on up to my neck. It was all I could do not to show it. I grinned and, having no idea where the sheath lay, kept the fighting knife loose in my hand. "What's the big idea?" I said. "You scared the wits out of me."

"It's good to be scared," Spanner said. His voice had lost its supposed Southern cant altogether. "Anyone says they're not scared, they're lying. Even your so-called hero. They all lie. It's the only way to make it. At first, it is ..." His rain slicker hung open. I saw the butt of my Colt sticking out his trouser pocket.

Horton kept staring down, at his feet.

"We got through the checkpoints," I said, trying to force eye contact out of Horton. "Your man Horton here did a fine job."

Spanner looked to Horton. "That right, goof?"

Still, Horton didn't look up. He only shook his head.

"Go stand down in that doorway, keep watch," Spanner said to him.

Horton looked up at Spanner with slow, tired eyes. He trudged down into the stairway, his boots dragging, and his shoulders shifting, his hands feeling at the walls.

Spanner unslung his tommy. He fired down the stairs, the punching roar like a jackhammer on steel, flames belching from the barrel. The shots tore through Horton's back and legs, smacking flesh and blood and soft chunks against the stairway walls with thwacks and thuds. Yet Horton held on. His hefty arms and legs had pressed to the steps and wall as if expecting the blow. He swayed, dripping, ragged, like a shredded drape. Spanner bounded over and kicked him out, the sound like a smack on mud.

I had dropped to the floor.

Spanner lunged at me. He pulled me up by an arm. "Take cover! Good. You know how. You know what to do. You might have made it past that first goddamn day up on the line."

"Jesus," I said. I still had the fighting knife, in my other hand.

Spanner handed me the sheath. "Here."

My will had seemed to dissolve once Spanner fired. It had gummed me up. I had gone numb, except for a heat in my legs. I might have pissed my pants, and I even glanced down to check. No, not yet. My muscles squeezed at my bones, wanting to snap them. I felt paralyzed inside, but so open to suggestion. So I put the knife back in the sheath, just as Spanner wanted. He took the sheathed weapon and slid it into another pocket.

I straightened up, hoping my petrified spine wouldn't snap. "What the hell are you doing here?" I muttered.

"What do you think?"

"I don't know."

"You know."

I looked down the stairway. The steam fog had cleared. I saw Horton's body out along the tracks, looking like a smashed sack of beets. Spanner eyed me, looking for a tell, so I shook my head and muttered, "All I know is, this was not part of the plan."

"It never is, son. That's the problem with going all in. Never goes according to plan."

"I see that."

"Do you? You got to. You got to keep moving. That's what you learn, up on the line. Never freeze up, bunch up. Fuck it up. Or you're dead. Everyone's dead."

"Horton's dead. Why?"

"Like I says: You know why." Spanner had re-slung his tommy gun so that it hung level, the barrel forward for shooting from the hip. He gestured for me to head down the stairs.

I kept my feet planted. "After you."

Spanner smiled. "Sure, sure." He went down, tiptoeing around the mess he'd made. "Careful, it's slippery," he said as I followed him down and out.

He walked me along the freight cars, to the first one. Ushanka and the engineer watched us from up in the loco cab but pulled their heads in when we got closer. I followed Spanner, stealing glances at the deep woods. The steam fog filled the spaces between tree trunks. Spanner might have guards out there. I could not be sure. I couldn't make a break for it. That was suicide. Tracking me out there in the woods would have been his delight. In such a place he had surely embraced the horror of war and discovered how much it fueled him, pushed him to his limit and beyond until he had become unearthly, warped, sociopathic.

He stopped at the doors of the first freight car, pivoting to face me. He handed me a key. "Open it. Go ahead."

I took the key, pulled myself up onto the steel running board, and unlocked the padlock hanging from the door latch.

"Pull the door open," Spanner said, looking up at me. "Watch out though, the contents may have shifted."

I grabbed the handle and pushed at the door, but something blocked it. I pushed harder, with both arms, legs. The door rolled open and banged to a stop.

I saw crates, trunks and suitcases, much like we had placed them, only a few dislodged. Something fleshy caught my eye. I looked down. A leg lay bloodied and bent in the wrong direction, the knee twisted. White bone protruded through cracked skin—a shin bone hung out. Blood dripped out the car now, thick and dark like a cherry syrup.

"Drag him out," Spanner said. "Swiss don't like it messy," he added, chuckling.

I had gone petrified again, and mechanical. Did what Spanner said. I leaned over the corpse. An Army blanket shrouded the body. He was naked under it. I knew who it was. I pulled the blanket away. It was Maulendorff. His face had bloated up on one side, so swollen that the eye had submerged. He was cut up and bruised all over, his body streaked with blood and soiled from what looked like mud, but I soon realized, with a harsh blast up my nose like ammonia, was his own shit. One foot was mangled, two toes missing. He was handcuffed. His stiff hands still clenched a black hood.

I was only glad for one thing: Spanner could not see my face from here. It had cramped up beyond my brain's control, my teeth biting down and wanting to gnash my uppers and lowers into chips, bits, a powder. My heart panged. I wasn't sure what would happen when the anger hit me. I had to hold it in, for now.

"I'm not gonna catch him." Spanner stepped back. "Just toss him out."

He was too heavy to pull out and had snagged on something. To get him loose I had to step further inside the car, almost slipping on the blood and foul smudges. I backed up against a crate marked "Melmer," using it as leverage to push him out. One of his arms had been smashed under a dislodged crate, I saw. I heaved the crate up an inch and kicked the arm free, but rigor mortis had started. The arm resisted. I forced it away with my boot and didn't like the sound it made. "Sorry, Freddy," I whispered, "I'm so sorry," not caring if Spanner could hear me or not. I had to drag him to the edge because the death rigor in his limbs wouldn't let me roll him there, and got on all fours to shove him out. He hit the gravel and tumbled away, off into the long grass along the tracks.

I climbed down. But Spanner, shaking his head, gestured for me to pull the door shut again. I climbed back up. I pulled the door closed, set the latch and locked the padlock.

The anger had found me, releasing my bones from their muscle clampdown and surging through my veins, nerves. I jumped down and should've broken an ankle but didn't feel a thing.

I squared my shoulders at Spanner. "Tell me why."

"Get back in the car first. We got to get a move-on," he said.

"Have it your way."

The locomotive rolled on, with fits and starts. Spanner and I had clambered back up into the passenger car, and here we rode. The trees had receded and then the clouds, revealing green valleys that sparkled from the rain still in them. The sun grew warm for the day, heating up our car like a greenhouse. I didn't want to hear it from him now, all his twisted bullshit. I sat on a bedroll, but the locomotive's black smoke swirled in and bit at my nostrils like burnt peppers.

Spanner sat next to me on the ammo box. I could smell the sweat coming off him, out from under that rubber slicker, a little sweet and sickly pungent, somewhere between rotting vegetables and the smell of Freddy's corpse. But I couldn't see a speck of blood or guts on him. For all I knew, he liked to do the deed as naked as his victims. That or he had a supply of rain slickers, one for every murder.

"I'll tell you why," Spanner said. "He said it was all his idea. He said no one was helping him. I didn't believe him."

"What was?"

"Ah, look. You can tell me. You did one hell of a swap, switching out those freight cars."

"I don't know what you're talking about. I'm doing a job for you."

Spanner sighed. He placed a hand on my shoulder, his right hand. I felt its warmth even through my Ike jacket. "And it is an excellent job, Kaspar. Fucking genius, you ask me."

"What?"

"It was not all his idea. He's not capable. He doesn't have the brass balls. Not like you."

Either I was a dead man or his Einstein. The goat or the hero.

"You're right," I said. "It was my idea."

"Good. Great!" He slapped me on the shoulder.

"It is? How is that?"

"It's smart thinking. It doubles the loot. Lets you do another deal. Just what I woulda done."

"It's fake. It's bogus. You do know that?"

"Who gives a shit! It's just commodity, son. Look. I know what you're thinking: Why are you not lying along the tracks back there too?"

I grunted.

"I gave you a chance to rub me out. You were holding a fucking M3 fighting knife in your hand. You did not assault. That tells me something. You're even smarter than I thought. You off Membre and then get to keep his spoils, fake or no, and go and double them to boot. That's one hell of a coup right there. And do not tell me you did not off him, because my hand could not have done it without your hand." Spanner pressed his deformed left hand to his heart, his claw-thumb tucked under. "I, Sheriff, am simply your humble deputy."

"Says you."

Spanner lowered his hand. He straightened. "Either that or you're just a goddamn coward. You're a fucking pansy. You can't take it. You never could."

He was forcing me into it. I was forcing myself into it. I would have to do it here, right now, somehow. It was like he wanted me to. But first, I had to bide my time, keep him thinking I was still his man and his cohort and no different than him.

I didn't have to feel for that pocket knife in my inside breast pocket. I could feel it stroking my heart.

Spanner said: "Now, all you have to do, is tell me where my real cargo is. Excuse me—*our* cargo."

"No. We have to renegotiate this deal," I said.

"Is that right?" Spanner grinned.

I was stalling. Then I wasn't. I did need something—there was one thing I had to be sure about. I said: "You have to tell me where Katarina is."

Spanner let out a deep breath and it carried that smell as if it emanated from his very gut. "I don't know what you are talking about."

"I know you. You gather bargaining chips, sure, stacks and stacks. She could be one."

Spanner smiled. "You want to negotiate? Parley? How's this? It seems CID uncovered a plunder ring. One insidious racket. They got all the ringleaders right around Heimgau. Sure. Half of them or more offed each other."

"And you still get away with at least half the take? I think you're bluffing. I don't think you got much pull at CID left, not any more. Times are changing fast, Virgil."

Spanner jerked back. It made him sit up, puff up. "Don't call me that. How do you know that name?"

"We all have secrets, Tercel."

His temple twitched. He leaned forward. "Now you listen to me. You don't know what I can do. Who I can alert. What will your parents think of the news? Your parents will be real proud of you. What are their names? Manfred, and Elise?"

"Fuck you. Where's Kat?"

"You're going to have to find out. Aren't you? Don't give me that smug look. You think that you're nothing like me. I was like you once. Now I'm not and good riddance to that fucking milquetoast do-gooder. You don't want to become like me, like this? You're going to have to do something about it."

I was going to have to kill him. I was going to die trying. It didn't clench up my asshole or clamp down on my bones or muck up my insides any more. Something had clicked inside me. A lever. Automatic. My own death was not a factor. Only taking action mattered. Keep moving, Spanner had said himself. So I would be his combat Joe. I would kill with robotic, unfeeling toil.

"Where's Kat?" I repeated.

Spanner stood. I stood. We faced each other in the middle of the car, our boots planted and legs shifting to compensate for the rocking, quaking rolling-along train.

"She's there, at the end of the line," he said. "I got word. She made it there in the baron's wood-burning cream puff. Oh, and her little refugee girl Marta came along. Tiny thing hid down in the back seat, apparently. Your Kat was none too happy about that part."

Were they dead or alive? He would not tell me, I knew that much. This was it, for good. He had clinched it. He was practically begging me to do it.

We stood about five feet apart. He still held his barrel out, pointed at my hip.

The car darkened. We had entered the woods again. Light and shadow flashed, painting and mottling our faces. Spanner smiled again, those big teeth flashing white.

"A Jewish gang has it," I said. "Ringleader by the name of Emil Wiesenberg. Death camp survivor. Cousin of one Abraham Beckstein, also a survivor. Until he got to Heimgau. To you."

Spanner's eyes blackened. He grimaced at me, the strings of his saliva stretching in the light.

Now I was the one forcing him into it.

"Stupid, stupid move," he said. "That's what they call a death wish up on the line. When a man's pushed too far. When he's all out of change ..."

The car lurched, and we stumbled into each other. We pushed back, found our feet again. We had come around a corner, and the train descended, the grade increasing, forcing us to shift our stances onto the higher hip. I glanced out, saw rocks of a ravine just feet from our passing car, then all dark forest again, the branches brushing at the windows with great slaps.

The car turned into another tight bend, the cacophony of creaking and screeching like below the deck of some ancient sailing ship adrift in a storm.

Spanner unslung his tommy. I tensed up. He tossed the machine gun down the stairway, where it clunked down against the door. In that moment I reached for my pocket knife, pulled it out, and got it yanked open somehow.

Spanner laughed. "Military Government issue, that's what that is."

I held it out in front of me. It felt even smaller like this.

Spanner drew my Colt from his pocket.

The train pitched, the cars banging together at their ends. Our car reeled. We tottered and staggered for footing.

I charged. He got a shot off, it ricocheted and I kept coming screaming with knees up and elbows out and I pinned him to a wall. Something seared me down low. He had the fighting knife out, I saw blood. The Colt had fallen away. I kept coming at him with all I had, kicking, howling, my elbows and fists thrashing. He got a grip on my neck, clamped his claw-thumb. I kept pummeling, stabbing.

I saw his knife skip across the floor.

I got on top of him. I kept stabbing, puncturing stomach, chest, shoulders. He gasped, shrieked. My hand was one with the knife, the blade a sixth finger, plunging, piercing, the blood sticky. Spanner kept shrieking, but the sound stopped coming out. I stabbed faster, thrusting into him, into hot wet flesh and thumping against bone, slimy ribbons flinging out, red strands of who knew what. My veins pulsed, my nostrils blew snot, my heart and lungs throbbed from the effort.

He wheezed, choked. His back had arched up. His right hand was pushing on my chest, but it lost its force. I pressed my body down on it, like stepping on a pedal. The blood sloshed inside his rubber slick, seeping out onto the floor under us. My vision had blurred. Blood had spurted into my eyes and onto his face, casting his skin with amok threads of red. He lowered all the way down, me pressing against his chest, feeling it give and soften against mine.

He eyed me, or rather pointed his eyes as if directing me. I came in close, my cheek pressed to his and inserted the short, dull blade into the base of his neck, prodding, twisting. I felt a spurt pass by my ear. My fingers had gone in, his tubes pulsing hot and slurping wet. I could have ripped the insides of his throat right out. I pressed the blade, depressing it. The tip resisted, and then could go no more. I must have hit the floor.

I pulled back. Sat up. Blood dripped as strings from my hand, both my hands, wrists. I threw the knife. I gasped a pop of air and another, and might have laughed.

His eyes had stopped on mine. He made a clucking sound, as if trying to get something out. Gurgles came up. Bubbles of blood.

"... a favor," he gasped.

His face turned to wax, and his mouth stayed open, gaping.

Twenty-Eight

AT LEAST IT HAD SOUNDED like "a favor." So I had done him a favor? That would have been about right. It had been too easy as if he had wanted me to do it. To become like him. He had gotten his licks in. My ribs ached, and at least one was probably cracked. My trousers were shredded along my left thigh. I cleared the blood with water from a canteen and saw a slice of flesh hanging off. The car had a first aid bag. I ripped open my trouser leg, cleared away more blood, threw on a sulfa packet and pressed a bandage to the wound. My neck stung and had stiffened up, whiplashed at the least. That grip of his was about to snap it. How many men had he killed up on the line like that? I wondered. Men more steely and fierce than me, I was sure of it, and only a few more scared and green than I. But he did not do it. Had he stopped himself? Did I really stop him? I could tell myself that I had taken him out just in time, that I had acted before he got set and ready. The truth was, I would probably never know.

"Shit, shit," I muttered. It only now reached me that I had killed a human being.

For Virgil Eugene Tercel, the war had finally ended. All his fingers had clawed up. His back had arched up again and froze that way as if stuck on a spike. Eyes open, the blood from his face pooling in them. I couldn't take looking at him anymore, and I sure as hell didn't want to deal with him when rigor mortis set in. I dragged him to the stairway, and I kicked him down the stairs. I grabbed the tommy, threw it back up into the car. I waited until the train hit the dark forest again. I forced open the door, the wind and branches rushing by, the loco steam swirling in the stairway. I heaved him up. I flung him out. He didn't make it all the way, and I heard his body clatter against train and track as he got swallowed down and under.

I sat there on the bloody steel steps catching my breath and shaking my head, wincing with pain, and wondering if the train was ever going to stop. I imagined forest animals dragging his parts off into the woods, for repeated feedings in relative safety. That was where he belonged. For the duration. The man would have bought it anyway if he would have stuck it out up on the line. The Ardennes and the Hürtgen were full of them, from the most sadistic killers to the smartest, kindest men who might ever have lived.

I got back up on the bedroll, too tired to think about clearing the mess and muck. I hugged the tommy like a baby blanket. I closed my eyes.

The next thing I knew, we were slowing. I slung the tommy, grabbed the Colt. I kicked open the stairway doors and jumped down and ran down along the cars, my leg stinging, the bruises burning in my neck and ribs. I climbed up into the cab.

I pointed the Colt at Ushanka the stoker. His hands shot up. I frisked him, and he gazed in horror at the sight of me. The engineer had frozen up, waiting his turn. I frisked him. The man's denim trousers were coated with coal grime and stunk of oil. In his pockets, I found two puny potatoes. I had expected grenades. We gaped at each other, the sweat streaming down our foreheads, noses, necks. Neither wanted trouble, especially from an American officer wearing combat paratrooper boots and splattered with blood and gore. They were hired to drive a train, these two.

"Just do what I say," I said, and they nodded and Ushanka wiped at his forehead, cheeks, and jaw as if washing with a washcloth.

The cab was hot and cramped, the air damp and gritty. I stayed with them there. This hellish little iron cave just seemed safer now. Ushanka shoveled coal on the engineer's command, humping the foul black chunks into the raging flame. The engineer stepped on another pedal, pulled back another lever. The engine's clamor deafened, gauges and pipes and levers and wheels met my eyeballs at every turn, the metal scarred with chinks, gashes, cracks. Jagged hot bolts prodded my sides. The muggy soot seared my eyes.

The engineer handed me a big canteen. I must have drank half of the water, but it only left me more thirsty. Ushanka handed me a tarnished little flask of vodka. The firewater only made me tired. He offered me spare overalls to cover my bloody deed that was all over me, but my weary limbs didn't want to step into it. I hunkered down on the little fold-down stool they had and leaned on the tommy gun, feeling ever weaker. My adrenaline had slowed; my powers had fizzled. I'm different now, I thought. I'm like Spanner and Tercel.

Like all my stateside buddies who had gone on to die in combat. Like all who survived and lived with the horror. Like all of them. I had gone through the grinder. It was only once, but that was enough.

Ushanka leaned out a cab window. We were heading into the wood near the village of Aschendorf. Directly ahead lay a wide bank of green and brown trees. I checked my watch. It was about noon now, and the sun high in the clearing blue sky proved it. I pulled in my head and sat, letting our ride jostle me. Feeling it. These rails were far worse than the main line; they teetered and sagged under our weight and seams sounded at uneven intervals; one went Click and the next Clack or Thud, as if the rails were busting up behind us, leaving no way out.

Katarina could be dead. Even Little Marta. I had to consider the fact. I had to steel myself. I was far from done with this. But my eyes filled with heat just thinking of Maulendorff.

The car darkened. We had entered the wood. We emerged back into the light. I peered out. Up ahead stood that warehouse, a rectangular mass of red brick—a behemoth version of that Dachau oven building, I couldn't help thinking.

At the far end, I saw a car. Freddy's wood-burning BMW 327 was parked there.

The brakes screeched and grabbed and a mighty jerk made me grasp at the handles. Then we were inching along. I tied the arms of the overalls around my neck, letting it hang like a silly cape, unslung the tommy gun, and jumped out, moving low like a crab, using the tree line as cover. Behind me, the locomotive had detached for recoupling. Ushanka was out signaling the engineer. Good men. And a good decoy. I neared the giant wood double-doors of the warehouse from the side. I knelt behind tree trunks to see if anyone came out. No one showed. The doors stayed shut.

The locomotive moved off down a sidetrack, and suddenly I felt nostalgic for the cramped shelter of that beast. Trees loomed all around me, a massive cage of lean gnarled trunks. I had to keep moving, keep on moving. I checked the safety was off on both guns. I sprinted for the warehouse and moved along its long brick wall, alone, just me and those locked double doors a few feet away. I crouched at the corner of the building. The locomotive had come back around and was shoving the freight cars nearer with squeals and howls, crashing, hisses of steam.

The doors slid open, to reveal a skinny GI and a burly Yugoslav, Savic. They had guns out, M1 carbines. The GI wore double-buckle combat boots but was a deserter, no doubt. Savic I'd seen in Heimgau, usually could be found shaking down elderly black marketers. My tommy trumped their peashooters, in theory, but I pulled back and crouched lower for now.

The skinny GI went back inside, and Savic stepped out along the rails to wave the cars into the warehouse as the loco droned and pumped steam with great thunks. The four freight cars fit inside with only feet to spare. The locomotive uncoupled, chugged off.

Savic stood alone, close to my corner. I rushed him. Savic swung around and poked his carbine at me, made a Broadway show of it. "Hands up!" he shouted.

"Drop it!" I screamed.

We couldn't hear each other over the roaring loco. We kept shouting, pointing our guns.

A great crack struck my head, my brain rung.

All went black.

I woke flat on the ground, one cheek in the dirt. It must have been only seconds later, maybe a minute. Waves of pain still rippled through my head like the worst funny bone. I could only see blurs and colors. I squinted to see through it. I stayed down, eyeing the double doors.

"Ah!" My ribs burned, tensed with pain and cramp. Someone had kicked me. Writhing, I saw those double-buckle boots standing next to my head. That skinny GI stood over me. Savic was gone, back inside the warehouse. The skinny GI must have seen me and had made his way around somehow to flank me.

His carbine barrel touched the back of my head.

I could not believe it. This was not happening. Well, there goes, I thought. For my last moments of life I tried to see as far as I could, out past those trees lining the clearing but the woods beyond were dark, extinguished. I needed something wonderful. I looked farther, higher. On the horizon puffy clouds glowed white, streaming along the blue. There, that was something. At least I was buying it outside. I'll be seeing you soon, Freddy.

I felt a great bang close to me, but my ringing head only heard it as far off, like a balloon popping yards away. Something dropped next to me, a body. A head.

The GI was staring at me, eyes open and not blinking, not anymore.

I looked up, over. Katarina crouched in the doorway wearing that raincoat and light orange scarf, just as she had standing over me in bed so early this very morning. Her hands aimed a short-barreled pistol, elbow cocked, knees bent. I blinked and squinted. Was this happening? She peered around like some paratroop commando. I opened my mouth, but I didn't know what came out.

Something flashed by, passed behind her. I shouted. She pivoted.

Savic had run past, trying to escape the warehouse. Blood streamed down his head, neck. He made for the trees.

Kat fired and fired, right over my head.

Savic went down face first, the rest of him following, crumpling, his knees up under his hips. Ass in the air. Kat fired one more to put it down.

Twenty-Nine

I LAY ON MY SIDE. I looked up and saw light streaming in from high windows. I heaved myself up on my elbows, but my head spun and it stung as if boiling water had been thrown on the back of my skull. I touched my hair. It was tender hot and sticky with blood. It had a bandage.

"He's awake, he's awake!" I heard in German.

A child's voice. Little Marta. There she was in her short pants and Peter Pan collar. Little Marta was here too? Was she a ghost? What was this?

She rushed for me. I smiled. Beyond her sat Katarina, at a table set up for a picnic. It even had a blue-white checked tablecloth. She stood. "Be gentle with him," she said to Marta, who slowed before me, sitting on her bent knees like only kids could do. She smiled at me.

I grinned. It hurt like hell. A rush of fear hit me. I cowered. I looked around for the tommy, my Colt, felt for the pocket knife.

"Harry, it's okay. It's over."

"It is? That was you. That was really you."

"Yes," Kat said.

My head felt so heavy, as if I was wearing a concrete helmet. I lowered back down, feeling behind me for my bedroll. They sat with me, holding me.

"Freddy didn't make it," I muttered in English.

Katarina pulled back, glaring at me. "He was on board?"

Little Marta looked at us, trying to make out our foreign words.

"He was, but he was dead by the time he got there. Same treatment the others got."

Katarina's head dropped to my shoulder, and she sobbed, squeezing my arm. My arm fucking killed me too, but I let her anyway.

"What is the matter?" Little Marta said in German.

"We lost a new friend," I said. "He had to go away, just when we got to know him."

"Oh. Well, I know what that's like. I'm so sorry," Little Marta said, and the way she said it sounded older and wiser than Kat and I put together.

Kat filled me in. Savic and the skinny GI, name of Gil, had been sent here by Spanner to watch over things. When Kat and Little Marta had showed up, Savic and Gil had frisked them and had them stay put till the train came. When it pulled in, Gil saw me making my move through the trees. He went around to flank me. He cold-cocked me, which put me back in my place—some soldier I was. That gave Kat just enough time to get her pistol out. When Savic backed into the warehouse, she had cracked his skull with the butt, and rushed out to me. To save my lucky life. I told her my end. Spanner had boarded the train to finish things off, and I did what I had to. I couldn't let him do his work on Katarina or Marta. I didn't have to tell Kat, I was lucky.

She stood behind Little Marta, brushing the girl's hair. "There was always the chance that Spanner would discover the switch. It was too great a gamble," Kat said in English.

"It wasn't about that. He was plenty beyond caring about things we would care about."

"In any case. We could have had Emil's group finish him off. Perhaps we should have."

"No. It wasn't their fight. I wouldn't have asked them to do it. It was something I had to do, me and me alone. And I almost think Spanner knew it."

Katarina had dragged Savic and Gil into the woods, covered them with underbrush. As for Ushanka and the engineer, they had just walked off into the woods, toward the village, looking like any other refugees. They hadn't protested, she told me. Apparently they had already been paid, and maybe were feeling a little lucky the American colonel had not escorted them all the way to the end of the line. Maybe they would get nice and drunk in the village, meet some girls to get them cleaned up. I sure hoped so.

Katarina had shut the big warehouse doors and locked them with keys she'd found on Savic. The freight cars stood inside with us, a black mass. The thousand-yard stare had found me, and Katarina and Little Marta waited it out. I couldn't shake it, snap out of it. I was back on that goddamn train with the colonel. I could smell the metallic sweetness of the blood.

"Wait," I said. "You had a gun. How? I thought they frisked you."

Katarina and Little Marta smiled at each other. Marta produced her long-haired, one-armed, one-eared teddy bear named Sally, and set the stuffed beast on my lap.

"Hi, Sally. Okay. I don't follow."

Little Marta held Sally straight for Kat, who plunged a hand into the elongated hole where the arm had been. Her hand came out, grasping a black Walther automatic, the smaller PPK model, less than a pound, with a short barrel and its edges so worn they shined silver. No wonder that bear was heavier.

"Little Marta has carried Sally with her a long time. She never told me where she got her, and I'm not about to ask."

Little Marta grinned at me.

"Me, neither," I said and pulled Marta close, aching ribs and throbbing head be damned.

They sat me at the table, along with Sally. The BMW outside had wood fuel and even some gas left, but Kat would not take me back until they decided I was ready. Set out on the tablecloth, they had dried sausage and soft cheese and a dense rye bread. I tore into all of it. This was going to be my victory feast at the Waldorf Astoria. But my stomach rolled. I ran to vomit out the side door, gushing like a pump hose. Viscous trickles of dry heave followed, the convulsions wracking my insides. Kat and Little Marta talked about this, watching me retch, and determined my purge was a good thing. Who was I to argue?

Thirty

FRIDAY, MARCH 29, 1946. Midmorning, about ten a.m. I sat in my City Hall office as always, manning my basic wood desk and Underwood typewriter, that same worn Persian area rug at my feet. Still, that smell like mothballs. I shook my head at that. What can you do? It came long before me and would linger long after. I had on my GE portable, as always, and Radio Munich was playing "I'll Buy that Dream" for the fourth time already.

> I fingered through the inbox, had the usual messages, reports, forms in carbon, nothing that couldn't wait till Monday. A folder lay before me. Inside was my ten-page draft of the "Annual Historical Report for Landkreis Heimgau," which I was required to send off to Frankfurt where it would be retyped, quadruplicated, and filed away. My intro was to the point:
>
> Military Government in Heimgau had its share of problems. Over time, however, with effective guidance and the proper re-establishment of local authority, the county and its capital appear to be adjusting to directives and conditions admirably ...

In tone it was much like all those combat units' after-action reports from the war, glossing over the degrading horrors and near disasters. Years later people would ask a man: What did you do in the war? I was on the front line, he might say, but I'm not going to talk about it. My report took the same tack. What did you do in the occupation, Harry? I got a town up and running and boy was it rough at first, but we got through it. This didn't exactly make things easy for historians, but that was not our problem. I read on, reaching for my good old red pencil.

Someone was at the door, again. "Yeah, come on in ..."

"Good morning, Harry."

Katarina Buchholz. She stood in the doorway.

I stood, knocking my knee on drawers. "Well. Good morning," I muttered. She wore slacks. Her hair was short now, the bangs and fringes curled under. Her eyebrows were thicker too; she'd given up all that tweezing and penciling. Seeing her here was the last thing I expected. Katarina and I had tried to rendezvous after the train job, but it hadn't felt the same. I told myself I'd been too busy playing CO, and that's why I never made the trip up to Munich. She never made the trip here. I could have written. She could have. Real phone calls were possible now, and passenger trains were back running. We had no excuses, neither of us. "You look swell," I added. "What brings you here?"

She leaned against the doorframe, smiling. "Why do you still wear the captain's bars? You're the permanent CO now. It is not major yet?"

"Maybe soon. I'm not counting the days. Come on in. Sit, sit down."

Katarina sat before my desk in the same ladder-back metal chair Winkl used, same chair they all used, but it might as well have become a chaise of feather-down the way she settled into it, crossing her long legs. I placed my brogues up on the desk, played the relaxed guy, flashed her a smile. "Plenty has happened around here, Kat. And a lot hasn't happened."

"Yes. So, how is Denazification going?"

"Oh, there's some good come of it. Most of Maulendorff's so-called monarchists went and skipped town. Except for Police Chief Jenke. Hear about it? Ate the barrel of his SS pistol, suicide. Next morning? I have reappointed Uli Winkl police chief. I personally 'edited' Winkl's *Fragebogen*. He won't have any problems."

"Good. Things worked out."

I shrugged and kept on talking, anything but look at her. I recalled how, about a month after the train job, I had hired a loco and crew to bring the freight cars back from Aschendorf. I gathered the artisans' top representatives—they had been starting to organize, with my blessing—and told them to have at it. But I had them leave the trunks, suitcases and bags bearing owners' names in white chalk, and trucked those back to Emil and his crew. Katarina nodded, saying nothing. She knew much of this; it was my way of stalling. We both stared out the window, though I couldn't have remembered what I saw. We listened to the radio. She said, "I like that song," and I didn't recognize the song or the songbird.

I have had nightmares about killing and being killed the way I had killed a man. In other horror dreams, I could not protect anyone from being killed, as hard as I tried. Sometimes I woke screaming, sweating. These nightmares had waned, for now. So far, so good.

I switched off the radio. "It's been a long while, Kat. You missed the good white snow."

"I haven't seen you in Munich either. You missed the good brown slush."

Silence. She shifted the other way, facing a wall. My map of Heimgau staring back at her.

"How are your parents back home?" she said.

"Better. The heat's off, so to speak. Commies and Reds are all the rage now. One fear all the time, it gets boring, wears off. You need a new one."

"Ever hear from your brother?"

"Max? No. And I'm still not looking." I pulled down my feet. I got up, went to the door, shut it and found my seat. Katarina stared into her lap. I watched her until she looked up. Our eyes met. Like this, the silence didn't drag on so long.

"I kind of miss it," I said finally. "I guess, I kind of miss you."

Katarina began to speak, leaving a pause where my name might have fit. "You do?"

"And then sometimes, when I'm feeling a little sour—when I miss you, I guess—I can't help thinking you knew something more about that train. On account of the life you led. Knew things a guy like Abraham Beckstein had to learn the hard way. Had an idea at least. But, that would mean a heavy price to pay, all around."

Katarina had crossed her arms across her chest. "I didn't come here for your interrogation."

I held up hands. "What can I say? It's been months. I've had time to collect my thoughts. Finish the puzzle." I went on with it: "Sure, your dad, your little brother, they went and revolted in the last days. They were heroes. Beckstein was on his own crusade. They do end up at the castle. That's how it started. Then someone, some interrogator, finds out who they are, who they're related to. So someone sends you—you personally—a message. Holds them hostage. At that point, it's got nothing to do with standing up. Has everything to do with loot."

Nodding, Katarina focused on the edge of my desk. She spoke slowly as if sounding out an American word new to her. "That someone, he was not the man calling himself Colonel Spanner. It was the SS. It was before I got here. The train was near here and they wanted it, thinking its worth could save them. They thought I knew where the train was. But I wasn't here, not yet. And I didn't know, Harry. I didn't know where the train was. In their desperation, they only thought I did, on account of my reputation. Just like you are thinking now."

"Hey. I'm just trying to clear it from my head. And Spanner?"

She shrugged. "He didn't care about what I knew by the time I arrived. He already had his train prize. It fell right into his lap. He had inherited what the SS started."

"Yeah. War will do that. Did you know that Spanner did the torture, the murder?"

"I couldn't be sure who did it. It was so hectic. All I knew was, an *Ami* colonel was here at the end. And then Major Membre, too. All so very hectic. I had made it back home, yet I was too late. Came too late. A few hours made all the difference …" A tear raced down her cheek. "That doesn't mean I didn't care for you. Loved you even. I wasn't after it. You weren't. Then this whole damn thing, it fell right into our laps."

"Like I said. War will do that. Did the baron know about any of this? He always told me he didn't."

She waved a hand. "Maulendorff? God, no. Of that one thing you can be certain."

We sat in silence. I watched her wipe her cheeks, one graceful swipe to each eye.

"About the corpses," I said. "They ended up along the road somehow."

She nodded. "Yes. I will tell you now. I cut a deal for them, to get them back. Colonel Spanner wanted the bodies removed, so I got to bury them my way."

"That's why you never asked me about their condition. How bad they looked. Because you already knew it. Not that I would've been able to describe it. What they looked like. Nasty work."

"I saw. I did. And I saw you from the trees, from where I hid and waited. You, in your jeep. I wanted to call out to you, scream, something, but I wasn't sure what you would do. Who you were."

"Smart thinking. I might've mucked things up worse. Was Horton your contact?"

A nod. "How they were left there wasn't talked about. I did not expect a hearse with flowers. But like that? The lazy pig, he heaved them out to the road like a bag of trash."

"The fee?"

"Some very fine jewelry," she said. "And, I shut my mouth or else. This was not a poor deal. I was able to live another day."

"You buried them, eventually. Meantime, I'd guess any cold cellar made a good morgue."

"Yes. But now they are finally buried here for good, together. My family is. Before, I did not think they'd be safe if I buried them here. Now I know they are safe with you here."

I held up my hands again. If only it was that easy, running this occupation. I had learned that much. "I had to know. I'm sorry for putting on the screws."

"I know. Don't be. I would, too."

She began crying again. I went out, got her a glass of water, gave her a couple extra minutes alone. When I returned she was sitting up straight, her cheeks glowing. I wanted to keep them glowing a little longer, so I told her: "Oh, the Red Cross team stopped by the other day. I asked about Little Marta. This time they'd gotten word. Her boat made it over, Kat. They placed her with a smart young couple in San Francisco. Turns out the father is an architect, does skyscrapers. I've never been to the West Coast. Maybe I'll stop by and see her someday. Or, maybe not."

"Perhaps she would rather not be reminded."

"Yeah. Sure." I opened my top drawer and lay a postcard on the desktop. On the front was a watercolor of a port city called Haifa. On the back, a message dated February 1946:

> We have made it, Mister! Thanks to you and your special gift. What are your future plans, my friend? We can use good men like you here in the days to come.
> Shalom,
> Emil

I pushed the postcard across the desk. Katarina ignored the watercolor and flipped to the back. The words made her smile, and she put a hand to her mouth. She flipped the postcard back over and smiled at the watercolor, her eyes searching it.

"Everybody's starting over," I added. "What's your game now?"

"Oh, I am busy," she said, placing the postcard back on the desk, "very busy. I've been cleared to teach elementary school, but I'm starting up my own side operation. I cut a deal with the Jewish relief agency, you see. I'll introduce orphans to Shakespeare and Schiller and the Brothers Grimm—"

"Where?"

"What? The Jewish relief office? It's the UNRRA one, in the Ludwigstrasse."

"Not the office. That's in Munich. You know what I mean. Where's the deal for? For orphans, say, in Palestine? For a port called Haifa?"

She took a deep breath. Her eyes darted around before landing back on mine. "I miss him, Harry. I miss them. It."

"A fight. That's what you miss. You're like the guy all bloodied in the ring, back to the ropes."

"As you say it, yes. I have to admit, I don't regret killing those two."

"You saved my life, Kat."

"I think we saved each others'." She stood. "Let's go out, all right? I wish to see my town."

I loosened my tie and slid on my sunglasses. Out in front of City Hall, the usual refugee kids were playing in the sidecar of my motorcycle. I had a new one now, a onetime Wehrmacht Zündapp I'd had repainted in glossy red and white like the baron's BMW. I had let Katarina take his car back to Munich and never had asked her what she and Emil did with it. It was warm for early spring, the breaking sun was drying out the cobblestones, and the air smelled of bark and flowers. We crossed over to the Stefansplatz, where a string quartet played to a small crowd. Katarina clapped hands together. "Wonderful! It's *Geigertag*?"

"Violin Day, yeah. Have 'em twice a month now. Brahms, I think. Bach? No idea."

"It's Bach." She put a hand to her mouth again, a new habit of hers. Fetching, I thought. It went well with the hair.

She led me to Cathedral Square. I lit a Lucky and watched her skip along up ahead. I took my time. She waited for me on the square, the cathedral looming behind her. Our frantic, crude tryst inside there came rushing back to me.

"Harry, stop. What are you doing?"

I was grasping her wrist, leading her away.

I sat her down at the cathedral steps. "Let's cut the bull."

"Yes. All right. Let's do."

"You helped Emil get out, right? To Palestine. And now you're going."

Katarina nodded. "Yes. I must try and visit him."

"Visit's one thing. You going to stay?"

"I don't know. I might not be able to make it back in any case."

"So you were seeing him. In Munich you were."

"Yes, but not like that, not the way you and I saw each other. I hadn't expected to find Emil in Munich. Alive. I thought he was dead. All of them, dead. But, we will see. He would love to have you come too."

I let her hands free. "And do what? Maybe I'm not so mad anymore. Since we're laying it all out here, the full confession? Maybe I'm not so starry-eyed either or aspiring in the way that gets a guy into trouble."

"I am still mad," she said. "I'm going to be mad for a long time."

I'd asked for this, so I had to finish it off. I took a drag off my Lucky and said: "We're too much alike, you and me. In plenty of ways. It doesn't seem like it now, but the farther we get from this war, you'll see it. And I just can't see you stateside. How you are going to like cooking for me every night, stuffing my pipe, chatting up the nosy neighbors."

"But that's not you either." She raised her eyebrows. "I could have acted there, or sang."

"Got enough Germans in Hollywood as it is."

She chuckled. "Yes. Why have a German Betty Grable when you have the real thing?"

"That's it. I was kidding about stuffing my pipe."

"What if you stayed here?"

"I'm no career soldier. I'll do my hitch and be done."

"And I'm no war bride."

"No. Get me? It wasn't meant to be. But that train job? That was laid out for us, up in the stars somewhere."

"Yes, I suppose that is true," Katarina said, and she stood, back out on the square. I stood. Facing each other as if to dance. She held me by the wrists with fingertips, and she kissed me on the forehead. I kissed her on the cheek. We hugged, probably a little too long for my own good. I breathed her in deep. She took a step backward, and another, and she turned, and she hurried off.

I ground out the Lucky under my heel. I sat back down on the cathedral steps and slouched, my head hanging right over my knees like a man trying to lose a vertigo. My thoughts stinging away. The girl wanted to believe she has a bigger debt to pay. So let her. I closed my eyes, but it only kept my thoughts locked in and banging around in there, going over it again and again. It was "up in the stars"—is that what I'd really said? What a crock. How could she buy that line? We'd shared so much more than that train.

I thought of her family. Now they are all here, together—that's what she'd said. Today.

I shot up and hustled down the alleys of Old Town, turning corners, crossing squares, and down more alleys until I found the Old Cemetery. Pushed through the black iron gate. A couple workmen rolled a wheelbarrow up the main path, the dirt in it fresh. Before I could open my mouth, they pointed to the work they'd just finished. I jogged on.

The two plots were so new the dirt sparkled in the breaking sun. I stood over the dark rectangles—a wider one for two and a single one. Double bed and a twin. A bundle of fresh flowers lay at each tombstone, purple and pink and yellow. Joachim and Frau Buchholz shared one wide tombstone, while little brother Gerd got his own nice slab. And for each, the finest marble I'd seen outside a baroque church. If there was still a Jewish cemetery here, I'd find one for Abraham Beckstein. But the Nazis had plowed over the Jewish cemetery. They made it a training ground for the local SA brownshirts to play army. I felt certain Katarina had found a good resting place for Beckstein and probably before I had even met her.

By the time I got back to the square, the March sun was out for good. It was all hustle and bustle there. They had a new News and Tobacco stand now. I strolled over, bought a *Süddeutsche Zeitung*, Bavaria's brand-new German-owned newspaper, and took a seat back on the cathedral steps.

"County-Level Elections Coming," read the headline. "Political Activity Allowed in US Zone: First Elections in Germany Since 1933." Again, I thought about the Baron Friedrich-Faustino von Maulendorff. This would have been his moment. He might have gone from mayor of Heimgau Town to Landrat on the Christian Social Union party list. Sure, he would have. It would have been a cinch.

Meanwhile, Heimgau was going to need another new mayor. I had brought in a good man with solid credentials, but he wished to retire. My man was old, and his heart was weak from years in Gestapo dungeons.

Two steps down, on the cobblestones, stood former and current Police Chief Uli Winkl. He saw my newspaper; he had one too. I waved mine at him.

"So, Heimgau will need a new man for mayor," he said.

"Don't I know it. If I only knew who."

"You know who."

"Come again?"

Winkl smoothed out his tunic. He looked around and cleared his throat. He rolled up his paper and shook it. "I know my Heimgau. I have the experience. And I can work with the Americans, can I not? You bet I can and I will."

"Sure, that's it, keep it going," I said and clapped and whistled, and several passersby stopped for more—two young widows holding hands, a refugee artisan and his wife, three scruffy schoolboys.

Winkl turned to them all. His voice rose to a confident holler: "Yes, citizens, it is true! Heimgau needs a good man for mayor, and that man can only be me!" He backed up those first couple steps, so they could all see him. He opened his arms wide and high.

Afterword

THIS BOOK MIGHT READ LIKE FICTION, but the story is based on simple truths and historical record. Justifications aside, the early US occupation of Germany was a type of Wild West in which a foreign autocrat caste had total power over the native inhabitants. On the frontiers of Southern Bavaria in late spring of 1945, US combat units had secured the war's unexpectedly calm closure. On the local level, however, the future peace and law and order remained far from clear.

Enter the US Military Government (MG) detachments, following the path of US tactical forces into cities and towns, villages and counties that were physically and socially devastated. Amid untold ruin and chaos, broken infrastructure and vaporized authority, the first MG detachments aimed simply to get things going again. Establishing order and ensuring public safety were primary duties. At the same time, MG officers performed a delicate balancing act that varied according to detachment make-up, intelligence on hand, a confusing mix of directives, and the inhabitants' cooperation. MG officers in smaller county and village detachments were often cut off in the first few months. This demanded self-reliance and inventiveness, but also invited confusion, scandal and infamy.

Some MG commanders made themselves the lords of their helpless, isolated communities, whether a town or a *Kreis* (county, district) or both. Such all-too-common types were dubbed *Kreiskönige*, or "County Kings," by fearful and sometimes grateful locals as their King often beat out rival MG detachments' communities competing for manpower and resources, shelter and food.

While performing historical research in Munich some years ago as a graduate student, I discovered the example of Miesbach, an unassuming capital of a rural *Kreis* between Munich and the Alps. US combat units had held back Miesbach's MG detachment until May 16, 1945, over a week after the capitulation. What detachment officers found there must have given them a shock. The MG report for May 13-20 described the local population as highly distressed at US Military Police "permitting SS officers and a limited number of enlisted men to remain armed with some freedom." Incredibly, the SS soldiers were able to shoot three civilians while at liberty, including a US intelligence informant. What's more, German army troops stationed nearby were allowed to operate with complete freedom. Their commander, a General von Hahn, reportedly addressed his men that "the war is not lost and another German Army will be formed."

Miesbach MG stabilized the situation, but as late as 1947 an MG investigator described a history of "careless enforcement" in Miesbach. MG there had appointed locals with distinct Nazi pasts to top posts. One deemed politically acceptable turned out a "paranoiac and a psychopathic mythomaniac." The investigator found the situation typical in such areas. Miesbach MG officers were flattered by officials with Nazi connections and reluctant to let them go, showing a lack of "judgment, intelligence and impartiality." He concluded: "It has been proved over and over again that the officer who is lulled into confidence by a surface obsequiousness is forgetting an essential fact: No people loves or trusts or essentially wishes to help the power that occupies it."

What intrigued me was how much scandal was implied between the lines, but had been lost forever, no matter how much research I performed. Musing about this would lead me to write a first manuscript years ago that, after repeated revisions, would become this novel.

Heimgau is fictional, but not unlike Miesbach, Landsberg, Bad Tölz or any number of towns in Bavaria or elsewhere in the US Zone of Occupation. I fictionalized my burg simply for creative freedom. Harry Kaspar, Major Membre and Eugene Spanner and the rest are fictional too, but real-life examples existed. Major Membre comes closest to one Major Towle of Boston, who commanded the Bavarian town of Eichstätt. Major Towle's MG reports made his rule there sound sensible enough, but in truth the major terrorized the locals while setting himself up as a minor eccentric tyrant, prompting Eichstätters to dub him "Major *Toll*," or Major Crazy, applying the German word for both insane and fantastic in place of an unpronounceable English name. Major Crazy carried a riding whip he slapped on his desk to scare any official questioning his decisions. A pleasure-seeker and a racketeer and obsessed with ancient Catholic power, Major Towle even had a papal costume tailored for himself, and brought in a top Munich painter to portray him in it. His German and American entourage of rakes and prostitutes and pimps took up over twenty houses in town that he had requisitioned. He shipped home hundreds of crates filled with finer plunder and forged art pieces. I could go on, but one gets the picture. There are many such examples. Indeed, MG and occupation duty seemed to attract a certain type of man who saw glory, not in combat, but rather in the power and patronage, mistresses and riches that martial rule provided. Even a common Joe could thrive, and all weren't criminals when considered in context. A 22-year-old sergeant named Henry Kissinger was a CIC agent tasked with finding and arresting former Nazis. As a CIC man, Sergeant Kissinger had more power than even the local MG commander. Calling himself "Mr. Henry," young Kissinger ruled over the town of Bensheim and surrounding county from a lavish villa and a posh Mercedes sedan. He reportedly enjoyed multiple affairs and extravagant dinner parties. The future US Secretary of State was already learning to enjoy the trappings of authority.

Lawlessness and plundering were widespread that spring and summer and went on at all levels, from the lowest German or Displaced Person to the highest levels of Allied authority. Some of the Displaced Persons, or DPs—foreign nationals liberated from forced labor or concentration camps—turned out to be the most violent, persistent and intimidating lawbreakers, and who could blame them? They had endured more than six years of brutal oppression. Others, whether GIs or German housewives, became (for drastically different reasons) small-scale smugglers and petty operators, part of the hordes of minor black marketeers. Meanwhile, the Americans with the power operated with shameless greed and impunity, a few punished only when matters got out of hand or made public. Among many such instances, the closest to this book is that of the Hungarian Gold Train. Sent west by Hungarian Nazis in the last year of the war to prevent confiscation by the Red Army, the train carried far more than gold; it held the expensive belongings and art of Hungarian Jews. This load was not the known museum collections and pieces that the US Army's vaunted Monuments Men units sought to secure, and as such proved all the more tragic. According to Kenneth D. Alford in *Allied Looting in WWII* (2011), at one point the train "consisted of 52 railroad cars, of which 29 were freight cars containing items of great value. The cars were sealed, locked with large padlocks, and guarded by Hungarian soldiers and gendarmes ...

[The cars] contained cases of gold, 60 chests of jewelry, and chests of the finest collections of Meissen, Dresden, and Chinese ivory figurines. There were over 5,000 handwoven Persian rugs, exceptional works of art, five large trunks full of stamps, over 300 complete sets of silverware and 28 large boxes of mink and sealskin furs. Other personal effects of the murdered victims included American dollars, Swiss francs, gold coins, small bags of gold dust, watches, rings, Bibles, skis, musical instruments, cameras, typewriters and—for some unknown reason—a solitary box of coal. One freight car contained diamonds; assigned to it was a special three-man guard detail ... In 1945 terms, the value of the train's contents was estimated at $206 million, which would translate to several billion dollars today." Under constant threat of attack from ground and air, the train made it into Austria as the war ended, where the SS and the trains' Hungarian guards fought for control. The train was meant for Switzerland, for anonymous bank accounts and profit-taking. It ended up in a train tunnel near Salzburg, Austria, where it fell into the hands of the US Army. Over the next couple years, certain unscrupulous American officers, empowered by victory and lured by easy wealth, began appropriating the contents from storage as the original ownership remained disputed between puffed-up policymakers. Much of the haul found its way to the states through boats and planes and back doors wide open.

Elsewhere, deserted GIs got in on the game and early, having found crime rackets the only way to stay free if not alive. It's known that certain crafty and determined deserters were able to set themselves up quite nicely and securely, especially in Paris and Brussels. About 50,000 American soldiers total had deserted in the European theater, many returning to duty, some never. Most had been broken by combat duty, given no respite from the front line, doomed "for the duration" (before the Army had instituted rest rotations) in units with casualty rates well over 100 percent counting replacement cannon fodder. Hell creates its own type of hero. It's not hard to imagine an enterprising sociopath like Virgil Tercel aka Eugene Spanner rising to the occasion, death wish and all.

And then there were men like Harry Kaspar, with special skills for MG, something big to prove, and a lot to dread down deep. Among the chaos, gangs of Jewish partisans and Holocaust survivors had their own agenda, with an eye to Palestine. I would like to think that, in real life, a man like Abraham Beckstein had actually survived to score his peoples' train.

Acknowledgements

This STORY FIRST EMERGED from research I performed on a Fulbright Graduate Research Fellowship in Munich from 1993-94 for a masters in history from Portland State University. For that formative experience I must thank the Germanistic Society of America, the Fulbright-Kommission in Bonn, and the overall promise of Senator J. William Fulbright's vision—may his grants always continue to be funded. Heartfelt gratitude also goes to Christa Rohnke (Niklas-Falter) and Prof. Dr. Jürgen Falter and family for making me feel at home in Munich. I remain indebted to the great and departed PSU professor and historian Franklin C. West, who advised me to follow my gut. As for the novel, I'm deeply grateful for all those who read and reviewed and put their faith in versions of this manuscript over the years—you know who you are. My agent Peter Riva stood behind this book through thick and thin and never stopped encouraging. Most of all, much love and thanks to my wife and reader-editor René for supporting me.

Suggested Reading

A NUMBER OF BOOKS COVER the early period of the US occupation, but few deviate from official history to stress the tough and at times scandalous tasks of MG detachments or reveal the realms of plundering and crime, greed and amorality. Edward N. Peterson's classic *The American Occupation of Germany: Retreat to Victory* (1977), introduced the grotesque yet emblematic Major Towle. *Allied Looting in World War II* (2011) by Kenneth D. Alford has many examples of US officers liberating finer goods, drawing from Alford's earlier works. Giles MacDonogh's hard-hitting *After the Reich* (2009) gives a broader look at the tragedies and offenses produced by the overall Allied occupation. In German, Klaus-Dietmar Henke's *Die amerikanische Besetzung Deutschlands* (1995) provides a detailed overview of that tense no-man's land between Germany's surrender and US occupation. For those eager to look, true accounts in various archives and contemporary books, magazines and newspapers offer buried surprises from a wild and brutal time that's been glossed over by idealized, selective and biased retellings of the history. For fiction, a little known novel by Steven Linakis, *In the Spring the War Ended* (1966), recreates the life of a bitter American deserter with no refuge left but crime, while another book, *The Spoils of the Victors* (1964) by Paul Edmondson, tells of American occupiers left to their own amoral devices in a far-flung corner of occupied Germany. The myriad challenges of reestablishing local administration and politics remains a vast topic in itself. Saul Padover's *Experiment in Germany* (1946) gives a contemporary, on-the-ground view of getting things going again. There are many other works, of course. Nevertheless, I imagine that an enterprising historian could find new ground to cover—a historian who doesn't switch to fiction, as I had.